UGLY GIRL

FAÎTE FALLING
BOOK ONE

MARY E. TWOMEY

MARY E. TWOMEY, LLC

Ugly Girl

Book One in the Faîte Falling Series

By

Mary E. Twomey

COPYRIGHT

DEDICATION

For my mom,

Who never let me believe that I was the Ugly Girl,
and loved me even when I was certain that's all I was.

WINNING AND TOTAL LOSS

*J*udah's laugh was music to my ears as he high-fived me, our pool sticks clanking together. "That was an awesome shot. We should've bet more," he said, eyeing the pile of twenties on the ledge that were weighted by a cube of chalk.

The atmosphere in the noisy bar was just starting to hit its sweet spot, with the blaring music enticing the college crowd to remember everything that was good about being young and away from home. We frequently came here after I finished a soccer game, yet somehow there were always a couple guys drunk enough to challenge us, even though we were undefeated at pool.

"Is it mean to take their money like this?" I asked, tilting my head at my best friend's dark curly hair that was slightly sticking up in the back. Neither of us looked in the mirror all that often, but relied on each other to either comb out the quirks, or decide if they should be left to add to our slightly off-center personalities.

Judah guffawed. "Don't you dare start with that pesky conscience tonight, Rosie Avalon. They were sober-ish when we started playing." Judah scrutinized the pool table, and I could practically feel him bisecting right angles and saying nonsense words like "hypotenuse" in his head. Gotta love him. He took his shot and sank the ball, beaming that we were still on top of our game of round robin. We laughed as we did our obnoxious Cabbage Patch dance, the brown curls of my ponytail swishing in time with my pool stick. The guys on my soccer team chuckled at our usual antics, but a few people on the fringes gave us weird looks.

Me. They gave *me* weird looks. Not that I could blame them. I had scoliosis, which resulted in a pretty sizeable hump on my back. Pair that with my lazy left eye, and I was ripe for receiving at least one grimace a day. One of my stellar nicknames in high school had been Baby Got Too Much Back. The other one was Crater Face, due to the painful acne that never went away. Judah was my other half because he'd never once looked at me like I was the ugly girl, and I'd never teased him about being super into Star Trek, spending his entire life at the top of the curve, or being Jewish. (I mean, come on, people. It's the twenty-first century already. You'd think the anti-Semitic comments would've died out before we were born, but there were always a few jaggoffs whose mission in life was to derail the evolution of the species.) I'd learned to accept the girl in the mirror and not hold back my personality. Just because I wasn't a blonde cheerleader didn't mean I was about to sit on the sidelines and sulk my whole life.

I was the starting striker for the Blue Hornets. The cheerleaders could have the blondes, for all I cared. I'd found my people long ago, and they didn't need me to be prom queen. Their main concern was if I could score, which I had no trouble proving game after game.

"Don't feel like foreplay tonight?" I asked, taking in our opponents' frowns of frustration. Our competition was droopy-eyed from their newly minted legal drinking-aged licenses, and not amused at our dance.

Judah tapped his watch, which also served as his day planner. "You've got to study for finals still."

I felt eyes on me, but I tried to ignore it. I pretended I didn't mind being talked about. It was the pointing that did me in. I rolled my hunched shoulders back as best I could, but no matter how straight I stood, I was still a little stooped. I did my best to push out the world and focus on the game. "Double or nothing if I make this shot blind." Maybe I was showing off just a little. I was in a great mood after the shutout, flying high off the adrenaline that kissed my forehead on the soccer field.

One of our challengers who was four beers into his night leaned against the table. "Not a chance. I've seen you pull that trick before. I still don't know how you do it."

"Magic," I teased, wiggling my fingers as I lined up my

shot. I paused to play with the locket on the thin gold chain around my neck. When my Aunt Lane had given it to me, she'd warned me to never take it off – it was my good luck charm. My luck tended to run freezing and scalding, but I placated her all the same.

Judah and I put them out of their misery quickly, since Judah was annoyingly right, and I did have to get home to cram for finals. It wasn't truly over until we finished off the chorus of Queen's "We are the Champions", which we nailed because we sang it at least once a week in this very bar after just such a victory. Our pool winnings kept our grocery budget firmly at a notch above ramen noodles, so we came here as often as we could.

I tried not to pay much attention to our goalkeeper, Kyle, who was arguing with his girlfriend, but they were hard to ignore. It was an hour after a victory, so their fight was right on schedule. Last time their clash was over him kissing her too hard, and smearing her Barbie pink lipstick. That had been one long night.

"I saw you looking at that skank!" Melanie's voice was shrill, which was the only tone I'd ever heard on the girl. I idly wondered what it would sound like if she ever whispered.

Kyle's indignation was so faked, I didn't even buy it. "Who? Women come to our games sometimes, Mel. They're half the population. I wasn't looking at anyone in particular. Just playing the game."

"Three times you laughed at a joke that girl told after the match. You think I didn't see it?"

Kyle scrunched his nose. "Who, Rosie? She's my teammate. Jeez." I was the only girl on the soccer team.

Melanie huffed, her arms akimbo. "I don't care if you joke with the ugly girl. It's the one in the halter top who you couldn't stop grinning at that I have a problem with."

My movements stilled as I leaned on my pool stick. Judah hadn't heard, because he was still being an obnoxious winner, dancing as he counted our take. It was just me who could stand in my defense, only I never wanted to in these situations. Melanie was right. I'd gone through many painful chiropractic treatments to try and straighten my hump, but scoliosis wasn't one of those things that went away with a simple crack of a spine. No matter how many times I went to the dermatologist, a heavy smattering of acne covered my cheeks, chin and forehead. I knew no guy ever looked my way, and over the years, I'd become okay with it. It helped me find out who my true friends were, and who not to waste my time around. Still, Melanie's words punched me in the gut. I wanted to believe the best in humanity, but sometimes it was a struggle.

Kyle's genuine displeasure at Melanie's slam made me stand a little taller, though he didn't say, "No, Rosie's not ugly," but rather, "Hey, she's my friend, and you need to cool it with that kinda talk."

I swallowed down the bad spot on an otherwise awesome night, working up a grin for Judah, who'd finally come down from his gloating. "You ready to go, Ro?" Judah asked, tucking our winnings into his pocket.

I put on my best fake smile and pounded my fist in the air. "I'm super way pumped to study!"

The crowd was thickening, hitting the point in the night where, if you hadn't already secured a chair, you were nursing your beer standing up for the rest of the evening. I held onto Judah's hand so we didn't get separated as we weaved through the college students who'd come to celebrate the end (or near end) of the semester.

I was starting to feel claustrophobic right as someone bumped into me from behind, knocking my hand out of Judah's. The bulky body bumped me forward into a woman, who turned to scowl, and then reared back with the infamous grimace when she saw what I looked like.

I held up my hands like claws and hissed, as if I was a hag who was about to put a hex on her, cursing her into decades of unending slumber. If I was going to be gawked at like I was hideous, I wanted to really earn the part.

Judah snorted a laugh at the girl's horrified expression. He gripped my hand tighter so we didn't get separated as we slipped through the crowd, finally making our way out onto the cracked sidewalk. The neon from the bar's sign lit Judah's smile just enough for his levity to migrate to me. "Did you see her face? I thought she was going to pee herself. I love when you do that. And if I didn't say so in there, good game."

I bowed under the streetlight to my adoring fan, grinning as I righted myself. The smell of exhaust and semi-fresh air was a welcome reprieve from the peanut shells and bottom-shelf beer I'd been breathing in all night.

Judah did a doubletake, his brows furrowing in confusion as if I was wearing a weird hat or something. He took three steps back, and then two forward to squint at me, pushing his Buddy Holly glasses further up on his nose. "Rosie, your face! Did you... Are you wearing makeup or something?"

My nose crinkled. "Huh? Why would you even ask me that? I don't even own any makeup. You know that."

For the first time in his life, Judah pointed at my face in distaste. "Your acne is gone. Like, you were normal just a minute ago, but now your skin is all... I dunno. You don't look like you."

"Who do I look like, then?" I challenged, hurt that he would point at me like the circus freak I often felt like.

"You look like your Aunt Lane! I mean, the similarities were always there, but now..."

My hand went to my throat to play with my necklace. I often did that when I wanted to soothe myself after being looked at like I wasn't pretty in a world where things like pretty mattered a little too much. My fingers touched the naked skin of my neck above my blue jersey, fumbling around for the chain that should've been there, but suddenly wasn't.

As if trying to pat down a fire, I felt all over my collar and my shirt, a panic rising up in me at losing the one precious thing I owned. "Oh, no! Judah, where is it? My necklace is gone!" I blinked rapidly as my left eye started to twitch while I searched around me for the sentimental treasure.

Judah frowned and turned on his phone to use as a flashlight, searching the concrete from where we stood all the way back to the bar. "I'm not seeing it. You sure you didn't take it off?"

I threw my hands in the air after shaking out my shirt and still coming up empty. "In all the years you've known me, have you ever seen me without that necklace? I never take it off! Lane made me promise to keep it on forever. Oh, she's going to flip." My vision started to swim, making the cars passing by look blurry, and then unnervingly detailed, disorienting me enough to take a step back. Rapid blinking made things clearer, but still didn't reveal my necklace anywhere in sight.

"I can't picture Lane getting pissed that you lost something. I can't picture her mad at you, period. It's an honest mistake, Ro. We'll come back in the morning and check the lost and found. It's probably on the floor in there. Chain was bound to break one of these days."

I groaned at the thought of people squashing the locket that had belonged to my long-deceased mother. My aunt had taken the locket from my mother's meager belongings and passed it down to me. "It's the only thing of my mother's that I have! Judah, we have to find it."

"Alright, alright. Don't worry. I'll help you."

My left eye started to itch as if there were phantom spiders running all over it, so I ran my index finger across my eyelid. I grimaced when I felt heat radiating out in a circle around that whole section of my face. I started blinking rapidly to clear away the foreign sensation, willing myself not to lose my cool and smack myself in the head to make the tingling stop.

When my gaze fell on Judah after my vision finally focused, he jumped back in horror. "Gah! What's wrong with your eye?"

It was the hurt that had never come from him until this moment. All the other kids in school had blanched at my lazy left eye, but Judah never cared that I looked different. Now he was acting like the woman who'd cringed in the bar when she'd gotten a good look at me. To have him comment on my wonky eye in the same minute he was acting all horrified by the rest of my face was a double whammy that made me take a step back. Anger welled up inside of me and spewed itself all over my best friend. "Are you just now noticing that I look like this? What's your deal, Judah?"

He seemed to remember himself and cleared the gap between us, hands raised. "I don't mean it like that. Your skin is totally as clear as a baby's, and your eyes are pointing in the same direction! It's freaking me out! How are you doing that?"

I felt my face and, sure enough, my skin was devoid of pockmarks. There wasn't even any of the scarring I'd acquired from acne gone rogue throughout the years. "Wha... Are you serious?" My optometrist swore up and down that my vision hadn't been affected by my lazy eye, but I began to notice that even though it was nighttime, I was able to see a little clearer – the edges of everything were a bit crisper. "Judah?" My voice came out in a pinched bleat of panic.

"I'm sure there's a totally logical explanation. Maybe it's a trick of the moonlight?" he suggested, though I could tell he didn't believe his conjecture.

I shook my head, feeling all turned around and border-line emotional. "A lazy eye doesn't just fix itself in a blink!"

"Okay, let's go home where there's actual light. Then we can see what we're dealing with. Maybe I'm wrong."

"Are you ever wrong?" I asked, incredulous.

"No," Judah replied apologetically. It was true. Judah was always at the top of the curve in school, but was blessed with the grace not to lord it over the dummies like me who were barely hanging on. His shoulders deflated when he took in the effect his unfiltered words had on me. "Come here. I freaked you out with my pointing. I wasn't thinking. I'm sorry."

Judah held out his arms, and I didn't hesitate to crash into them, resting my trepidation on his shoulder in hopes it would evaporate there. "Don't point at me like that anymore," I said quietly, letting him know that he was my safe place, and taking that away would be a devastation I wouldn't recover from. "Everyone else can, but you? You're my..." I fished around for the right word, but landed on shtick. "You're my pimp daddy."

Judah snorted into my hair. "You're totally right. I'm sorry, hot mama. Are you okay?"

"I lost my necklace, so no. Everything else can take a backseat to that. My acne is really gone? I saw myself in the mirror after the soccer match, and I was still me."

"Not a trace of it, Ro. And your left eye is pointing straight now. It wasn't that way when we were playing pool in there just a few minutes ago."

I was about to crack a lame joke to ease the seriousness, but a sudden ache in my back forced me to roll my shoulders through our hug. A gust of air thrust out of me when it felt like something suddenly shoved me from inside my spine. The push held enough of a punch to catch me off-guard, changing the most basic things about my appearance, and freaking me out when I was already on the brink. "Oof!"

Judah scrambled to hold onto me as my legs gave out. I whimpered pathetically when my back decided to be a total wuss and start spasming. "Hey, what's wrong? What's happening?"

"My back hurts! Oh, man! Super way painful. Give me a second." I tried to stand on my own, but my spine was in full-on contortion mode. Judah held me, despite my protest and my torso bending away as it tried to center itself.

A terrifying crack sounded, rippling down my spine.

Judah and I cried out in alarm as one voice, but he held me until I was finally able to find my footing. I slowly stood with a bit more stability, rolling a kink from my shoulders.

Judah hopped back with alarm clear on his face. He lifted his finger to point, but remembered himself and lowered it. Instead I followed his eyeline and patted my shoulders in fear.

The noise from the college kids passing by blurred into the background when my fingers reached over my shoulder and landed on... nothing. I pulled in a deeper breath than I'd ever managed before, my lungs expanding with extra room that came from standing up straight.

Only I'd never stood up straight before.

"My hump," I whispered, amazed and terrified. My mouth fell open when I realized that I was seeing the world from a vantage point of about two inches higher than usual, due to not being stooped anymore.

Judah shook his head, his hand over his mouth. "Rosie, your hump is gone!" He looked like he was about to say something else, but the newfound air that dragged inside of me was pushed out in a forceful gust.

Something heavy pulled at my chest, making the whole area feel bruised and unsteady. Discomfort mutated to pain as I moved my arms over my chest. I'd always had a flat chest, with no breasts to brag about. That, I'd been grateful for, though. Having immobile A-cups meant you could run faster on the field without being bogged down by weighty body parts.

My mouth fell open as dread colored my cheeks. Beneath my banded arms, I could feel my chest growing at an alarming rate. The whole area ached so bad I had to bite down on my lower lip to keep from screaming. Inches and inches expanded faster than I could conceal them, my skin stretching grotesquely as the elasticity of my sports bra was tested to its limits.

And then both straps snapped.

Never in all of our years as friends who'd seen each other through puberty had Judah ever glanced at my chest. He gawked like a teenager with no thought of social propriety as I scrambled to hide my spontaneous breasts. "Did those just... Are your..." He couldn't say the word "boobs" to me, which was good, because I might've imploded on the spot from mortification if he did.

"I'm going to go look for my necklace!" I shouted, horrified and utterly drenched in confusion. I worked the tattered remains of my bra over my hips and discarded the sad fabric in the nearest garbage can, flummoxed and a little terrified that I was morphing into something... not me.

I didn't wait for him, but barreled back into the bar, holding my bosom in place with my arms crossed. Goose-bumps were covering my arms, and tears of angst threatened to spill out of me. My shoulders and my chest felt like someone had taken a baseball bat to them, but the terror at the suddenness of it all hurt far worse. I pulled out some cash in my haste to find my necklace, and slapped it on the bar top. I rarely drank more than a beer or two, but my back ached, and my chest felt like the skin might tear at any moment. Frankly, I was surprised it hadn't. I slammed the shot in hopes it would be my pain reliever.

I'd never cried in a bar before, and was firm that tonight wouldn't break that trend. I didn't know what was going on with my body, so I decided I would deal with all of that later when I had a mirror and, I dunno, a sedative or something. My nerves were on the brink of a total breakdown.

My necklace. I have to find it and get out of here.

I renewed my focus, determined that I wasn't leaving until I had the locket around my neck once more. I was great at finding things. I was always the kid who had the most Easter eggs in my basket. I'd never lost my car keys. Not once. I was a human GPS who could find true North blindfolded. I followed my gut, and it led me to whatever I needed to find. It was how I landed so many flawless shots. My gut told my pool stick where to aim, and I never had a problem. I inhaled the stench of beer that stank like it had been soaked into the walls, warning my gut that it was go time. Judah came in a few minutes later, shaken but ready to be helpful in my quest to find my locket and get the crap out of there.

Three hours later, the bar was closing and we were being pushed out on to the street with a promise that the owner would call if they found anything.

Judah didn't say a word, but kept his arm around me as

we walked, my eyes on my shoes and my hands blackened from running them over every inch of that disgusting, sticky floor. I had one family heirloom. One. My Aunt Lane salvaged one thing off my mother's body before it had been cremated. The locket was gone now, and though I had no memory of my mother, the fragile connection I had to my roots was gone with it.

2

STRANGE BODY AND OLD DUDES

*T*he park was my favorite place to hide when life grew too confusing to navigate without a roadmap. The one just off-campus was geared toward kids, and showcased copious amounts of playground equipment. There was a runner's track stretching the perimeter, but the trees were my favorite part. They were a little piece of nature, smack in the middle of civilization. Tall and varied in color and trunk thickness, they gave a home to many a critter who saw me coming a mile away. It was a peaceful place, and even after the week I'd had, I could still feel nature calming me in that way only the best parts of life could.

It wasn't just the hippopotamus of pressure from exams that pressed down on my chest, it was a whole new chest that troubled me. I glanced down and tugged my light zip-up sweater tighter over my breasts. In the span of a week, I still hadn't gotten used to my face without the shroud of acne, my hump being gone and my eyes pointing in the same direction. Strangest of all were my breasts, which had burst from a solid A-cup, to actual double D's that I couldn't stuff gracefully into my normal clothes. They had kept growing in the days after we left the bar, but thankfully, seemed to have tapered off. I was surprised I didn't have stretchmarks, and that my bruising seemed to be mostly faded. Every morning since then, Judah had a freaked out look on his face when he woke up next to me, just as perplexed as I was that my entire body mutated so dramatically. I was too embarrassed about it all to call Lane and tell her all that had happened quite literally out of nowhere. So I hid in my hoodie, which wasn't quite the invisibility cloak I was wishing for.

My hand moved to my throat, seeking out the locket that was still missing. It was the thing that anchored me when life grew too confusing. Now when I truly needed it because I barely recognized my strange body in the mirror, it was nowhere to be found. Yesterday, my Chem professor had actually stopped me, saying that they weren't letting in new students to audit the class. He hadn't recognized me, though I'd never missed a lesson.

I ignored the bench and sat under my favorite knotted tree, setting down my book and opening up the loaf of bread. I didn't have to snap my fingers at the squirrels. I didn't have to be super still for the birds to land on the toes of my black indoor soccer shoes. They knew to come. No sooner had I dug the bag of birdseed from my pocket did twenty birds land near or on me, hopping with their tiny two-toed feet and vying for attention with their dainty chirps and chipper greetings. They were telling on the squirrels that evening, where they usually just sang me pretty songs and told me about their favorite places to build nests.

I felt eyes on me, but I shook off the paranoia. I kept my hoodie cinched tight around my face now, weirded out when people looked at me. The pointing had been replaced by appraising glances. I wondered if this was what normal felt like, and wasn't sure if I liked it or not.

"Calm it down, guys. I brought enough food for everyone. Tell me everything I missed." I worked up a smile for them as the squirrels started arguing with the birds over who had stolen whose twigs.

No, I'm not crazy. I know it's not normal to hear animals speaking to you, but from the time I could make out Lane's voice, I could also understand the entirety of the animal kingdom. They have no one to listen, so I let them unload. The squirrels made themselves at home tearing apart the slices of bread into squishable handfuls. I always bought the kind of bread with nuts in it, since that's what my squirrels preferred. Judah had thought it was crazy when we'd been younger, but he was used to me by now.

The birds were super talkative, and the squirrels were

downright rascally. Two of them started fighting over half a piece of bread, yelling at each other until I tsked their bad behavior and picked up my loaf. I peeled off my sweatshirt and hugged the bread to my purple *Princess Bride* t-shirt, which featured André René Roussimoff in his prime. "Cool it, guys. I mean it. If you two start fighting over food again, I'll take this bread and eat the whole loaf myself right in front of you."

"No! No, we'll be good," one of the squirrels named Randy promised.

The two backed down, Tubby's fat belly dragging on the grass while Randy fluffed his black tail to keep from lunging at the big guy on the yard who always tried to steal his nuts. "There's enough for everybody, so chill."

I reached for Penelope, who was never shy about climbing into my lap. She skittered over my shoulders and flicked my cheek with her gray tail, and then cozied up on my neck like a scarf to keep me warm, though it was decently toasty spring weather out. She chittered in my ear, begging for some good girltalk. *"Tell me about Jake again."*

The hottest guy on campus didn't even know I was alive, though we'd had three classes together. Jake was premed, wore skinny jeans and listened to my favorite band, Lost and Forgotten. I liked to add little embellishments when I told them about human life, so Jake was transformed into a pirate with a curved sword and a devil-may-care grin he whipped out just for fair maidens like myself.

Sure, Jake wasn't a pirate in real life, but that didn't matter. In my imagination, he had a bandana and an eyepatch and said things like "I'll have a shot of rum in that" (that last part I'd actually heard him say at a party once, so the pirate adventure wasn't too far off the mark).

"Will you ever get to go off on the pirate's ship and find buried treasure?" Penelope was always asking if I had any new stories about her favorite pirate.

"Sorry, sweetie. A life of adventure isn't for me. Besides, if Jake knew I was alive and invited me onto his pirate ship, I wouldn't be able to hang with all of you, would I?" I tried to keep my voice chipper, but my animals always saw right through me.

Penelope tried not to scrape me with her tiny claws as she hugged my neck. My favorite girl squirrel was always good at squeezing a smile out of me.

"It's fine. Wasn't meant to be. I've got too much school-work to do anyways. I don't have time for pirates. I'm learning how to take better care of all of you. That's way more important than being the princess." I tried to declare my future with gusto, but I couldn't lie.

My squirrels gathered closer around me, as the birds started singing the bedtime song Lane used to sing to me when I was little (and a few times I'd been homesick in college. Don't judge). My furry friends so wanted to soothe my heartache. It was the Beach Boys "Wouldn't it Be Nice", and they nailed every bar, as usual. My hand went to my collar to finger the locket that wasn't there. I felt naked without my necklace, and dreaded telling Lane I'd lost my favorite thing she'd ever given me.

The squirrels kept coming until the usual forty-three were gathered around me, intermingling with the two dozen birds and the skunk. My skunk always skulked in the background, like the exchange student who didn't know how to ask if he could sit next to you on the bus. "Come on, Wilbur," I offered, waving him forward. I'd never been sprayed before, and I was pretty certain Wilbur just wanted a friend. In that respect, we were the same animal. He was like a shy kitten who just wanted to be loved on, so after spreading out enough bread and seeds for everyone to have a snack, I kept one hand on Wilbur while I opened my textbook.

The familiar anxiety swelled up in me at reading aloud, but I knew my babies wouldn't judge me if I got a word or two (or three hundred) wrong. I came here a few times a week to practice before work, and they hadn't kicked me out yet. Wilbur snuggled into my shirt, nuzzling André Roussimoff's smiling face that stretched perhaps too tight now across my chest. I scratched Wilbur under his chin, smiling when he purred at the attention I paid him. *"I love you, Rosie."*

"I love you, baby doll." I knew how much he hated that people shouted when they saw him. He loved me because I didn't see a freak of nature when I looked at him. The animals treated me like I was their prom queen, and not the dyslexic ugly girl who didn't belong at the cool kids' table. It's a powerful thing to be so thoroughly loved for being who you are. Now that my body didn't look like mine anymore, I clung to the familiar feel of their love all the more to steady myself.

I stared the letters of the book down, daring them to make me cry. It was too much to hope that straightening my lazy eye might erase my dyslexia. I tried not to wish for things that would never happen, but every now and then, being at the bottom of the curve started to get to me. Forget overnight boobs; I'd trade my new big girl bra for the ability to read any day. "'The smell?' No, that's not right. 'The sm…sm…smallest atom in the d…d…d…'."

I felt someone's eyes on me, but I brushed off the paranoia and went back to my homework. "'The smallest atom in the d…d…d….'"

I stopped when I heard a set of footsteps running in my direction. I wasn't perched near the running track, so I wasn't quite sure what was going on. I tried to shoo my friends away, but they remained with me, taking on a protective stance. The birds formed a line to my right where the footsteps were coming from. Their heads dipped, readying to take flight in the direction of the newcomer, instead of flying away from the intruder. My squirrels started running laps around me, as if they thought they could form a static fence that would keep the trespasser away from their story time. I clicked my tongue to tell them to calm down; they usually didn't get so worked up with strangers.

"Rosie? That's gotta be you behind that tree. Only you'd be surrounded by a million little critters."

"Hey, Judah." I relaxed at the sound of his voice. "Have you come to escape the super cool people at the super cool complex?"

Judah groaned. "It's like just because some of us are finished with finals, they assume no one wants to read ever. The apartment below us I swear has some sort of major wrestling event going on."

"Whatcha reading?"

"The library had a huge used book sale, so I cleaned up. Can you believe I got all these books for twenty bucks?" Judah excitedly opened up a book from the top of his stack, rifling through the pages till he found the right one. Judah was a master at books. He educated me on most of the things my teachers threw up their hands trying to teach me. "See this font? They don't make it like this anymore. I mean, it's called the same thing, but the top loops are completely different looking." He yanked his phone out of his pocket and typed in the modern version of the font he was looking for. "See the difference?"

I nodded, though we both knew I was bluffing. Judah was my best friend, and had been my tutor since the fourth grade when my nickname had gone from "Rosie Posey" to "That Stupid Girl" when it got around that I couldn't read yet. "Very cool," I said, convincing neither of us that I understood what he was talking about.

Judah picked up my pointer finger and traced a letter

in the book with the tip of my nail, taking his time and going down each curly slope. "Okay, that's the old one." Then he froze the touchscreen option on his phone and traced the same letter (probably) with my finger so I could *feel* the difference instead of trying to *see* it. He got me, and what's more, he didn't mind spelling things out to help me. And respelling them. And respelling them. "This is the new one. The tail on the end is curvier. Totally different, but it's still called the same thing. Eleven years, Ro. That's all it took for them to evolve this font into something almost unrecognizable. Isn't that crazy?"

"Totally shitbat." I always got a kick out of the weird things that excited Judah. Most people didn't get his quirks, but I did. He had one minor flaw, though: tunnel vision. "Dude, tell me you left enough money for dinner. It's your night to cook."

He winced and then slowly looked over at me. His sheepish half-smile made his wider nose crinkle only on one side. "How do you feel about soy dogs and macaroni?"

"*Again*. How do I feel about soy dogs and boxed macaroni *again*," I complained.

"Come on. What's going to feed you better – books or a measly meal that we eat, and then it's gone? Books are forever, baby." We were leaning on the same stretch of bark, our heads sharing the tree as our own upright pillow.

I narrowed my eyes. "Hm. When your stomach is growling tonight, I'll just tell you to put some ketchup on page eighty-nine. Sound good?"

"I'm going to Jason's tonight for D&D, so you're on your own. Speaking of which, I'm still not abandoning my theory that your locket was magic, and losing it made your body morph into this new one. I'm thinking there was a spell put on it that gave you your hump and whatnot." He waggled his fingers at me, his eyebrows dancing at being able to work his story games into conversation organically. He pushed his glasses up his nose with a grin.

Judah's imagination usually ran somewhere between The Shire and Mordor. "That's a pretty solid theory. Is that backed by the Medical School of Vampire-Elf-Tinkerbell?"

"It is, actually. Doctor Peter Pan himself endorsed my conjecture."

I raised my eyebrow at him. "Wait, you're gaming tonight? Aren't you going out with Jill? It's your anniversary. Five years, dude."

Judah grimaced. "Oh, man! You're right. I totally blanked. Do you think I can pass off any of these books as an anniversary gift?"

"Um, being that she's hoping for an engagement ring, I'm guessing a used book on graphic design would be a giant step down."

Judah paled. "She's not expecting a ring. Why would she think we're ready for something like that?"

"I dunno. Five years together is a long time. Plus, her roommate just got engaged."

"Yeah, but Tonya's a senior. We're juniors. We've got

years of time before conversations like that have to come up. Why can't we just leave well enough alone?"

I smiled and clasped my hands together under my chin, gazing up at the white, puffy clouds. "One day, I hope to have my very own boyfriend who dodges the 'where is this going' speech at every turn. Totally dreamy." I balked when Judah opened his book again, and flipped through a few pages. "Are you seriously going back to reading when you've got nothing planned for your anniversary tonight?"

"I seriously am. Jill has no reason to think I'm proposing tonight."

"Sure, but she might be hoping for flowers or something that says you appreciate that she's stuck around for five whole years."

Judah shrugged, avoiding my penetrating stare by burying his nose in his book. "Quit with the nagging. Be my hot mama and just enjoy the afternoon with me." He always used ridiculous terms of endearment when I was pissed at him, or when he wanted to make me laugh. We liked to pretend we were the shiz. Our own VIP party for two suited us well, though it made the rest of the world raise their eyebrows at us.

"Okay, pimp daddy. I'm just trying to make sure Jill doesn't murder you. It's not a bad thing that a woman wants to spend her life with you. Sooner or later, you're going to have to either make a commitment or set her free."

Judah put his book on his knee and turned so I could

look into his dark brown eyes, which were framed with the thick black plastic rims of his glasses. "Rosie, for better or worse, till death do us part, you're my best friend. That's about as committed as I'll ever get."

I smiled at him. "Aw. That was sweet. Thanks, Player."

"Anytime, Boo."

I turned my attention back to my studying. "Jill's still going to murder you dead if you show up with a used book instead of something relationshippy. Fair warning. I like my BFF in one piece."

"Which piece would you like? I can have Jill send it to you, because I don't have enough for something nice for her."

A twig snapped a ways behind me, alerting us that we were not alone. Judah stood so we didn't look so couply, and I watched his expression twist into confusion. "Can I help you, man?"

The footsteps quickened into a swift march. They were heavy and determined as they neared us. When the mid-seventies-aged man filled my vision, I decided he was definitely not a runner who'd skipped off the trail. The black cloak that hung off him looked Red Riding Hood-ish (except, you know, it was black). The stranger stood tall over me, even though he was stooped with age. His face was scarred on one side, like he'd suffered through a painful acid burn. It left the cheek pock-marked and lined with what looked like permanent claw indentations.

Wilbur left my lap when I stood, and I knew he was

waiting for me to move away from the stranger before spraying him, which I appreciated. "Sorry. We were just leaving. You can have the tree." The good tree. The one that curved perfectly to my body and had a root system that felt like a cozy chair and fit my hips like a hug. I stood, scooping up my book and dumping the rest of the bread and seeds out of the bags for my buddies to eat.

"Are you the daughter?" he said with too much intensity, his blue eyes boring into my matching ones. His breath stank like rotting kitty litter. When he reached out to clutch my shoulder, his gnarled fingers bent around my bone like steel that didn't fit with his old man physique. "Are you her?" he demanded.

"Whoa! Hands off, buddy." Judah gripped the much bigger man's arm, and was rewarded with a hard shove that actually made him stumble back, trip and fall on his backside.

Pure anger rose in me whenever anyone was nasty to Judah. "Hands off!" I warned. When old dude didn't comply, I wriggled and shoved him as hard as I could.

Old dude's scarred face barely registered any offense. He didn't budge, his fingers still digging into my shoulder. "Oh, the reward I'll get for coming back with you!"

I tried to shake him off as the squirrels ran around me to create a living, breathing barrier, making sure that though his hand could get at me, the rest of him couldn't. His skin was covered in yet more squirrels, who attacked and bit into his flesh with vigor, defending me with everything in their arsenals. "Back off, dude! I don't know who you're looking for, but I'm not her. Get lost and leave us alone."

"The animals! I know you're the Lost Daughter of Avalon." His tone was accusatory, as if he was announcing some big scandal. "Finally! You're coming with me."

"Okay, now I'm pissed. You're hurting me!" I tried to struggle free, but surprise and the beginnings of fear started flooding into my pores. I didn't want to hurt the old man, but I also didn't like strangers putting their hands on me. I reached out and popped him in the chest with the flat of my hand, torn between guilt at shoving an old dude, and confusion that my shove had little effect. When that did nothing, I took a swing and socked him across the jaw. In the next second, I was immediately horrified that I'd struck a senior citizen. "I'm sorry!"

Judah scrambled to his feet and lobbed a punch at the guy, missing the mark and letting panic fuel his punch more than calculated rage. The man jabbed Judah in the stomach, and I watched with dread as my best friend doubled over in pain he'd not been seasoned to shake off.

I wasn't quite so delicate. Judah was more the book type than the muscular type. I was more the bar brawl type when someone crossed Judah and put their hands on me. Despite the fact that he was an old man, my conscience muted and I saw red. My fist launched from my body and knocked the old dude across the face once more, but again, the power I packed behind my punch did nothing but irritate him. I was temporarily stunned. I'd decked a few guys in my time, and none of them had behaved like they were being annoyed by a fly. This old dude was no joke. I was beginning to see that Judah was a liability, and that I wasn't a huge asset either.

3

ANGEL OF VENGEANCE IN FLANNEL

"*H*elp!" I screamed, alerting no one. I told the squirrels to move, and then kicked out at his stomach, but he was determined I should stay where I was in his clutches. I kicked at his knee with my best soccer goal thrust, feeling horrible that I was attacking an elderly man who was clearly off his meds, and most likely ate spinach every day to maintain his Popeye-like strength. The kick finally allowed me to break free, so I bent down and picked up my heavy textbook. I didn't hesitate for my conscience to slow my swing as I bashed an entire year's worth of theorems against the old dude's temple.

I'd always wondered what Popeye would look like as an old man. Trade in the black cloak for the sailor outfit, and this salty jag was a dead ringer for a seventy-year-old Popeye.

My squirrels took my attack as a green light to unleash

on him once more. They skittered up his body, scratching at what was unmarked on his face and swiping at his eyeballs. He howled, batting at them as he stumbled about like a drunken, well, sailor. I wanted to stay and fight with my animals who were coming to my aid, but Wilbur gave me the ominous head tilt that told me it would be tails-up in a hot minute. I hoisted Judah up, turned and ran with him toward the street, seeing two guys charging for us to come to our aid.

Well, whataya know. There still are decent people who come when they hear a cry for help.

"Bastien, go after him!" The guy running towards me wore a plain brown polo, nice jeans and looked to be an African-American dude in his early thirties. "It's alright! We've got you!" he called to me, meeting me in a hug I didn't have the wherewithal to question. He was half a foot taller than me and built like he was made for answering cries of distress. His friend, Bastien, I'm guessing, who charged the old dude, was built like a tank wrapped in red flannel, and whipped past me in a blur. I remained in the stranger with the brown shirt's arms while Judah keeled over and held his stomach, moaning. It was the longest hug I'd had from a guy who wasn't Judah since I'd happened past a Green Peace meeting on campus that dismissed as I was walking by. Those pacifists were quite the affectionate type. "I'm Reyn, and you don't have to worry about Armand anymore. Bastien will handle him."

I ducked out of the hug sheepishly, hating that I looked

like a teen who threw up drama over nothing. "I don't know what he wants! He just came up to me and told me I needed to go with him. He..." I felt embarrassed to be tattling on an attack from a senior citizen. "He's stronger than he looks. He grabbed me and I couldn't get away. He punched Judah!"

Reyn patted Judah on the back and led us toward the street, his arm around my shoulders to keep me tucked into his side. "I know he's strong. I'm surprised you managed to get away at all. Don't worry. Bastien will take care of him."

"You know that guy? Armand is his name?"

Reyn nodded, his black hair frozen in its short and naturally spindly style that stood no more than an inch off his scalp, and was buzzed short around the sides. "Unfortunately. I should've guessed he'd be tailing us instead of doing his own search for you. It's lazy, is what that is."

I balked at Reyn, the shock still rolling through me. "He's after *you*? Then what the flip was he doing harassing me?" I heard grunts of a fight near my favorite tree and turned to look, but Reyn corralled me toward the street, squaring my shoulders to face ahead so I didn't see who was winning. His other arm patted Judah's back in a "hang in there, champ" kind of way.

Judah groaned, rubbing his stomach. "I've never been punched before. This is probably some sort of rite of passage or something, but all I feel is pain."

Reyn led us faster away from the brawl that was

growing louder and more violent, if the grunts and howls were any indication. "We have to get you out of here. If Armand tracked us down, there's no telling who else might be on their way here."

I shook my head at myself. "This isn't right. I can't let your friend take him on by himself."

Reyn managed a weak smile that didn't touch his green eyes. Against his dark skin, the green shown brightly, making him look that much more expressive. "Bastien can handle himself just fine."

I ducked out of Reyn's half-embrace and ran toward the mayhem. It wasn't in me to leave someone to fight my battles. I wouldn't have a stranger get hurt because he was being a Good Samaritan.

My animals were yelling at me to run, but they knew as well as I did how stubborn I could be when I was keyed up. I grabbed a fallen two-foot long thick branch off the grass and gripped the hilt like a pro baseball star. After eight years of softball, I had my fair share of experience.

Bastien was huge – an action hero if I ever saw one. He dwarfed my five feet six inches by almost a foot. He wore a red flannel shirt with his jeans, the sleeves rolled halfway up his arms to reveal a wrist tattoo of a hammer and a lion. He also bore a matching neck tattoo that had some scripty kind of lettering across the left side.

Armand was no match for him, but the strange thing was that Armand didn't raise a hand to Bastien. He simply stood there with his arms raised, unsure if he should strike.

My heart seemed to slow and my veins felt frozen when I saw Bastien pull something that looked like an eight-inch thick stick from his back pocket. He clicked a switch on the side and popped out a jagged blade that looked more pirate than hunter. He didn't hesitate at my scream, but plunged the steel into Armand's stomach. The steel tore upward, like Bastien was puncturing a pillow in hopes of spilling the feathers all over.

Only it wasn't feathers that trickled out. Thick red ribbons trilled down Armand's torn shirt and pants, painting him in gore. I wanted to look away from the macabre scene, but my whole body seemed to be frozen to the spot.

My scream was on repeat; I was in such a state of shock that I didn't even hear myself at my top volume. I kept going back to my favorite movie, *The Princess Bride*, hoping my sweet Wesley would never have been so brutal. Reyn trotted over to help, and lowered Armand down, laying him facing the sparse clouds above. Then he covered Armand's face with his cloak almost reverently.

Bastien turned to me, blade at his side like an angel of vengeance, wrapped in flannel. My animals scattered to watch the scene unfold from their various perches, but when Bastien closed the distance between us and cupped his hand over my mouth to stop my scream short, the birds started up their angry rants. They chirped with the foulest language at the scandal of a stranger putting his hands on me. Bastien smelled like masculine sweat, cinnamon and Christmas trees, his caramel eyes boring into my blue ones to make sure I could focus enough to hear him. "Shh. We have to get you out of here. If Armand found you, there's no telling who else might be coming." Bastien had rounded cheekbones and a wide, stern jawline that was peppered with what looked to be three days of forgetting to shave.

Penelope threw a nut at Bastien, chittering at him to keep his hands off me. Girlfriend always had my back.

"You need more proof? It's her," Reyn said, moving away from the old, dead Popeye, who would never again eat another can of spinach.

4

ROLLING AND BOOKING

"I don't know that guy," I admitted, goosebumps erupting on my skin too swiftly for me to suppress a shudder. "He just grabbed me out of nowhere." I stopped before emotion became apparent in my voice. I'd never seen someone murdered right in front of my eyes before. It was scarier than it looked when I'd seen the occasional stabbing on TV shows or in movies. This was sadder, and infinitely more finite. "Are... Are you okay? Bastien, is it?"

Bastien nodded. "You alright? Armand didn't hurt you before we found you, did he?"

I shook my head, horrified at how the evening had unfolded. I touched Bastien's arm, but retracted when he flinched. His eyes widened and he moved a foot to the left while we walked, as if my mere touch unnerved him. "I'm sorry. I just... Are you hurt? How can I help? He was so strong. Did he get in any punches?"

The corner of Bastien's mouth twitched upward, clearly not used to being fawned over. "Not a single swing."

"Seriously, thank you for intervening. You were incredible."

Bastien met my gaze of gratitude and bobbed his head once, tilting his chin downward, as if uncomfortable accepting praise. "Don't mention it. You looked like you were handling him alright before I got involved. All you were missing was a decent weapon."

I straightened with pride that he'd assessed my prowess as more than capable. "Well, lucky me that you showed up with your butter knife."

Bastien chuckled, and then stopped the sound abruptly, his eyebrows furrowed. It was as if he wasn't comfortable laughing, but somehow I'd coerced it out of him. He frowned to remind himself of his personality, and introduce me to how his face no doubt normally looked. He cleared his throat. "Good that you're safe."

"Here, let us give you a lift," Reyn offered, his large hand flat on the back of my shoulders.

Under any other circumstances, I would never have accepted a ride from two strangers, but all I could think about was getting some distance from the dead body. I nodded, and Reyn walked beside me, leading me toward a blue Prius. There was a fifty-something man with salt and pepper hair behind the wheel who didn't turn his head to greet us. I wondered if he'd been too scared to get out of the car and help. I didn't much blame him.

Judah was too shaken up to ask questions. He followed us, a hollow look on his pale face.

When I slid into the backseat between Reyn and Judah, and Bastien took the passenger seat, Reyn gave the driver a pat on the shoulder. "Alright, then. Head east."

"I work just a mile up the road at the pet shop. If you could drop us there, that'd be great."

"Sure," Reyn replied, leaning back in his seat after the driver locked the doors and started off. Reyn turned to look across me to Judah, who was still coming down from the excitement. "You alright, brother? You took that punch like a warrior. Didn't even throw up."

Judah quirked his eye at Reyn in question to the congenial address. "Thanks, man. I hope that's the last time it happens. Did that guy really... Did he really just die? Did you really kill him?"

Bastien nodded from the passenger seat. "He was gunning for your girlfriend, so he had to go."

I rubbed my arms, trying to smooth out the goosebumps. "This is my friend, Judah." I twined my fingers through Judah's, and he squeezed back harder than usual. He wasn't used to physical fights, and no doubt this one had shaken him up.

"You killed it out there, Ro. If I was your old softball coach, I'd give you a gold star, for shizzle." Judah adjusted his thick black frames on the bridge of his nose, leaning against the door to give me a little more space.

Reyn watched our exchange with his arm draped across the headrest behind me. "So you're the Daughter of Avalon. In the very flesh. Elaine of Avalon hid you well."

"You mean Lane Avalon? Sure. She's my aunt who adopted me. Do you know her? Are you from her gym or something?" Bastien looked like a bodybuilder, and Reyn had a runner's physique. It wasn't a left-field guess. Lane was a personal trainer, but her gym was two hours away back home.

The two nodded uncertainly, as if unsure what they were agreeing to, or even what a gym was. Bastien kept his eyes ahead as he spoke. "Um, yeah. From her gym. She sent us here to talk to you. Good thing we showed up when we did. Otherwise it'd be little girl guts all over the place." Bastien scratched the back of his neck.

"'Little girl'? Hello, I'm twenty-two."

Judah sat back, trying to center himself. "Who was that guy?"

Bastien ceded the question to Reyn who, of the two, seemed more amiable and prone to gentle smiles. Reyn sat straighter, and spoke like someone who'd had a lengthy education. "Armand is the pet of Morgan le Fae of Avalon. She sent him to look for you. Actually, she sent quite a few looking for you. We're fortunate to have found you first."

"You were looking for me?" I shook my head. "Wait,

Morgan of Avalon? You mean Morgan Avalon, right? That was my mother's name."

"It still is your mother's name," Bastien argued. "She didn't change it."

I swallowed. "I guess that's true. I just meant that she's dead, so whatever Morgan Avalon you know can't be the same one."

Bastien and Reyn exchanged wary looks before Reyn took the bullet and said the thing they were both thinking. "Morgan le Fae of Avalon isn't dead, and she *is* your mother. She rules over the whole of Avalon, and she's searching for you. We can't let her find you, though. She's bent on..."

Bastien shook his head, and then rubbed a kink out of his shoulder. "None of this would make a lick of sense to you, so just trust us that Armand is a bad guy sent by the worst queen. We found you to hide you from her. If she uses your magic, there's no telling what she could do to the rest of the Fae. Bad news all the way around."

Judah's mouth dropped open and he cast me a "let's get out of here and away from the lunatics" look. I couldn't have agreed more.

I glanced from Reyn to Bastien and took in the listless expression of the driver who had yet to make a sound. He wore a long rope necklace that didn't suit his sweaty white dress shirt and red tie. "Um, o-kay," I said slowly. "I think I can walk from here. The store's just up there." I pointed, but the driver didn't slow down. "Um, sir? Can you drop me off here? I'm sorry, I didn't catch your name."

"He doesn't need a name," Bastien told me. "You can call him whatever you like. He won't obey you, though."

I quirked my eyebrow at flannel shirt's dismissive tone. "You sound like an entitled jag when you talk like that, you know."

Reyn let out a snort of amusement. "'Entitled jag', eh? I rather like the sound of that."

Bastien turned in his seat and glowered at me, all sense of our previous budding camaraderie gone. "Our driver's taking us to the gate. He won't stop unless Reyn tells him to."

"Huh? What gate?"

"The gate to Avalon. Do you always ask this many questions?"

"Only to people who don't bother making a lick of sense."

"We're taking you to Avalon," Bastien said slowly, as if I was dumb. "Are you trying to be stupid or something?"

No matter how many people called me that awful word, it never stopped feeling like a sucker punch to the gut. The air left my lungs in an inaudible gust, but I kept my mouth shut, absorbing the pain like friggin' Mike Tyson.

Judah came to my defense when my sore spot took a beating at one of my trigger words. "Hey, watch your mouth. She's not stupid."

I squeezed Judah's hand, my head clearing a little when he didn't let go. "Avalon. Is that in the state?" I asked, starting to sweat at the caged-in feeling that crept over my shoulder and settled in my chest. "Look, I really have to get to work. You just passed it! Turn around, guys."

Reyn looked ahead, unperturbed. "We're taking you to a place where Morgan's people won't come looking for you. And the truth of it is, we need your help."

Bastien hissed at this admission. "Give her the advantage, why don't you? You don't have to say it like that."

"How else would you say it? We're basically kidnapping this poor little half-pint and her friend. The least we can do is tell her why."

Bastien shook his head. "She's not a little anything. She was handling Armand pretty well back there. Watch her, Reyn."

My heart started banging around like a silent alarm that I couldn't believe wasn't audible. I had to get us out of here. The rescue was starting to feel like a well-timed trap. We were only going thirty miles an hour down the business-lined street, but I knew I still might get pretty banged up if I did a duck and roll out of the car. Judah's hand inched toward the handle, making eye contact with me as we silently agreed on the same crazy escape plan. We knew it would be risky. We knew it would hurt.

It was worth it.

The guys probably expected me to throw a fit, cry, reason with them and ask a litany of questions, but that's just not how I roll. Apparently, I'm a decent roller, as is Judah. After silently popping open the lock on his door, Judah gripped my hand with fingers meant for typing and painting. He waited until the car slowed for a stop sign and made his move, ignoring their shouts of surprise that I wouldn't be their magical Patty Hurst.

I played my fair share of soccer. Growing up, I'd been so introverted that my Aunt Lane signed me up for every sport and afterschool activity I could squeeze into my schedule. Soccer was the only one that stuck, and I still played with an indoor team on the weekends. It wasn't clubbing, but it was fun to me.

Judah was not a runner, but he was sufficiently motivated not to get kidnapped, so he was faster than his usual barely-a-jog pace.

We whipped past bus stops and businesses, wishing there were more people on the sidewalk at sunset to witness the insanity and call the cops. I didn't look back, but charged as fast as I could go with no plan at all other than to run. In my experience, the giant muscle-bound guys were only barely decent at cardio. Lane and I ran half marathons every year together. I only hoped Judah could hold the pace of the initial sprint.

I heard Bastien closing in on me with his heavy pants and growls of frustration at having to track down his prey, and sorely wished I'd stayed in karate past the few lower belts. I stopped on a dime, turned and swung my fist up toward

Lumberjack Bob's throat, cutting him straight in the center of his Adam's apple. "Run, Judah! Go!" It was satisfying to watch Bastien double over as he choked, but I only caught a glimpse before I had to move on. I ran down the street after Judah, who turned the corner and didn't stop until he reached a store that was still open. We hid in the back aisle furthest from the window, making note of the fire exit in the corner.

Judah was white as a sheet, breathing through his teeth as he bent over at the waist to hold the stitch in his side. "Who are those guys?"

"I don't know! I've never seen them before in my life. You alright?"

Judah looked at me like I was the biggest idiot he'd ever seen. "Um, no! I've been punched in the stomach and just ran like, a hundred miles! I'm not okay! I won't be okay until we lose those guys."

"Take a breath. Go to your happy place." My heart was pounding and my hands were trembling, but I started singing "My Favorite Things" from the *Sound of Music* soundtrack. "'Girls in white dresses with blue satin sashes. Snowflakes that stay on my nose and eyelashes. Silver white winters that melt into spring. These are a few of my favorite things.'"

Judah glared at me through his panting. "You know I hate that song!"

Grateful to have sufficiently distracted Judah from his pain, I pulled out my phone. It was only then that I realized I'd landed myself in the one type of store I usually tried to avoid.

I was smack in the middle of a bookstore. Which, coincidentally, was Judah's version of his happy place, and also was my personal Hell. I tried not to look at the titles that begged me to read them, some of the books daring me and taunting me with their bold colors and stupid fonts that made decoding a chore. I closed my eyes so I didn't get too overwhelmed and pressed my phone to my ear, nearly squeezing out a tear when Lane's voice came to me. "Hey, Ro." Then she started singing her favorite song by the Spice Girls. "'Ro, I'll tell you what I want, what I really, really want. Ro, tell me what you want, what you really, really want.'"

Her casual voice calmed me down so I could at least get in a full breath. "Two guys! Chasing me. They said they knew you from the gym, but I'm pretty sure that was a lie. And the old guy died! But he attacked me first. It was self-defense!" I leaned over, bracing myself on the bookshelf to steady my nerves. Judah was shaking his head slowly back and forth, no doubt reliving the murder he'd witnessed me taking part in.

"You didn't punch, hit or kick anyone," Judah ruled. "I'll swear to the whole thing. We were on the sidewalk the entire time. No one's taking you to jail."

Emotion welled up in me at Judah's pledge. Though I knew it was self-defense, the fact that Judah would lie under oath to save my skin reaffirmed that he was my ride-or-die best friend until the end. "I love you," I whispered.

Judah's firm nod was all he could muster.

Lane's voice turned sharp, and I could picture her pink lipsticked mouth pulling in a tight line. "Tell me what they look like."

"Bodybuilder on too many steroids. Tall. One in a brown shirt, the other in a flannel. Tattoo on the lumberjack's neck. Bastien. Late twenties, mid-thirties." Another detail popped into my mind. "Reyn! The brown shirt guy said his name was Reyn." I forced out a high-pitched laugh that made me wince with its fakeness. "They called you 'Elaine of Avalon' instead of Lane Avalon. They killed Armand, the old Popeye guy who attacked me, so I thought they were good, but then they tried to kidnap Judah and me! They said I'm the Daughter of Avalon, and Lane, they knew Mom's name! They think she's still alive, but she's some evil queen or some nonsense. What the flip is going on? Judah and me? We're pretty well freaking out right now!"

My aunt swore, which was a thing she didn't do unless she dropped something heavy on her foot or was caught off her guard. "Okay, listen to me, Rosie. Tell me exactly where you are, and then stay there until I come get you."

"But you live two hours away!" I shook my head. "No. I'm fine. We'll wait it out here until I'm sure they're gone, and then we'll head to the police station and file a report."

"You're not fine! You have no idea who those guys are."

"Think of the gas money, Lane. It'll cost you a ton to drive all the way out here. I shouldn't have called. I'm sorry. They just... I've never seen someone die before!" I closed my eyes, keeping my voice quiet so as not to confess my crimes to any eavesdroppers, though it looked like we were the only ones in the store. Judging by the empty cash register, I guessed it was smoke break time. "And I helped! I took swings at the old Popeye dude so Bastien could kill him! I helped kill a man!" I whispered.

"Shut up!" Judah scolded me, looking over his shoulder to make sure no one heard my admission.

Lane acted as if I hadn't spoken. "Where are you? I'm getting in the car right now."

"Oh, jeez. I don't want that. Never mind. Seriously. I'll go straight to the police station once I'm sure they're gone."

"Tell me where you are!" she yelled. Lane never yelled. Not even the time I accidentally nicked the mailbox with the fender of her precious Honda that I could hear purring in the background.

I bit my lip, wishing she was here. Though, really if I'm wishing for things, I should've wished I was there, and then those guys wouldn't be able to find me.

Lane had given up everything to raise me when I'd been willed to her as a child. She'd been only seventeen at the time, and saddled with a one-year old. Somehow she'd made the best of it, and though money was always tight, we were tighter. I felt terrible at making her come all the way out just so she could walk me two blocks to the police station. Though I wanted to protest further, part of me needed her. I was such a mommy's girl. I took a deep breath to calm my erratic nerves. "We're in Halston Books on Fifth and Main. Not more than a few blocks from the pet shop."

Lane's voice was determined. "Good, baby. You stay right there and get down. I'm on my way."

I should've been paying closer attention. I shouldn't have stopped moving until we made it to the police station. There were probably a million things I should've done to make my life what a life should be, but none of that mattered when Bastien snatched the phone out of my hands and wrapped me in his tight grip with his free arm. Reyn slid out from behind the rack to block Judah with what looked like a kindly scolding on his rounded features. His hand went over Judah's nose and mouth quicker than either of us could combat. Though my bestie was a few inches taller than me with a slim build, he looked very small as he inhaled something he wasn't supposed to. Judah started to go limp, fighting to get to me, begging me with his drooping eyelids to make it all better.

I wanted to. I wanted to save Judah, but Reyn dragged him toward the fire exit that led out to the alley. I screamed into Bastien's hand as he moved me toward the back exit, closer and closer to my doom.

5

FIGHTING THE BRICK WALL

I wasn't fighting for my freedom at all anymore, but for Judah's. He had canvas to paint. He had fonts to super care about. He had a degree he was working towards. I struggled against Bastien, kicking and thrashing and throwing my elbows like a wild woman.

Holy crack on the cement, but the man was strong. Bastien's bicep tightened around my chest, and I could barely breathe as I jerked around to no avail, exhausting myself but not him. "Elaine of Avalon?" he breathed into the phone. His voice ragged, probably because he sucked at cardio, and was a kidnapping bastard. "Would you stop it?" he grunted at me, squeezing tighter.

"Oh, okay!" I replied sarcastically, ramping up my struggle. "Get off me!" I shouted for help, but Bastien dragged me out through the back exit before the store clerk came running to see what the commotion was about. Of all the stores we had to duck into, bookstores these days were the desert island of commerce. I'm inclined to blame Michael Bay with his flashy movie productions, but since he's a fellow dyslexic, I gave him a pass to make as many movies as he wanted that mutated readers into movie-goers.

The alley was far darker than the street, but I was determined not to get murdered next to the dumpster like a statistic. Reyn trotted back and snatched the phone from his friend so Bastien could muffle my screams with his hand. I continued my quest to fight with all my might, determined to make his life miserable if he was set on keeping me hostage. I stomped hard on his foot, plunged my elbows into his abdomen, and scratched and bit at random.

I heard Lane shouting on the phone, calling down every filthy curse imaginable if they didn't let me go right that second. Reyn's voice was calm, as if the whole thing was a PR mess. "Elaine of Avalon?" He waited while Lane ranted some more, and then spoke with a low threat that sent a chill through me. "This is Reyn. I'm the judge's son from Province 2. I've come from Faîte to collect the daughter of Morgan le Fae." I heard my aunt going ballistic, but Reyn paid her no mind. "Morgan wants her, and no matter how much you hate me right now, the one thing we have in common is that we don't want Morgan to find her daughter. I know that's why you've hidden her here. I know there's no other reason you'd choose to exile yourselves up here in Common."

I was growling and trying to rip myself free from Bastien's iron grip, scraping at him with my nails and biting him until I tasted blood while I stomped on his instep. Bastien didn't even flinch, the Frankenstein. "Dude, you're pissing me off," I warned him when I finally wrenched my mouth free. Then I shoved my elbow into his abdomen again, wincing at the immoveable muscles that barely budged at my attack.

"A little to the left," he cooed, as if this whole thing was funny.

I stomped down hard on his left foot, satisfied at his slight wince. "Like that? Did that feel good?"

"Tickled a little."

"Laughing, are you?" I tried my hand at popping my backside into his hips to attempt hefting him over my shoulder, but dude was a brick wall.

"Who knew the Lost Daughter of Avalon could fight? That one might've worked, if you weren't going up against me. I'm too tall for that to push me off my balance. But if you're fighting someone else next time, make sure he's not backed up to an alley wall, so you can get some real leverage."

I was livid that he was calmly giving me pointers. "Don't patronize me! I'll end you!"

Reyn flicked my ear, grinning like a little boy who knew he wasn't supposed to tempt the pit bull, but who also knew the dog behind the fence couldn't do anything to get at him. "She's a fighter, but if you could just explain to her that we're not going to hurt her or her little friend, that would make my life so much easier. It would also help us get her out before anyone else from the Queen's Army finds her. We're your best bet for keeping her hidden right now."

I bit down on Bastien's finger and ripped my head back and forth, smearing his blood on my cheek. I could feel his frustration that I wouldn't go quietly. "Ah! Would you stop it?" He clutched me tighter, his hard muscles making my many attempts at freedom seem like a joke. I was finally making a dent, making him wrestle me to keep his hold. *Point, Rosie.* "If you'd just settle down, I could tell you that you're fighting the wrong guy." Then he started smooshing my cheeks so that my mouth opened and closed on his command. When his high-pitched voice came out in a poor imitation of me, I stomped down harder on his foot, accomplishing nothing. "Oh, Bastien! Thanks for showing up like that and saving my neck. You're so strong and handsome." Then he switched his voice back to his own deeper cadence. "Aw, you don't have to say that. I live for rescuing damsels in distress."

"Bite me, you jag! I'm not a puppet! I'll bash your head on the cement if you don't let me go right now!" I finally ripped my head away from him and thrashed around as best I could, but dude was ripped. I bit Bastien harder on the inside of his middle finger, not stopping until I drew more blood, letting it drip down my chin like a savage.

Reyn continued his conversation with Lane, shaking his head at the two of us. "We just saved her from Armand, Morgan's favorite pet. If he's here, more are coming. You might want to consider going further into hiding, your majesty. In fact, if Armand found her, you might not have much time to relocate. I'd get out now. Pack a bag and run, Duchess. If you come meet us, we can protect you and keep you hidden."

I heard Lane quiet down as I listened to the strangest conversation I'd ever heard. Her answering tone sounded like the whole thing wasn't all that confusing to her, which scared me more than the whole being abducted thing.

Reyn nodded a few times. "Alright, then tell the Lost Daughter of Avalon that. She's trying to run away, and we don't have a whole lot of time before the others find her." He mustered up a friendly smile to contrast my wrath as he put the phone to my ear.

"Rosie? Hun? Are you okay? Are you hurt?"

"*I'm* hurt!" Bastien unclamped his hand from my mouth and sucked on his finger to stop the bleeding, complaining loudly. "Does anyone think to ask good old Bastien how he's holding up? No! Rosie bit me! I saved her life, and she bit me! Your girl attacked an Untouchable, I'll have you know."

"I'm okay." Tears pricked my eyes as I struggled against Bastien's looser grip to get closer to the phone, as if that could get me nearer my maternal source of comfort. Lane would somehow find a way to make everything better, I just knew it. She had that way about her.

When no one had asked me to the homecoming dance senior year, Lane went as my date. We'd gone to the thrift store and found a couple of not too shabby dresses that we doctored up to look like the dream come trues we would've bought if we'd had the money. We did each other's hair in fancy twists and made a day of having the most fun being girly and young. She was always a ball of optimism and life, pushing me out onto the dance floor until I came out of the turtle shell I so loved cozying up in. Surely she could find a way to make this chaos better, too. "Laney? Tell me you're right around the corner and can make this all okay." I closed my eyes, knowing even she couldn't sew and bedazzle me out of this mess.

"Baby, I need you to listen to me. There's a lot you don't know about your parents. Your mom... Well, I didn't tell you the whole truth. Actually, I outright lied. A whole heap of lies to keep you from looking for her." I could hear her frustration as she spoke through her teeth. "And I don't even have the time to tell you all this gently, because Avalon's probably on their way to me right now! This isn't how I planned on telling you any of it."

Shock. Buckets of cold watered shock poured down on me. "You lied to me?" I squeaked, my whole worldview shifting like a Rubik's cube. It wasn't an accusation, but rather a plea for any other explanation.

When Bastien sensed my shock was too great for me to run away, he released me, so I could hold the phone on my own.

"I did. I lied to keep you safe, babe." I could hear her rummaging around in drawers, no doubt having driven back home to pack in a hurry. I was upset with her, sure, but underneath was a note of fear that someone might hurt her, and take away one of the few constants in my world. "Morgan? Your mother? She's a bad one, and if she's looking for you, it's for nothing good, I can promise you that. Go with the guys. They'll take you somewhere away from the danger, and I'll meet you there as soon as I can. Can you do that for me?"

I was thunderstruck. "Are you serious?"

Bastien shot me a superior "I was right" look, which earned him a hard slap across the face he only grinned through. It was like he enjoyed being slapped, and was used to women being so pissed off at the sight of his mug that they attacked without warning. This, of course, only got me a crushing bear hug when he spun me around so I was facing Reyn, my back pinned to his flannelled chest once again.

Lane's voice grounded me. "I so wish I wasn't serious. Rosie, go with them. They'll take us to Faîte. I'm meeting you at the gate. Think Narnia, but with immortals and Fae and all sorts of things that'll make your head spin."

My mouth was dry and my nose red. "My mom's alive? Why would you... I... You're all I have, and you lied to me!"

I knew my accusation hurt her. We never fought. Not even when I'd pulled a teenager on her and threw a fit about not being allowed to get my driver's license the day I turned sixteen. She handled me with a cool shrug and a hug that ended our feud in a matter of minutes. She was good like that.

But she couldn't hug me now, and Bastien's restraint was a poor substitution. Though his hold was still firm, it wasn't nearly as bruising once I stopped struggling so much. His hands were too big for typing, his fingers splayed across my heaving ribs to keep me secured to his torso.

Lane's voice came back repentant. "I did lie, and I'm sorry. When I meet up with you, I'll tell you everything, even the ugly parts. I kept the truth from you because the truth is awful, and you don't need to be around something so terrible. I want good things for you, hun, and your mom? My sister? She's... she's not a good thing."

I closed my eyes, reining in all the fury I wanted to rant. It would have to wait for an in-person showdown. "I don't want to go with Bastien and Reyn. Bastien killed a man right in front of me!"

Bastien hissed at my issue with him. "What was I supposed to do? Let Armand kill you or abduct you? I don't think you understand danger. Or a hero's welcome. I saved the day, you know."

"They drugged Judah and shoved him who knows where!"

Reyn kept his polite expression in place, smiling lightly at me as if I was being dramatic over a puddle in the middle of the sidewalk. "Judah's tucked safely in the trunk. He'll be just fine."

Lane was forcing her voice to sound calm, but I could hear the anxiety tightening her speech. "I know, but they're our best bet right now. Judah will be alright. The guys can hide you, so listen to them. It's a life and death thing we're facing, here, and we don't have other options."

I waited too many beats, wishing I had words to tell her how deeply she hurt me, and how scared I was at being asked to walk with the lions into their den. Finally I closed my eyes, consenting to whatever fate I was being pointed at. "Okay. I'll go with them."

Lane gusted out all the tension in her body. "Good girl. Thank you for trusting me."

I don't trust you. Not anymore, I wanted to say, but I bit back the hurtful words I knew I wouldn't be able to unsay. Reyn took back the phone and spoke in a low voice to Lane, making arrangements to meet during the half-moon at some place I'd never heard of. I didn't understand a crack of it, but I guessed that mattered very little.

6

BLOOD AND LUCK

I slumped in Bastien's arms, trusting that they were strong enough to hold me upright if they were powerful enough to restrain me. The alley was unlit, which suited me just fine, covering my tears as I broke down past what was socially acceptable to do in front of strangers. I felt Bastien's discomfort as he squirmed behind me. "Alright, alright. It's fine. Your aunt just told you it's fine, didn't she?" I could tell he wasn't used to comforting girls. He patted the top of my head awkwardly, like a giant holding a rag doll. It was sort of like being slowly knocked by a bear's paw. "Are you going to run?"

I shook my head, though I was still on the fence. Bastien released me, and I made a mental note that if I wanted to escape him again, all I'd have to do was turn on the waterworks. He put a healthy eight inches between us, looking away from my face as if I was wearing an embarrassing hat or something, the crackfish.

"Let's go," he said to Reyn, starting down the alley and out onto the main street. He looked both ways for threats as we walked down toward the car. I wasn't sure if that made me feel safer or more endangered. "Keep your head down. I don't want anyone getting a good look at you."

Dipping my chin downward helped to obscure my tears, I obeyed, wishing I could disappear altogether. "Where are we going?"

"Faîte. Your aunt just told you. Weren't you listening to anything?" Bastien snapped as Reyn ended the call with Lane.

A sharp upswing of anger flared in my gut that anyone could possibly be impatient with me under these circumstances. I stopped, waited for Bastien to turn and face me, and then socked him square in the nose. A number of curse words spilled out of him, matching the flow of the blood that ran down his chin.

"Ah, man!" Reyn rolled his eyes at his friend, apparently expecting Bastien would say something that deserved a good crackdown.

I held my finger in Bastien's face as he blinked rapidly to try and regain his vision. "You'll watch your mouth, you raging butthole. My whole world just got smashed, so I don't want to hear a disparaging word about any of the millions of questions I've got coming for you. Now look me in the eye and say, 'I deserved that, Rosie.'"

Bastien glowered as if he wanted to return my assault, but knew he couldn't. I could tell it wasn't because I was a woman, but more because I was the commodity they needed. "I could have you hanged for that, I hope you know."

"Bite me."

"Whatever. Run your mouth to Reyn. I saved your life, by the way. Any of those things you want to say to me have a 'thank you' laced in there?"

"You've got to be joking. Thank you for holding me against my will? Thank you for abducting me?"

"You're welcome!" Bastien shouted.

Reyn opened the door and ushered me inside with Bastien, taking the passenger seat for himself. "Head East," he instructed the driver, who obeyed like an emotionless puppet.

"Hello! Get Judah out of the trunk!" I protested as we drove down the street. Sure, *now* I saw pedestrians. Where had they been when I was calling for help? Lame.

Reyn shook his head, checking in the rearview mirror to make sure we weren't being followed, and that I wouldn't jump out of the car again. "He's got more room back there than with you. I put him on a blanket. He'll be out for a long time, anyway."

"How long?"

"A day maybe? Half a day? Depends on how much he inhaled before he passed out."

I lunged forward and socked Reyn in the temple, but

Bastien jerked me back before I could go in for another. "You keep your hands off of Judah!"

Bastien growled low in my ear. "You don't like it when your Judah gets messed with? Well, Reyn is my Judah. Punch him again, and we're going to have a problem."

"Bite me!" I seethed, unapologetic.

Reyn held up his hands. "Okay! I'll never drug him again. I promise."

After I settled into my seat, Bastien leaned his head back and motioned to Reyn. "Give me something for my nose, man."

Reyn fished around in the glove compartment and pulled out a stack of napkins for just such an occasion. Bastien started choking as he dabbed at his nose, sucking in the blood.

"You'll make yourself sick doing that," I commented, watching him struggle through swallows and gulpy breaths like most people did when they leaned their head back on instinct through a bloody nose.

"I don't need advice from a Commoner on anything. Man, you popped me good. Suckerpunched me when I wasn't ready."

"That's the thing about pissing me off. You want me to warn you next time before I knock you one? Being that you abducted me, I hope you're not expecting an apology." I wasn't usually so confrontational, but Bastien seemed to bring out the worst in me.

"Hello, I'm bleeding over here! You want to tone down

your mouth?" Bastien scowled, marring his rugged and masculine features that would've been handsome, were he not so surly. And if he wasn't, well, a kidnapping murderer from Narnia. He had lots of visible scars, I'm guessing from women fighting back in the throes of him abducting them.

I shouted in his ear just to disorient him. "What?!" It probably didn't speak well of me that I giggled when his mouth dropped open as he winced. His eyes shut while his head swung to and fro at my too-loud voice in his ear.

"Oh, man! Why, Reyn? Why couldn't we have dosed *her* and shoved her in the trunk instead of her little boyfriend?"

"Play nice, kids." Reyn was unperturbed by our fighting. He had the well-bred air of sophistication that came from someone born into a higher class than Bastien or me.

"Shut up." I huffed and rolled my eyes at Bastien's ineptitude to deal with such a minor affliction after successfully pulling off a murder. I could tell he wasn't used to being bested by a girl, or bested at all. His pride looked equally as wounded as his nose. *Good.* "Here. Give me that. You're going to make yourself sick." I took two napkins off the top of the pile resting on his thigh and batted his hand away, scooting closer to his parted legs and sitting up on my knees to reach his unshaven face. I pinched the bridge of his nose and tipped his head forward. The gentle pressure from my other hand on the back of his head told him to let me take charge. He swatted at me, but missed. When he could breathe through his mouth without choking, his shoulders relaxed. I patted him lightly on the back in a "hang in there" kind of way. "Despite the punch to the face you totally deserved, I am grateful you helped me with that Armand guy."

"That doesn't sound like 'I'm sorry I broke your nose, Bastien.'"

"I'm not sorry, and I didn't break your nose, you big baby. I wanted to teach you a lesson, not send you to the hospital."

"Baby?! We've been searching for you for almost a year to try and save your life, and when we finally find you, you punch me and call me a baby?"

"Um, you might've gotten better results if you hadn't tried to abduct me. Kidnapping and rescuing aren't exactly the same thing."

"Bite me," he breathed, coming down from it all still.

"I already did. Bit through the skin on a few of your digits, and I'm not apologizing for that, either." I braced myself for his tart reply.

Bastien paused, but the fight died between us when he chuckled into the napkin, which made him choke on the blood he'd already swallowed. "I didn't think you'd do that. You got me pretty good back there. You've still got some of my blood on your face."

I itched to wipe it off, but held my ground. "I think I'll leave it there for now. Remind you what's in store if you try anything rough like that again."

He picked up one of the napkins that had fallen to his

knee and reached up with a clumsy hand to dab the blood from my face. He was gentle, which I didn't expect him to be. My hand pinched his nose while he swept the blood from my cheek with slow, gentle strokes. A few inches closer, and we would've been hugging. He studied my face with curiosity that had almost a graphic intensity to it. I tried not to be drawn in, but parts of me that usually were content to live out their days muted began to urge me toward action, confusing the crap out of me.

When he balled up the napkin in the palm of his hand and reached his finger to trace my cheekbone, I couldn't help my intake of breath, nor the blush that swarmed up where he touched me. No man had ever touched me like that before. My eyelids lowered involuntarily, goosebumps breaking out on my skin when he ran his finger along the tips of my lashes.

Bastien retracted his hand a few inches, his eyes wide, and looking like he'd been caught farting in church. "I was trying to get you out of there before Armand could send word to the others that he'd found you. You have no idea how relentless they are."

"You're right on that." I lowered my voice, speaking with a steady gentleness I willed myself to feel. "I don't know anything about any of it because you snatched at me without explaining a thing. Does that seem like a good idea now?"

"You're annoying when you're trying to be right." Despite his prickly nature, Bastien let his forehead rest in my hand as I pinched the bridge of his nose. His shoulders relaxed when my hand gently stroked from the back of his head downward, calming the beast with a simple touch.

Trees whipped by us, announcing the beginning of spring to the world with their brightly colored green leaves to the night, laughing at winter for giving up so soon. I worried about letting the guys keep Judah in the trunk. He'd never done drugs before, and I hoped whatever roofies Narnia had to offer weren't all that strong. Or maybe I hoped they were strong enough so Judah could sleep through the whole thing, and wake up thinking it was all a bad dream. I couldn't decide.

I looked up, ignoring Reyn's look of utter shock at the two of us playing nice after such a fight when I saw a trickle of blood coming out of the driver's right ear. "Um, that doesn't look so good. You alright up there, chief?"

Reyn glanced over at the driver and swore. "Pull off the road and park somewhere," he instructed the emotionless man, who seemed unperturbed by his own blood. "This one's done. We've got to switch up the guide so we don't kill anyone else." The driver pulled off the freeway and into the parking lot of a rest stop. There was a smattering of trees shielding us from behind, and your standard shabby, but not disgusting, rest area in front of us, with no other cars in the lot.

"'Else'? How many people have you killed?"

"Just a few. Trial and error. I mean, we've been scouring Common, searching for you for nearly a year now. We're still learning." Reyn turned to the driver and looked the guy in the eye. "After I take off the necklace, you'll go call a friend or someone to come pick you up. We're keeping your car, and you won't report it stolen. You'll be alright, but you won't remember a thing about this. You blacked out and woke up here. Nothing more." He pointed to his chin. "Do you remember this face?" The man shook his head. "How about those two?" Reyn jerked his thumb in our direction, and the man shook his head again. "Alright, then. Have a nice life." Reyn reached out and removed the rope necklace from around the man. He waved goodbye as the guy exited the car and headed for the restroom area, where there was sure to be a payphone.

"Go get another one," Bastien said, his head tilted downward, and resting in my palm. His words were muffled and nasal.

"I know, I know. It's just such a pain." Reyn sighed heavily, as if gearing himself up for some arduous task.

"Get another what? Driver?"

"Yeah. We don't know how to use this thing." Reyn slapped the dash twice. "We're not from your world, remember? We need a guide." He displayed the necklace. "This helps. It's one of the few charmed items that holds its magic up here in Common. It was around before the higher magic was taken from Avalon. Most magic doesn't work up here in Common. This has a *cerveau* charm in it, but if a person wears it for too long, it starts to melt their brain after a while."

"Well, keep it away from me." I removed my grip from Bastien and picked up his hand, molding his fingers around his nose so he could keep the napkin in place. "Pinch it hard, and it'll clot just fine, if it hasn't already. Keep your head forward, or you'll swallow too much blood and you'll puke. Not fun. Got it?"

Bastien nodded. "You're not going anywhere, though. Don't get any ideas. Just because you got in a lucky shot doesn't mean I won't take you down if you run."

I rolled my eyes. "Jeez. Unclench your butthole." I jumped when Reyn let out a loud laugh that filled the beige interior of the stolen car. "What's so funny?"

Reyn clapped his ebony hands three times, the corners of his eyes crinkling with delight. "'Unclench your butt-hole!' I've never heard anyone say that before. Oh, I'm using that one."

"Spread the love with my blessing," I allowed magnanimously. "And give me the keys. I can drive us where we need to get."

"No," Bastien ruled. "You're a flight risk."

"Actually, I came with you all by my little self. Lane said to go with you, so that's what I'm doing. I don't want you melting anyone's brains. No one else needs to get involved in your Harry Potter world of craziness. Leave my world be."

Reyn cast Bastien an apologetic look. "We really don't have the time to keep switching guides."

"It's settled, then. I'm using the restroom, and then we

can hit the road." I pointed an accusatory finger at Reyn, who held up his hands in surrender. "And you're getting Judah out of the trunk. You're going to make sure he's nice and comfortable in the backseat by the time I get back."

"Yes, ma'am."

Bastien's hand batted at the door before it landed on the handle. "Not out of my sight."

"I'm not bolting, and you're not following me into the women's bathroom."

Bastien didn't argue, but he didn't listen, either. He followed me as I walked under the glow of the streetlight to the restroom, and didn't stop when I entered the vacant ladies' room.

I turned and gave him a light shove to the chest. "Gross! Get out!"

"I said you weren't allowed out of my sight. We made it this far and finally found you. I won't throw it all away now."

"You are so dramatic," I huffed, slamming the tan stall door shut. He turned on the water at the sink, and I heard him scrubbing his face and neck. I came out and washed my hands in the sink next to him when I finished, looking at the handful of streaks of red staining his flannel shirt. I gasped and looked down at my own shirt when it dawned on me that my favorite t-shirt might be ruined. "Oh! I hope you didn't get any blood on André."

"Who's that? Was that the guide's name? Did you know him?"

I cocked my head to the side, realizing that only people who didn't know how to drive cars didn't know who André René Roussimoff was. "No. It's the guy on my shirt. This is my lucky t-shirt, but it doesn't look like it's stained. Thank goodness." I let out a sigh of relief as I washed my face of the rest of Bastien's blood smears. It was one of the few shirts that still fit me after my hump vanished and my boobs sprouted with a vengeance. André's face was stretched to distortion over my chest, but I could still see his smile that had only ever charmed me. "You thought I was a pill before, but you don't want to know the damage I'll do if you mess with André."

My eyes caught on my reflection in the mirror, and I flinched, temporarily confused that this was what I looked like now. No more acne – not even any scarring or pockmarks. My hump was completely gone, and I looked, well, like one of the cool girls who ate lunch at the cheerleader and jock table. It was off-putting, to not immediately recognize yourself in the mirror, to say the least.

Bastien rolled his shoulders back, looking at himself in the mirror in that self-satisfied way only the insanely good-looking people can. "Lucky t-shirt, eh? I never put much trust in luck."

"Well, my lucky shirt ran me smack into you guys, so I guess it's losing a little of its mojo." I dried my hands, trying not to be thrown by my reflection that I still wasn't used to. It was like someone had hired an actress to play me in the real-life version of my biography. Totally trippy. "How far is the drive?"

"Two more moons probably."

"That means nothing to me. Miles. How many miles?"

Bastien shrugged and wiped off his face. "We'll get there when we get there, Princess. The trick to not getting caught is to keep moving. We should go." His stubble was clean and devoid of the violence I'd spilled on it, but the nose that matched his stern jawline was puffy at the bridge.

I winced, hoping I hadn't broken it. "Oo. That looks bad."

He sniffed a couple times, and we were both a little relieved that his nose still served its basic function. He splashed a little more water on his face. "That didn't feel like your first fistfight. I hate to compliment the girl that gets one in on me, but that was a good shot. A lucky shot." He narrowed one eye at me while his face dripped over the sink. "The luckiest of your life. It's not likely to happen ever again, so don't get cocky."

I grinned at him. "Whatever helps you sleep at night, Princess."

"You're the princess. I'm the muscle."

"I don't like being called that. It suits you far better. You want me to carry you over any puddles we come across on the way to the car?" I teased, tearing off a few beige paper towels from the dispenser on the wall. I took a chance and dabbed at his face instead of simply handing him the wad of paper towels. There was something about him that made me want to lean closer, despite my better judgment. I could tell that he was equally confused that he'd let me into his body space, but neither of us pulled away. My hands were gentle as I blotted the water from his cheeks and chin, but my heart was working up a pounding rhythm that made me question my sanity. He studied my face while I let my hands linger long past any sort of practical need. His face was dry, and suddenly so was my mouth. My fingers grew a mind of their own, deciding with their sentient powers to take up residence along his jawline. His lashes fluttered shut, allowing me to study his features without having to own up to the crime. He had a notch taken out of his left eyebrow, a scar running clean through it from his hairline downward. Instead of recoiling, I leaned in closer to get a better look.

I froze, suddenly all too aware of how forward and downright reckless I was being. Bastien's eyes opened, and he seemed to be thinking the same thing about his own actions. He cleared his throat. "What were we talking about?"

I stepped away and tossed the paper towels in the trash, rolling my shoulders back as if nothing freakish had just happened between us. I'd had a crush on Jake for two years, and I hadn't been able to get within three feet of him without running away like a giant chicken. I turned and straightened my ponytail in the mirror. "We decided you would be the pretty princess, and I'd be the knight in shining armor."

I could hear the tease in his voice. "Is that so?"

"Don't you worry. If the big kids start picking on you, just tell me and I'll take care of it."

He mimed laughing, clutching his tight abs and tilting his head back before casting me a simpering look. "Hilari-ous." Bastien walked next to me as we made our way back to the car through the crisp night air. I felt the animosity between us dying down in layers.

Reyn handed me the keys and sat in the passenger seat next to me, with Bastien spreading out in the back next to a slumped and unconscious Judah, who'd been buckled in. I started the engine and pulled back onto the freeway. "Okay, guys." I cleared my throat and tried to feign a calm I didn't feel. "Tell me what I'm about to walk into."

BROWNIES AND BASTIEN

"You're telling me you're a Brownie? Like, a Girl Scout?" It was nearly half an hour into their "the truth is out there" speech, and I was no closer to understanding any of it.

Bastien gave a derogatory grumble, but Reyn was patient. He was leaned back in the passenger seat, with his hands folded behind his head, as if he was lounging on the beach. "We're not girls. We're men. Are the genders really so difficult to spot in your world? I can tell you're a girl easy enough."

I pursed my lips and shook my head as I held tight to the steering wheel. "That's not what I meant. Never mind. I know you're men. What's a Brownie, then?"

"Bastien's a Brownie. See his brown hair? Brown eyes? It's one of the races in Faîte. There are three different types of Fae. Bastien's the Brownie kind."

"What does that mean? Like, does that come with perks?" All I could think of to equate it with were video game stats, fantasy fiction and sci-fi movies. Judah was big into those, so I'd learned enough to fake my way through a conversation about RPGs, LARPing and whatnot.

"It's mostly the normal Fae stuff," Bastien answered, sounding bored as he stared out the window in the backseat. "Most of our more impressive magic was lost a long time ago. We're not all that different from Commoners."

"You say you're a fairy, right? All that tells me is that you live inside of flowers, fly around and sprinkle people with glitter. The only fairies we've got around here are the fictional kind in books and movies. I assume you don't live inside of a tulip, right?"

Bastien blinked at me, catching my eye in the rearview mirror. "You've got to know how little any of that made a lick of sense to us."

I shrugged. "Well, we don't have super powers here. Not sure if you've noticed, but we don't have fairies that aren't fictional. Start at square one."

"Square one? Okay. If I'd had access to the old magic that isn't around anymore, I could've turned myself invisible if I was very powerful," Bastien offered.

I looked in the rearview mirror. "Let me see." I slapped my knee and giggled. "Get it? I couldn't see if you were invisible." My laugh trailed off without the other two joining in, but I didn't care. "Whatever. My jokes are awesome."

Reyn eyed me as if I was a peculiar bug who'd just told him she was really an elephant. "You're much better company than the last guide. They can't talk when the necklace takes their will, so it makes for a pretty boring trip."

"Yikes. The more you talk about your necklace and its powers, the less I like it, and the less good I feel about you for using it on some poor, unsuspecting victim."

Reyn shrugged, unperturbed. "I'm okay with that. We were talking about Brownies."

"Ah, yes. Tell me all the things that make Bastien sparkle and compensate for the short end of the stick personality he got stuck with."

Reyn chuckled, casting me a sidelong glance before continuing. "Well, when we're in our own world, he's even less sparkly, if you can imagine."

I raised my nose in the air. "I simply cannot picture Bastien without a hefty dose of I'm-so-pretty."

Reyn smiled at me. "I'm a Rétif, which is the second kind of fairy. There are Brownies, Rétifs and the rest of the Fae."

"Hit me with it." I gripped the steering wheel, trying my best to keep my head above water as the bottom of my reality dropped out from under me. I kept my chin up, not wanting to be caught crying or cowering again. We were equals now. They had superpowers, but I was in the driver's seat. Ka-blam.

"Brownies are known mostly for being house

guardians. They can give themselves to a household, and they'll help make it function. Milk the cows, clean the house, look after the kids, keep the home safe. Things like that."

"Makes sense. So who do you work for?" I asked.

Bastien and Reyn's intake of breath told me I'd said something offensive. Bastien's answer came back in a verbal slap. "Brownies don't work *for* anyone. We can leave whenever the family grows ungrateful or treats us like their slave. It's a noble profession. Brownies aren't nursemaids."

I raised my eyebrow and looked at him in the rearview mirror, sizing up his flaring attitude. "Fine. Who do you work *with*?"

"No one. That life's not for me. It drains a lot of magic out of you when you take on a household. Calling a family your home? No thanks. I don't want to have to go to sleep to recharge my magic. I like it on tap." Bastien went back to staring out the window, looking every bit like the lone cowboy his flannel shirt reflected.

"Huh? Recharge your magic?"

Reyn filled in the blanks. "People in Faîte generally don't sleep unless they've drained their magic. Brownies sleep regularly, once they start feeling loyalty to a family and take on a household. It keeps their magic fresh. Brownies have the most magic left inside of them after the higher magic was taken from Faîte, since they usually look after a house."

"Okay, so Bastien's only regular powerful until he takes on a family, and then he's Super Bastien?"

Reyn smiled at me. "Something like that."

Bastien leaned forward. "How has Elaine of Avalon not told you any of this? You can't possibly be this far behind." He leaned back and folded his arms across his chest, eyeing the sparse clusters of bushes that lined the freeway in the night. "Ignore her, Reyn. She's just playing stupid."

I had a sore spot for being called the s-word. "Dude, do you want me to punch you again? Because it felt pretty good the first time."

"You got in one lucky shot. The luckiest shot of your life. Enjoy your moment, Lost Daughter of Avalon. It's not likely to come around again."

I chewed on the inside of my cheek as I drove, seething silently until I found a tone of voice that betrayed none of my anger. "Look, I'm not the Lost Daughter of Avalon or whatever. My name's Rosie Avalon, so don't fancy me up to fit into your Lord of the Rings realm of crazy. Secondly, I know nothing about your world. My aunt told me zip. And she's not Elaine of Avalon. She's Lane. If you want to blame someone for me 'playing stupid,' aim that noise her way. It was her call to keep me in the dark, so either be helpful or shut it."

My phone rang, interrupting whatever idiotic thing Bastien opened his mouth to say. Reyn took out my phone from his pocket like it was a bomb that might go off at any second. "Why's it doing that? I hate when they do that."

The phone was playing a classic – a booty shaking tune that encouraged the guys at the club to grab what they could while they could get it. Judah liked to go in and change my ringtone at random every now and then to surprise me. "Give me that." I snatched my phone from Reyn, told them not to make a sound and turned the call on speaker, setting the device in the cupholder so I could drive without holding it. "Hey, Jill. What's up?"

"Hey, Ro. Is Judah with you? I've been trying to call him all evening, but he's not picking up." I batted away Reyn's mimed warning to keep my mouth shut about them. Like I was really going to explain the freak show I'd been dragged into. "Say you know where Judah is. It's our anniversary, and I'm starting to get worried."

I cringed that Judah was unintentionally leaving his girlfriend duties with me. "You tracked him down, but he's asleep."

There were a few beats of a pause that made me squirm before Jill said, "Do you think you could wake him up, or drive him over here?"

"Actually, I'm not coming back to the apartment tonight. We're headed home. He didn't tell you?" I smacked away Reyn's emphatic "what the flip are you doing?" gestures.

"Tell me what?"

"We're on our way home to stay with Lane for a few days. Maybe longer."

Jill's voice caught in her throat, and I wanted to

strangle Judah for forgetting her on their anniversary. Not like he could go on any date now, but still. "Are you joking? He's leaving town on our anniversary?"

"It's my fault," I offered, coming up with a lie on the spot. "My mom injured herself at the gym. He's coming home to help me take care of her. Lane broke her leg. Totally laid up in the hospital until we come and get her. I pretty much kidnapped Judah to make him come with me. I'm sorry, Jill. I forgot it was your anniversary."

"But the rest of your finals are tomorrow! How are you going to take them if you're two hours away?"

I bit down on my lower lip, cringing that she had a very valid point. If I got zeroes on my finals, I might still pass the classes, but I would lose my scholarship for sure. "I can't think about all that right now. Family comes first." I inhaled, taking a leap to pacify Jill, who was sweet, and deserved better than Judah's absentminded professor routine. "Judah mentioned wanting to go back home and see his mom to ask her for something."

"Wait, to ask her for something?"

"Yeah. An heirloom, I think?"

Jill's voice was pinched with excitement. "A ring? Do you think he's asking her for his grandmother's engagement ring?"

I knew Judah was going to tear me a new one for this, but the lie was beyond my control at this point. "I'm not sure. It's possible."

"Oh, Rosie, you're the best! If you see it, can you take a picture and send it to me?"

"Sure thing, babe."

"When are you coming back? A few days?"

Reyn shook his head and spread his hands out as if measuring the length of something to indicate our journey wouldn't be over anytime soon. "Um, it'll be longer than that."

"A week?"

Reyn shook his head again, stretching his hands out further. "No," I answered. "Probably a bit longer than that."

"Have him call me when he wakes up, okay? And tell Lane that I'm sending up positive vibes for her."

"Will do."

"Oh, and my roommate wanted to know who did your boobs. They look amazing."

I guffawed. "What?"

"Come on, Ro. It's me. You can admit you had a boob job. It's the only explanation."

My voice turned squeaky as I fumbled with my phone. "I'll talk to you soon." Then I ended the call, feeling horrible as I turned off my phone. The awkward silence rang throughout the gray sedan's interior, and I knew I should've risked the traffic ticket rather than let them in on Judah's mess. I tapped my thumbs on the steering wheel, wishing I was a Fae with loads of that higher magic, so I could be invisible. "So... How about them Yankees?"

8

RUNNING AND DITCHING

*R*eyn wrinkled his rounded nose as he took in my discomfort. "Sorry about the... that whole thing."

I motioned outside to the darkness that was lit only by intermittent streetlights on the side of the highway. "You can apologize to Judah for sabotaging his relationship when he wakes up. Why don't you guys grab some sleep? I can head east well enough without you having to tell me to keep going in the same direction."

"We don't sleep," Reyn reminded me.

"Right." I gripped the steering wheel, choking it to keep myself in check. "Could you pretend?"

Reyn closed his eyes and started snoring loudly, peeking at me to catch me slipping into half a smile. "Did I do it right?"

I nodded, my shoulders loosening as I shifted in my

seat. "Like a true human." My eyes flicked to the backseat where Bastien was scratching his neck. "You're not going to fake sleep?"

"I don't need to pretend for you. You have one use right now – driving. That's all I care about. Drive, and keep your little friend's drama away from us."

There weren't any other cars in sight, so I did what I'd always pictured my dad doing when my perfect fictional family went on road trips together in my imagination. Of course, I had never seen a picture of him, but I imagined my father looking like Superman, complete with chin dimple and the ability to straighten out the bad guys who fell out of line. We would go on long car rides, and Lane and I would start being annoying about something. Maybe we'd fight over which kind of fast food to stop for, or sing Britney Spears' top hits too loudly. Then Dad would threaten to pull the car over if we didn't knock it off.

It was my turn to be the dad. I pulled onto the shoulder of the freeway and cut the engine, taking three deep breaths so I didn't open my mouth and start shouting. "Is there something you want to say to me?"

"Um, yeah. Let's go." Bastien clicked his fingers a few times just to infuriate me.

"Try again."

Reyn gave us both a heavy sigh. "Come on, Bastien. Think of Roland. This isn't helping us get to him any faster."

Bastien surprised me by reaching his left hand around

my shoulder, gripping my chin from behind as he leaned forward, turning my head so my eyes met his. "The longer we sit here, the more likely we are to get caught by another one of Morgan le Fae's people. Whatever little problems you think are a big deal, they're not. Trust me when I say you've never met anyone like your mother, and you don't want to. We'll be lucky if she gives up and declares you dead. That's best-case scenario."

"Jeez, Bastien." Reyn glared at his friend and shook his head, but Bastien didn't let go of my chin, giving me the full force of his coldness up close, so there was no mistaking him for a good guy.

Hot, angry tears pricked my eyes when his cruel words mixed with his bruising hold. When he finally released me, I grabbed my phone, and threw the keys in Reyn's face. "You're a cracked dick to say that to me! You know I've never met my mom. Of course I've 'never met anyone like her.' And you hope she thinks I'm dead? This is my life you're obliterating! Drive yourselves off a cliff! Then my mom will never look for me!" I didn't care that Lane had told me to go with them. I popped open the door and ran forward toward the sign that said... something. I was too upset to decode, but I knew there had to be an exit nearby with gas stations and places to hide out for a while. The moon did precious little to illuminate my path, but I hopped over highway debris with little problem, even though my eyes were cloudy with unshed tears.

I heard both of them running after me, but I didn't

look back. Their chase only fueled my rage, pushing me forward as I pumped my arms and used every bit of my soccer training to take my edge where I could get it. I heard one of them trip and felt a mixture of relief and guilt. Reyn seemed like an alright guy; I hoped he wasn't hurt.

I'm not sure how far I ran before Bastien caught up to me, heaving like an elephant as he grabbed the back of my shirt. I flung my elbows out as he slowed me down, hoping to nail him anywhere that would hurt. I felt the thrill of vindication when my hit rang true, my elbow sinking deep into his gut and making him keel over as he struggled for breath.

I would've kept running, but Reyn sidled up beside me, the knee of his jeans torn from when he'd fallen on the uneven pavement. He grabbed my arm, but he didn't have the same note of aggression Bastien did, so I slowed, letting him catch me. Reyn held up his hands and spoke as if talking a jumper from the ledge. "We're never going to get anywhere like this. We have to work together if you're going to live through it all."

"Save your lecture for this one, because I don't need it! I was cooperating just fine before he started running his mouth. I'm not your human chauffeur here. I don't do your bidding. He's the one who put his hands on me, like I need to be threatened."

Reyn helped Bastien to stand up straight and slapped him on the shoulder harder than could be comforting. "Go get in the car and shut up. This one's on you, brother. I'm used to you, but she's not."

Reyn waited it out through Bastien's glare, and then stood with me in the night while the foul jag skulked off to the car to pout it out. Reyn put his hand on my back and led me to the nearest streetlight, examining my face under the glow with careful hands. "I don't know much about humans, but I know he was too rough. Bastien's used to bounty hunting. He doesn't actually work with other people all that often, least of all young women."

"You don't say." I tried to make my voice sound light, but emotion snuck into the last word. "I don't care what Morgan le Fae does or did or will do. I don't need him running his mouth about her when I've never even met her. He doesn't get to make decisions about my mother. I do. I decide if I hate her or not."

Reyn looked deep into my eyes as if trying to communicate something he couldn't find the words for. "You can wait until you meet her someday, and then make up your mind. But for your sake and all of ours, I pray that day never comes."

I shook my head, whispering next to the stillness of the freeway that would be jammed in a few hours. "That's a terrible thing to say to me."

Reyn leaned his forehead to mine, his breath tickling my nose. He smelled like grass and unwashed clothes. "I don't take any joy in breaking your heart, only in keeping you alive." He brought me in for a hug, wrapping gentle arms around me in a way that made me feel safe, despite the fact that he was a total stranger, we were on the side of the freeway in the middle of the night, and I had no concrete idea of where we were, or who was chasing us.

The safety made me itch for space, so I pulled away, avoiding eye contact and nodding wordlessly when he asked if we were all good to go now. I wiped any traces of emotion away so Bastien didn't know he'd won the fight. Reyn opened my door for me like a gentleman and walked around to his side, shutting himself in and fastening his seatbelt after casting a grim look into the backseat.

Bastien sighed dramatically as I fished through the keys on the ring for the right one, and shoved it into the ignition. "Do you need me to apologize?"

I kept my eyes on the road as I pulled forward behind the only other car on the freeway. "I don't need you to lie to me, no. But keep your hands off me for like, all of eternity." I reached forward and flicked on the radio, fishing through the presets until I found something palatable. My favorite band in the universe was Lost and Forgotten. They were straight rock, with a little extra violin and instrumental variety to them. It was too much to hope for one of their familiar songs to play its comfort into my soul. I didn't mind the harder rock; it kept me awake and didn't whine too much. "Hear this? This is our own little brand of human magic. If we don't want to talk to each other, we can listen to music and tune out the world." I turned up the volume to drown out Bastien's response. It wasn't terribly loud, just loud enough so I didn't have to deal with him. Or anything. I could just drive and not have a complete and total breakdown in front of two men I didn't know.

Reyn leaned back in his seat and let the yellow lines on the highway hypnotize him into relaxation. Eventually Bastien did the same, stretching out on the backseat next to Judah, who was still unconscious. Every now and then I caught Bastien watching me in the rearview mirror. One of the times that I didn't flick my eyes away immediately, he held my gaze and offered up a humble nod of apology for being such a tool. I returned the sentiment with a bob of my head. It was our best communication to date.

"Can you turn this down? It's really loud back here."

I lowered the volume so the guys could talk if they wanted. "Better?"

Bastien made a face. "Your music is terrible. Do you always need to sing about your feelings? Ack. Is this what all human songs sound like?"

"Nah. Here, fish around for what you like."

Reyn studied the presets warily. I imagined being in a car for them was the equivalent to being on a submarine for me. You want to touch all the buttons, but know you can't, in case one of them launches a missile or something, when you're just trying to turn on a little Salt-N-Peppa.

Reyn accidentally cranked on the air conditioning, adding a chill to the car that spooked him. He panicked, and started pushing buttons and turning dials at random. "I'm sorry! How do I undo it?"

"It's alright. Just like this." I turned the knob and watched him visibly relax. "Now that we're all calmed down, why don't you tell me a little more about what I'll be walking into?"

9

MAGIC FAMINE

*R*eyn opened his mouth to speak, but Bastien beat him to it. "What do you want to know?"

I shrugged. "Big stuff, small stuff. The things that'll make you both not so annoyed with me when we get to wherever it is we're going. You've been in both worlds now. Tell me the differences."

Bastien folded his arms over his chest. "Well, our music sounds like music, for one. And we don't have cars."

"What do you use? Horses?"

"The wealthier families own horses, but the rest of Faîte gets around on foot. Main jobs for men are at the mill, goods trading, or in the Queen's Army. Almost everyone from my hometown does one of those options."

"But you're a bounty hunter?"

Bastien nodded. "I was in the army up until a couple years ago. Hunting suits me better."

"What kinds of crimes do your people commit?"

"Stealing, murder, skipping out on the army. You know, stuff like that."

"I don't know much about fairies. Only what Peter Pan taught me, which I'm guessing isn't on the mark."

"Is Peter Pan your boyfriend or something?" Bastien inquired.

I smirked. "No. He's a little young for me."

Reyn folded his hands on his lap. "I'm a Rétif. See? Green eyes." He pointed to his startlingly emerald irises that shone brightly against his dark skin.

"So Brownies have brown eyes, and Rétifs have green?"

"You've got it. The rest of the Fae have blue or gray eyes. Rétifs have a few enhanced abilities from your average Fae: an aptitude for charms, for one. Some say we're more prone to trickery, though that's highly debatable. Lots of abilities used to be on tap, but most of the more impressive skills went away, what with the magic famine that's swept Avalon. Magic is connected to vitality – making the crops grow and keeping everything in nature running smoothly."

"Magic famine?" I inquired. "That sounds ominous."

"Master Kerdik, the creator of Avalon, saw we were getting too powerful, and wars between the regions were starting to erupt. There used to be all sorts of magical creatures and beasts – Vampires and Werewolves and whatnot. To protect us from them, he took away all higher magic, leaving us with the dregs. When he took a portion of our magic to vanquish the dark creatures, he created a sort of famine."

"So you should be able to have superpowers, but because of the famine, you only have medium powers? The bad creatures getting put away meant that some of the good magic had to accidentally be taken, too?"

"That's exactly right. My magic's been broken for a while now, but Bastien's got enough to take care of those around him. The magic's held out longer in the Brownies, because like I mentioned earlier, they usually take care of a household. Nature favors the protectors."

I didn't know how to respond to this, so I offered up a lame, "Dude, I'm sorry your mojo's broken."

"Thank you." Reyn continued like the patient teacher he was. "After the famine started, there was a powerful Fae who stole most of the natural resources, keeping them in her province so that others would flock to her, and she could have more subjects to rule over. As the magic gets harder to reach, people seek out refuge in her province, giving up their rights so they have food and water."

"Who's the evil witch lady?"

"That's one of the reasons we've been searching for you." Reyn paused as if steeling himself to say his next piece.

Bastien spoke up from the back, his voice low and unpleasant. "She doesn't need to know the rest yet."

"She has every right to know that we're not just taking

her to save her life. She deserves to know what she's walking into."

I closed my eyes for two seconds to center myself before the blow. "Oh good. This sounds like I'm going to love it. Alright, crack me with it."

"Morgan le Fae's had control of Avalon for too many years now. She's been seizing land from the other rulers who couldn't take care of their people, and forcing them into the Forgotten Forest."

I swallowed, chiding myself for not expecting this. Of course my mother was the evil witch queen. It seemed the only way I could possibly forgive Lane for keeping me from her. The frustration that could've morphed into anger quickly dissipated into something sadder, and I wasn't sure if that was a good thing or not. "So my mom's not dead, she's alive and super mean. She sucks away people's rights, takes over neighboring lands, and shoves the defeated leaders into the woods. That sounds just the right amount of grim. So where do I fit in with all of it? Am I the peasant? The dragon? The huntress?" I tried to think up other fantastical elements.

"Actually, you're the princess," Reyn answered quietly. "It's one of the reasons Armand was trying to bring you in. We're hiding you so that Morgan doesn't use you to further her plans to claim more of Avalon."

I quirked my eyebrow at Reyn. "I feel like you're holding back because you think I'm going to freak out on you. I've got news for you, pal: if I haven't hit the roof yet, you're not going to tip it all now."

Reyn rubbed his palms down his pants, as if gearing himself up for a hard truth. "The Forgotten Forest is a place that you can choose to go if you're at the end of your rope. Once you go, it's impossible to ever come out. About a year ago, Morgan wanted to claim our friend Roland's province, so after a long bout of trying to ruin his life, she took the land by force, and sent Roland to the Forgotten Forest. No one's seen him since, nor ever will again, most likely." Reyn's gaze shifted from Bastien to me. "If you're willing, we'd like your help getting him back."

10

BLESSINGS BROKEN WITH GREED

"Oh! Reyn, that's terrible." I reached over the console, and even though I didn't really know him, my heart went out to the poor guy. My hand rested atop his, wanting to comfort him or save him from such a terrible life that was no doubt filled with the fear of losing the people he loved.

Reyn gave me a full-blown smile of appreciation that I was starting to understand their plight enough to empathize with it. He clasped my hand between both of his. "Thank you... May I call you Rosalie?"

"If I'm in trouble, sure. I go by Rosie."

He gave me a gentle smile. Reyn looked prone to kindness. He was the sort of guy I could picture writing sonnets, and telling a girl she looked lovely with no hint of irony. "Very well. Thank you, Rosie." He jerked his chin toward the backseat. "Bastien and Roland have been my best friends forever. It's been a rough year. The people in Province 4 were taken to Province 1, where they live under Morgan le Fae's rule now. She's the sovereign over Province 1, which is now the largest region in all of Avalon."

Bastien's tone was devoid of anything pleasant or good. I could tell he was speaking from a place of deep hurt, so I listened silently to respect their pain. "We fought with Roland's army, stayed with him in his palace, but the Cheval Mallet found Roland in the dead of night. I chased that cursed thing, but eventually he outran me."

Reyn kept my hand sandwiched in between his, like we were old friends who did that sort of thing when needed. I drove with one hand and my knee, but it was worth it to show him a little sympathy. Reyn glanced over his shoulder to his friend. "You couldn't have caught the Cheval Mallet, Bastien. It's not possible. You should stop blaming yourself."

When several seconds passed with no one filling in the blanks, I asked quietly, "I'm sorry. I really am, but I don't know what that means. We don't have that here. Who or what is the Cheval Mallet?" All their special words sounded French, so I tried my best not to butcher the pronunciation.

"It's a pure black horse," Reyn explained when it seemed Bastien could not. "It's got a white lightning bolt branded down its flank, and you only see him if you're desperate enough to leave your life. Then the Cheval Mallet comes to you. If you get on it, he rides you away to the Forgotten Forest, and you're never seen or heard from again. Some call it the Horse to Nowhere."

I was quiet. I mean, really, what was there that I could say? I wanted to say the right thing or reach out to Bastien in some way, but I didn't want him turning surly again. If my read on him was right, he got bratty when he felt things that made him uncomfortable. When I finally opened my mouth, there was very little volume to my voice. "How long has Roland been missing?"

"Just over a year. We searched everywhere, but like everyone before us, you can't follow the Cheval Mallet. The horse finds you, not the other way around." There was a long pause in which we let the moment of silence hang in the air on Roland's behalf. Then Reyn cleared his throat. "There was rumored to be a blessing put on the only child of Morgan le Fae." He squeezed my hand. "When you were born, there was a kingdom-wide celebration. I was only a boy at the time, but I remember the music and the dancing that lasted for days."

I sat up straighter, confused. "Wait, are you talking about me? I'm supposed to be this daughter? There was a party when I was born?"

Reyn rubbed his thumb over my knuckles. Now he was the one soothing me. He could sense my heartbreak over hearing about a life I couldn't remember. "The whole kingdom was waiting for you. You were the daughter of Morgan le Fae and King Urien. Everyone loved Morgan back then, and many still follow her without question. Your birth was a big deal. It ensured Morgan's reign would live on through her heir. Women sit on the throne in Avalon, with men at their sides. To give birth to a girl meant our kingdom was secure."

"Okay, I feel like you're making stuff up now just to see how far you can take this. A queen? A princess? A king? Seriously?"

"Very serious."

I motioned to my outfit with my other hand, driving with my knee. "Hello, look at me. I think I would know if I had royalty swimming around in my veins."

Reyn stiffened and dropped my hand. "Okay, I don't know much about your cars here, but I do know you have to use that circle to steer them with." When I grinned and held my hands up, steering with my knee, he began to fret. "Put your hands back on the wheel!"

I broke into a light laugh, still navigating the car with my knee while my hands did a crazy dance just to tease him. "It's alright. I've been driving for years." I placed my hands back on the wheel just so he'd calm back down and tell me more about kings and princesses and the fairytales that I knew couldn't possibly be real. But, man if they were... I cleared my throat and sat up straighter. "Back to the story. So I got blessed as a baby? Is that like someone says nice things and people write happy thoughts in a baby book or something?"

Reyn quirked his eyebrow at me, as if silently questioning my mental state. "No, nothing like that. Blessings have magic in them, just like curses. You were given the ability to find things. In case the kingdom's moral compass got lost, Master Kerdik blessed you with the ability to find anything. So along with 'Daughter of Avalon', people started calling you 'The Compass'."

My nose scrunched. "So knowing how to get places is a gift? Huh. I mean, I've never been lost on the road." Even though I couldn't rely on reading road signs, I still had never been lost. I'd never thought much about it, but maybe there was something to that.

"Your other blessing was that he gave you a hidden language. It's one only you can speak. Can you think of what that might be?"

I racked my brain. "Um, I took two years of Spanish, but I didn't do all that great in it. You got me. What's the language?"

"You can talk to animals. We saw you doing it at the park. It's how we were certain it was really you."

I fidgeted in my chair. "I mean, I don't know if that's totally true. They don't *talk* talk to me. I more just kind of understand what they're thinking." I swallowed hard, keeping my eyes on the road. "Only Lane and Judah know about that. And that's only because Lane raised me, and

Judah caught me doing it too many times for me to explain it away." I started to feel too under the microscope and shifted uncomfortably in my seat, wishing to disappear. Judah was still unconscious in the backseat, and I was scared he'd been out too long for your average commercial drug-induced sleep. "Could we keep that little detail quiet?"

Bastien spoke up, coming out of his funk. "Everyone in our kingdom knows it already. We wanted to find you because yeah, Morgan's evil. She needs you and sent her people looking for you, so clearly she can't have you. But we also need your help finding Roland."

Revelation dawned on me. "Ah. Right. Because I can talk to horses, and can apparently find anything. So I can reason with your Horse to Nowhere, and I can find Roland wherever the Cheval Mallet took him in the Forgotten Forest." I cast a look over my shoulder to Bastien, whose face was set in a hard frown. He needed my help, but didn't want it so clearly spelled out for my scrutiny. "I mean, if I can help, I'll give it a shot, but it sounds like I'm supposed to know how to tap into these abilities, and it doesn't work like that. If an animal wants to tell me something, I listen. If I need to get somewhere, I just go. There's not a science to it, so I'm not sure how well it'll work if I try to use it on purpose. But I'll help you find Roland if I can. Poor guy." I pursed my lips. "For the record, explaining this to me? Totally different than abducting me. In the future, best opt for conversation rather than full-on Patty Hursting me from my life."

"Noted. There's actually something in it for you if you help us," Reyn said, reaching for me. He drew my hand to his thigh, holding my fingers like we were good friends. It was nice. I liked how casual he was and how easily he took to me. It calmed my nerves through a pretty confusing situation. There was nothing romantic to his touch, only kindness, which I desperately needed a dose of after all the fighting. "Roland is the son of the late Duchess Heloise and Duke Isengrim. Heloise was Morgan le Fae's sister. So Roland is actually your cousin. Morgan le Fae and King Urien ruled Province 1, and Roland took over for his parents when they passed, ruling Province 4." He let out a heavy sigh. "But now there is no Province 4, since Morgan took it over and sent Roland to the Forgotten Forest."

I chewed on my lower lip, unsure how to process the blow that I had not only a mother, but a father, too, plus a cousin. My voice was small when it came out. "Could you tell me about my dad?" It was too much to hope my dad really was the Superman he'd been in my dreams, but as I held my breath in anticipation of Reyn's response, I realized that's exactly what I wanted to be true.

"King Urien rules alongside Morgan le Fae in theory, but not really," Bastien added. "Your dad's been too sick to assist in Morgan's rule for at least two decades. About a year after you were born, actually. You went missing right after you turned one, and he got a lot worse. Morgan's been ruling by herself ever since. It was all so innocent in the beginning, but I'm sure you can guess my theory on that. She's a power-mad lunatic."

I followed his logic to the evil queen conclusion Disney had well-trained me to expect. "You think my mom poisoned my dad or hurt him somehow so she could rule the kingdom without his input?"

Reyn nodded. "That's exactly right. He was usually the vote against warring between the provinces. Morgan was always trying to shut him up. I haven't talked to Elaine of Avalon, but something tells me that when we do, she'll tell us she took you to keep you from the same fate that found your father."

"Tell her about Master Kerdik," Bastien suggested. "She needs to know the truth so she doesn't get her pretty little head turned around once we get to Faîte."

I don't know why his jabs had the edge of a compliment buried in them, and why the compliment sounded insulting. "Kerdik's the dude who created Avalon, right?"

Reyn settled in, as if telling a campfire story. "Master Kerdik's a very old immortal. Some say Rétifs were created by him."

"Like you?"

Reyn gave me the stink eye. "I'm thirty. That hardly qualifies as very old."

"I meant the Rétif part. Sorry, Grandpa. Go on." I smirked at him when he shook his head.

"Anyway, Master Kerdik is a very powerful man. He's the immortal who gave you your birth blessing."

"I'll be sure to send him a thank you card."

"The magic he could wield? No one in our generation has ever seen his equal in Avalon. His main focus was vitality. So he had a fair say in crops growing, people procreating, things like that. Legend says that he grew so powerful that he began to fear himself. So he put a portion of his magic into nine jewels, capturing his ability to make the land and the people fertile in each stone. Then he divvied up the gems between Queen Diana and King Lucien's nine daughters. Each daughter was given a stone, called the Jewels of Good Fortune. They spread out all throughout Avalon (one of only two continents in Faîte), so the whole nation would be blessed."

"I'm sensing a 'but' here."

"Very intuitive."

I shrugged as I switched lanes. "Not really. I just watch a lot of fantasy fiction. Judah's a huge fan of anything with superpowers. Evil queen, magical stones – you're doing well on your fantasy checklist. Go on."

"Morgan le Fae is the oldest of the nine sisters. She wanted what all people want for their land and their people. She wanted them to prosper. When the first sister died, no one thought much about it, other than the grief, of course. It wasn't until the Duchess was buried that anyone noticed her jewel was missing. Her province started growing less bountiful, the women had a more difficult time getting pregnant, and it soon became apparent the jewel had been stolen. It wasn't a big secret who took it, because Morgan le Fae's province began to flourish."

"Yikes. Hard to hide that kind of thing, I guess."

"Indeed. One after the other, Morgan took jewels from her sisters, killing them or simply taking it and leaving her sisters with nothing. Province 1 thrived, so the barren regions started to fight back. They've waged wars, kidnapped, raided, you name it. The blessing Morgan le Fae was supposed to be bringing to her province has turned out to be the biggest curse she could've brought down on her people. War is a manmade curse she wasn't counting on."

I put the pieces together in what I hoped was the right order. "So I'm supposed to be some super amazing compass, right? I'm guessing one of the reasons you found me was so I could find where Morgan stashed the jewels. You want me to steal them back, don't you."

Reyn was quiet, but I could tell I hit the nail on the head. Bastien finally spoke. "We were hoping Duchess Elaine of Avalon still had her jewel, and could bring a little life back to some of the struggling provinces."

I mentally face-palmed myself when the skip over the obvious hit me. "Right. Because she's Morgan's sister. Lane has a jewel? What does it look like? Lane doesn't wear jewelry."

"They're all different. Duchess Elaine's stone was an emerald." Reyn held up four fingers in a large circle to indicate the circumference of a ping-pong ball. "About yea big."

My mouth dropped open. "Um, no. She doesn't have anything like that. I think I would've known if we had a gem that size lying around."

Reyn's face fell as Bastien swore. Reyn recovered first. "That's alright. We can ask her when we meet up to see whatever came of it. With a few of the gems unaccounted for, the fertility of the land started to go awry. Hence the two-to-one ratio of females to males. It didn't used to be so unbalanced. Having Duchess Lane's emerald back in Avalon might help even out the population a bit. Some of the men are growing a bit... restless."

My voice was quiet when it broke the stillness inside the car. "It sounds like my mom wanted to do the right thing by her people. She just took it a little too far."

Bastien scoffed. "A loyalist already. Great. No, oh wise Princess of Avalon, Morgan brought down a world of suffering on her people when she made them the target for the other provinces. And the rulers are supposed to care about *all* of Avalon, not just the ones who bow to them."

"Jeez! Take a pill already. I'm allowed to have opinions, jackweed."

"It's a nice idea, her using more power over nature and magic to help Avalon. I can see why you'd wish for utopia." Reyn patted my hand. "I think Kerdik hoped the daughters would do exactly that with the gifts he gave them. I don't think he anticipated the damage Morgan could do, or the sad state the world would fall into when he gave them prosperity. Good plans tinged with greed always lead to ruin," Reyn said sagely.

I went quiet, as was my usual pattern when something too giant threatened to crush me. I wasn't sure what to make of my family being the villains Bastien was painting them. I wasn't sure about anything anymore. Reyn was compassionate, rubbing my hand as I drove through the night and on until morning.

11

VEGETARIAN, KOSHER, AND POISONOUS HOT DOGS

I stopped to refuel at a gas station, tired and wired from driving all night and being stuck in rush hour for way too long. The traffic had been bumper to bumper, so I ditched at the nearest exit, claiming defeat until everything cleared up in an hour or so. I went into the convenience store to look for anything edible, but knew I wouldn't find anything but junk inside. Bastien was my constant shadow. He didn't have the same note of aggression in him, now that he knew I wasn't going to bolt, but he watched me everywhere I went.

"Are we really in that much danger of being found that I can't shop without you hovering?" I made sure not to let my tone sound bratty, so we didn't get into it again. I don't know why he was so easy to fight with, but I was too exhausted for another round. Stores were a medium amount of stressful even on a good day, because every single item for sale had about a billion words printed all over it. The bags of chips seemed to mock me, sending me to the back of the class for being an idiot who couldn't read words like "potato" without getting it wrong three times first.

"We're probably not in as much danger anymore," Bastien admitted, examining the candy wrappers with curiosity. "They're all still looking for you. No one knows we actually found you, and they'll most likely be searching around where you lived. But still, you've been missing for two decades. I'm not about to let you out of my sight now."

"I can understand that. I've found a flaw in your master plan, though, chief. You may not sleep, but I do. I'm guessing when we get over to your side, it'll be more running and hiding, right?"

"Yup. We have to find your aunt, locate the Cheval Mallet, and go get Roland as soon as we can. Then we hide out where Morgan can't find us until we come up with a plan for what you want to do from there. Maybe we'll do us a little Jewels of Good Fortune stealing." He waggled his eyebrows, like he was up for a good bout of evil master-minding. Every now and then his non-acerbic personality highlights seeped out, lifting the corner of my mouth whenever the boyishness painted the man. "Since you're The Compass and can find anything, we might actually have a shot at cutting Morgan off at the source of her magic."

"I'm guessing there won't be much time for sleeping until then?"

Bastien scratched his five o'clock shadow that was slightly thicker than when I'd first met him. His red flannel shirt was rumpled and his hair was sticking up in the back. "Probably not. How long do you have to sleep every day?"

I shrugged. "Humans are supposed to get in eight hours a night. I'm a little overdue. I can drive a bit longer, but I'm warning you, a crash is coming soon. Either me, or the car, or both at the same time. Not good."

"But you're not human. You're Fae."

I scrunched my nose, considering this obvious fact for the first time. "I guess you're right, but I still need to sleep like a human. Not sure why, but it's not something I can just power through."

Bastien ran his hand over his face, factoring in the new information. "Man, we didn't work that into the plan. Do you have to sleep right now?"

The allure of sleep seduced me like a gorgeous tempter in a tight t-shirt and butt-hugging jeans. "If it's possible, then yeah. If not, then I can truck along for another hour or two."

He cast around, a hopeless grasping at straws look on his face. "Can you show me how to work the car?"

I shuddered as I pictured the damage he could do behind the wheel. "Um, no. You have to take classes and get a license. It's a whole big thing. Not something you can learn on the fly." I stretched my arms over my head and twisted at the waist. "It's fine. I can drive a little longer."

"But not long enough to make it to the gate. It's not exactly around the corner."

I shrugged. "Then I'll get us a hotel. I'm guessing you don't have any money?"

"Only what we nicked off the guy whose car we borrowed."

I closed my eyes. "You stole money from the guy you mind-controlled? You gotta know that's lowest common denominator kind of stuff. Shouldn't you be hunting yourself down right about now, Bounty Boy?"

"You're forgetting murder. I killed Armand, too. That was a long time coming. Cross that one off my life's to-do list."

"Congratulations. Petty theft, grand theft auto, kidnapping, plus murder. That's a full rap sheet. When you get home, you should arrest yourself right quick." I thumbed through the various types of single-serve trail mixes that would do in a pinch.

"I'll be expecting a royal pardon once you're properly instated." He cast me a sliver of a smile, the corner of his mouth lifting slightly as he took in my tone that was more playful than antagonistic. "The last driver got us burritos. Those were alright."

"Oh, right. What do you guys eat?"

"Deer, elk, rabbits, potatoes, vegetables, fruit, grain. Things we can hunt and grow." He motioned to the prepackaged high fructose corn syrup varieties laid out on the shelf. "Not quite the same."

"We have all that too, just not here." I grabbed all the trail mix on the shelf and took it to the counter. "Two hot dogs and a coffee," I said, adding food for the guys to my order. Then I looked over at Bastien again, taking in how much bigger than me he was. "Make that six hot dogs." I paid for our food, filled up my coffee with enough cream and sugar to make it not disgusting, and walked out of the store with Bastien, passing the guys three hot dogs apiece. "Sorry. This is sort of the worst food our world has to offer. Convenience store hot dogs. Ick. But it's better than nothing, so there you are."

Bastien raised his scruffy eyebrow at me. The cut dividing through the horizon of his left eyebrow made him look just the right amount of unhinged and charming – though I couldn't imagine him putting the moves on anyone. "You're not eating? I feel like it's a trap if you're not going to have one."

I held up one of the bags of trail mix. "I don't eat meat," I announced, waiting for the barrage of questions or jokey insults that usually came when you told heavy meat eaters and hunters you were a vegetarian.

Bastien scoffed. "Funny. That's not a thing. Everyone eats meat."

I lowered my voice and leaned in. "Not everyone. Would you be able to eat a deer or a cow after having a conversation with him? They're not the same to me as they are to you. I can hear them. I know their feelings and their dreams. It's not just picking off the lower rungs on the food chain. For me, it feels more like cannibalism." I shook my head, embarrassed at their dropped-open mouths. I'd never spelled it out like that for anyone, except Judah and Lane. It felt strange to have my inner workings so exposed. "Eat up, though. I'm not poisoning you. And I'm not preachy about it, so eat as much meat as you want. I don't care, so long as I don't have to eat my friends."

Reyn's eyebrows furrowed, his angular features softening as he watched me fidget at being so exposed. "That's horrible to feel. I never thought of your gift like that."

"It's fine. Lots of humans are vegetarians without having my talking to animals thing going on. It's really not all that weird here."

Bastien shoved half a hot dog in his mouth and grimaced. "I think this is definitely poisoned. It doesn't taste like food."

Reyn handed his to Bastien. "Well, I can't eat them now. Not in front of her. Not after hearing that. Maybe Judah can eat mine."

"Judah's kosher, so he doesn't eat hot dogs."

"Huh? What's that?"

I waved my hand. "Never mind. And seriously, it's fine for you to eat meat in front of me. I don't care."

Reyn straightened, puffing his chest gallantly. "Well, I do. I won't go against the Lost Daughter of Avalon."

I lowered my chin and cast Reyn a mildly exasperated

look. "Okay, you're going to have to cool it with that kind of talk. I'm nothing as special as you're making me out to be. So far my awesome skills include driving a car."

We piled back into the vehicle, and instantly I was hit with a wave of exhaustion. I checked on Judah, who was still sleeping in the backseat, the lucky duck. My hands were on the wheel, but it took me a full rendition of the chorus of Lost and Forgotten's "We Can't Handle the Silence" before I put the keys into the ignition.

"You alright, half-pint?"

I leaned my head back on the headrest and turned my chin in Reyn's direction with a sleepy smile. "That's a cute nickname. Much better than Lost Daughter of Avalon. My coffee's too hot to drink yet, but I need some caffeine if I'm going to drive much longer. I really need to sleep, guys. Tell me when it's safe, and I'll pull over."

"It'll never be safe," Bastien ruled, absolute in his dogged wish to get us to Roland. "But I guess if you can't go any further, we could always use the necklace on another human to take us to the gate. Can you sleep back here? I can scoot over."

"I could probably sleep standing up at this point, but I'm not okay with you warping someone. It's not cool. That guy probably has a family and a life, and you sent him back bleeding from his ears. No. I can get us to a motel or something. I'll nap for a few hours and be good as almost new." I shrugged off the protests I knew were coming. "Best I can do, guys."

"No. We really shouldn't have stopped even for this."

"If that's your way of thanking me for feeding you and paying for gas, you suck at it," I said to Bastien.

"Thank you for feeding us," Reyn offered. "If word gets out that you're still alive and we actually found you? There are people who don't like Morgan le Fae, Rosie. People that hate her so bad, they'd kill her heir to make sure her reign ends."

"And you're taking me into a world full of these people? Thanks a lot!"

"Not full," Bastien amended. "Just scattered in there. You'll be fine. We're here, and we know how to keep those kinds away from you. The best way to do that is to keep driving. Keep moving. Find the Cheval Mallet and get ourselves good and lost in Avalon."

I rubbed my forehead. "I... But... What you're doing is wrong!"

Bastien shrugged, turning my exasperation into a glower. "I don't really care about that. Give me the necklace, Reyn. I'll go get us a new driver."

"No!" I shook the sleep off my body as best I could. "I'm fine. I can get us there. How much longer?"

Reyn watched me pull out of the parking lot dubiously. "Um, are you sure? It's at least another day. Maybe longer. It's hard to tell with your sun."

I whimpered, but sat up straighter, gripping the wheel as I pulled back into the worst traffic I could've picked to keep me awake. I rolled down the windows to let the fresh spring air revive my senses, and took the lid off my coffee so it would cool faster. I turned on my phone out of habit and saw I'd missed fourteen calls from Jill and one from Lane. I called Lane, knowing Jill would only say more things to make me come home, and I didn't have that option anymore.

"You scared me! Don't ever leave your phone like that! Are you alright?" came Lane's harried greeting.

"I'm fine. We just stopped to get gas."

"Where are you?"

I pulled the phone away from my ear and tried to focus on the sign in the distance. I was too tired and too far from it for the letters to make any sense. "Reyn? What's that sign say?" I handed the phone to him.

After Reyn answered her, and gave a few perfunctory status reports, he gave me back my phone. Lane's voice sounded scared, which I didn't like. Fear never suited her. She was too heroic for that. "I'm a few hours behind you, but I'll be there. I don't know how this happened! Your locket was supposed to keep you hidden."

My mouth went dry. "I lost my necklace after the game last week! I'm so sorry. I meant to tell you, but I was hoping it would've turned up by now. Then my body sort of went crazy, but with finals, I went on radio silence so I could study. So I didn't call you, but maybe I should've."

Lane swore, which she didn't often do. "Well, that explains it. Your necklace is special, baby. It conceals your abilities. It lets you talk to animals without allowing your magic to be tracked. It does a few other things, as well."

"Oh." I'm sure there were other things I could've said, but my mind was sufficiently blown. She'd given me my mother's gold locket on my first day of kindergarten. It was engraved on the back with the simple phrase, "You are my Sunshine, My only Sunshine." It was supposed to remind me that even while we were apart, Lane was still with me. I'd always had a bit of a mommy complex with her, running to her arms when life grew too confusing to handle alone. Whenever I got scared or lonely, I touched my locket, and imagined my best girlfriend by my side. It was her love that made it feel magical. Now that there was real magic to the jewelry? Somehow that made the whole thing feel less enchanted. Funny how that happens.

"Talk to me, Ro. I know you're upset."

I ignored the elephant in the car and went with the most pressing issue. "Lane, I can't keep driving much longer. I've been going all night, and I need to sleep. What are my options?"

Lane paused. "Give the phone to one of the guys."

I handed my phone to Bastien, who held it away from his face like a toddler might. "Duchess Elaine of Avalon? This is Bastien of Province 1." I eavesdropped on the conversation, but Bastien's side made little sense to me. "Oh, that magic's not around anymore. I'm sure you're right, that it's the best, but Avalon hasn't had access to those charms in years. We might be able to do the magic concealment one, though, if you can walk us through it."

I kept going until Bastien told me to pull off at the next exit. All that time, and we'd made it exactly one exit. I parked in the lot of a diner, and their waft of breakfast food had never smelled better. I rolled up my window so I didn't lunge through it to get at the delicious food. My trail mix was beginning to lose some of its appeal. They'd only had the kind with soy nuts and wasabi peas – like it was made by people who didn't like trail mix to begin with, so they just threw whatever they wanted to get rid of in there. *Gross.*

Bastien handed me the phone when he finished with the call. "She said to take us to a market. We need to buy a few things that can help us hide you from anyone who's using a magic tracker."

"Huh? I thought your magic didn't work on our side."

"Most of it doesn't, but magical objects can hold onto their power, hence the necklace," Reyn explained as I started up the car again. "How do you think we found you?"

"You used a tracker? But I don't have magic."

"It's not a normal thing to be able to talk to animals. You lit up like a beacon when you started doing that. What you do takes up a lot of magic." Reyn threw his head back. "That must be why you sleep. Normally Fae don't sleep unless they're using a huge chunk of magic, like if a Brownie takes on a household. Those things take a lot out of the person, so sleep is necessary. Your animal thing must work the same way."

"Oh. My bad." I drove through the side streets and parked in the superstore's lot, gearing myself up for going shopping. "Crack me with the list. I'll go pick up whatever you need so we can hide me."

"Like I'm letting you out of my sight. Let's go, Princess." Bastien opened his door, making the decisions and taking charge. I wasn't so sure I was liking him, but I was too tired to protest more than an inaudible grumble.

12

BASTIEN'S BUTT

*T*he motel was skeevy, but I didn't have any expectations it wouldn't be. I had a limited income that didn't budget for lavish hotel rooms, so we set up camp in the brown carpeted room that smelled like pot and unwashed man feet.

Whatever. All I saw was the big, glorious bed. I tossed the keys on the nightstand, pulled my wavy brown hair from its messy ponytail and flopped onto the mattress. I hugged the pillow as I kicked off my shoes. Then I burrowed under the maroon comforter and pen-marked off-white sheet. Bastien carried Judah in and laid him down on the floor, then he stood up to stretch his back through my protest. "No, no. Judah shouldn't sleep on the floor. Can you put him in the bed with me?"

Reyn raised his eyebrow. "I thought you said he wasn't your husband."

I turned abruptly at the weird statement. "Um, he's not. What's that got to do with anything? Judah shouldn't be sleeping on the floor like that. He's a person, not a dog."

Bastien threw up his hands. "Sure. Why not? I'm the pack mule. I'll put a man in bed with the Lost Daughter of Avalon. No danger there."

"That's a good little pack mule," I teased him in my most patronizing tone. "And what danger are you talking about?"

"Of being labeled a loose woman, like your mother," Reyn explained while Bastien carefully placed Judah on the furthest edge of the large bed from me. Both of them cast Judah and me uncertain looks. "It's not acceptable in our world for a young woman to share a bed with a man unless they're married. Since your father took ill twenty-one years ago, your mother's filled her castle with dozens of the most attractive male servants Avalon has to offer. She's scoured the country for the best of the best, and she takes them into her bed at her whim."

I put the pillow over my face so I could muffle my growl, wishing just once that I'd get a sliver of information about my birth mother that didn't make me cringe. "Look, Judah's got a girlfriend named Jill. Judah and I live together off-campus to save money. Judah's my oldest friend. We share the bottom bunk at our place, and have slept in the same bed probably the same amount of nights we've slept apart. He grew up down the street from me, and both our moms are single parents, so we slept over at each other's places all the time. Never anything funky going on between us." I positioned my pillow under my head and flexed my toes under the sheet. "Why am I explaining this to you? Don't make my life sound weird. I'm going to sleep. I don't care about my reputation as a loose woman or whatever. I care about sleep. That's all."

Reyn sounded wary, but tried to keep the urging in his voice diplomatic. "In Avalon, the men outnumber the women two-to-one, so courting is a serious matter. Sleeping in a bed with a man who's not your husband just isn't a thing good girls do."

"I get it. I'm a loose woman of questionable morals. Rosie the Floosy. That's what they should call me." I scooted to the middle of the bed so I could be closer to Judah. I always slept best when his steady in and out lulled me to rest. I touched my hand to his arm and closed my eyes.

Reyn and Bastien set to making their potion or whatever, talking to each other in hushed tones to give me the space I needed to drift off to sleep.

The peace didn't last long. A hair was yanked out of my head, jerking me awake. "What the flip? Why?" I rubbed the spot with a drowsy frown.

Reyn's voice was further away, so I knew Bastien had been the one to do it. "We need your hair for the protection charm. Your aunt said it's how she's been able to keep you hidden this long."

I rolled over, my eyes closed. "Lane never woke me up

by yanking hair out of my skull. Dude, I don't think you understand sleep." In the next breath, something wet snuck into my ear. My body jerked and I recoiled from the intrusion, eyes wide when I took in Bastien's mischievous grin. He had dimples that were deep enough wells to be seen through his stubble, though it didn't appear as if he exercised them often. He had a fantastic smile. His brown eyes were a milky caramel in the dim lamp's light.

"You don't sleep with someone's wet finger in your ear? That's odd. That's how they do it where I'm from."

"Oh, shut it."

"I'm bored. Been in the car for too long, and now we're going to have to just sit here and wait, hoping this spell works while you lie around."

I wasn't the best person when I missed too much sleep. I didn't have that sunshiny glow that could last through all-nighters, like Jill did. She could go out partying all night and show up for class the next morning without missing a beat. I was ninety, apparently, and Bastien was strolling straight into the lion's den. I rolled onto my back to stare up at him, my shirt twisting under the covers. "Look, crack-fish, hand me that remote there." When he looked around in confusion, I pointed. "The black thing right there." I clicked on the TV with it and flipped around to find a channel that played old sitcoms he could easily follow along with. "Have a seat."

Bastien looked around as if willing imaginary furniture

to become real. There was the bed and the old upholstered chair with too much dust on it to be comforting. Plus, Reyn was sitting in it, leaving Bastien to skulk around the room and put his finger in my ear. I patted the side of the bed with lidded eyes. Bastien raised his eyebrow at me. "Uh, are you sure? That's not a thing in Avalon. That's more of a proposition."

"I propose you sit anywhere you feel like so long as it'll get me some peace and quiet." Perhaps I shouldn't have closed my eyes, but I wasn't expecting Bastien to sit down on my head. "Ah! Get off me!" I pounded on his butt with both fists until he got up, laughing.

"You said I could sit anywhere I wanted." He held his stomach, having a good old hardy-har-har at my messy hair and grouchy expression. He held up his hands in a truce when I threw my pillow at him. He picked up the pillow and then did something so sweet, I had to remind myself this was the same guy who'd just squashed his butt to my face. Bastien tucked his hand under my cheek and lifted my head a few inches, sliding the pillow underneath, and laying my cheek back down on the fluffy haven. Then he kissed his thumb and silently pressed it between my eyebrows, rubbing out my frown where he saw it playing on my features.

The precious act was so strange that I merely gawped at him. Finally, I patted the space on the empty side of the bed. "You can sit here. Not on my head. Right here."

He smacked his forehead in revelation. "You humans and your tricky customs."

"Bastien, I have to sleep. You don't want to know me when I start to get crabby."

"Start? You mean this has been the pleasant version of you? Yikes."

"No, this is me being attacked by an old man and abducted by two tools, and then driving all night. Crabby is what will happen if you don't let me sleep. Villagers will scatter. Houses will burn. It'll be bad news."

"Well, we can't have that." Bastien watched me for a few seconds, and then sat down on the floor next to where I lay on the mattress. His knees were bent up so he could rest his elbows on them. He looked like a sentry, a gargoyle sent to make sure no evil elves or Cookie Monsters broke in to disrupt my slumber. It was kind of sweet, how seriously he took my safety. I watched him visually check the double bolt on the door, touching the hilt of the knife on his belt a few times as he vacillated between being a gargoyle and relaxing.

I took the spare pillow and slid it between his back and the wall. "Is that better?" I asked quietly.

Bastien turned his face to examine mine for signs of a whoopee cushion or a box of dynamite concealed in the gift. He seemed confused at the simple gesture, as if he needed to argue with it for no reason other than to show me he didn't care about trite things such as kindness. He pursed his lips as he studied my face, which was illuminated only by the dim glow of the television once Reyn turned the lamp off. Finally Bastien worked out a gruff, "Thank you."

I nodded, holding his gaze to steady him in his venture into polite behavior, lest he fall and break a bone.

Bastien cleared his throat, and then leaned back against the pillow. His shoulders unclenched as he rested his head against the wall. "What's this show about?"

I closed my eyes through a yawn. "Watch it and find out."

"Does it get louder? I can barely hear it."

"I will straight up punch you if you keep talking to me."

Bastien chuckled under his breath. "This is going to be fun. I thought you were going to be all royal and proper when we found you. This is far better."

"Glad to hear it. I'm not totally surprised to hear you like when girls punch you. Now shut up. You're conversing with a loose woman. There's no telling how unladylike I'll get if you keep bugging me."

He snorted out a silent laugh, settling in to get more comfortable. He smelled like day-old clothes, cinnamon and pine, which wasn't a bad thing. He almost smelled like a Christmas tree, though not quite so concentrated. I'd crashed at a few of my guy friends' places every now and then, but they didn't smell anything like Bastien, nor did Judah. I felt like I was sleeping under a Christmas tree, and that childhood nostalgia lulled me more than his abrasive mouth ever could.

Finally I was granted a few minutes of peace, which was all I needed to drift off into a hard sleep.

13

OLD FRIENDS, NEW ENEMIES

*W*hen I awoke, Christmas was all around me. The pine filled my lungs, and though I knew when I opened my eyes I wouldn't see brightly wrapped presents under the tree, the thrill of anticipation teased me all the same. I was warm, holding onto something that had all the inner peace of a childhood teddy bear. I stretched like a cat against the pillow, not letting go of my treasure. I yawned and burrowed my cheek into the supple snuggle, feeling not a single worry in the twilight of my wakefulness.

"You finally up?" Bastien asked, breaking me out of my dreamy haze.

"Mm-hm. Mostly." I ran the comforting thing in my hands over my cheek, nuzzling it to prolong the moments before I would have to deal with the world again.

"I might need my hand back at some point."

My eyes flew open, my gasp flying out of my lips as I took in the thing I was snuggling to my face, which was most certainly not a beloved childhood toy. I was hogging Bastien's left hand, my cheek pressed to his curled knuckles. I dropped contact, as if recoiling from a scorpion. "Oh! Oh, screw it all! I'm sorry. I didn't realize you were... I didn't mean to... I'm sorry!" I climbed out of the bed, ignoring Bastien's and Reyn's snickers as I straightened my shirt and fought through my barely awake blur to collect myself. I smoothed back my hair and pointed my finger down at Bastien's grin. "That didn't happen. I'm going to go hop in the shower, and when I come out, that won't have happened. You should've said something!"

"Said what? That I was right next to you? That was no secret. You reached out in your sleep and grabbed my hand."

I hugged myself around the middle, utterly mortified. "Okay, so um, super sorry about that. Feel free to push me away if I try to hold your hand while I'm sleeping." I cringed. "So embarrassing." I was about to apologize yet again, but then gasped at the empty bed. "Judah? Judah!" I shouted through the small room.

Judah strolled out of the bathroom, his hair wet from a shower. "You miss me?"

I didn't hesitate to throw myself into Judah's arms. "I was so scared for you! I don't know anything about the Narnia drugs they've got! You've been out for so long! Are you alright? Let me look at you."

Judah chuckled as he held me, squeezing my waist and rocking me from side to side. "I'm alright. Sore, but that's the worst of it. Lane filled me in on everything over the phone. Yikes."

"I know! Everything was normal, and then it all turned upside-down. I'm so sorry you got dragged along for the ride."

"Are you kidding me? A wicked queen, a lost princess, and a magical horse? It's the best LARP ever!"

I laughed into his damp shoulder. "I knew you'd find a way to geek this up. No Live Action Role Play. Just Live Action, I'm guessing."

"Even better. I'll be the knight, saving you from the evil queen." He took one arm away from me and flexed his modest bicep. "Never fear, Judah the Heroic is here!"

Though we were at least five seconds past what I usually felt was acceptable hugging length, I clung tighter to him. His bravado calmed as he rocked me in his arms that radiated safety. I needed him now, if for no other reason than to make me feel sane again. Judah could give me something normal when I was surrounded by unicorns, and right now, normal was a beautiful thing.

"Hey," he whispered. "Hey, now. It's alright. Lane explained it all. And Reyn seems like an alright guy when you get past the drugging thing. Sounds like we'll go find your cousin on the fancy horse, defeat the evil queen, and we'll be home in no time."

"I don't think it's quite that simple. What about Jill?

Your mom?" I pulled back and narrowed my eyes at him. "That's why you're so chipper and forgiving of the guys who drugged you and threw you in a trunk. You don't want to face Jill, and the dreaded 'where is this going' conversation."

"Well, that is an upside to consider."

I shook my head at him and stomped into the bathroom, muttering under my breath about the state of the male conscience of convenience. I washed the day and night and half day off of me, wondering if I'd be able to get my hands on some clean clothes anytime soon. After drying myself on the too-small towel, I twisted my hair into a messy bun atop my head and redressed in the same clothes that were starting to lose some of their appeal. André René Roussimoff had definitely seen better days, but if he could get through it, so could I.

When I came out into the room, Judah was sitting on the bed, touching his thumbs to each of his fingers, making his way down the row and then starting all over again – a thing he did when he was stressed. "You alright, chief?" I asked him.

Judah shook his head, keeping his eyes on his hands. "I have to tell you something, Rosie."

"Oh, jeez. Why do I get the feeling the roof's about to cave in? Out with it."

"I was on the phone with Lane while you were in the shower. I had a few concerns, and she... I asked her if I could explain it to you. Might be a softer blow coming from me."

My senses were on high alert, so I took a tentative step backward. By the looks on Reyn and Bastien's faces, they didn't know which bomb Judah was juggling, either. "Hit me with it."

"That necklace you always wore? It didn't just keep your animal mojo from being tracked. It also changed your appearance. I gotta be honest, it shocked me to watch you outside of that bar, morphing into someone completely different." He paused, and then scratched the back of his neck. "On the upside, I was totally right about the whole cursed necklace thing."

My mouth tightened, and too many rage-filled emotions swept through me. "You're telling me the necklace gave me my hump?"

"And the lazy eye, the blemishes, and the..." Judah waved his hand over his chest, and then cleared his throat three times before saying his piece. "The way Lane explained it just now is that she put an old charm in the necklace, that apparently doesn't even exist in that Avalon world anymore." He held his hands out to mime having breasts, and then motioned to my body guiltily. "You went from flat-chested to some serious jugs not five minutes after losing your necklace. I've been freaking out ever since. I mean, it's still you, but with some major alterations."

Reyn tsked Judah's crass assessment of my curves, but I didn't care about that. My mouth hung open, floored beyond words. "Lane did this to me? I have my chiropractor's home phone number all because of her? I was the Humpback Whale and Baby Got Too Much Back because of something she did to me? But she's my mom!" I covered my mouth and let out a bleat of betrayal. So very many things began to roil in my gut, filtered through this new light. I'd cried to Lane about being the brunt of so many jokes. My second-grade nickname had been the Humpback Whale. Third grade had been Lazy-Eyed Susan. Fourth grade had introduced Remedial Rosie. Fifth grade had settled us back to either Crater-Face or Remedial Rosie, and there we landed until college gave me a break. College kids mostly left you alone, giving my self-esteem a little time to rebound. Whenever the kids in junior high had done impressions of me, they'd always been cross-eyed, with their shoulders stooped. It was hurtful, as if all I was, and all I had to offer the world was being the ugly girl.

A million responses flooded through me, varying from shock to outrage. So many years of questioning myself to the point where I'd given up trying to look nice altogether, resorting to jeans and t-shirts because no guy ever looked my way with that special glow. My greatest ambition some days when I was younger was simply to blend in.

But Judah had been my constant, not once caring that I looked different. True, he had never been attracted to me, but amid the sea of hurling insults, Judah had been my faithful friend, shutting people up and sticking by my side.

Judah's best friend was the Humpback Whale.

While I'm sure there were many other things that needed addressing with Lane, I cleared the distance between us, drew Judah to standing, and threw my arms around him. "You loved me, no matter what I looked like."

Judah held on tight, embracing me to let me know he loved me for all the right reasons. "You've always been perfect. Wouldn't change a thing, Hot Mama. Your old body or this new one, you're still the coolest girl a guy could have for a best friend."

My eyes welled with tears, but I sucked them in before they fell. "I'm the luckiest, to have you. I love you, Pimp Daddy."

Judah chuckled, making a farting noise with his mouth when I squeezed him tighter. "Love you too, Ro. Hey, no ditching me now that you're all, you know, without a hump."

I don't know why that made me laugh, but I belted out a loud one, stepping back to smile at the guy who'd seen me through the best and the worst. "Promise."

I refused to meet Bastien's eyes. I could feel him studying me, though I knew he was watching our exchange with too much scrutiny. Bastien shoved his hands in the pockets of his jeans. "If we're putting it all out on the table, I'm the one who stole your locket. I'd been tracking you for a year, and was positive it was you, even though you didn't look enough like your mother. I recognized the insignia on your locket, and yanked it off you when you were in a bar last week."

I balked at him. "That was you? Well, give it back!"

Bastien shook his head. "Couldn't if I wanted to. I destroyed it. I had to know if you were really the Lost Daughter of Avalon. Then when I found you again, you looked like this." He motioned to me with the flat of his hand. "Spitting image of your mother."

I didn't know what to say to any of it, so Judah did the decent thing and wrapped his arms around me, holding me tight in the hug I needed when life shifted so uncertainly around me.

"Are you guys ready to get back on the road?" Reyn asked, standing with the hint of levity on his lips. He handed me a convenience store cup of coffee with a slight bow.

"Thanks. Yeah, I'm good to go." I took a sip and grimaced at the cold disgustingness that ran down my throat and threatened to come back up. "Oh, that's this morning's, huh."

"Yeah. Is that not okay?"

"I take it they don't have coffee where you're from?"

"No. I'm guessing the drink has a drug that helps you stay awake?"

"Yup. I'll get some more when we check out. I think I saw a pot behind the counter."

Reyn packed up the small scattering of random objects we'd bought at the store for his charm, while Bastien hosed himself off in the shower. We left the motel and the large bed for the office to turn in our keys and beg for coffee. "It's for employees only," the gum-popping mid-forties woman with overplucked eyebrows informed me as she tapped with her acrylics on the computer's keyboard.

"Okay." I looked around at the brochure tower and saw a hole in the stack. "Do you happen to have a brochure of the nearby attractions? We're not sure what we want to do today."

She looked up at me, communicating with a bored glare that she hadn't felt like showing up to work this afternoon at all, and I was only making matters worse. "Fine. Hold on."

I waited until she disappeared into the back room before I hopped up on the counter and swung my legs over, ignoring the guys' whispered protests. "Cover me, Judah," I answered, pouring coffee from the pot into my emptied cup. I handed the cup to Reyn and climbed back up on the counter, taking Bastien's extended arm as an offer for help to get down. I wasn't all that graceful at accounting for my boobs yet, and accidentally brushed his forearm with them. I jerked away when I noticed his right fist was gripping his jagged knife. "Jeez! Put that thing away."

"You said to cover you! In our world, you steal and you could lose a hand. This coffee better have some serious magic to it."

"Oh, it does." I waited until he pocketed the knife

before I leaned into his strong arms and hopped to the floor between the guys. I tried not to enjoy the feel of his musculature, nor the scorching heat his simple touch grazed me with. The Employee of the Month came back with a stack of brochures a fistful of seconds later and handed one from the top of the stack to me. "Thanks. Just what I needed."

"Whatever. Have a nice day," she said by way of a "get out right now so I can go back to farting around on social media."

It was evening time, and the sun was just starting to set in the distance. I walked toward the car with Judah, but paused when Bastien stopped, looking to his left and his right with obvious hackles raised. "Something... I feel someone. Stay close. Put your head down." He pulled his knife out from his back pocket and flicked the switch so the handle shot a thick, angry jagged blade from the hilt. "Try not to look... like that."

"Like what?"

"All pretty and stuff. It draws the eye."

I stopped short at the almost-compliment. "Hello, you stole my necklace! I'm not trying to look like anything. This is just my face."

"Well, stop it!"

"Oh, you drive me crazy. If it's a person from my world, you can't just up and stab them, you know. We have rules, and it's not kill or be killed."

"Keep your head down and get to the car with Reyn. Both of you."

No sooner had I left his side to tuck myself under Reyn's outstretched arm, did footsteps come pounding toward us. Bastien turned as Reyn shoved me toward the car. "Get inside and lock the doors!" he yelled to Judah, pulling a knife out of his belt and running to help Bastien.

I wasn't really the hide and wait it out kind of girl. When my soccer buddy Kyle was getting picked on by a few older fraternity higher ups with too much beer in them, I didn't run when the bar fight broke out. I hopped on the biggest one's back and choked him until he went down, while the other girls screamed.

Today was no exception. I didn't wait for the guy running toward Bastien with an actual sword to see how things played out. I'd seen enough slasher movies to know the unarmed girl who runs always gets tracked down and captured. I searched for my own weapon, popping the trunk when nothing in the parking lot seemed like a good fit. I ignored Judah's loud, "Get in the car, Rosie!" The man who owned the car kept things pretty pristine, leaving only a gym bag, blanket, jumper cables and a tire iron in the sedan's mid-sized trunk space.

Good enough. I snatched up the iron and hung back, knowing I didn't have the upper hand in a sword fight. The man who fought with Bastien was bald, but the non-hair style didn't look like a choice or the misfortune of old age, as he appeared to be in his late twenties. It looked like his scalp had been burned by that same kind of acid that deformed Armand's face. He wore burlap pants and a peasant-like loose brown tunic that swished around his toned stomach as he fought with Reyn. The stranger was a seasoned fighter, his sword thrusts long and elegant, like a Musketeer or something.

Bastien threw himself in front of Reyn. I expected the fight to continue, but Baldy stopped mid-slice, as if he was afraid to take a swing at Bastien. "You can't fight me, Silvain!" Bastien warned as Reyn dodged a slice from the sword that looked heavy but well-wielded. "We were friends at the Academy! You know I'm Untouchable!"

"Of course I can't fight you, but you've got the Lost Daughter of Avalon! You know Morgan le Fae needs her daughter back. She belongs to our kingdom, not this world. I have my orders."

"Then Morgan can come up here all by her little self and fight me for her. Funny how the Lost Daughter's been missing for twenty-one years, but Morgan only just sent out her soldiers to search for her. You know she doesn't care about the girl. You know she only wants her because she's The Compass." The two circled each other, making half-moves on the other to see who would lunge first. Bastien looked primed to strike, but Silvain held his sword back almost in surrender.

The words stung me; I'd been trying not to think those very same thoughts. Why had my mother waited until now to try and find me? I understood why Bastien and Reyn were trying so hard all of a sudden. Their friend had gone missing. But I'd been lost from my mother and father my whole life. Why now?

"You don't want to do this," Bastien said, a note of pleading in his voice when Silvain turned his attention to Reyn. Bastien didn't sound afraid of getting hurt, but more wary of how badly he might have to hurt his old Academy buddy.

Silvain gulped. "Then don't make me do this! Give me The Compass, and I'll leave you be."

"You know I can't do that. If Morgan gets her hands on The Compass, the people don't stand a chance. You're fighting for the wrong team."

"And you're just fighting. Same Bastien you've always been. Fighting on the losing side just for an excuse to use your fists." Silvain's puffy lips curled into a snarl. "Be glad you've got your Untouchable status. You don't want to know how strong I am since taking the Queen's Loyalty Oath."

Reyn was at his best when smiling, but as he looked on Silvain with utter sorrow, I sensed there wouldn't be much optimism left after the showdown. "Be reasonable, Silvain. You know Morgan's behind the attacks on the Duchesses."

Silvain shook his head in exasperation. "Why would she turn on her own sisters? You're just like the other crazies, talking up conspiracies just so you have something to be mad about."

It might've been a valid point, but Bastien was done

talking. The Musketeer knew how to use his sword, but Bastien knew how to fight dirty. He went wide with his jab on purpose so he could twist around behind Silvain and stab him with his dagger from behind. It was so quick, I barely saw the whole dance.

I would've thought that's where Silvain would be munching on concrete, but apparently these Avalonians were made of tougher stuff than the average Joe Human. Reyn lunged to stab Silvain through his stomach, but Silvain shook Bastien off of him and dove for Reyn, nicking him on the arm and drawing blood. Bastien sprang forward to help Reyn, his knife still buried in Silvain's back, leaving him unarmed.

I didn't know the odds on the next college basketball game, but I could guess the odds on a fight between a kamikaze soldier with a sword and an unarmed guy who didn't understand the terrain like a native. Bastien was in a vulnerable position now, and I wasn't about to let that stand.

Silvain took another swing at Reyn, but ended up slicing Bastien's bicep. Silvain paled, as if cutting Bastien was a crime he was unwilling to commit, but cutting up Reyn was fine and dandy. It was hard to understand the politics of these people. Bastien didn't cry out at the offense, but he let out a deadly growl as he crouched like a wrestler, ready to pounce. That was all I needed to spring into action.

I ran toward the fight, swinging the tire iron like a base-

ball bat, letting loose a satisfying crack to the back of
Silvain's skull. I jerked the knife from his back on an angle,
knowing I didn't have it in me to stab a person, but that I
could cause a lot of damage taking out the blade if I pulled
to the left where a vital organ lay waiting. His right lung
was no doubt praying I would pass over it and leave it
unscathed. The tip snagged on something on its way out,
and Silvain screamed as I slid Bastien's knife across the
concrete, returning the weapon to its owner.

"Get back!" Bastien shouted, running Silvain through
the gut with his knife just as Reyn pushed me out of the
way to cut a slit across Silvain's throat, spilling blood out
onto the pavement, and coating Bastien's hands in red.

Bastien's face mutated from warrior to little boy in the
time it took Silvain to collapse in Bastien's arms. Bastien
lowered his old school buddy to the black pavement,
shushing him like a father comforting his child. Silvain
choked with wide eyes on his own blood.

"Are there others coming? How close are they?" Reyn
demanded, standing over the two. We all watched with
identical grim expressions as Silvain gave us a terrified
nod.

Silvain was now beyond being able to talk, and probably past the point of understanding anything but the fear
and the agony that painted his scarred face. Bastien was on
his knees next to his old friend, clutching his fist while
Silvain struggled out a few last gurgling breaths. Then I
heard Bastien whisper something that sounded like a

rehearsed prayer. "'Beyond the clouds there lies a home for the brave at heart to rest and roam. Your weapon's sure, your body best, but now you've earned a warrior's rest.'" He closed his eyes as Silvain's last gust escaped his quivering lips. Then he went still.

Reyn bent over and smoothed Silvain's eyelids shut. Then he pried Bastien's hand off his friend, so he could drag the body over by the small clearing of trees to conceal the carcass to keep it from view when the sun rose again.

Bastien looked lost, forlorn in his grief. I couldn't even begin to understand the pain that must come with having to kill a man you knew and had palled around school with. I dropped to my knees, and though I didn't know Bastien all that well, I wrapped my arms around his neck, pulling him into a hug I knew he'd never ask for. Bastien slumped into my arms, allowing me to hold him together while he tried not to fall apart in the middle of the parking lot.

14

HAMISH'S NUTTY ADVENTURE

*B*astien had killed his friend for me. Trying to keep me safe. *Me.* I'd cost him a friend.

"You were so brave," I whispered, pressing my lips to his temple. "I'm sorry it had to go down like that."

Bastien didn't answer, only let the grief wash over him in waves as I held him. When Reyn came back, Bastien was pulled up into his friend's strong arms. Reyn gripped him in a hug that possessed more years of understanding and compassion than I could throw together on a dime. Bastien's arms remained at his sides, permitting the hug, but not returning the affection. It wasn't until his eyes moistened that Bastien's hands wrapped around Reyn, squeezing as he let out a muffled shout into Reyn's shoulder. It was beautiful and horrible to watch, so I turned my face downward as I stood, taking in their injuries and reasoning that we probably needed a needle and thread.

I spun on my heel and went back to the office, snaking the keys to our room back off the hook when I saw the receptionist was nowhere in sight. I walked until I found the utility closet, opening it to find the maid's cart, stocked full of the things I would need. I grabbed a few sewing kits, bottles of water, soaps, shampoos, mints and anything else I didn't have a use for just then, but might down the road. I didn't have the guts to turn on the light in the utility closet, so I squinted in the dark until I found a first aid kit. I swallowed my guilt at the theft and ducked out of the closet, making my way out to the guys and motioning for them to follow me back to our vacated room.

When the door closed behind Reyn, his voice was quiet but firm. "We have to leave."

"I know. Let me patch you up, and we can hit the road. It won't do to have you both lose more blood on the way."

Reyn pulled his shirt over his head to inspect the damage. There would be a few bruises by morning, but my concern was the gash on his arm. I opened the kit, pulled out the antiseptic and sorted through the bandages, guessing Reyn's was probably not deep enough to absolutely need stitches. "We can probably get away with this, if that's okay with you." I held up a larger patch bandage, and he nodded.

"As quick as we can, then." Reyn held out his arm, hissing when the bite of the antiseptic spooked him. "Is it supposed to burn like that?"

"Yeah. Sorry. I forgot your medicine might be different

than ours. It's cleaning out the cut so you don't catch an infection." I cleaned out his wound and stuck the bandage on. I'd had worse on the soccer field, so I knew he'd be okay.

Judah stood watch, peeking out the curtain to make sure Silvain was the only one who'd followed us. His fingers were quivering on the maroon material, and I could tell that whatever LARPing expectations he'd had for this journey, he wasn't prepared for seeing an acid-deformed man get stabbed by two otherworldians, and bashed over the head by his BFF. He'd seen me in fights before, but he always looked away. He'd never had the stomach for it, which was probably a good thing. I'd had my locker vandalized too many times with the meanest graffiti, that I'd lost the ability to turn away from a fight that was aimed in my direction.

I decided right then and there that I wanted more for Judah. He wouldn't be crossing over into Faîte. No, he would stay here and have a nice summer. He'd sort things out with Jill. He'd paint and geek about graphic design. He wasn't meant for bashing people over the head. I wished I wasn't, but that seemed to be the mud I was stuck in. At least Silvain hadn't spray-painted "Retard" on my favorite hoodie while I was in gym class. I still remember the feel of Shannon McJeski's nose breaking beneath the wrath of my emotional fists when that whole mess went down. That was back in junior high. I was calmer now, after years of yoga and self-defense classes with Lane. I knew to pick my battles. Now I only fought back when acid-torn men came out and tried to snatch me up. Progress.

Bastien's cut was far deeper than Reyn's, and still seeped a few drops through his ruined shirt. He didn't look at me as Reyn and I helped him work his flannel off his shoulders, nor did he say anything when I gently tugged the white t-shirt beneath over his head. I gasped when I took in the damage done long before he'd found me. I couldn't even focus on the wonder that was the hard body of the seasoned warrior shirtless, so many were his scars. There were angry slashes across his chest in patterns of three, looking like claw marks from a vicious animal. He looked like he was a creation who'd been opened up and sewn back together badly, and too many times to count. Bastien had scars on his forearms that stretched in a wave over his shoulders. There were a few that looked as if someone had tried to tear off his collarbone. I forgot all about his grumpy jokes and saw only the terrifying figure that made me want to run and gawk simultaneously. He had thorny tattoo swirls that attempted to cover over some of the worst of his scarring, but it was clear that Bastien's body had been through just plain too much.

My fingers traced over a particularly deep scar that looked like it had been sewn on the fly across his heart. His intake of breath told me he wasn't used to having his bare skin touched. It took me a minute, but I steeled myself and looked up into his caramel eyes, whispering, "Ouch" to him in lieu of something that might actually help.

Bastien caught my wrist and turned his head slightly from side to side, telling me with a hard expression not to ask questions, not to pity him, and not to linger on his pain. My heart thudded unnaturally, and though I wanted to listen to him tell me about each scar, I knew he wasn't going to talk. I nodded, swallowing the lump in my throat as I turned to his bicep. He didn't hiss through the sting of the antiseptic. He didn't flinch at the stitches I'd only ever done on animals and myself before. He didn't look at me once while I wrapped the bandage on his arm, preferring to remain lost in his grief over killing his friend.

I took a chance and moved into his body space, coiling one arm around his waist. I knew Reyn was watching from the doorway of the bathroom, but I didn't care. I wanted to be there for Bastien, to shoulder some of the burden he was intent on carrying in silence. His palm lifted to rest on the small of my back, participating in the hug as much as his gruff demeanor would permit.

I pressed my ear to the scar over his heart, confirming the steady metronome of the organ. It was still there, buried beneath the fights that seemed to keep finding him. He was an acerbic butthole, for sure, but he'd let me hold his hand while I slept. Perhaps I didn't need to hear the gong-gong-gong of his heart to know it existed.

He dropped his hand and stepped back, unwilling to look at me. It wasn't until I tried to work his t-shirt back over his head that he snapped back to life. "I got it. Jeez. Go mother someone else."

I took a step back, bumping into Reyn, who wore a matching frown to mine. "Sorry. You just looked a little out of it."

He shoved his arms through the holes and rolled the material down his torso, covering the scars. There was a hint of self-consciousness that made him turn surly, like he hadn't wanted me to see his body. He had that same cagey way about him that I'd worn in the locker room when girls would gawk at me while I changed to get a better look at my hump. I didn't want to be just the ugly girl to people, and judging by Bastien's self-protective glower, I could tell he saw himself as the ugly boy because of his scars.

I should've known he'd bite. Most wounded animals did. "I told you to get in the car and lock the doors, didn't I? I didn't need your help murdering my friend. That one's useless, but at least he listens." He motioned in Judah's direction.

"Are you serious? I think the thing you're searching for is 'thank you, Rosie.' You're welcome, Bastien. You're welcome for not leaving you to die on the pavement. And don't you dare run Judah down in front of me."

"I killed Silvain because of you! Don't you get that? If not for you, he'd still be alive. And I don't need your help for anything other than finding Roland. That's your one use. Not hitting people on the head. Not stabbing my friend in the back. Find Roland. That's it."

I blinked, stepping back as if his words had grown a

hand and shoved me. "Look, I didn't mean for your friend to come after me. I'm sorry, okay?"

Reyn tucked me behind him as he moved back into the small space, glaring at Bastien while I set to cleaning up the tools from the counter with shaking hands. "You want to blame someone? Blame Morgan le Fae. Blame the oath her battalion took to serve her until death. Don't tear up the girl just because she saw your scars. You did the same thing to Rachelle when she saw them. You yelled so loudly, she cried for a week."

"Who's Rachelle?" I asked stupidly.

"My sister," Reyn answered at the same time Bastien said, "My fiancée."

My head snapped up to Bastien, shocked at this new information that colored my minuscule attraction to him in a new off-limits light. "You're engaged?"

"I'm a whole lot of things that have nothing to do with you. Be The Compass. That's your one job. Not mothering me. Not hitting my friends in the head. Find stuff, that's all."

"You need to go cool off, brother. It's enough." Reyn pointed his finger toward the door imperiously, one hand on my arm to keep me distanced from the anger.

Bastien seethed at Reyn while I finished gathering everything up and all but ran back to the car, Judah in tow. I wanted to cry. I wanted to tear Bastien a new one. I wanted to strangle him so he'd stop being such a pill and just deal. But I knew that some people just couldn't change, and it was hopeless to try and make them see reason. It may sound like a silly straw to let break the camel's back, but a camel can only take so much. Judging by how easily Reyn pinned Bastien's verbal swings, I guessed this was too frequent an occurrence for me to try my hand at combatting.

Judah was my soothing balm. "Don't listen to him, Ro. He's a jerk who's pissed about losing his friend. You did the right thing, helping like you did. I wish I'd thought to do that."

I let Judah's pat on my back serve as the hole I wished I could crawl into so I could have a minute to recuperate. "Thanks. Let's just get this over with." We walked out together, hand in hand. I shoved the contraband into the trunk, and then made my way to the driver's seat.

"I don't think so, Hot Mama. You drove across who knows how many states. My turn." Judah was firm, and though I wanted to argue, part of me knew I had no reason to. If I could catch a few more hours of sleep in the back, that wasn't something to sneeze at.

"Yeah, alright. Thanks, Pimp Daddy." I slid into the back, finding my coffee at the perfect temperature. "Here. You'll need this more than I do." Now I wouldn't stay awake for hours, mulling over how my mom wanted to find me so she could use me, and the guys rescuing me from her only wanted the same thing. I was a tool, nothing more. I'd worked so hard to be more. I studied more than anyone when I'd lived in the dorms. I passed on parties and staying out late with the guys so I could earn a degree. Now I was missing my finals, which would cancel my scholarship for sure. I might still pass most of my classes, thank goodness, but it would be a hard road next year.

If I made it back. If they let me come back.

I looked out the window to Bastien, whose head was bowed over the bushes where Silvain rested. Reyn looked like he was saying a prayer over his body or something. "Judah, can you see if there's a phone charger up there? My battery's pretty low."

"Sure." Judah fished around in the glove box and found a car charger that matched my phone's model. "There we go." He plugged in the device so I could call the one voice I used to trust above all else. The one who'd lied to me about pretty much everything.

When Lane answered over speakerphone with a harried, "Are you okay?" I almost broke down in embarrassing tears.

"I just needed to hear your voice."

Lane started sobbing, and I could tell she'd been holding back as well. "You're still talking to me? Oh, baby. I'm here. It's alright. I promise when I get to you, we'll hash it out. I'm so sorry. It's all on me. It's my fault completely. I should've told you years ago. I shouldn't have lied. Unforgiveable."

I nodded, but knew I couldn't speak without the waterworks I wouldn't be able to clean up in time. "Mm-hm."

"Are you guys close? Where are you? I'm still about three hours out."

"Where? I still have no idea where we're going."

"Montana. There's a tract of land that's got the well in it. The gate to Avalon is down inside the well."

Judah spoke up. "A well? Seriously? That doesn't sound so spectacular."

"Hi, honey. You doing okay, Judah?"

"I'm hanging in there. Tell me more about this well."

"It's not so deep. You just sort of lower yourself down, and land on the other side."

My stomach dropped. "Okay."

"Rosie, please tell me that one day you'll forgive me. I didn't want to tell you who your mom was because she wasn't a good person. She didn't deserve a daughter like you. You're amazing. You're my best friend, and she never understood how to love or take care of things without breaking them."

I nodded, though I didn't want to. "I really can't get into that right now. I don't want to get upset. It's already too much over here. Silvain? Some friend of Bastien's from the Academy? He found us, and it got bloody. He's dead now." I saw a squirrel watching me in the parking lot to my right, so I cracked my door open, waving him inside. On long treks home when I needed a driving buddy, I usually took Penelope or Wilbur with me. This new guy was a stranger, but when he scurried through the door that I popped open to let him in, I knew I'd chosen well. He chittered on my lap and butted the top of his head against my abdomen, grateful to have made a new friend. Animals were funny like that. Didn't take much for them to be cool. People weren't as easy to navigate.

I named my new buddy Hamish. He had big eyes that were perpetually wide, a brown bushy tail he was quite proud of, and an eagerness to inspect everything on the inside of the car after jumping up on my shoulder to nuzzle my neck. My eyes watered, and I knew I couldn't hold the emotion back much longer. "I think I helped kill a man, Lane."

"Oh, Rosie. Baby, you didn't have a choice. Trust me. With the army, it's kill or be tortured and then killed. I'm sorry you had to do that, though." Her tone changed to irritable. "Those idiots probably did the spell wrong. I should've known. I'm sorry, hun. Just get to the gate as soon as you can. Who's driving?"

"I am," Judah said. "I told her about the *visage* charm. You might have some 'splaining to do, Lucy."

Lane's voice was penitent and quiet. "I altered your appearance because you're the spitting image of your mother. I'm sure Reyn and Bastien can tell just by looking that you're Morgan's daughter."

My reply was no-nonsense. "You gave me a hump, Lane."

"And I'd do it all over again if it kept you alive and away from danger. I'll let you hate me forever if it means you're breathing."

I wasn't sure how angry to be with all of it. It was too much to process. "You know how rough it was for me in school. You fed me to the wolves, Lane."

"I love you, and I'm sorry for my role in it all."

Crap. If only she'd argued a little bit, then I could maintain my anger. As it was, I couldn't feel much beyond the shock. It was still too fresh to put my emotions in proper order.

Judah saved our uncomfortable lull. "Is it true Rosie's a human compass? Remember when I got separated from you at that carnival? She was the one who found me. You think that was her Compass kicking in?"

"I know it was. Let me give you the address so you can make a straighter shot with the GPS, and that way Ro doesn't have to use her abilities to navigate."

"Hit me with it." Judah pulled out his phone and turned it on. "By the way, your daughter's got a squirrel in the car."

"Yeah, I figured. Rosie, don't get rabies. You don't have time for a hospital stop."

"Roger that." I eyed Hamish. "Do you have rabies?" He chittered to me his indignation at being asked such an insulting question about his hygiene. "He says he's clean."

"I feel so much better." Lane rambled digits to Judah that I tried to remember, but they jumbled in my overcrowded brain. Hamish ran up to Judah and tapped the coffee cup with his tiny paws, but when there wasn't a nut inside, he left it alone. Hamish took up residence on

Judah's thigh, once I confirmed my BFF was cool. Hamish stood at attention with his hands on the right side of the wheel as he'd seen humans do. He wanted to drive, unafraid of the adventure. I wished I could say the same.

Hamish sensed my impending emotional breakdown and ran back to me, hopping up on my chest and examining my face with grave concern. *"It'll be okay."*

Though I wanted to believe him, he was a squirrel, and couldn't be sure of such things. When a tear squeezed out of the corner of my eye, Hamish dabbed at it with his tail, sensing my discomfort at the public display.

Bastien slid into the backseat a healthy distance from me, and Reyn took the passenger side next to Judah. I swiped at my tears, but knew it was no use. I'd been caught caring that I'd been hit too hard. Bastien didn't deserve to know how on the mark his aim had been when he'd taken a verbal swing at me. "We gotta go, Lane. They're back, so we'll see you soon."

Lane was irate. "Hand the phone to Tweedle Dumbass."

"Which one's that?"

"Whichever's closest." I handed the phone to Reyn, who was directly in front of me. Judah turned the keys to drown out the sound of Lane chewing him a new one for screwing up the spell. Reyn took her anger in stride, using his judge's son diplomacy to calm her faster than her usual tirades permitted. By the end of it, I could even hear a hint of a flirtation in her voice. I don't know how Reyn did it. Dude was smooth.

"Do you have any family?" I whispered to Hamish.

"No. I live alone, and there's hardly any nuts nearby. It's terrible here."

"Do you feel like relocating? I have a long way to go, and I could use a buddy."

Hamish was so excited at the idea that he perched on my shoulder and hugged my cheek, taking care not to scratch my face with his tiny claws. His tail hooked around my neck, warming the parts of my soul that I feared might grow cold over time.

Judah drove onto the freeway, sipping the coffee with one hand and driving with the other, while Hamish pointed out all the things he'd never seen at such a high velocity. He told me which trees were his favorite until we got into uncharted territory. Then he was mute with rapture, blown away at how suddenly the world grew far larger than he'd previously understood it to be.

When Reyn finally hung up, I took my phone back and turned on the cell station to cheesy nineties hip-hop, which was the best kind. I didn't have to think, and they didn't have to like it. I turned up the music and rolled down the windows. Judah and I loved hip-hop, the more ridiculous the better. We had epic dance-offs and rap contests when we ran out of normal ways to entertain ourselves. When the song hit the chorus, our heads moved back and forth in the same gangsta rhythm. Judah took the hook with, "'I love it when you call me Big Pop-pa. If you got a gun up in your waist please don't shoot up the place. Cause I see some ladies tonight who should be havin' my baby.'"

Judah looked in the rearview mirror to make sure I chimed in with the echoed "Ba-by." He offered me a small smile that let me know that if I could be Notorious B.I.G., then this Compass/Avalon crap was nothing. Judah was good at putting things into perspective for me.

Reyn quirked his eyebrow at either us or at the crass lyrics, I'm not sure, and then fished the vial of the stuff they'd concocted to keep me hidden. "Can you make it quieter?" he shouted over Judah's rapping that matched the singer perfectly. Judah was the rap master. I was a close second, though I didn't have the levity in me that evening.

I turned down the volume to a respectable level using my phone, and remained silent in lieu of asking Reyn what he wanted when he turned around.

"Elaine of Avalon told me that we made the potion right, but we were supposed to keep it on you, not near you. So can you put this in your pocket or something?" It was a small vial, but I knew I couldn't sit in the car for hours with something hard like that in my pocket, so I took it and shoved it down my shirt, working it between my breasts where I knew it wouldn't move or be too annoying. Reyn and Bastien cleared their throats and made a point of looking straight ahead after gawking like teenagers. *Whatever.* "Well, that works too, I guess."

I didn't answer, but kept my eyes on the scenery outside my window. The vibrant greens burst out at me with new life, waving in the wind to tell me about the possibilities that lay before me. I tried not to be afraid. I tried not to feel the sting of being with two guys I didn't know enough to avoid their personality traps. Then there was the one great guy, who I knew like the back of my hand couldn't handle a trek through Mordor or wherever.

"So we're just going to finish out the drive without talking?" Reyn asked, exasperated at the quiet.

I nodded, trying to drown out his words with the provocative and kind of funny lyrics from the next rap song I never tired of. I settled into my seat and idly wondered whatever happened to good rap. It was all blingy and boring now. Blarf.

Twenty minutes later, Bastien blurted out, "I can't take your music anymore! You've punished me enough, okay? I get it, I was a jerk. You win. Now turn it off."

I didn't answer, only turned up the volume, my eyes on my window and my face devoid of expression.

"Come on! I said I was sorry."

Of course, we all knew he'd said no such thing, but bringing that to light would necessitate talking, and I saw no point in that.

Reyn spun dials trying to adjust the volume, but he only managed to turn on the air conditioning yet again, which we didn't need. I helped him out and leaned forward to crank the music back down to a reasonable level. "Thanks. Bastien shouldn't have said those things. He gets like that when he's... but he shouldn't have. You didn't deserve that. You've been nothing but helpful once we got over the initial bump. I mean, we didn't know what to expect when we found you, but you're nothing like the royals in our world. You're one of us, and you didn't deserve to be barked at like that."

I responded with a shrug, but didn't look over at either of them. Hamish understood enough of the fight to scurry up and sit on the headrest of my seat. He raised his fist at Bastien, chittering up a storm and letting him know just who had the smallest nuts in the group.

"Okay, call off your minion. That's creepy." Bastien backed up in his seat behind Judah, eyeing Hamish and me warily.

I didn't feel the need to make things less uncomfortable for him, so I let Hamish yell until he exhausted himself, the poor puppy. After a while, he curled up on my thigh and took a little nap, scooting closer to my stomach when I reached down to comb my fingers through his tail. His even breathing soothed me, and though I still felt the disquiet of fear, I tried to let Hamish calm me as much as a squirrel was able.

15

NO JUSTICE FOR THE JUDGE'S DAUGHTER

*J*udah drove through the night in silence, and I felt no need to ease the tension. I kept vacillating between nodding off and forcing myself to wake. When the sun began to rise, I saw the Montana landscape in new light. There were pink hues from the sun that lit up the mountains in the distance, highlighting the greens and browns of the towering nature. Majesty surrounded us on both sides of the highway and off in the distance we were headed toward. We were almost out of gas again, so Judah pulled off at the next exit and parked at the gas station, refueling in silence while everyone took turns with the bathroom. I bought myself another coffee, though I knew I could only fend off sleepiness for so long. The road was hypnotizing, and the silence was too quiet to keep me awake without stimulants. "You've got to take the next shift, Ro. I'm starting to see cross-eyed." Judah demonstrated his dilemma with his eyes crossed.

"That's fine. I'm getting my uppers now." I held the coffee cup up as a visual aid.

I used the restroom after the guys and splashed water on my face to wake myself up, not looking in the mirror so I didn't have to confirm that the hurt I felt deeply was still etched all over my face. No matter how much we had tried to be buddies through our trip, I was a tool to be used and thrown away. My mom knew it. The guys knew it. Maybe I had always known it, too.

Hamish perched on the sink that had too many stains and cracks in the surface to be less than twenty years old. He saw my pain for what it was and promised me he wasn't using me to get to a better venue for nuts. He was along for the ride and wanted to be my friend.

The best friends were always animals. I scooped him up and let him cling to the back of my shirt, hoping he didn't leave permanent tiny holes in the purple material. André Roussimoff was still with me. That had to count for something. My favorite wrestler hadn't written me off as a lost cause. In my imagination, André, though deceased, got to see the world via me when I wore this t-shirt. He went on adventures with me, and laughed at the same jokes that made me giggle. He would never use me, but went on escapades with me.

I walked out to the car and stretched before climbing into the driver's seat, turning off the GPS to give my internal Compass a crack at navigating. Two hours, and I could see Lane again. Despite all the lies, I still wanted to find her. She would make everything better – that was her way.

Reyn got out of the car and came around to stand next to me. He didn't say anything, but waited until I turned to face him. I gave him a baleful expression that told him I wasn't in the mood for more of his "let's all be friends" BS. He slowly pulled me out of my seat and wrapped his arms around me, bringing me to his chest in a hug I tried not to need. He rubbed the middle of my back, taking Hamish's lecture that they didn't deserve me in stride. Reyn kissed my forehead, and I knew he was trying extra hard to make things okay, to compensate for his jackweed of a friend. "It's how he gets when something hurts him too bad for him to deal with," Reyn whispered into my ear.

"I'm aware he's got the emotional range of a two-year old. But I don't have to look the other way like you do. He's not my friend, and after I find Roland for you, you two will never have to see me again."

"Now, now. That's not what I want."

"It's what you're going to get. I'm not a tool. I'm a person. I shouldn't have to be around people I have to spell that out for. Bastien's your problem, not mine. He's not marrying my sister." I pulled out of his embrace and shut myself in the car.

"Look, I said I was sorry," Bastien said quietly from

behind me as Reyn made his way back to his side of the car.

"No, you didn't, and I already told you before that I don't need you to lie to me. I don't need your fake apology. I need to get your friend back and find a way to get myself good and lost so your people can't get to me anymore. I need you to leave me alone so none of your other friends have to die when they try to kidnap me. That's what I need."

"Fine!"

"Good!"

Judah buckled his seatbelt, settling in behind Reyn. "Ah, the sound of Rosie fighting to the death. I never thought you'd meet someone who could push all your buttons enough to make you lash out like you used to before you calmed down, but here he is. In the very flesh."

I shoved the key into the ignition and peeled out of the lot, jerking the newbies to the side of the car. "That's my reminder for all of you to put on your seatbelts."

Hamish was concerned with my behavior, so he sat up on my thigh and hugged my stomach. *"I won't leave you. I know you're mad, but I'll help you find some nuts. I'll share all my best nuts with you."*

"Okay, stop it," I whispered, my hand brushing down over his thick, brown fur. He was too thin for my liking, and I made a mental note to give him some of my trail mix when we got there. "I'm alright," I assured Hamish, who knew better than to believe me.

"That's so strange you can talk to them," Reyn commented, pretending there was no fight or tension in the car for the moment. "I mean, the whole kingdom knows you can do it, but it's crazy to watch it play out. Do you have to talk aloud to them? Because sometimes it looks like he's answering something you didn't even say."

I bit my lip, not wanting to divulge things I'd never shared with anyone except for Lane and Judah. "I don't want to talk about it."

Judah stepped in, opening the locked box when I clammed up. He was good like that, knowing when to step in and when to let me stand my ground. "She can do either. Sometimes when she doesn't want other people to hear her, she can talk to them in her mind if she's known the animal for a while."

"That's incredible," Reyn mused.

I kept my eyes on the road, not wanting to see the look-at-the-freak expressions I was sure the guys were wearing. "Okay, I know it sounds like I'm insane, but I can hear them pretty clearly. Not like I can speak squirrel or anything, but I can understand what they say to me, and somehow they get me."

"You can talk to us, you know," Reyn offered kindly.

"No, I can't. Animals are easier. They don't lie to me or piss me off on purpose. I've never once had an animal treat me like that." I jerked my thumb over my shoulder to Bastien. Hamish stood up on my thigh and raised his fist at the guys, yelling at them for their bad behavior.

Bastien was exasperated. "Would you just let it go? It's been hours! So I snapped at you. So what?"

"Why do you care if I'm quiet? What's it to you? You're still getting everything you want out of this deal. I'm still helping you find Roland. Why do you care if I like you or not through it all? Leave me alone!"

"This is how I'm going to die. This woman right here. You're going to be the death of me with all this drama!"

"Hello! You're the drama queen. I defend you when you're caught in a fight, I help patch you up, I hold you when you're going through the crack of it, and you bite my head off! No animal has ever treated me like the dog you must think I am. I don't care how you are with Reyn, your fiancée and your buddies who are used to you. You don't get to skate by after treating me like that. Now shut up and let me drive, or so help me, I'll pull this car over right now!" My fury reached its crest when I realized I sounded like my imaginary Superman dad on our infamous road trips to nowhere. I smiled to myself, and Hamish sat his butt down on my thigh, his arms crossed as he stood guard to make sure Bastien didn't run his mouth anymore.

Reyn broke the silence. "Silvain was from the Queen's Army. Can I assume you don't know much about them?"

"You can assume I know nothing about your world."

"Very well. The Queen's Army serves all sorts of purposes. They help rebuild cities that need it, they distribute food to the needy, and they defend our territory from any creature that threatens it, theoretically." I waited for the "but", and Reyn let it fly. "But in the last few years, they've grown aggressive. Less concerned with keeping the peace and more concerned with just keeping. Sometimes taking what isn't theirs. Land, food, women, you name it."

"That's awful."

Judah chimed in. "We've had a bit of that in other parts of the world, or in history books, telling how things were centuries before we were born."

I finally tore my eyes away from the road to glimpse Reyn's barely controlled pain. It pulled down the corners of his mouth into a twisted grimace of memories that still tortured him as if they were fresh. "What did they take from you?" I asked quietly.

"I told you my father is a judge. Well, he threw a few soldiers into the stocks for roughing up a farmer who wouldn't hand over his crops just because they demanded it on their march through the city 'for our safety.' My father never cowered before that, but he's not the same man anymore. I can't imagine anyone would be after how they retaliated."

"I'm afraid to ask."

Bastien answered when the prolonged pause indicated that Reyn could not. "They took the judge's daughter, Rachelle, and gave her to Captain Burke. He raped her, impregnated her and abandoned her in town square, disgraced and beaten."

I was so shocked that I almost veered off the road. I couldn't let that piece of horror go with a simple, "I'm so sorry," so I pulled onto the shoulder and flung open my door, ignoring the few cars that whipped by in the dark as I ran to Reyn's side and threw open his door. It was my turn to pull him out of the car and hold him. I wrapped my arms around his waist as he cradled my head to his shoulder. "Reyn, that's the most awful thing I ever heard. I can't believe your government allows that! What happened to your sister? How'd she deal?"

Reyn combed his long fingers through my curls, comforting me through his pain. He was strange like that. "They sent her back barely alive, trapped in a deep sleep with a spell. We've tried everything to wake her, but it's been a year, and nothing."

"A year?! What happened to the baby?"

"Died inside of her. But not before my sister's honor was questioned throughout the city."

I shook my head, trying to add up all the variables that I knew about Avalon. "But I thought you lived in a matriarchal society. My mother wouldn't allow that." I tried to state the obvious with certainty, but Reyn's carefully composed compassionate expression gave me pause.

"Any ruler – male or female – lets their people fall to ruin if they hold no love for them in their heart. Morgan le Fae cares only for herself and expanding her territory. If the soldiers are happy in their depravity and she looks the other way, then they follow her, ever more loyal. All she has to do is nothing – an act she's perfected over the years."

Dread sank low in my gut. I wanted my mother to be a

defender of the downtrodden, but it sounded like she didn't give a crap about any of it. "Your sister... Reyn, I don't know what to say."

"Bastien stood up for Rachelle when her good name was being dragged through the mud. He went to my father and offered to say he'd marry her to save her name. To save my father's name. Rachelle doesn't even know she's engaged. I doubt even she knows what her older brother's best friend did for her. I doubt she can hear us through her slumber."

I mulled over the facts while I remained in Reyn's arms. Despite everything, there was a wave of safety I felt being near the man I barely knew. "That's a terrible story, Reyn."

"It is. Bastien's hard to understand, but there's enough good there to make up for the difficult spots. Be patient with him. He's not used to someone like you."

"Like me?" I scrunched my nose. "What am I like?"

"You're like him."

I pulled away, my mouth hanging open at the words that rang in the air around me. Surely that couldn't be true. I decided to ignore the parts I didn't want to hear and gave Reyn's hand a squeeze. "We should get going. I didn't want to make you tell me your awful story without someone to hug you through it."

The corner of Reyn's mouth twitched upward, and he looked down at me with unconcealed appreciation. "And I thank you for that. Shall we?"

We got back in and drove in silence until the tug in my gut told me we'd arrived. At a tiny ranch. In the middle of nowhere. Nothing ominous about that. I called Lane, who told me we needed to park and hike inland toward the mountains for five miles, and that she'd find us when we got close. The guys put their packs on their backs with all the things they'd traveled with over to my world. I shoved my trail mix into Reyn's backpack and tried not to let my frayed nerves show when my exhaustion coupled with the prospect of going into a whole new world I knew nothing about. I didn't know how to feel about my mom and dad, so I tried not to think about them. I had a cousin, though, and the promise of meeting Roland drove me forward. Maybe Roland loved soccer, too, and we could play together in the backyard of his castle, once we rescued him. Maybe he would take one look at me, and instantly see the sister he'd always wanted in his family. Having a cousin sounded super amazing, and though I was worried about the actual extraction of him from the ominous Forgotten Forest, part of me wanted to go there at a run, and reclaim the family I'd never known.

I'd always wanted a big family, though I'd never had the heart to confess that to Lane. She'd been family enough to fill those gaps on the surface, but beneath my skin lay cracks and holes that had been spackled over but never fully filled. I had a real, live cousin, and maybe a few aunts lurking about. We could go Christmas shopping together and pick out matching sweaters to wear. I wondered if my aunts were as fun as Lane, or if Lane was a true original, as I'd always thought her. I began to plan dance parties, and candy-centric events that I could share with my new family.

Hamish scampered along beside me, talking away and pointing out the things that stood out to him. Squirrels saw the world mostly in shades of nuts. This kind of tree produces this kind of nut, that tree was good for hiding these types of nuts, and so forth. Hamish was a chatty one, and I welcomed the distraction. When he asked if I was hungry, I shook my head. I was too nervous to eat.

"What's wrong? You're shaking your head," Reyn said as he walked next to me. Reyn and Bastien were on either side, sandwiching me from whatever harm they were on high alert against. There was nothing but dirt and mountains surrounding us, but apparently they still needed to hover.

"Nothing. I was talking to Hamish."

"Hamish?"

I pointed to the squirrel, who put his hands on his hips to give Reyn all kinds of attitude to make sure he never forgot just who Hamish was ever again. I kinda liked how feisty my little guy was. He had words when I didn't. "Hamish is my squirrel. He's coming with me as far as he feels like."

"That's weird," Bastien stated flatly. "It's like you have people you talk to in your head. You've been having whole conversations with a squirrel while ignoring us."

"Ignoring *you*. There's a difference. Reyn can say whatever he wants to me. Judah and I never argue for more than half a day. You can talk to the voices in your head all you like. See if they can knock some sense into you."

"This reminds me why I never lived with a woman. So much crying about nothing."

"Can I say I'm not terribly surprised no woman could stand to live under the same roof as you?" I stomped on ahead and let Hamish yell at Bastien until he got a little too offensive on my behalf. "Hamish! I appreciate it, but you don't need to talk like that. I'm still a lady, and I can hear you." I did my best to feel like a lady, but that image always fell flat. I was married to my soccer shoes and owned exactly zero dresses. Something told me that a legit lady would own at least a skirt.

Bastien lost his fight to a chuckle. "I guess I really was wrong if I made your guard dog this angry." He held up his hands in surrender. "Fine. I said some things back there that I shouldn't have. I knew Silvain well and didn't think he'd... It doesn't matter. You were fine, and I was... I shouldn't have..." It was like he couldn't work out an entire apology without choking on his words.

I eyed the confusing act of Bastien humbling himself, and slowly bobbed my head. "Alright. Me too, I guess. Truce it out?"

Bastien offered his hand in apology, and I shook it without any underlying note of aggression, though I wasn't sure how much I was trusting his surrender. "I wasn't expecting Silvain. Seeing him like that really threw me."

"You weren't expecting your old buddy to show up in another dimension and attack us?" I gave him a wry smile to ease the fight between us. "For what it's worth, I'm real sorry it all went down like that. I can't imagine if one of my friends tried to get the jump on me. I probably wouldn't handle it all that gracefully."

Bastien shook his head to scold me. "See? You're doing it again."

"What?"

"That nice thing. I was a jerk. You can say it."

I tilted my head up at him. "Do you want me to think you're a jerk?"

"No."

I shrugged. "Then don't be one. Easy-peasy."

Bastien smirked at my phrasing. "'Easy-peasy?'"

"Careful," I warned with a faux frown. "That sounded almost cutesy. If people hear you talking like that, they'll start expecting smiles and songs from you. Best keep up that surly front you've been working so hard to perfect." I mimicked his glare with my eyebrows pushed together and my shoulders tensed in preparation for a fight from a butterfly.

Bastien rolled his eyes at me. "Yeah, yeah. Let's go, you ridiculous girl."

"Funny, I was just about to call you the same thing." I smirked at his mimed laughter at my dig.

Hamish scampered to my side, scurrying up my leg, on my hip and onto my shoulder so he could get a free ride and remind me he was my best friend. "I love you, too, buddy." Love was easy to give and receive with animals.

People were trickier.

16

MY LOVE FOR JUDAH AND LANE

"Where are we staying when we get to your world?" Judah asked.

At this, I stopped, turning to face him. "Judah, I can't have you crossing over with me. I want you to take the car and go on home."

"You can't be serious. This is Middle Earth we're talking about."

"Yes, and it's a world where the military doesn't give a crap about people's rights, and where I'll be hunted for who knows how long. I won't put you in the thick of that. Would you let me come if the situation were reversed?"

Judah didn't pause to see it from my point of view. "You're not going in there without me. I'm coming, Ro. We've never lived farther away than you could throw a baseball."

I tilted my head at him, shoving my hands in the

pockets of my jeans and tapping the toe of my shoe to his. "I don't want to live somewhere new without you, either, but if something happened to you? Because of me?" I shook my head. "This is where you jump off the train and ride off into the sunset, cowboy."

Judah's thin lips were set in a line of defiance. "It's not your call. Lane can decide."

"Alright. We'll see how much she's going to want to risk your life. You have a family, Judah. Your mom needs you to get a degree and get a good job. Think of all she's sacrificed for you! And Jill loves you. You should go back to her and make things right."

"You're saying goodbye, but I haven't agreed to up and abandon you."

"I don't know when or if they'll let me come back. You'll really ditch Jill and your mom like that? This isn't just some adventure that's over in two hours. It might be weeks, or even longer. You're willing to drop out of school for this?"

I saw the hesitation, and though I wished for my security blanket to travel with me everywhere I went, I knew it was time to cut the cord if I wanted to save the baby. I reached forward and pushed his glasses up his nose. "Judah, you know you can't come. Let's blame it on school."

"Stupid school." He tapped the toe of my Sambas with his sneakers.

"Yeah. Stupid school."

Reyn played his role of peacemaker well, breaking the tension with neutral conversation. "We've got a friend who's waiting on the Avalon side of the gate. When we get there, he'll let us through. He's part of the guard, so he'll let us in without alerting the army." When no one had anything to say to this, Reyn continued. "When we get to Avalon, Bastien and I can get us safely out of the barracks, so stick close to us."

"Where do you live?" I asked Reyn, unsure what to make of their veiled conversation.

"A few houses down from my father in Nanti. Bastien lives just outside of Louche, deep in the woods. It's closer to the gate, and there aren't so many upstanding citizens who'll report you if they happen to catch onto who you are. People tend to leave each other alone in Louche. It's mostly hermits and grumps like Bastien."

"Very funny." Bastien turned to me. "Plus, we don't know the judge's stance on you, so it's not a good idea to bring you too near him. Puts him in a dangerous position if Morgan le Fae found out he knew about you being in Faîte and didn't bring you straight to her Province. So for now, Hermitville is where it's at."

"Alright. That's fine. Then what? How do we find this horse?"

Reyn shrugged. "We don't really have a plan for that. I'm hoping your pal Hamish can help. Maybe you can talk to a few animals or something. Plus, you're The Compass. You're supposed to be able to find anything. If the animals don't know where Roland is, then maybe you can just start walking and end up there."

"Well, with a solid plan like that, who can complain?" I tried to sound cheery, but it fell flat.

"You guys have no plan," Judah stated, calling them on all the BS I was too tired to bother with. "You're expecting her to give up her life here and run after yours so she can fix it. Am I reading that right?"

Bastien ground his teeth together. "You got something to say to me, kid?"

"I do, as a matter of fact. You're pushing Rosie around like she owes you or something. Well, she doesn't. If she's the daughter of a queen, that means her place is above yours, right?"

Reyn nodded thoughtfully. "Her place is above mine. That's correct. But if she can keep quiet about her title, she'll stay free longer."

"Fine, but when she's around you two, make sure you both remember that she's the best thing that ever came into your lives. She doesn't owe you a thing. She's a princess, and you'll treat her like one." The declaration with which he spoke my fake title was so sincere, I couldn't help but gape at his conviction. "Rosie, don't let them jerk you around, alright?"

"Okay, Judah. Thanks." I watched him nod and knew exactly why he'd been my closest friend through the years.

Judah addressed Reyn, as if giving him the keys to the kingdom. "If she says she's fine, check for broken bones or blood. If she says she's hungry, it's because she hasn't eaten in like, a day. If she gets quiet, it means she's yelling inside. She gets pretty violent when someone's getting picked on, so watch you don't push her too hard."

I balled my toes inside my shoes. "They don't need a play-by-play. I'll only be around them long enough to find the horse, then I'll come back home. That should only take, what? A day? Day and a half?" I kidded.

"You'd better." Judah shook his head. "I don't like this."

We walked in silence for a couple more miles. I was so tired, but knew I couldn't say anything, for fear of being the weakest link. Hamish butted the top of his head to my jaw to offer some comfort, letting me know he saw me, that he heard me even when I kept my mouth shut. It's a solid friend who can do that.

I saw Lane in the distance, and despite my weighted body, I told Hamish to hold on as I broke out into a sprint, running toward her as if she was my only lifeline. Some days, that's exactly what she was for me. We met in a crash of the greatest hug on earth since the last time I came home from school on mid-winter break. She held onto me as if she needed me there so she could breathe properly. I knew the feeling. "I was so afraid I lost you! I should've been the one to tell you the truth about it all. I know you must hate me. I'm sorry, Rosie! I'm so sorry!"

I clung to her, pulling her tighter to me as if she was the only thing holding me to the planet, which, let's face it, some days she was exactly that person in my life. Lane was my best girlfriend, my touchstone. "I promise to be really mad at you when this is all over. Until then, no more secrets, okay? No more lies."

She nodded into my shoulder, and I felt her pain at our temporary separation and sudden rift. "I was the one who fixed your bike when you were a kid. I told you it was Santa, but I lied right to your face." She held me tighter when I broke out into a laugh. She smelled like lemon balm, as she always did. It was the lotion that she made herself, and I missed the way our home always smelled like her. She was only three inches taller than me, so we fit into the same clothes and had shared one dresser after I hit eighteen. She clung to me, and I felt just how scared she was that she'd almost lost her best friend, too. "I used to take your homework out of your folder after you'd finished it and fix it so you got a better grade. I shouldn't have done it, but you worked so hard, and I knew you knew those answers! But I cheated, and it was wrong."

"I missed you, Lane."

"Oh, Ro. I only missed you like I miss breathing."

"I only missed you like I miss rainy days and hot tea," I admitted.

"Let me get a good look at you." She pulled back, but still gripped my hands, letting them swing between us. Her eyes sparkled with wonder and borderline trepidation as she drank in my features. As much as my new appearance had spooked me, I could tell there was an additional layer of anxiety that hit Lane. "You're just as beautiful as you've always been."

It was the lie only a mother could get away with. I looked nothing like my former self, but then again, she had always told me I was pretty, even when other people shuddered at my appearance. "I look like you," I observed, amazed at the striking similarities.

Lane nodded, swallowing hard. "All the Daughters of Avalon look similar. I'm having a moment, here. You look... I mean, you're the spitting image of Morgan."

Lane and I had always shared the same heart shape to our face, the same chestnut hair, the same petite but muscular bodies, and a grin that shined for cheesy jokes. But now we had the same unmarked cheeks, since my acne had cleared up. We had the same upright posture, with the disappearance of my hump. We could probably borrow each other's bras, now that my curves were more in line with her feminine form. Though her eyes were green and mine blue, our eye shape was the same, curving up at the corners when we smiled, which we were fortunate enough to do often.

Lane was still crying as the guys sidled up beside us. Bastien looked awkwardly toward the trees to avoid the horrendous display of affection and emotion, while Reyn studied our connection as if trying to figure out what made us tick in the same offbeat rhythm only we understood. Lane was sixteen years older than me, but she was the type to look younger than her age, due to constant smiling and living off of corny jokes that made us both laugh. Though she was thirty-eight, she didn't look a day over thirty-two. I felt about a hundred, so we were a good match overall. "I'm sorry," she whispered again, wetting my hair with her tears.

I squeezed her in lieu of speaking.

"If we're offering up confessions, I did the whole fixing your answers thing a few times myself," Judah said, earning a laugh from both of us.

Lane pretended to be appalled. "You're her tutor! I paid you good imaginary money to make her brilliant."

"And I spent every last fake dime on women and booze." He grinned at his second mom. "Hey, Lane."

"Get in here, boy. It's been too long. I haven't seen you in months! How much have you grown? A foot? Two?"

"Seven feet, actually. They're saying I'm a medical marvel."

"You're my own personal miracle, is what you are," Lane said, hugging Judah tight. She turned to me, holding my hand. "Looking at you like this... I mean, I always knew you'd turn out looking like Morgan, but it's spooky. Pretty much spot on from how she looked the last time I saw her. You alright?"

"So my mom's still alive, but she's some evil queen or something. Is that true?"

Lane hesitated, and then nodded, her curly, chocolate-colored ponytail bobbing up and down. We looked so much alike now, I had to remind myself we weren't actually sisters, or a biological mother and daughter set. "I took you because I was convinced she was behind a lot of bad things going down. She used to... When you were a baby she... I couldn't sit back and do nothing. I couldn't let you get used like that. It was the only way."

"You kidnapped me," I stated flatly, the words in my mouth tasting sour. "You kidnapped me and told me my mom died in childbirth, and that my dad ran out when my mom found out she was pregnant." Twenty-two years of self-hatred bubbled up inside of me, igniting on the one spark of truth I finally was given. I didn't want to spew fire and ire at Lane, but that's exactly what shot out when I opened my mouth. I punched my fist to my chest, feeling the vial snuggled in between my breasts moving from side to side. "All these years, I thought *I* was the reason I didn't have a family, but it was you. I thought I killed my mom! I thought my mom died alone because dad left when he found out about me. All these years, I was certain there's a man out there who knows all about me and wants nothing to do with me. I thought he hated me so much that he left us! Left my mom to die and abandoned me! You have no idea what that feels like!" I didn't know how many tears I'd reserved for this very conversation until buckets of emotion began to pour down my cheeks.

My rage was painful to say and even worse for Lane to hear. I expected her to shout back, to argue with my feelings or to throw her own fit, but when her arms gripped me in a tight hug, I didn't know what to do. Darn her intuitively spot-on responses. "Keep it coming, baby. I earned it. Don't hold back. I told you a lie so you wouldn't go looking for them. Be mad at me." I struggled to get out of her grip, but she only held on tighter, squeezing yet more tears out of me.

"Every birthday I've ever had has been terrible! All I can think is how I killed my mom on my birthday! You did that to me! You put that in my brain!"

Lane was horrified. "Why would you ever say it like that to yourself? That's why you like to go camping every year instead of have a party?"

"What's there to celebrate? My mom supposedly died in childbirth, and my dad didn't give a crack about me. *You* put that on me, Lane! Why? So you could have a daughter? A daughter who wasn't yours? I wasn't yours, Lane! I'm not yours!"

That was the slice. It was the pivotal moment I pushed the truth too far. I'd cut her in a place I knew wouldn't heal, but still she held me. Bastien, Reyn and Judah finally moseyed on ahead to give us some space.

"I did everything I could to make you mine. Morgan had a plan, Rosie. There's a set of jewels."

"The guys told me about the Jewels of Good Fortune, yeah. Do you have yours? I've never seen it."

"It's safe." The finality of her tone told me there was nothing more she would say about it.

"Well that tells us nothing. Where is it?" Bastien wasn't

quite out of earshot, apparently, and whirled around to stick his bossy nose into our conversation.

"Somewhere safe. It's no concern of yours."

Bastien reared back, affronted. "Are you kidding me? It's the concern of everyone in Faîte! Does Morgan le Fae have your jewel or not?"

"Of course she doesn't have it. I said it was safe, not safe in the hands of the enemy."

Bastien's hands flew out in frustration. "Where? Avalon needs it! We've got people starving, kids dying, magic withering. If you have one of the jewels, you have to bring it to Avalon."

Lane reached up and gripped his scruffy jaw with one determined hand, squeezing his face so his lips parted in a smoosh. Her gaze was steel and her tone deadly as she brought his face down to be level with hers. In that moment, I saw the carefree silly girl façade fade away; it was replaced by a ruler who didn't take crap from anyone. "Listen, you punk kid. You don't know the first thing about protecting the Jewels of Good Fortune. Rosie doesn't even know where I stashed mine. Do you really think you're going to annoy it out of me? The second I show my hand, Morgan's army will come running. We have to take her down first, then I'll bring the stone to Avalon."

"Fine." Bastien glared at her, but didn't protest from his position of submission to my tall, slender aunt. "I'm an Untouchable, not some 'punk kid'."

"I couldn't care less what you are right now." Lane

released Bastien, who rubbed his face as he pouted. Her hands were gentle as she placed them in mine, squaring her shoulders to me to make sure I heard her completely. "Morgan was going to use you to find the other jewels as soon as you learned to walk, baby. The only time she wanted to see you was when she was showing you pictures of the jewels, telling you stories about them. Then she left you with me. *I* raised you, even in Avalon. You were a tool to her, but I loved you. The only kindness I could think to say to you was that she was dead. I didn't know you'd read into it that you killed her. You didn't! And your dad loved you, babe. King Urien?" Her voice quieted to a whisper. "Urien saw what Morgan was doing. When he confronted her about being a shoddy mom, she started slowly poisoning him so he started to lose his mind. I tried to find a cure for the poison, but I couldn't help him! I went to Master Kerdik and begged him to cut Morgan off from the power, to take back his jewels, but the snake wouldn't listen!" The confession poured out of her as if it had been stuffed inside a lockbox for decades, and finally had its chance to spill out and breathe.

Reyn and Bastien both gasped. Reyn was the more diplomatic of the two, so he spoke what they were both thinking. "You've seen Master Kerdik? You've spoken with him?"

Lane shrugged. "Well, sure. Twenty-one years ago before I left with Rosie. Why? Is he not as social anymore?"

"Kerdik hasn't been seen or heard from since the

Princess of Avalon was lost. How soon before you left did you see him?"

Lane touched her forehead, then her chest. "I don't know. Maybe a day or two before? I told him what was going on with the jewels, and what Morgan was doing to Rosie. When he washed his hands of the whole thing and basically told me it wasn't his problem, I went to the castle and told Urien. That's when Urien said we were doomed, and to take Rosie and run."

"What?" My voice was quiet, but it felt like my shock was heard across the world. "My dad... That Urien guy... He... he didn't walk out on us?"

She leaned in and gripped my face with gentle hands, ignoring the guys who were gawking from a safe distance at the new information. "In the last days Urien was himself, he begged me to take you away. He told me to hide you where Morgan could never use your abilities. So I took you here, to Common, which is what people in Faîte call Earth. I assumed you'd lose your abilities, like how I lost mine. It's why no one from Faîte comes up here. Common mutes most of your magic." She pressed her forehead to mine, and both of us closed our wet eyelashes in unison. "Urien loved you. He loved you enough to give you up when you were in danger. He loved you so much that he would rather suffer and die alone than see you hurt another day. You are the daughter of a great man." Her blue painted fingernails squeezed my face.

When I finally found the words, they came out in whispered vows of familial loyalty. "I'm sorry I said I wasn't yours."

"Oh, kid. You don't get to apologize. You get to be as mad as you want for as long as you want. I'll never leave you. Spice Girls until the end." She hugged me again, and this time I let myself cry harder than I meant to. I hadn't killed my mom. My dad wanted me. And I still had my best friend through all the changes. Through all the bad spots, there were enough pieces of good for me to hold tight inside my heart.

17

THE RABBIT HOLE TO AVALON

*R*eyn was a gentleman, taking a handkerchief out of his pocket and handing it to Lane when I passed on the offer. I turned away and pretended there was something interesting on the toe of my shoe.

"Thank you." Lane dabbed at the smeared black eyeliner she always wore the right amount of too much. She could work that smoky eye look like nobody's business. I had colored chapstick I wore on special occasions like sports banquets, but that was about it. She handed back the damp square, but Reyn wouldn't hear of it. "But it's yours," Lane insisted.

His long, dark fingers closed over hers, bunching the fabric in her fist. I didn't need ears to hear the zap of electricity between them that jolted Lane's eyes wider. I'd never seen Lane look at a man like that, but there it was – the beginnings of a crush. Reyn tilted her chin up in a move that was super intimate for people who were meeting for the first time. He was gentle as he spoke, as if his words grew a hand he could caress her upturned face with. "And now it's yours. We're going back to your home country. Something tells me you're going to need it again when you see how far we've fallen without you." He motioned to a stone well still a ways off, and wrapped an arm around Lane to guide her there. "I think it's time."

I'd never seen Lane with a man's arm around her before. She was celibate, always putting me as her top priority. I felt horrible for yelling at her, saying things I didn't mean, or at least shouldn't have said aloud. Reyn was a few inches taller than Lane's regal 5'9", and she fit under his arm perfectly. I watched the two and walked behind them with Bastien, Judah and Hamish, musing quietly to Hamish how I'd never seen her comforted like that. I wondered how often she'd needed a shoulder to cry on that was sturdier than mine. I did my best, but there was something different about a guy giving you his handkerchief and letting him shelter your shoulders from the world's weight that made a girl's problems seem just a little bit smaller.

"I'm not doing that," Bastien said, clearly uncomfortable.

"Doing what?"

"I don't carry a handkerchief around for girls to cry into."

I rolled my puffy eyes. "What the flip are you talking

about? I'm not the kind of girl guys do that sort of thing for."

"Good. Just so long as you know that. When we get back to Faîte, I'm promised to Reyn's sister. I have to play that part."

"Well, I'll just be crying myself to sleep that you're not pining away for me."

His eyes darted to me and quickly looked away, pained at my appearance. "You look terrible."

"Yeah? You look like a grown man who should know better than to say that to someone who's just gone through the crack of it. I don't care how I look. I'm not entering a beauty contest. I'll be in hiding, tromping through the woods with you guys. What do you care how I look? You're engaged. You're not supposed to be looking at me anyways."

Judah groaned. "I'm almost glad I'm not going with you now. There's two of you. Best of luck to Faîte."

Bastien paused, and I wondered what the next jerkish thing he was going to say to me would be. "I didn't know that about King Urien. No one does. That he knew Morgan le Fae was using you, so he sent you away? It's noble. It's the king the generation before us remembers. He's been sick for decades. Some guessed he was being poisoned by Morgan, but no one took those conspiracies seriously." He looked ahead, still offended by my ugly crying, the jag. "We have to do something. Now that we know? We have to save him. I wish I knew what the poison was."

"Was he a good guy before he stopped ruling?"

Bastien's cheek dimpled. "He was the king the kids all made up songs about. King Urien the lion-hearted. King Urien the brave. Things like that. We'd make swords out of sticks and fight over who got to be King Urien, and who got stuck being the bad guy." His eyes grew unfocused as he recalled his childhood. "Silvain always made me be the bad guy. I guess that's sort of fitting now."

I winced at the awful blow. "Oh, Bastien. I'm so sorry."

Bastien shrugged, apparently satisfied with the small venting he'd done. "Urien was a great ruler. Everyone loved him, and we didn't have nearly the problems we do now when he was watching over Avalon. Your dad was a good one."

I mulled the new information over as we walked toward the well, fiddling with the hem of my t-shirt as I bit down on my lower lip. "You really think there's a way to help him? After all this time?"

"I think we have to try. Would you be satisfied finding Roland and going back to your life here if there was a chance to save him and get your father back?"

"I guess not." My stomach started churning at the prospect of meeting my dad. Not the deadbeat who didn't want anything to do with me, but the one who'd been at death's door for twenty-one years. The one who loved me, and perhaps needed me. I didn't know what to do with that information.

"Okay, could you stop that? I didn't even say anything sad, and you're crying again."

"Am I?" I wiped at my eyelashes, but it was just old tears that hadn't dried yet. My lashes were long, so tears tended to stick around even after they'd been disinvited from the party.

"I think it's a problem if you don't even know you're doing it. Girls crying? It's... Just stop it."

"Oh my word! Could you be more of a sideways butt-hole right now?" Hamish yelled at Bastien as I moved to Judah's other side to get a few more feet of distance from him. "No wonder the only girl you can get is in a coma."

Reyn looked over his shoulder to frown at Bastien. Then he shot me a "Dude, quit harshing the vibe I'm working on your aunt" look.

Judah tutted me. "Now, now, kids. Let's keep the hair-pulling for later."

"Come here," Bastien sighed. He tugged me to the side, letting the others march onward as he delved into his pocket and pulled out a handkerchief. He looked around, as if he didn't want to be caught in a scandal of... owning a handkerchief. "Here."

When he shoved the damp off-white square at me, I stared at it blankly. "I thought you didn't carry these around."

"I don't. There will be no mention of this, and if you start blubbering again, don't look at me to give it back to you."

I gulped, taking the offering and dabbing at my cheeks. It was like Bastien had seen other guys act like a gentleman, but had no idea how to pull off the routine organically. "Thank you?" I considered blowing my nose loudly into the material just to be a jerk, but decided on the high road and handed it back to him after a quick obliteration of any tear tracks. "You didn't have to do that."

Bastien nodded and put the handkerchief back into his pocket. "I don't like it when you cry," he admitted. "You've got this look that makes me... Just don't. Caring about how all of this affects you doesn't get the job done, and that's what we've got to do. Do you understand?"

"You're saying that you would care that my life got dumped out and broken into a million pieces if there wasn't a world to save?"

Bastien reached out and tucked a stray lock of hair that had come loose from my bun behind my ear. He didn't say anything, but met my eyes with a look that told me he wanted to know my secrets, yet tell me none of his. He had that guarded way about him that warned all who attempted to penetrate his thick exterior not to bother trying. "Reyn says I'm not good with people. That I need to be nicer."

"Nice isn't a bad thing."

"It doesn't get the job done," Bastien argued, though I couldn't tell you why.

"Depends on the job. If you want us to work well

together, you might want to dust off those manners and give not being a jackass a try."

Bastien snorted at what he wrongfully assumed was a joke. "Okay, then. I should probably ask you to stay close instead of yelling at you that everywhere you go, you might be in danger."

"Asking instead of yelling is always a good thing. Might even be in that ridiculous 'nice' category Reyn was talking about."

Bastien shoved his hands in his pockets, looking down as he tried to find the words. "Walk with me? I know you don't want me hovering, but I'm worried too many people are looking for you. I don't like you out of my sight. You may not like me, but you'll live longer if you stay by my side."

"Careful," I warned, the corner of my lips curving upward. "That was pretty nice. Next thing you know, you'll be throwing around words like 'please' and 'thank you'."

"Let's not get carried away." Bastien extended his arm to me, breathing easier when I slowly moved to his side. He exhaled as his hand found the small of my back, as if protecting me soothed some unrest inside of him. That small touch was a constant reminder of his mammoth strength as we walked forward to catch up with the others. The mountains in the distance were enormous, and towered over nature with a foreboding air that felt suspiciously like doom. After Armand's attack, and then Silvain's, I began to see spots where bad guys could conceal themselves as they waited for us to have our guard down. For all his antagonism, I was grateful for Bastien's protection. Though he didn't like anything about me, he was bent on making sure I got through all of this alive. I moved tighter into his side, my eyes darting around the dusty landscape warily.

When we made it to the well, we gathered around and watched as Bastien picked up three rocks nearby and threw them in one by one. The well was old, and it was so deep I couldn't see the bottom of it, or even where the water came up to. I heard the first plop and saw a glow light up and then fade, revealing stagnant green water several stories down into the earth. I looked at Lane to make sure this was the way in, but she was still peering down into the deep abyss. "Ro, could you tell the rats to get out of there? It really creeps me out."

"Rats?" I bent over the edge of the well and squinted down, but couldn't see anything. "Hey, guys? Could you give us a few minutes? Then you can have your house back. Promise." It took some time, but eventually the scurrying feet found their way to the surface. Twenty-seven rats in all came out of the well, all in various states of covered in fungus. "Aw, guys! You really shouldn't live down there. It's too wet, and you'll get sick." I listened while they squeaked to me that there were vultures that swooped down and tried to eat them when they were out in the open. I saw the glassy film over their eyes and knew they couldn't see well enough to know there were trees not too far off. "Hamish, could you show them a good tree to hide in? They can't see their way."

"Okay, but only if you promise you won't leave without me. This is my adventure, too." Hamish was tired of parking lot life. Unlike Judah, he didn't have anyone waiting for him back home.

"Go ahead. I'll wait."

"I don't care how fine Reyn is with it, we're not taking your critter to Faîte," Bastien ruled, his hand migrating to the small of my back again.

"Funny that you think you have any sort of say in what I do. Hamish stays with me. I don't need to ask for permission to be who I am," I reminded him calmly.

Reyn drew up the ropes from the pulley system that hung above the well, revealing not a bucket but a wooden board stretched across two ropes like a small swing. "Bastien and I signed out, so there can only be two of us that come back. Our man knows to report only two coming back, but that means only two trips can happen. I'll take Lane down. Bastien, can you handle taking Rosie? Can the two of you fit?"

Bastien nodded, and I swear I could almost hear his internal gulp that matched mine. Reyn took his time figuring out the best way to get two adults on the thin board. The well wasn't all that wide, so space was an issue to consider. He finally settled on straddling the board so Lane would have a little more security. Bastien held her hand and guided her onto the board, her hands shaking and feet uncertain as she slid onto the space between his legs, her back to his stomach. Every movement sent down an echo that told us all just how steep the drop was. There seemed to be a skyscraper of distance between the grass and the underworld. Lane shot me the best look of forced bravery she could muster as she gripped the rope. Her shaking subsided a little when Reyn's arm slipped around her slender waist to keep her from wobbling. He looked over at me and winked, knowing exactly the moves he was putting on my aunt, and the likelihood she'd fall for them. They were cute smooshed together on the swing.

Bastien cast Reyn a serious look of warning. "Don't use any magic to try and conceal her, Reyn. I'm serious. It won't do to have you lose it halfway home."

"I've got this," Reyn replied through gritted teeth. There was something to Bastien's worry about Reyn's ability to wield magic that I planned on poking into later.

Reyn waited until Lane stopped shaking, and then used the pulley system on top to slowly lower them down. Their heads disappeared as Reyn made a joke I couldn't decipher, and Lane gave a nervous giggle in answer. I imagined the well mutating into a monster's mouth, devouring them whole, like a trap set up in a video game. Bastien and I both watched them as they went down into the dark, holding our breaths as several minutes ticked by.

18

WELL WISHES FOR KISSES

*H*amish climbed up my body and peered over the edge, expressing his concern over how deep the well was. "You can always stay here, Hamish," I told him, but I knew he wasn't having any of that kind of talk.

"He *should* stay here."

I ignored Bastien. We waited until the bottom lit up with a green glow. Bastien informed me that was the sign they'd made it safely to the other side. Bastien pulled up the swing, and I could tell his arm was bugging him. "You alright? Your stitches holding up?"

"Yeah. Your medicine's different than ours, so I'll give it another look when we get back. It's fine, though. Just stings a little." When the swing finally appeared above the top of the well, it looked smaller than it had when Reyn sat on it. Instead of going sideways, Bastien took his time situating himself as if he was swinging under a tree on a summer's day in sunny Montana. His feet were on the lip of the well, and his hand was beneath him on the opposite side of the stone circumference. I hoped this would make for a steady seat I was expected to climb on. "Come on. Nice and slow."

"I gotcha, Ro." Judah held my hand, giving me a reassuring nod that he wouldn't let me fall to my death.

I met my bestie's eyes and swallowed hard. *Heights.* Not my favorite. In fact, it was my super least favorite.

"It's just like anything else. You do it, and then it's done," Judah assured me.

I chewed on my lower lip as I climbed up to stand on the stones that had been flattened on the top, but were not quite level enough to let me catch my balance with any sort of confidence. Though I liked to think of myself as decently athletic, I began to understand why Lane had been so shaky on the precipice. I was only four feet off the ground, but the drop in the middle was a whole tall building's worth of difference. I tried to tell my feet where to go, but there wasn't any room on the seat for me. The possibility of a quick death flustered my cool.

Bastien leaned back, offering his lap. "Just one step, and you're here. I'll catch you if you slip, alright?"

I nodded, too scared to tell him that I didn't trust his ability to catch me if I turned into Olive Oyl during the precarious step. I felt a slight breeze that teased me, threatening to push me in. "There's nowhere for me to step but on you!"

"It's fine. Just aim for anywhere that's not my face, and you're good."

Hamish chanted encouraging words to me, taking on the role of being my own personal cheerleader, echoing Judah's, "It's alright, Rosie. We won't let you fall."

I started narrating my actions so Bastien knew what to expect. "Okay, I'm stepping on your thigh, then, just for a second until I get situated."

"That's good. You won't fall, little Daisy," Bastien teased me with a playful smirk. Then he met my eyes with a promise. "I've got you."

I froze, and something important and warm flooded through my chest, melting any stoic and cold parts of me. I don't know why I needed to hear that small vow, but it unwound some part of me that needed somewhere safe to rest.

I grabbed onto the steel bar that held the pulley system over his head and used it to lower myself down as slowly as I could, melting onto his body and threading my legs inside the ropes, so my thighs wrapped around his waist. My hands looped around his shoulders in a hug, and my trembling ankles locked at the small of his back. Hamish made me look like a fool when he scurried up the bar, down the rope and onto Bastien's shoulder, and then hopped onto my knee with no qualms whatsoever. Bastien grumbled, "Seriously? I said we weren't bringing him."

"He can't understand you." Okay, that was a lie, but I

didn't have the brain space to argue just then. I was too focused on not plummeting to my early death.

Judah tried to iron out the anxiety in his eyes, but I caught the fear he could never hide from me. "Hey, be safe, Ro. Call me the second you get back. I'll take care of your stuff and make sure you have a bed to sleep in when fall semester starts."

I gave him a look that told him just how scared I was that I might never see him again. "I love you, Judah."

Judah touched his heart, watching me with too many years of knowing me to let things trail off without a proper goodbye. "I love you, too, Rosie. You're my best... You know."

"I know. You should go. I can handle it from here, Pimp Daddy."

"Okay. See you soon, Hot Mama." He steeled himself, like he was going to say something else, but deflated, waving as he turned and jogged toward the car.

I was shaking, my forehead buried in Bastien's sternum with my eyes closed before we'd made the first move downward. When Bastien raised his arms above my head to start lowering us, something happened and the swing jerked to the side. "Whoa!" Bastien cried out, rocking backward on the seat a few inches as I screamed. He righted us in the next breath and wrapped an arm around me, clutching me tight to his chest. "Hey, I was only kidding. I don't know why I thought that'd be funny. We're fine. It's all fine. I've got you." He rubbed my back, scooting me up his body so my head rested on his shoulder.

"Don't do that to me!" I gripped him tighter, wishing I could slap him without the possibility of death by well. Not that I could unclench anyway. I was so racked with fear that I couldn't let go of him if my life depended on it. "I'll cry, Bastien! I'll do it, I swear! I'll cry all over you right now and make you so uncomfortable you'll wish you never messed with me!"

"Deadly threat, that is." There was a tease in his tone, and I could tell he was smiling, though I couldn't open my eyes to see it. He pulled his head back to watch me. "Hey, look at me." When I shook my head into his meaty shoulder, he started rubbing up my spine until his hand reached my cheek. His other hand held the rope that kept us from plummeting. I felt the rough pad of his thumb stroking my face. It was nice – so nice that I exhaled a portion of my nerves, deflating slightly in his half-embrace. Bastien being sweet to me was so confusing that I didn't focus so much on the impending doom or the slight breeze that made me feel like I was standing on top of a skyscraper. All I could feel was his thumb tracing the side of my face down my jaw. When I lifted my head to look up at him, he caressed my lower lip, watching the curve with a fascination that made me blush. No man had ever touched me like that. Finally his eyes met mine, and I saw no trace of the antagonistic tool who loved to make things harder for me.

I couldn't feel the breeze anymore, though I knew it was still there. All I felt was his breath on my lips when he lowered his mouth to rest an inch from mine. Cinnamon. His breath was a cinnamon intoxicant, and I was getting drunk off the allure. His arm wrapped back around me, and my heart picked up a new rhythm it didn't know, and had never practiced. It was uneven and had no clear thread of direction I could grab onto, so I held tight to Bastien, hanging in midair while we breathed in each other's confusion.

When he finally closed the gap between us, I let out a pathetic whimper when the side of his mouth grazed mine. It wasn't a kiss, but it was something. Something too big and messy to look at up close. But Bastien stayed close, rubbing his cheek to mine, his stubble scraping my skin and sending a thrill through my spine. His piney scent was concentrated in the crook of his neck, so I took a chance and breathed him in, flooding myself with thoughts of Christmas and presents and happiness. The Christmas muted out the mustiness of the well below that I could feel nipping at my toes. He pressed a slow, melty kiss to my heated cheek, his sculpted lips teasing me and turning me to Jell-O. He was a sexy lumberjack, and way out of my league. I nearly lost myself when he whispered in my ear a quiet, velvety and deep, "I've got you, little Daisy."

Confusion tornadoed with lust inside of me. I didn't know what to do with any of it, so I simply clung to him and nodded.

His left arm reached to the side to work the pulley with one hand, while his right arm remained fixed around me, holding me close as we started our descent. Every few feet he stopped, holding us steady while he paused to kiss a different part of my face, always missing my lips and lighting a bigger fire in me that I couldn't begin to get ahold of. He was so mean, but here he was in the dead of the dark, holding us in limbo so he could steal a few seconds to almost kiss me. It was romantic, which I didn't think he'd had a whole lot of experience with. Sex, sure. I mean, dude was ripped and gorgeous in that dangerous motorcycle cowboy "Sure, you can fool around with my girlfriends, and I'll forgive you" kind of way. But romance? I didn't think he had the softness in him.

"I can tell you're blushing," he whispered in his husky manner, like he was calling out my secret that was supposed to be thoroughly hidden in the dark.

"You cannot. It's too dark down here."

His teeth captured the apple of my cheekbone, and I shivered. His bite slid off and mutated into a kiss to my cheek that made my lashes flutter. "I can feel the heat in your cheeks. So much heat."

It was cold and dank in the cylindrical stone prison, but my body was on fire. A thrill raced through me at the small bite. It felt like finally living, after a lifetime of pretending I had no libido, just to escape the crushing loneliness that came from never ever ever ever being asked on a date. I was the dude friend, the asexual teammate, and yet Bastien had me practically purring as I straddled him on the swing like a stripper. "You're driving me crazy," I admitted into the black when his nose traced a line down my neck and up the other side, making my head loll back.

"Then I'm doing it exactly right."

Right, but it was all wrong. My eyes flew open and I stiffened out of the seduction. "But it's not right. You're engaged." I shook my head as he deflated, and took the moment along with him.

"But you know it's a sham. Rachelle doesn't even know we're betrothed. It's hardly as scandalous as you're thinking. No one can see us in here."

"I can barely think straight right now, but I know I can't have my first kiss be with a guy who's got a fiancée."

"Wait, what? Your first kiss? You mean *our* first kiss, right?"

I cringed and buried my face into his shoulder to escape his scrutiny. "No, *my* first kiss. I've never kissed a guy before."

"But you're twenty-two! You're... Have you seen you?"

A smile played on my lips. "Thanks. But I didn't start looking like this until last week. I never found the right guy, and now it's built up into this big deal thing. I don't want to cut that ribbon just yet with a guy who's promised to someone else. Conscious or not, I don't want to move in on someone else's man. That's not me." I clung to him, suddenly afraid he might throw me off into the abyss. "Could we not talk about this right now? I'm like, vulnerable on top of terrified on top of bursting into flames. You're really screwing with my brain, here."

I thought he would take his arm away from the loop he'd made around my waist. It would certainly make lowering us easier if he used two hands. But Bastien held me as my head remained attached to his shoulder. When his cheek pressed back onto mine, I softened against him, glad he hadn't decided to be a prick about the whole thing.

"It's okay. I've got you."

Again, that delicious and somehow precious warmth flooded through me at his simple promise.

His arm took on a protective hold now, clutching me to him to shield me from the world. I finally started to feel safe, despite our harrowing position. Of all the places I expected to find solace, Bastien's arms wouldn't have been on the list. Yet I couldn't stop wanting to get closer, hold him tighter, and touch more of his skin. My lips wanted to kiss him for hours and days and whole years, but my conscience couldn't commit to the effort. Bastien wasn't mine, though he held me as if I was his. His grip was solid, gentle, and carried with it a command for me to understand that everything would be okay, because he would make it so. It was heady to be wrapped around that much strength.

"If I can't kiss you, can I at least think about it?" he whispered as we lowered down a few more feet. Hamish answered for me in angry rants and a lecture about all the ways Bastien didn't deserve me. I laughed in time with

Bastien, our chests moving against each other's and increasing the sexual tension we knew we weren't allowed to feel. "I think I've been around your squirrel too long. I understood the spirit of that one. Can I ask you a question?"

"No." I knew he'd ask things I didn't have answers to.

Bastien ignored me. "How come you never kissed anyone before? Is that normal where you're from?"

"No. It's very not normal. And I never kissed anyone because the guys in my life see me as a guy. Plus, I study and work a lot. Not much time for anything else."

"You must be top of your class. I don't know anyone that dedicated."

"You say that like there was a line of guys I was ignoring because I had my nose buried in a book. Whatever. It is what it is, and it'll stay that way until something changes. Something big." I shifted on his lap, and I heard him hiss in the dark. "Did I hurt you?"

His voice came out low, seductive and borderline pained. "Daisy, you're killing me."

"That's a cute nickname." I was used to the cruel nicknames. I smiled into his shoulder, making it my new home away from home as he lowered us with painstaking care down until his toes touched the water.

The green light took me by surprise when it shone beneath us, lighting up the fear on my face and the determination on his. He set into business mode, taking over as the authority, now that we would be in his world. "Okay, when we go through, you have to hold onto me. Stay quiet and keep Hamish on you, otherwise he'll be seen. We don't have squirrels in our world."

"Okay." I held tight to him, and for a few seconds we hugged each other in the glow of the green water that lit only half our faces. There were flickers of shadows, and they played on the secrecy of the moment that would remain forever ours. Before he plunged us down into the water, I clung tighter to him. "Bastien?"

"Yeah, Daisy?" he answered, brushing his nose back and forth against mine.

I leaned up and planted a delicate kiss atop the dimple in his left cheek. "Thanks. That was probably the sexiest thing I've never done."

He chuckled into my ear. "I think we can raise the stakes next time around, yeah?"

With that, he plunged us down into the glowing water that wasn't wet when we touched it, but merely a mirage. I held on tight, not knowing what life would hold as we landed crack in the middle of Faîte.

19

NEW WORLD, OLD FOES

I'm not sure what I was expecting, but this certainly wasn't it. We landed in a building that had a mixture of plaster and mud walls that led to larger rooms. I could hear men shouting in unison and stomping. It sounded like angry calisthenics.

"Great. We landed right in the middle of rounds. Quiet as you can, okay? And keep your head down." Bastien lowered me slowly, letting me slide down his body until my feet touched on the gravelly dirt that served as their flooring. Though I could've stood next to him, Bastien held my head to his chest. I felt the fear rising in him, and realized that just getting me out of the military building and into the populated city would be more work than he anticipated.

There was a soldier in brown leather armor standing behind a podium to our left, scribbling on a piece of parchment with a quill. An actual quill. I wanted to touch it, but knew now wasn't the time. He wore a deep red long-sleeved shirt with what looked like a snake in gold on the shoulders. Bastien whispered to the soldier, "Good to see you, Macon. Did Reyn go on ahead?" He moved me to stand behind him, shielding me with his far larger body.

Macon wasn't nearly as tall and muscular as Bastien. He had the build for pencil pushing, which was exactly what he was doing as he scratched the parchment with his quill. His hands were dainty, almost feminine. He wrote down Bastien's name as he whispered, "He got in fine and went on his way with his passenger. Do you have the package?"

"We're in. Write down our arrival time as earlier this morning."

Macon bowed his head over his podium, his eyes on his parchment so he didn't draw anyone's eye. "Your majesty. I offer you my sword, should you ever need it."

Bastien nudged me, and I realized Macon was talking to me. Bowing to me incognito. Like I was important or something. It was too weird. I was the girl in the back of the class, baseball cap on and head pointed downward, praying the teacher wouldn't call on me. "Um, thanks, man. Thanks for keeping things quiet, too."

I could feel Bastien's internal groan at my lack of decorum. "Let's go, your majesty," he said with a hint of exasperation.

I shifted to his side, keeping one arm around his back.

He moved my free hand to grip the buckle of his belt under his flannel, so I for sure didn't get separated from him. "Ha. You have to be nice to me here," I teased him in a whisper. "'Your majesty.' You're too funny."

"Oh, shut up." He started walking forward down the hallway, hugging the wall and darting into an open doorway when two soldiers made their way past us. He led us upstairs on the balls of his feet so our footsteps weren't heard on the wooden steps. I could feel his nerves building as we snuck past doors with labels on them I was too frazzled to attempt to read. One door made him particularly unsettled. He paused, his arm holding me tight – in part to shield me from whatever harrowing menace awaited inside, and part to have a friend to cover him through the old wounds that hadn't quite healed. He clutched me tighter to him, his brows furrowed in what looked like remembered pain that was both physical and emotional. We heard footsteps inside, so Bastien darted us into the room a few steps down the hall, letting us peek through the gap in the doorjamb.

When the ominous door opened, a hook-nosed man with skin so tan it was almost orange came out, sniffing the air like a dog. Bastien froze, and then reached into his pocket for his knife. I could tell he was readying himself partially for if we were found out and part because he just plain hated the guy.

"Pierre?" the man called, looking down the hallway right past us.

Hamish clung to my shoulder, even his tail refusing to twitch. He told me he didn't like the hook-nosed man as his claws dug into my shoulder. Animal instincts were rarely wrong when it came to danger, so I kept myself completely silent and thought invisible thoughts.

Bastien's thumb stroked the button on his knife's hilt to slide the blade out when the man came all the way out of his office to walk by, but he refrained, keeping our cover that much longer. When the hook-nosed man passed us, I smelled a waft of what I could only describe as pancake makeup. Lane had convinced me to go out for the junior high musical, but I'd been too shy for the tryout. I ended up being a grip, which basically means you move things around all night on and off the stage. The bubbly, giggly actresses had fun costumes and wore that thick, vibrant makeup. It smelled chalky and a little like old people, and was impossible to wash off. It was then I realized the hook-nosed man was wearing pancake makeup all over, even on his hands. For what purpose? I couldn't begin to tell you. All I knew is I wouldn't be hugging him and risk ruining my André Roussimoff t-shirt.

Bastien let out an inaudible breath when the hook-nosed man turned the corner. "Captain Burke," he whispered in my ear.

I kept my gasp muted when I realized we were super way close to the man who had ruined Reyn's sister and put her in a coma. Bastien's grip was tighter on me, and I knew he was worried that the worst was not over yet. We walked in-step together down the hallway, and just as we passed a fork where the hook-nosed man had turned down, a hand shot out and snatched at my hair. I bit off a scream and held onto Bastien, unsure if I should put my energy into fighting or running.

Bastien gripped my ribs and without a word clicked his knife, driving it downward into the hook-nosed man's makeupped forearm. The man cried out in anger, not just pain or surprise. I would've thought that was enough for him to let go, and enough for Bastien to pull back his blade so we could bolt, but it was only the beginning. The blade stayed perpendicular in the man's arm until Bastien ripped the hilt up toward the man's elbow, unzipping his skin and spilling out more blood than I knew what to do with. Bastien leaned over me to growl above the man's screams, "That's for Rachelle. I'm coming for you tonight, pig. Take my time when I gut you nice and slow."

Captain Burke drew his sword clumsily with his good arm, but I wasn't about to let the two devolve into a sword-fight. He'd attacked Reyn's sister; I didn't need any more of the story for my rage to start boiling. The man opened his mouth to yell for backup, so I whirled in Bastien's arms and punched the guy in the throat twice in rapid succession to buy us a few seconds before the alarm was raised. Bastien scooped up my hand and punched the man so hard with the butt of the blade in his fist, I was pretty sure he broke the dude's already wonky nose. That had to buy us a minute or two. I'm not sure that was enough to get us to safety. Bastien had the same thought, and punched three more times with his Hulk-like fist, knocking the man clean out.

Bastien's hand found the small of my back, claiming the intimate space for himself. He cradled my body to his so he could whisper in my ear. "If I'm here, you don't have to do any fighting."

I clung to his flannel and leaned up on my toes to whisper a shaky, "I wasn't about to let him take a swing at you."

Bastien's eyes flitted to me in confusion, as if he didn't understand why anyone would fight for him. "I'll take care of this. You just stay close to me."

My heart thudded in my chest, and I worried that any second, our crime would be known and I would be found out. I was shocked no one had seen us or heard the man's cries above the calisthenics that were now echoing through the long building. Bastien moved my hand to the back of his belt and dragged the hook-nosed man by his ankles back to his office, leaving a trail of blood that wouldn't do us a lick of good in keeping a low profile.

Bastien wasn't concerned with time anymore. He wanted justice for Rachelle, and I couldn't blame him. As soon as we were tucked inside the office, Bastien took out his knife and gutted the man, spilling his intestines out onto the floor in a pool of gore I was unprepared for. I let go of Bastien and turned away from the horror, shocked at the stark difference between his world and mine. I let out my silent screams into my hand, wishing I could run, but knowing I had no way out. I would have to go deeper into Faîte. Hamish hugged my neck, not caring all that much about the violence, but more about my emotional upset. Hamish was a good guy.

Bastien wiped his palms off on the man's pants and then gripped my hand. He bolted down the hallway with me, his arm shaking. We stopped caring about sneaking, and worried far more about getting the crack outta Dodge.

20

DAHU AND ABRAHAM LINCOLN

We hit the open air just as an alarm sounded throughout the building, alerting the world that we were murderers. Well, that someone was a murderer, and Bastien's name was on the roster as having been inside the building with Reyn. We walked swiftly down the street, keeping our heads down to avoid the villagers who walked through the tented market square to our left. They all wore expressions of varying degrees of disinterest and zealous haggling, and paid us no mind. There were trees I'd never seen before, dark emerald leaves with equally dark green trunks, instead of brown. They had long umbrella tops for shading the grass, dirt and rocks we traveled along.

Bastien slowed when we reached the woods that were finally thick enough to shield us from the villagers. "I have to cover myself. My name's on that roster. My place will be the first they check. I've got to show my face, but you still can't. Stay here." He looked around, hating the idea as much as I did. "Sit down and keep your head low. I mean, low. I need to get you a hat or something. Everyone's going to know you're the Lost Daughter of Avalon by your face alone." He glanced over his shoulder to peek at the village. "Don't talk to anyone. I'll be back in five minutes, okay?"

I nodded, though nothing about the plan felt okay. "You've got blood on you!" I pointed out. I handed him a few leaves that had a bit of dew on them for him to wipe off his hands and wrists.

"Thanks. If anyone takes me in for questioning, run straight down the path until you see the house with two green chimneys. That's Marie's place."

"Who's Marie?"

"A friend. She'll take you in if you tell her Reyn sent you."

"Why can't I say you sent me?"

"Because she's a jealous wench who'll take one look at you and won't let you past the door because she'll assume we're together. I mean, look at you! Five minutes. I'll be right back." Before I could answer or fully process what I'm pretty sure might've been a compliment, he leaned in and kissed my cheek before he jogged toward the village. My heart fluttered, but I worked to quickly calm it. I heard his voice greeting a few of his friends in the distance, totally devoid of the nerves I'd seen him shaking with mere moments ago.

I ducked down and positioned myself behind a thick chartreuse tree trunk, trembling as I came down from the horror of my entry into Faîte. The bliss of almost having my first kiss with the most infuriating guy I'd ever met clashed with the fear of nearly plummeting to my death in the well. Follow that up with watching the guy whose bones I'd just wanted to jump gut a man, and I was overwhelmed. It was a lot to process.

Hamish was in awe of the newness of the nature around him. He wanted desperately to go exploring, but I held him back. "You can't go running off here. There are different predators, and we don't know the lay of the land. We don't even know where we are! No, no. Wait it out, little buddy. I've got more trail mix in Reyn's bag that you can have until you meet some friends who can show you what's safe to eat."

"I can tell all that without help," he spouted, but remained in my lap all the same. He knew I was scared, so he crawled up on my knees that were pulled to my chest and leaned in to nuzzle his nose to mine. He promised not to leave me, and silly as it was, I needed that comfort.

When I heard rustling in the bushes behind me, I stiffened, trying to remain silent. I closed my eyes, as if that would help me go invisible, and rubbed the belly of my lucky shirt, hoping André René Roussimoff would help shield me if I wished it hard enough. I'd made many a wish on good old André. In my imagination, he was sitting next to me, his back up against the tree, his eyes scrutinizing our surroundings so he could get an accurate read on the land.

When the rustling came closer, I realized it was four paws, not two feet. My shoulders slumped and I gave good old André a grateful pat that we were facing an animal, and not a person. I turned to my right and bit my lip through a silent scream when a two-headed dog-like creature came poking around my tree, sniffing the air around me curiously. The left head geared up to howl, but the right one stopped short when I held my finger to my lips. "Please, guys. I can't be seen here. Tell your owner or friends or whoever that you didn't see anyone."

I was scared my animal-speak might not translate here. I'd never talked to a two-headed pit bull before. Their sharp eyeteeth were malformed and jutted out from the bottom, almost like a vampire's, if the fangs sprouted from the lower jaw. The two noses sniffed me and Hamish, who had gone completely still. Hamish gave me stiff-jawed apologies for blowing off my earlier warning that we didn't know the terrain well enough to go exploring just yet. The left dog sniffed my shoes, pausing when I tsked the right one for sniffing Hamish with too much interest.

I gusted out a sigh of relief when the dog (or dogs) sat down in front of me with their four paws and placed a head each on my knees, tongues lolling as their tail wagged playfully. "Thanks, guys. I really can't have people knowing I'm here. That cool?"

I heard more rustling of four-legged creatures and

squinted off into the thick of the woods. I grinned when I saw a pack of five antelopes with legit unicorn horns jutting out two feet from the middle of their foreheads. They walked tilted, and I noticed that their left fore- and hindlegs were two inches shorter than the right side. Despite the wonky slant, they were elegant and didn't trip. "Whoa! Hey, guys. Come on over." They neared with caution, sniffing my feet before they sat down in front of me, their legs folding gracefully beneath them – nature's ballerinas. "Hey, guys. Well, aren't you gorgeous? I've never seen anything like any of you. Wicked horns." They exchanged conspiratorial looks, and I started to pick up on bits of their conversations.

"Is she a person, or an animal? Is she one of us?"

"She looks Fae, but talks like us."

"I'm a regular person, but you can talk to me if you want. I could use a few buddies to clue me in. My guide's busy at the moment." The unicorn deer responded by bowing their heads as if offering their horns for my service. "That's just cool," I mused while I reached down and pet the left head of the pit bull. The right one grew jealous, so I took one hand from Hamish and stroked them both. "Can I touch your horn? I've never seen anything like you in my world."

The uni-deer in charge nodded, offering himself up for perusal to set the example of peace for the others to follow. "You're super way lovely, you know," I complimented them all.

The head uni-deer opened his mouth, his speech low and gravelly with too much breath to it. *"Who are you?"* he asked. He raised his long neck, looking regal with the white, unspeckled flank showing itself off to me, while the others remained bowed.

"I'm Rosie. I mean, I guess I'm supposed to be the Lost Daughter of Avalon or something. I'm new to your world. I come from Earth, or Common, I guess." I was impressed with myself that I'd picked up enough of their lingo to make sense to them. "I have to stay hidden here. Can you make sure that happens? I mean, don't go to super amounts of trouble, just if you see someone sneaking up behind me, give a girl a heads-up."

"You're the Voix? *You can speak for us to the queen?"*

I looked from side to side, seeing more uni-deer slowly approaching, their horns bowed as they tuned in to our conversation like hitting a dial on the radio. "Um, I'm actually trying to avoid the queen right now. And I don't have any real power to help you with. From what I understand, the queen might not like me all that much." I cleared my throat as the self-inflicted wound stabbed me through the heart. "My mom, I guess. But if you want someone to listen to you, I'm your girl. I can't help much, but I can at least do that."

The one in charge met my eyes and nodded. *"If that's what you can give us, that's enough. Remember us if you do stand before the queen."* He threw his head over his shoulder and shouted, *"All hail the* Voix!"

The uni-deer mob echoed with a rousing, *"All hail the Voix!"* Then they bowed, scaring the crap outta me.

"Um, you really don't have to do that. Honest. I'm happy to listen to you. What's got you down?"

The leader rose, but everyone else remained on the grass, their heads bowed in reverence that made me itch. *"I'm Dahu of the Three Pines. My tribe is being hunted by some of the soldiers in the province. They don't hunt for food, they hunt for sport, and they keep my people's heads as trophies."*

I grimaced, knowing what Dahu's opinion of hunting in my world would be. "That's not cool. If I run into any soldiers, I'll be sure to tell them to hunt only for food."

"Thank you. There's also the problem of the water," he added, turning his head to the right. I didn't see a body of water, but I took him at his word. *"The Mousseuse River used to be pure, but Province 3 has been dumping something in it that's making some of our fawns sick. They vomit for days, and then they're listless. Some of them have started to die off. The others are barely themselves, and they've yet to recover."*

"Oh, jeez! How long has it been going on?"

"Two full moons."

I wasn't totally sure if that meant two days or two months, but I nodded. "Just that river? Is it affecting the people, or just the animals?"

"It affects the weaker walkers, but they aren't figuring it out that it's the water from the Mousseuse River. It's going to keep poisoning the young until a whole sea of them die. It'll be too late by the time the walkers figure it out."

"*That* I can spread the word about, no problem. I've got friends who are walkers here. They can take care of at least telling their people. Can you keep yours away from the river until the queen sorts it out?"

Dahu lowered his elk-like nose and cast me a dark look. *"The queen is no friend of ours. Telling her will do nothing. It's because she stole Province 3's Jewel of Good Fortune that they attack us at all. We're on the border between the two districts, so we pay the highest price when they war. Morgan would merely have to give their jewel back to end the battling between the Provinces, but she won't. So we die for it."*

I covered my mouth with my hand as I took in the scope of the damage. "Crap. I didn't realize there'd be full-on corruption my first hour being here. I'll do what I can, but I gotta warn you, I don't have any power here, and I can't actually let the queen know who I am."

"I understand." We shared a smile at the layers of meaning in his words. *"The birds have told us there's an unpoisoned river several moons east of here, but we can't get there without passing through the East Village where many of the soldiers live. If you would grant us safe passage, then we could survive."*

"I'll talk to my friends and see what we can do. I'm not sure the soldiers will be cool with me, but I'll give it a shot as soon as I'm not in hiding anymore."

The uni-deer stiffened when a predator ambled into the thrum from behind them. I held up my hand to the newbie, my eyes wide when I saw it was a bear cub. A real bear cub. The other animals had weird nuances to them, but this was a straight up brown bear that looked like he would've fit in fine in my world. He whined to me too loud for comfort. *"I need you!"* he cried. *"My mama got taken by the soldiers, and now I have no one! Can I stay with you?"*

I waved my hand for the others to let him through, and I saw them all stiffen as the top of the food chain bounded up to me and rolled onto his back on the grass at my side. I took a chance and rubbed his belly, softening as he almost purred, grinding the top of his head into my thigh. I'd always wanted to pet a bear, but Lane forbade trips to the zoo sometime around the second grade. Something about me getting the animals too worked up. "You can stay with me, so long as you don't eat anyone here. That cool? And you have to be careful not to scratch me or Hamish with your paws. You don't want to hurt me."

"Mama," he crooned, melting my heart as he named me the most precious label he could think of. The pit bulls growled low in their throats, but I gave them a disapproving look that shut off that nonsense right quick. I didn't like it when animals fought in front of me. If I had my way, there would be a happy pink bubble around everyone, and no one would think angry thoughts, or war in any way. We'd talk about cotton candy and have skipping contests. André Roussimoff would still be alive, and we'd have parades in his honor. We'd eat jellybeans all the livelong day, and he could teach me his best wrestling moves. Ah, bliss.

Hamish sniffed the bear and gave in to his daring. It was his one chance to play with his own personal dragon. He jumped on the bear's belly and gave the guy a cuddly hug. I was proud of him for being so brave, and even more proud of the bear for not mauling Hamish. The bear was the size of a fat, round German shepherd, and I knew if he wanted to, he could tear me up with his heavy paws inside a minute.

When I spoke, I was quiet, scared that too many were congregating too near me, and that they would draw attention. I hoped we were far enough hidden in the woods that we wouldn't be seen. "I need some help, guys. I'm supposed to find the Cheval Mallet. The Horse to Nowhere. You heard of him?"

They all nodded uncertainly, but Dahu spoke for the group. "*We know of him, but he's not from our woods. He doesn't answer to anyone. You can't follow him,*" he warned.

I shrugged. "I kind of have to. I have a cousin who wasn't supposed to end up there. I don't have much choice. So if you see him, could you send him my way?"

The animals all had something to say about this, telling me with wide eyes that if I followed the black horse, they'd never see me again. They wouldn't allow their voice to be taken from them so permanently.

"It's a chance I have to take. I have to find my family. The Cheval Mallet horse is the only one who might know where Roland is. I have to try. You'd do the same thing if it was one of yours."

Dahu lowered his head somberly. *"We'll see what we can do."*

I heard stomping coming from behind me and stiffened, closing my eyes when I realized it was two feet, not four paws. The footsteps stopped when the uni-deer all stood and formed a barrier between me and the intruder, their horns sticking out like unadulterated weapons of doom. It was that simple act that gave me faith that perhaps I'd found my people in this new world. Granted, animals weren't technically people, but to feel loyalty enough to defend me after a single conversation? My heart warmed to the creatures that couldn't be found anywhere in the nature I knew. They'd found me, which meant that part of me wasn't so lost after all.

"Rosie?" came Bastien's uncertain voice.

"Oh, good! I was worried someone else would find me first." I stood, picking up my weighted bear, cradling him like he was a fat baby. Not to be ousted from his place of prestige, I let Hamish perch on my shoulder. The pit bulls growled at Bastien, remaining at my side like the sweet puppies they were. "Oh, it's okay, guys. This is Bastien. He's the one I'll talk to about helping you all out. If anyone can fix your problems, he's your best shot."

Dahu sized up Bastien and the threat he represented before taking a step back. *"He's an Untouchable, your majesty. Are you certain you're safe with him?"*

I sized up Bastien curiously. "Mostly sure. He brought

me here in the first place. If he wanted me dead, I'd already be six feet under."

Bastien quirked his eyebrow at my half of the conversation and raised his hands in surrender. "I won't hurt her. I brought her here to help Avalon."

Dahu ventured a step towards him and sniffed Bastien's flannel. He ran his horn along Bastien's chest in warning, snagging on the buttonholes. *"Very well. If you say you're safe with him, we'll leave you to talk."* He turned and came up to me, brushing his nose to my arm while I held my new beary special baby. *"Be safe, Queen of the Woods. Be careful to stay hidden from the Queen of Avalon. Should you need us, send word through the birds. They can find us quickly."*

"Thanks, Dahu." I watched the uni-deers walk away with their tilted gaits, but the two-headed dog remained by my side.

"Rosie, very slowly come towards me. Do you know what that is?" He pointed to the slobbering pit bulls.

"It's a dog," I shrugged.

"It's a *sosie chien*. They're very dangerous. One wrong move, and he'll tear you up. See his collars? He's got a master he'll obey in a heartbeat. They're killers. Trained for guarding a house to the death. I used to have one myself."

I reached down and set my bear on the grass. I scratched behind both the dogs' ears in the middle with one hand, smiling as they wagged their tail at me. "It's alright, buddy. Go back to your master, but make sure you don't tell him you found me or Bastien. I have to stay hidden here for now. Got it?"

Bastien hissed as they licked my hand. He was visibly relieved when they ran off, his shoulders rolling back. "I'm not sure I'll ever get used to that. Now tell the bear to go away, and we can head to my place."

My bear reached his arms up to me, a lost boy in need of someone to care for him. I lifted him up and situated his furry body on my hip. I closed the gap between me and my guide with my cub firmly attached to me, like a toddler clinging to his mom. "I can't do that. He's coming with me. This is..." I fished around for a decent name. Something grand befitting a prince, not an orphan. "This is Abraham Lincoln, and he doesn't have a mama, so I'm his mama now." Abraham Lincoln responded by leaning up and snuggling the top of his head under my chin. He was so soft and cuddly. I couldn't bear to leave him in the woods without someone to sing to him at night. (Couldn't *bear* to leave him? Get it?)

Bastien reached out to press his hand to the small of my back. I could tell he was nervous, letting me be so close to the bear, and inching closer himself. Hamish ran from my shoulder to perch atop Bastien's, curling up on the larger seat Bastien's body offered to hitch a ride to our new home. "I don't know about this. Actually, I do know about this. It's dangerous, Rosie. That bear's not a household pet. It'll tear your face off just to have something to chew on.

Even if you're playing around with him, he could do serious damage."

"Oh, I do this all the time. I just have to let them know how to treat me, and they're usually fine about it."

"Don't think I didn't hear you say 'usually'. Maybe Lane can talk you out of this."

"Aw, that's sweet you think she's not completely used to me doing this by now." I bumped my hip to his, to show him how not big of a deal this was.

He hesitated, taking in the bear's cuddly demeanor and the look of "this is happening, dude" on my face. "Can I pet him?"

I beamed, nodding and taking Bastien's hand so Abraham Lincoln wouldn't be frightened of the foreign touch. "Of course. Like this." I showed him how to stroke my baby's fur – slowly, and in a way that Abraham Lincoln could always see his hand before it touched down.

"That feels nice."

"He likes you."

"This is surreal." He kept his eyes on the bear as he spoke to me. "Stay close, okay? My house isn't too far from here. I'd rather we get there without being seen."

"Lead the way, mister."

Bastien coiled his arm around me, holding my waist with his large grip that made me feel petite and precious. I leaned my head in his nook, and he pressed his lips into my hair on our walk through the woods. It was sweet, like we were a couple who went for walks in the woods all the time. I could tell that the commerce and hustle of my world had made him uneasy, but being in the woods made him feel master of his domain. His shoulders were rolled back, and because we were alone, he had no problem keeping me close for no good reason. I mean, it's not as if someone was going to snatch at me in the middle of nowhere.

We walked together through the woods toward his home, staying hidden in the trees that were green from root to tip. Everything smelled like vibrant nature, making Bastien look and feel like a true wild man in his element. It was nice to see ease rolling through him, when he'd been on alert for so long.

Abraham Lincoln sensed my growing affection for Bastien, so he climbed further up me to give Bastien's stubble a lick. Bastien froze, unsure if he was about to be bitten, but softened when Abraham Lincoln nuzzled his neck and then went back to hugging me. His head looped over my shoulder and his paws held me tight.

Bastien narrowed his eyes at me, as if Abraham Lincoln and I were ganging up on him, which we kind of were. "Okay, okay. He can stay for now. But I'm serious, one wrong move, and he's out. And you have to hide him. I don't have any nearby neighbors, but if someone happens by, it'll raise a few flags if I have a bear around the house. A billion animals in my home is a dead giveaway I'm harboring the Lost Daughter of Avalon."

"That's fair. Everything okay at the marketplace?"

"Yup. Made sure to be seen by the biggest gossips first. Hopefully the guards will stop by my house and clear me quick. Can Abraham Lincoln run alright? Is he injured? Because we should get home before any soldiers find my house empty."

Abraham Lincoln clung to me, letting me know that though he was able to run, he wasn't giving up his new mom for anything. "He's afraid to be put down. I can keep up holding him just fine."

Bastien removed his hand from me as we jogged together through the woods, hopping over fallen branches and sticking close. It was as if we were made to run through nature at each other's side. We jogged for nearly half an hour, laughing as we tried to outpace the other. It wasn't exactly a hard job for Bastien to beat me, I mean, I was carrying a friggin' bear, but he played along all the same, sometimes letting me take the lead. When we finally reached the forest's edge, I was grateful we were stopping. Abraham Lincoln was no squirrel.

Bastien pressed his hand to the small of my back again as I caught my breath, tucking me into his side and leading me forward toward a dirt path that veered to our right. The walk was beautiful, the trees forming a canopy along the path that was almost romantic with its seclusion and late-springtime warmth. The shrubs lining the path seemed put there purposefully to add beauty to the trail, and I wondered if Bastien had done that. I didn't see him as an aesthetic gardener, but when we reached his home, I saw yet more bushes that yielded berries, and trees that bore football-shaped fruit surrounding his quaint home. The door was made of roughly-hewn wood, and had been painted green to match the trees that surrounded his property. It was a quaint cabin in the woods, and couldn't have been more perfectly suited for the lumberjack at my side.

21

BUSTED MAGIC AND BIG BABY

*B*astien walked through the door, heaving out a gust of relief when his eyes fell on Reyn. Lane stepped away with a blush, looking guiltily at her hot pink gym shoes.

"What's that doing in here? You can't keep a bear, Rosie. Especially not in a house! Bastien, you're going to get her killed! Be sensible!" Reyn chided us. His eyes were bloodshot and his long fingers looked somehow thinner than when I'd last seen him earlier that day.

The bear clung more tightly to me, closing his eyes to fend off the sting of immediate rejection. I ran my hands down his back to soothe him. "It's fine, Reyn. This is Abraham Lincoln. He's my baby, and he's staying with me."

Reyn put his hand to his forehead. "He's not your baby. You're Fae. He's a bear. You can't keep a bear as your baby."

"You feeling alright? You look... I dunno. You look like you're getting a little sick."

"Really? I've never felt better." It was an obvious lie filled with too much bravado. I felt bad for outing him in front of Lane, who he was clearly trying to mac on.

Bastien moved to the kitchen area and slid out a chair from the table. "Sit down," he ordered. When Reyn glowered uncharacteristically at him, Bastien smacked the back of the chair with his palm. "I'm serious. Sit down and rest. I can tell you tried to use concealment charms to muffle your footsteps. It used up too much of your magic, and you know it."

Lane looked between the two of them, trying as I was to decipher all the hidden meaning beneath what they were saying. "I'm sorry, Bastien. It's my fault. I haven't used magic in twenty-one years. I'm a little rusty."

"It's fine. But if you need anything to do with magic, you come to me next time. Got it? Reyn shouldn't be doing that. I only let him do it on the way in because I couldn't fit both of you on my lap in the well."

Reyn was livid, which was a strange color to see on the genteel dude. "Bastien, jeez! Everything's fine. I can provide for her well enough." There was a clear undercurrent of manliness Reyn was defending, but it looked as though Bastien wasn't having the same argument. His scarred eyebrows were furrowed with genuine concern for Reyn's health.

I tried to catch up with the social cues, confused that

magic was something a man wanted to be seen as being able to provide. The fact that Reyn's magic was less perhaps meant that he wasn't a traditionally desirable catch in Avalon terms. I didn't care about that, though. He was a nice guy who looked at Lane as if she was the most beautiful woman on the planet. Magic or not, Reyn enchanted us with his sweetness.

Bastien disappeared out the back door with a pitcher in hand, and came back a moment later with it filled with water. He poured a cup for Reyn and shoved it in his face. "Here. Rest up before the army comes looking for us."

Reyn tilted the cup of the water to his mouth, and Dahu's warning came screaming into my head. "Wait! Don't drink that!"

"Huh?" The cup stayed frozen on Reyn's lips.

"Dahu. The unicorn deer? He told me something's wrong with the Mousseuse River. Their fawns are getting sick after they drink it. It's a slow poison. A lot of their babies are dying, and the ones who live aren't doing so hot. If you're getting sick, your immune system might not be able to handle whatever poison's in that water."

Bastien and Reyn both gaped at me in shock. "Are you serious?" Reyn balked.

"Too serious. Dahu asked me to help him find a way to cross over from this territory into Province 2, so they can have fresh water to drink. But apparently there are some soldiers there blocking the way? They're hunting the unicorn-deer for sport, not for meat. So they'll need our help to get somewhere safe. It's either all their babies are going to die, or they'll all die at the soldiers' hands trying to cross over to unpolluted water. I'm guessing for the hunting society you guys are, it would be a very bad thing to lose the unicorn-deer population." I hiked Abraham Lincoln up and rubbed my cheek to his furry one. "Dahu said it's already affecting the Fae children, but none of the Fae knows what's making them all sick, so they keep drinking the water and the babies keep getting sicker. Job one's gotta be spreading the word that the water is tainted. It was Province 3 who poisoned the water, if that helps. They're pissed at Morgan for stealing their Jewel of Good Fortune. Job two needs to be helping the animals cross over into Province 2 or wherever if we can't clean up the water."

Bastien shook his head slowly, rubbing his forehead, as if just me talking was giving him a headache. "You know, every time I think I understand what we got ourselves into bringing you here, you open up your mouth and a whole new batch of horrible crazy spills out."

I huffed, indignant. "Well, *I* didn't poison your river. I'm just telling you how to fix your country's problem."

"I had a drink from the river on our way in," Reyn admitted. "Maybe that's why my magic is draining so quickly."

Bastien looked at Reyn with a lost expression hollowing out the brash haughtiness in his eyes. "You've been so healthy when we were in Common."

"It's because we didn't have access to magic, so nothing was draining me."

"Maybe there's something to the water thing. You look worse than you did before we left for Common last year."

Reyn put the cup down in the sink. "I'll call a meeting of the Council. If they know to test the water, surely they can do something to fix the poison. If it's Province 3, then Bayard can deal with it quickly. That's easy enough to fix, once you know what you're dealing with. Then the animals won't have to leave, and people won't get sick like that." He scratched his head. "We've been in Common for nearly a year. Children are really dying?"

I nodded. "That's what Dahu told me. I've never had an animal lie to me, so I'd take that as solid truth and make a plan. Your Council can really fix a poisoned river?"

Reyn nodded and then looked to Bastien, lost. "Twelve months, and this is what we come back to. I don't know why I hoped for Avalon to work out its problems while we were away. Instead they've only created more."

"I can't imagine an Avalon where there isn't some kind of battle going on between the Provinces," Bastien admitted. "But we know what we're up against with this problem, at least. It's fixable, brother."

Reyn offered Bastien half a smile at the familial term. "You're right. Perhaps I've despaired too soon."

Lane cooed and sidled up beside me to change the temperament of the room, holding her hand out to show the bear she was safe before petting him. "Aw! Hi,

Abraham Lincoln. I'm your Aunt Lane. You're a precious little guy, aren't you. What a love bug." Her eyes flicked to me. "Can I hold him yet?"

I loved Lane. She understood me through and through. She was used to me bringing home odd animals and making friends with them. She had a house rule they could only stay one month apiece, and then they had to be on their way. I had a feeling I could get my bear a permanent residence out of the deal, now that Bastien was in charge. For all his brash gusto, I saw the softy beneath the muscles. Plus, Lane was in doghouse mode after all her lying came to light. I wasn't above cashing in on that guilt to get myself a brand new teddy bear.

Lane sat down on the wooden floor in the middle of Bastien's main room. His whole place seemed to be made of one bedroom off to the side, and everything else was in the big room we were congregated in. There was no paint on the walls, and no decorations in the kitchen area. The wooden walls were cemented together with black pitch. I saw a fireplace in the kitchen I guessed was used for cooking, and a chimney to complete the picturesque scene. It made me feel cozy, and a little like I wanted to curl up by the fireplace, kindle up a few flames and listen to a good audiobook. In my imagination, a rugged lumberjack would come stomping home, a basket full of vegetables from his garden in his beefy arms. I tried to keep the dream man's face nebulous, but he had the flavor of

Bastien to him, despite my best efforts at keeping things platonic.

I lowered myself onto my knees next to Lane and tried to pry Abraham Lincoln off my midsection, but he was reluctant to jump ship just yet. My big baby clung to me, remaining on my lap until I finished talking him into giving Lane a try.

"I don't like this!" Reyn blurted out. He drew his knife with a shaking hand as I transferred Abraham Lincoln onto Lane's lap.

"Oh, put that thing away. You'll scare him and hurt yourself. He's a baby," I scolded Reyn, as if he should've known better.

"He's a bear! Bastien?" Reyn turned to question his friend, arms akimbo. "You can't honestly tell me you're considering this."

"We've got more important things to worry about right now. We ran into Captain Burke while we were sneaking out. He grabbed Rosie, so I stabbed him."

Reyn was horrified, and then he ran to Bastien's room, flung open the bedroom door and shouted to Bastien from inside. "I'll pack you up. Take the girls and run!"

"It's fine. I killed him before anyone saw. But our names are on the list, so they might be stopping by here to investigate. I made sure I was seen in the market on the way back, so that should help. I also had Macon change our arrival time to this morning, so it's not quite as suspect."

Reyn poked his head out, his brows furrowed. "Are you alright?"

Bastien shrugged, but his jaw was stiff. "I'm always alright. Didn't think I'd have the guts to take the bastard down, but I guess I did. Rachelle's avenged. I got him back for everything he put me through. It's done."

Reyn crossed the room and gathered the larger man up in his arms, hugging Bastien even though it looked like Bastien wasn't well-practiced in the ritual. Reyn wasn't offended, squeezing Bastien tighter until Bastien exhaled in his arms, finally dealing with the monumental kill that had shaken him up. "Thank you, brother."

Bastien nodded, but didn't look like he wanted to talk any more about it. He went to the kitchen area and pulled out a clear bottle with green liquid in it, and took several long gulps, closing his eyes in relief to get a taste of whatever his drink of preference was.

"Bastien," Reyn said in warning. Whatever was in that bottle made Reyn's lips tighten in a protective way that Bastien's had when Reyn had used his magic to the point of hurting himself.

It was then I realized that whatever Bastien was drinking was the same thing – a way to hurt himself.

When Reyn surrendered the bottle from Bastien after too many glugs, Bastien started washing his hands, pouring water from the pitcher into a basin and scrubbing with hard soap over and over. His hands, wrists, forearms and elbows took the brunt of his anxiety, and though they were beyond clean, he started all over again, lathering and punishing himself as he went.

It was hard to watch. I stood, leaving Abraham Lincoln in Lane's arms and crossing the blond-colored wood floor to stand next to Bastien, who refused to look at me. I took the towel that hung off a hook on the side of the hanging cabinets, silently encouraging him to finish his ritual of self-flagellation.

Bastien was silent as he let me dry off his arms, not even pulling away when I ran the prickly cloth between his fingers. He'd killed Armand without a second thought. Silvain had shaken him up inside, but this kill looked like it haunted him. He stared at me without seeing my face. He was somewhere far away in his mind, and judging by his hollow expression and lifeless eyes, it didn't look like a place he visited often, or that brought him any joy. Bastien didn't speak as he watched me dry his hands. When I finished, he pulled away and took another drink from the green liquid, snatching it out of Reyn's grip. His breath smelled like hard liquor and licorice, and I wondered just how strong that stuff must be.

When Reyn wore a look of utter flabbergast on his face, Bastien didn't hear the follow-up questions Reyn pelted at him to confirm the orange big bad baddy was, in fact, gone. "He's really dead? Like, you saw him die?"

I answered for Bastien, who looked beyond words as he drank a few gulps more, leaning his backside on the edge of the counter. "Yeah. That's a good thing, right?"

"Burke's the captain of the Queen's Army. He's one of the men who ordered the others to scar up Bastien when he left his post and wanted out of the army. Burke's part of the reason Bastien's an Untouchable."

Bastien hissed. "You don't have to go telling her all my business. It doesn't concern her. Tell her your business, and stick to that."

Lane shook her head, disappointed at the aristocracy system she'd washed her hands of. "Morgan's army is more like a military gang, Ro. You don't just leave or retire. You fight your way out, and if you live, you can leave. So many tried to fight their way out, but it's an entire army against one man." She stood with Abraham Lincoln on her hip, and motioned to Bastien's neck tattoo. "He's an Untouchable. So Bastien can get away with lots of things now. Short of murdering a royal, there's nothing he can be hanged for. And if anyone lays a hand on him, they face the gallows. He's above the law. He doesn't have to pay for things, either. Anything he wants is handed over without question." She crossed over and tapped the hammer and lion tattoo on his wrist that matched the one on his neck. "Magic in Avalon goes on a trickle-down system. First the royals get their share, then Untouchables, then army commanders, then the rest." She studied his face. "How strange that you don't need to heal the magic in the land – I mean, you've got it on tap – yet you risked it all, lived as a Commoner in our world so that you could find us and set things right for Avalon. Some might call that heroic."

I nodded, grateful someone had explained all of his scars without me risking Bastien's temper to ask. My mind was reeling at the messed-up system I'd stepped into.

"I've never known anyone who fought their way out." Lane placed her free hand on Bastien's forearm, softening him with her sincerity. "You're lucky to be alive. I had no idea it was even possible to survive leaving the army. That you did? Well, I can overlook your mouth, knowing how well my Rosie will be protected if you're nearby."

Bastien mouthed, "thanks" and told her with his eyes just how bad the beatings actually were. He turned his back to us and drank some more, wiping his mouth with the sleeve of his shirt. I shuddered as I remembered how patchworked his torso was.

Lane turned back to me and hiked Abraham Lincoln up into a tighter hug he seemed to perpetually need. "Morgan markets it as loyalty to the throne, but really it's stay or die." She looked up at Bastien with Abraham Lincoln in her arms and sincere regret shining in her eyes. "I'm sorry for what my sister's army did to you."

Reyn crossed the room and wrapped his best friend in a tight hug that was strong enough to hold him together, should he let himself fall apart. "You don't know. Burke and his lieutenant are like the fathers of the soldiers. The men love their commanders. Would die for them. Bastien was Burke's right hand before he left. To have someone you think of as your father order the worst beating of your life? To have him watch while you're inches from death and do nothing to save you? To have the man you risked everything to protect order your death?" He squeezed Bastien so tight, I worried he wouldn't be able to breathe. "I should've gutted the bastard years ago. Both of them. All the military leaders should watch the shadows for daggers now. Tell me you made it slow and bloody, brother."

Bastien closed his eyes and rested his chin on Reyn's shoulder before patting him twice on the back in a "thanks, but get off me" kind of way. "It's fine. Burke's dead. There'll be lots who will be out for my head if I'm found out, but since I can't be killed, they'll go after anyone I'm close to. That's you, Reyn. I'm not so untouchable that I can kill Burke with no retaliation. Judgment won't fall on me; they'll come for you."

Reyn nodded. "That's fine. Tell them it was you, and that's that. I won't leave your side until we bring Roland home."

Bastien nodded, his eyes darting to mine to gauge my level of falling to pieces. I took a chance and moved into his body space, wrapping my arms around his middle to hold him through his moment of being reminded that he didn't enjoy falling apart. "I'm sorry, Bastien. I'm so sorry."

I felt him bury his nose in the top of my head and inhale a deep drag, taking in the scent of my hair. Then he stiffened, and I could practically feel him slipping away, trading in the camaraderie for a scowl. "It's my business, and shouldn't be on display. I'm fine. Get off me with your hovering. All of you." He straightened, exhaling whatever softening smelling my hair had done to him. His breath didn't smell like cinnamon anymore, but stank of the sweet liquor that scorned my nose. I didn't have to look up to see his gruff demeanor sliding back into place. He stepped back, shaking off my hug as if he was allergic to the touch he'd just been leaning into. "When the soldiers come to ask me questions, you two have to be out of sight." He moved to the bedroom. "Well, get in here!" he barked.

I could've put money on him turning sour on me. He'd been publicly vulnerable, and now he would make me pay for it. He stomped his foot on the wood plank near the far wall. There were no windows in his bedroom, and no bed, actually. There was a chest for clothes and weapons that he slammed shut when I glanced at it, and a sturdy wooden chair in the corner. The plank he indicated had a small notch on the corner that he bent down and used to lift up a sizeable square of flooring. "Get inside. Man! Do I have to spell everything out for you? The army's probably already on their way. I've got security set up around the place, but if they trip one of my alarms, it still only buys us a minute or two. We don't have time for whatever whining you feel like doing."

I knew I could argue back or recoil from his bite, but neither option seemed like they would lead to anything productive. This was the bear I'd chosen to bunk with, so I shouldn't be all that surprised when he turned on me. I spun on my heel to get Abraham Lincoln, but Lane was right behind me with my teddy bear. "I know you don't think you're yelling at my daughter like that." Her head swiveled, and attitude the likes of which could rival any Miss Thang rolled off her in waves. "Apologize right now!"

Bastien sneered down at Lane, his brute strength up against her royalty card – two mules breathing through their noses at each other. Hamish came in and shook his fist at Bastien, shouting at him to behave, or he'd make the big guy cower. Finally Bastien spoke in a deadly growl. "Fine. I'm sorry I saved her and brought her here. She clearly can't handle our world."

"I can handle it, guys." I pushed my way to the front and eyed the hole Bastien had revealed in the floor of his room, unable to see how deep down into the ground it went. "I'm getting in. Come on, Abraham Lincoln. In we go, Hamish." Abraham Lincoln was a big scaredy cat, for all his animal strength. He asked me why Mama and Daddy were fighting as Reyn readied to lower me down into the ground. I shot Abraham Lincoln a we-can-do-this look. "He's not your Daddy, baby. It's okay. I'm still here."

22

STUCK IN A PHONE BOOTH WITHOUT SUPERMAN

*I*t felt like the earth was swallowing me whole as my feet touched down on the dirt. The wood floor of the house was a good two feet above my head. The dirt walls were packed tight in the narrow space that was only slightly wider than a phone booth. What little light filtered down through the opening informed me that I would be bunking with fat earthworms, spiders the likes and size of which I'd never seen, and various beetles who scurried away from the light into their little hidey holes. I whimpered, knowing my gift of talking to animals didn't extend to bugs.

"Pull me back up!" I begged, panicking and pleading as I gazed up into Bastien's hard expression as he stared down at me over Reyn's shoulder. "I need some bug spray or something! Reyn, there are spiders down here as big as baseballs!" I heard a hiss and all but screamed for Reyn to get me out. "There's something else, too! A snake or some-thing! Get me out! I can't talk to snakes! My magic doesn't work on them!" I'd tried when Judah and I were camping once, and happened across a small garter snake in our tent. I'd never seen Judah run that fast before.

Bastien folded his arms over his chest and sneered, "Quit complaining, your highness. It's the best I can do."

Reyn scowled at his friend. "Shut up, Bastien. They're actual royalty, here. You just shoved the Lost Princess into a hole in the ground! Have some sense." Reyn was on his knees reaching for me, but froze when he heard a bell ring, announcing someone had tripped Bastien's security system. "I'm sorry! I'll try to get rid of them quick." He turned to Lane, who lowered Abraham Lincoln to my trembling arms. Hamish had no qualms about the bugs, but jumped down and made himself at home in the all-you-can-eat buffet, scooping up beetles and handing a few to Abraham Lincoln, who was whining like the little baby he was.

"Shh. It's alright, sweetheart. Mama's here." I hugged him to my chest, letting his nose drape over my shoulder as he held onto me for dear life. I knew he could see in the dark, and that he ate bugs and wasn't afraid of them; what spooked him was Bastien and me fighting.

Reyn carefully lowered Lane down next to me, and we held each other in the dark, claustrophobic space. I began to wish for my pretend father, who was clearly adept at making the most out of the limited space in a phone booth, since he was Superman. Lane's arms wrapped around Abraham Lincoln and me as Reyn slid the flooring in place over our heads and placed the chest atop it. I didn't make a sound after I told Abraham Lincoln he couldn't cry anymore, or the men would come and take him away from me forever. Hamish stopped his feasting temporarily when the front door opened and let in a series of heavy boots, the severity of which scared me more than I could compartmentalize enough to keep from the animals.

Something slithery crawled across my shoe and up my pant leg. I bit my lip to keep from screaming when it slipped up to my calf and curled around the bone. I could tell it was waiting for me to react, so I remained perfectly still. Lane didn't know about the snake, so she rubbed my arms, thinking the soldiers were the only problem.

Suddenly the snake on my calf wasn't at the top of my list of worries. A second snake joined him, twining himself with his scaly buddy, and wrapping three times around my leg just under my kneecap. The squeeze started slowly, the coil tightening almost like a hug. I sobbed silently in the dark as I heard the men talking just above us and to the left. I heard Bastien getting mouthy and Reyn's diplomatic calm that seemed to quell the soldiers' aggressive, indiscernible tones.

Then the snakes bit me. I could barely stand, and the vicious jackworms bit me. I felt four sharp entry points digging into the muscle on the back of my leg under my knee pit. I screamed in my mind, but remained perfectly still until Abraham Lincoln decided he wasn't too scared to be useful. He dropped down and waited for Hamish to help roll my pant leg up before ripping the snakes off of me and sucking them down like gummy worms.

"I have to call for Daddy!" he whined quietly.

"Shh! No, baby. It's fine. We have to wait until the soldiers leave, and then Uncle Reyn can give my leg a look."

Sweat began to bead on my forehead and slid down the back of my neck. I heard the beetles skittering in and out of the walls all around us, and then my hearing started to get away from me. It felt like I had cotton stuffed in my ears, and when Lane pulled my face closer so she could whisper in my ear, I couldn't hear any of it. My leg began to go numb, starting at the exact point of the bite and slowly crawling upward toward my knee. The sweat was pouring off me now, and it was hard to keep my balance in the dark that disoriented me. I clutched Lane and whispered through slick lips, "Snake bite!" Each word took up an entire breath, and I worried at the labor simply breathing caused me.

Lane stiffened and asked me a series of questions I couldn't hear or answer. I started wobbling and took in another ragged breath as my leg gave out. It didn't hurt; it didn't feel like anything as the cold made its way through my veins like an IV. I couldn't feel my left leg up to the top of my knee, and the slow crawl with which the numbing was creeping up my leg struck a terror in me I had not known much of in my life. I was so close to meeting my parents. My cousin. I was so close to seeing their faces. Superman's chin dimple swam in my mind's eye, and I begged him to save me, to swoop in and Lois Lane me straight out of here. He could fly me around the world, showing me where the very best ice cream was made. We would go see operas and pretend we totally knew what the point of it all was. We would kick the soccer ball around in the backyard for hours while he asked if there were any new boys in my life. I'd roll my eyes and say, "Oh, Dad," pretending to be exasperated, but secretly pleased that he cared whose car I was getting kissed in.

Superman, my mom, my cousin, Lane and the world started fading from view as I collapsed in Lane's arms. She was shaking, or I was. I couldn't tell anymore. I felt her breath on my face and knew she was whispering to me, but I couldn't hear any of it. I couldn't feel her warmth that always managed to find me, no matter how icy my heart got.

I closed my eyes as a violent shudder ripped through me, nearing me closer to the edge of unconsciousness. One more raspy breath in and out. Then there was dark.

Then there was light.

23

MOMMY FAINTING

*T*hen there was pain. Searing, blinding agony jerked me back to the world where there was no mom, no Superman, no cousin and no thoughts in my head other than one giant scream that echoed off the walls of Bastien's home.

I wasn't in the hole anymore. I was in the main room near the kitchen on the floor, and someone was covering my mouth while a strong pair of hands was pushing on top of my chest, anchoring me to the ground while my body jerked around without me telling it to. I was slick head to toe from sweat, and all my bones felt like they were caught in a vice, down to my pinky finger. My left leg was stiff as a board, but I felt something tugging on it. Though I couldn't really feel much of my leg, each movement shot lightning up through my body and made me feel like I was slowly sizzling from the inside out.

The hand over my mouth was removed and something was shoved past my lips too far down my throat. On top of burning alive, I was choking to death on a man's fingers as they spread some kind of thick paste over my tongue toward the back of my throat. It tasted bitter, and like fingers. Come to think of it, that last part was probably the fingers.

I heard Reyn calling my name while Lane sobbed. Reyn was the one pinning me down, I realized, now with his whole body. I didn't much care for a man forcing me onto the ground, but something told me to trust him, so I did. My body spasmed uncontrollably. If I knew how to tell any part of me to calm the flip down, I would've, but my body would've given myself the finger and kept on seizing anyway.

The paste turned sandy in my mouth, and my head was lifted so someone could tip water down my throat, washing the bitter flavor through my digestive system. I'm not sure how long it took for my stomach to figure out what to do with the paste. Since pain was the only thing I could feel, all my faculties went to addressing the agony that ripped through my body like little Hot Wheels cars on fire, racing through my veins for the gold medal.

I screamed, silently this time, into the hand I could tell was Lane's. She lowered my head back to the wood floor and pressed down on my forehead to steady my senseless thrashing. I heard Abraham Lincoln crying, his howls filling the room and tugging at my heartstrings. Though I couldn't even control my own body, I wanted to hold him, to lie to him and let him know I was okay. That he wouldn't lose another mama. Lane had fainted once in the sauna at the gym. I still remember the terror that raced through me at my mommy lying there for an eternity of seconds before she finally roused. I saw my whole life flash before my eyes that day, and knew that if she was gone from my world, there would be no more world to speak of.

I didn't want to scare Abraham Lincoln like that.

I could tell people were shouting, but I couldn't make out a word of it through my ears that still felt stuffed with cotton. I tried to make sense of the random images that filled my vision, but when my eyes landed on an olive-skinned stranger in his mid-forties with thick lips and kind eyes, I gave up on figuring out what the crack was going on. He wore a black cloak like Armand's, but he bore none of the scars. Lane opened my mouth for him to look inside, and his fingers poked at my tongue, rubbing something else on it that tasted like the same kind of bitter salve, but didn't dissolve into sand on my tongue. The paste stuck to me until I manually swallowed it down, and with the introduction of the foreign element to my system, my body started to slow its violent seizing.

The relief of not moving was bliss. All my body felt was floating, melty bliss. I was bliss.

Then I was gone, and the world faded to black again.

24

WOBBLY LEGS AND MISSING TONGUES

I was a pretty healthy kid growing up. For all the sports I played, I never broke a bone. I really only caught the once a year sniffles and moved on from those as quick as I could orange juice myself out of the bed. There was one time when I was in junior high that I caught the flu, and my temperature got high enough for Lane to forego her look of bravery and break down by my bedside as she pressed ice packs to my arms and forehead to cool me down. She didn't go into work, didn't shower, didn't eat, didn't do anything or go anywhere until my fever broke and I was on my feet again. I remember how very safe I felt, even though I knew I should be scared. I had Lane there, so I knew everything would somehow figure itself out. She'd always been my very best friend, and even while I was puking my guts out, she'd tell me how beautiful I was, and that she was the luckiest girl in the world because she had me.

When my eyes opened, I expected the first face I saw to be hers. I turned my head left and right, stretching sore and barely mobile muscles. I hissed at a crack in my neck that sounded too unsettling to be healthy. I wasn't in Bastien's house anymore. I wasn't sure where I was. All I knew was that I was in a room by myself without Lane, which didn't feel right. I swallowed hard, my throat too dry to work normally.

I took my time sitting up, finding myself in a room with a single window hole near the top of the wall, too high for me to see out. The light that shone through let me know that I was in an empty wooden room on a straw mattress that sat on a low frame. I stretched my legs, shocked that I could feel them again. Slowly I sat up, confused to find that I wasn't in my jeans and purple *Princess Bride* t-shirt. I wore a long flannel shirt that looked about Bastien's size. It was blue and brown and went down to my knees, revealing bare legs and a bandage covering my left calf. I remembered sweating up a storm, but I was clean now. I hadn't showered since the motel, but running a clumsy hand through my brown tangles, I could tell my hair had been washed.

"Three more hours, and then I should rewrap her leg. I need that guérit *root, though. Where's Bastien? Reyn should've been back hours ago. I can't leave the Lost Princess."*

I heard the man's voice as if he was just outside the

bedroom, and I wondered if it was the thick-lipped man who'd shoved that bitter paste down my throat. Gingerly, I picked up each leg and set them on the cold floor. Cold was good; it meant I could feel things. My nervous system wasn't totally damaged, then. I wished for Hamish to calm me down, but he was nowhere to be found. I was terrified something had happened to him, that some animal or someone had discovered him and taken him from me. I was his home. He needed me, and in that moment, I needed him.

I tried to push myself off the mattress to stand, but I overestimated my healing speed. Agony ripped through my left leg, causing me to cry out as I fell sideways onto the floor, landing with a thud that jarred my aching bones.

The olive-skinned man burst through the door. *"No! What's she doing out of bed? Great, Remy. You have one job to do. Bastien's going to be angry. Angering an Untouchable? Deadly."*

"I'm trying to walk, is what I'm doing, but apparently I suck at it today. It's okay, Remy. It's my fault for walking when I wasn't sure I could. What's going on? Where am I?"

"Oh, where's my quill? Does she even read our language? Come on, Reyn! Where are you?"

"I don't need you to write it out. Just tell me where I am, okay? Tell me how I got here."

"Bastien the Bold carried you here, to my home. Nearly bit my arm off when I tried to dress your wound. Where's my quill?" He looked around the room, wringing his hands as

he cast around for what he needed. There was a desk in the corner, but I didn't see a quill or parchment on it.

I tried to soothe his unease, waving my hand from my position on the floor. "Bastien's always biting people's arms off. I wouldn't take it personally. Did you need to leave him a note or something?" I straightened my legs and tried to rub feeling back into them, but they were still pretty numb, my skin cold.

Remy's straight, black, shoulder-length hair had been pulled back into a short ponytail. He froze at my words, his eyebrows furrowed as he studied me. *"How did she..."*

I scooted ungracefully back to the mattress. "Give a girl a hand? My leg's still totally useless. Feels like my arteries are filled with sand or something. Fun times."

Remy seemed to come to himself and gingerly lifted me to sit back on the straw mattress that rested on a hand-made wooden frame. He knelt before me and silently asked permission before picking up my left leg to inspect the bandage and the wound beneath. His head was bent over my knee as he pried off the bandage with long fingers. He worked with great care not to hurt me. *"Guérit root. We need some* guérit *root, or the poison won't come all the way out. The* souillement *is keeping the damage from spreading, but we need the* guérit *root. Come on, Bastien!*

"What's *guérit* root? Is it somewhere nearby?"

Remy's head shot up, staring at me with his pale brown eyes that were almost devoid of color, they were so glassy. *"How did she hear that? Is she... Is she listening to me?"*

It was weird to watch him talk. His lips didn't move, and yet I heard him perfectly. "I mean, I can hear what you're saying to me, but how are you talking without opening your mouth? Is that a magic thing?"

Remy lowered my leg to the floor and leaned forward to grip my shoulders hard. A jolt of fear hit me that I was basically wearing a long shirt, underwear and nothing else, sitting on the bed of a stranger, letting him get a good look at my leg. I tried to shake his hands off me, but my body was still too sluggish for ninja extractions. "Dude, hands off! Let me go!"

His eyes bored into mine, his lips still not moving as he spoke to me. *"I need to know if... Can you hear me? Can you understand what I'm saying?"*

"Of course I can hear you. I just can't figure out how you're talking without moving your lips. Let go!"

Remy finally realized his hairy hands shouldn't be on me, and retracted them. He remained a few inches from my face, transfixed. He examined my features with intensity that made me want to hide. *"If you can hear me, then tell me who you came here with."*

I bit my lower lip. "Um, I'm not sure if I'm allowed to talk about that. No offense, but I've got no clue how I got here or who you really are. Can't you just pick a number and ask me if I can hear you say it?"

"Very well. Thirty-four."

"Dude, I know you're older than thirty-four."

Remy gasped and stood, pacing on the wood floor. His

mind was consumed by half-sentences that all had a note of wonder and confusion to them.

"Hey, not to disturb your freak-out, but where's Reyn?" I wanted to ask where Lane was at, but wasn't sure if Remy was supposed to know about her.

He started to point to the door, but then realized he could just tell me. The revelation sizzled like something precious in his chest. Like hope. I didn't understand the buildup, but at least the vibe I was getting from him wasn't creepy rapist or something. Bonus. *"Reyn and Duchess Elaine of Avalon are trying to find more* guérit *root. Bastien has your animals. He's summoning a second healer to see if he's got more herbs to stave off the danger that's spreading from the bite. We went through all of mine. The poison had been in you too long for a regular dose."* He paused, watching my face with anticipation that softened my concern. *"You really heard all that?"*

"Every word. But how are you talking without talking? Can you teach me? That's dead useful."

Remy shot me a look of disbelief, and then light dawned on him. His eyes began to sparkle with moisture. *"You must not know about the goings on of our world, then. Everyone here knows about the silencing of the healers."*

"Yikes. That sounds super bad, whatever it is."

Remy's thoughts skipped around, overjoyed at being able to talk to me, but utterly woebegone about whatever the silencing was. He knelt by the bedside in his jeans and long-sleeved green t-shirt, scooping up my hands and looking into my eyes like he was making a pledge. His olive skin against my sun-kissed fingers looked pretty.

It was a little intimate for me, but I swallowed down my confusion and discomfort and tried to be polite. "Hey, it's okay. Whatever it is you want to tell me, I'm all ears. Go nuts."

I could hear his elation in the silent laughter that lit his long features. He had rounded cheekbones, like Reyn, but longer ears and nose. When he started to explain things to me, his face fell. *"A few years ago, the healers were asked to rehabilitate the soldiers who'd taken the Queen's loyalty oath to Morgan le Fae's throne. The potion was barbaric, melting the men's skin and leaving some dead if they didn't 'pass her test.'"* He shook his head, his plump lips in a firm line as his black ponytail swooshed back and forth.

"Yikes. I think we ran into one of those dudes. Silvain was all acidy like that, and so was Armand."

Remy nodded vigorously, enraptured that we were having a conversation. *"Yes! They were two of the many who took the oath and survived. Us healers decided we couldn't be part of the ritual in good conscience. We as a group refused her, some more vocal about the dangers of the potion than others. The people we told passed on the warning to others, and pretty soon soldiers were starting to take their names off the list, refusing to undergo the swearing of her oath."* Remy opened his mouth, revealing teeth and... nothing. There was a gaping empty space where his tongue should have been.

I gasped, covering my mouth in horror at the clear

injustice. Then I realized I was being super rude and toned down my shock as much as I could. "Dude, what happened? Where's your tongue?"

"She took our tongues to silence the uprising that was starting against her." He clutched my hand, holding my fingers tight. *"I haven't spoken to anyone since. None of us have. We use hand signals and quills with parchment. Right now you're not hearing my voice; you're reading my thoughts."*

My worry was clear on my face that I'd intruded on something so private. I would be horrified if someone read my thoughts. "I didn't mean to! I swear! I just heard you talking as if you were saying it all out loud. Remy, that's horrible! How could Morgan do something so vicious?"

"Bastien told me, but I admit I wasn't sure. It's said the Lost Princess of Avalon could hear unknown languages. We all just assumed that meant you could speak to animals, since they flocked to you from birth. You're Morgan le Fae and King Urien's daughter. You're the Compass, the Voix. Rosalie of Avalon, the Lost Princess."

My neck shrunk into the collar of the flannel shirt as I tried to hide from the fairytale labels. "Well, when you say it all together like that, it's going to sound like some grand title, but I only just found out about all that lineage and whatnot like, not even a week ago."

Remy remained on his knees with unshed tears sparkling in his eyes. Then he lowered his shoulders and bowed to me. Actually bowed. *"Daughter of Avalon, if you can give me a voice, I swear to you this day I will follow you to the ends of Faîte. I will fight beside you and win battles in your name. I'm utterly at your service. Please allow me to take the Vow of the* Guardien."

I grimaced, completely confused and out of my element. I hadn't even been able to get someone to do the seesaw with me in the first grade, but this dude wanted to follow me to the ends of his world? "Whoa! That's not necessary. I'm not my mom. I don't need you to sign your life away to me. I don't even know what the Vow of the *Guardien* is. I'm happy to help you talk to people whenever you like. Just tell me, and I'll translate. It's really not a big deal. I just don't understand how I'm hearing you, but no one else can."

"Whatever miracle made it possible, I'm grateful for it. I've been silent for so very long."

He was still on his knees, head bowed, so I leaned forward as gracefully as I could manage and placed a clumsy hand atop his midnight hair. "I'm here now, and I won't be mean to you like my mom was. I'm a safe place, alright?" I gave his scalp a sumptuous scratch to lighten the mood, and tugged on his ponytail. "Now tell me all about yourself. I'm listening."

25

THE VOW OF THE GUARDIEN

I'm not sure I said more than two words after that. Remy remained on his knees before me until I insisted he knock it off when he finally paused his rant of elation. "I really don't need you to kneel like that. Maybe we could sit at a table or something?" I suggested, hinting at the fact that I was starving and hadn't eaten a thing in who knows how long. At least I got a nap in. That's the upside of being knocked out. They let you sleep.

"Here's fine. May I?" He sat next to me on the mattress and scooped up my hand. I'd never been much for hand-holding. Lane and I did sometimes when I could tell she'd been having a bad day. Judah and I sometimes did in our sleep, but that was under the covers, and let's face it, totally embarrassing to be caught needing my Judah-blankie. Remy examined my knuckles carefully as he told me more about his life and his thoughts. He'd grown up

the oldest of seven children, five of whom became healers.

"Whoa. Five out of seven are now totally mute? That's terrible. Your poor parents. Poor all of you."

"Yes. We used to have fun together, but now we're a grim bunch. The youngest of us is a soldier in the Queen's Army who actually took the Queen's loyalty oath. Don't think that hasn't caused a fair amount of tension."

"But how could he serve her after what she did to all of you? How could anyone?"

"You forget that there is no way out, except near certain death. He didn't have to sign up for the loyalty oath, though. Bastien was the first Untouchable I ever met. I was barely able to keep him alive after he escaped the Queen's Army, but he survived, which is more than I can say for the others who defected. Faîte didn't use to be like this, but it's gotten far more forbidding in the past few years."

"So I don't get it. If Morgan le Fae's clearly so terrible, why are there people who still serve her? It makes no sense. Who would possibly still be on her side?"

"Those who want power gravitate toward power. Morgan le Fae is the most powerful ruler we've ever had. And she's done a fair amount of good things, too. Every time she does something gruesome, there's something benevolent that comes about around the same time to distract the public. When the healers were silenced, she lowered the taxes. When the horrid effects of the oath became clear, she made sure everyone in Avalon was fed, not just her district. It's brilliant politics, actually. Though *she's done what she's done to me, even I have to see some merit in many of her actions."*

"Yikes. That's a pretty bold statement, man."

"Decades ago when I was just a boy, before the Jewels of Good Fortune, things were overall fine, but poverty was an issue. The land wasn't giving us crops as often as we needed."

"But then the jewels showed up, and Morgan got greedy."

"Morgan le Fae found a way to fix many of our kingdom's problems. At what cost? We never fully know. She's taken so many of the jewels from neighboring provinces over the years. Other lands whither while hers flourishes. She welcomes the stragglers, destitute and starving into Province 1. They don't even care that she's the one responsible for depleting their land by taking their Duchess' gem; they only care that someone will feed them. So Province 1 increases in size, and never dips in prosperity."

"I guess that makes sense, but yikes. So far, not a fan of all the criminal activity from the Avalon higher-ups."

"Indeed. The Queen's loyalty oath was to give the army gifts of speed, strength and determination to carry out her will. We were to have a super army of soldiers who could dig new wells as needed, build homes for those who required help, and protect our people from the creatures that have always bested us. The downside is that the potion left many of the men deformed or dead. If a soldier died, she ruled that he must not have been loyal after all. I have yet to see how her soldiers will benefit us. There have been no new wells, no houses built for the poor.

Some use their superior strength to terrorize the locals. She has them on a mission, though I shudder to guess what that might be."

"It's me," I said quietly, my hand still sandwiched between Remy's. "They're trying to find me. They tracked me down in my world and tried to take me to her. Apparently I'm some compass or something? I'm supposed to be able to find things."

"You're not *supposed* to be able to find things, you *can* find them. It's part of who you are." Reyn stood in the doorway to the bedroom, holding Lane's hand, who was at his side.

Lane smiled at me, looking on my bedraggled face as if I was her sun and moon. "Reyn's right. And when you've had a little training, you'll be able to turn it on and off. Really tap into it."

"That's wicked cool, Lane. You have to teach me."

"How about we get you to stand first?" Her eyes fell on Remy, and she frowned, her tone turning sharp on a dime. "You'll not hold my daughter's hand on your bed, Healer. She's a princess. Don't forget that just because she does."

Remy was embarrassed, but he didn't drop my hand. He moved back to kneeling in front of me on the wooden floor, my fingers squished between his palms in supplication. *"Forgive me, but I can't be parted from you. I haven't had a voice in so long. Permit me to stay with you! Please, Princess Rosalie! Let me take the Vow of the Guardien."*

"Okay, everyone needs to chill out. First off, I'm not

Princess Rosalie. I'm just Rosie. Second, Remy and I were having a friendly moment, Lane. Nothing weird. He's been catching me up on the drama with Morgan and the healers. It's all pretty intense."

"Well, be intense with someone your own age. Remy's older than I am."

I rolled my eyes. "You gotta know how silly you sound. Not intense like that, but thanks for making it all awkward. It's nuts in here because I can hear him. We're having a conversation."

Reyn spoke slowly, taking in Remy's humble posture and reverent demeanor. "How do you mean? Remy can't talk. The Queen…"

"I know all that. Remy told me."

"You mean he wrote it for you?"

"No, he told me. I can hear him talking in his mind as clearly as I can hear animals. He wants to stay with me. With us, I guess. He wants to take some kind of oath of the guard or something."

Reyn and Lane (first time it hit me that their names rhyme) both gasped. Then they barreled into the room all the way to start talking at me in harsh instructional tones I couldn't make heads or tails of because the three of them were all jabbering at the same time. Finally Lane held up her hands to quiet Reyn and garner Remy's attention. "Remy, we appreciate the offer, but I don't want anyone taking the Vow of the *Guardien* for Rosie until she knows enough about Avalon to make that decision. You can join us, but that's the extent of it. I won't have her living with a man I don't know, who's twice her age."

My eyebrows furrowed and my nose crinkled, but Bastien was the one to speak. I didn't even know he'd come in. He stood behind them in the doorway, caramel eyes wide in shock as he took in the conversation with a few bundles in his arms. "You're considering a Brownie? You're taking a protector?" He stared at me with the sting of betrayal in his eyes before the hard edge took over. "Why shouldn't she have a guard? It makes sense. With how often she gets hurt, it's not a bad idea. Clumsy enough. It'd make the job easier, for sure." Abraham Lincoln and Hamish made to come for me, but Bastien whistled them back. "Not yet, guys. Not until she can actually get out of bed." They pouted, but sulked back into the living room. Abraham Lincoln whined while Hamish tried cheering his furry buddy up with a song. They were kind of precious together.

Fire burned in me when I remembered how pissed I was at Bastien. "Don't you dare talk to me about being clumsy! You threw me in a dark hole in the ground! I got bit because of you! I told you there was something down there, and you shoved me in anyway. I should take a protector to save me from you!"

It was the fight Bastien had been waiting for. Now he didn't have to apologize. He didn't have to feel bad. He could just be mad, and that would be the only thing he'd focus on. I'd walked right into that one, and berated myself for being so stupid. "Oh, you need saving from me? I guess you really are a little princess." He spoke the word like a dig, and his verbal shovel cut me deep.

"Take that back! I'm not helpless! I'm not weak. I've gone along with everything just fine. I don't need your mouth. You got me to Faîte. Great job. I'm alive. Reyn can help me find Roland. You're dismissed."

"I'm *what*?" He reared back as if I'd slapped him.

"Sure. If I'm the princess, then I have the power to dismiss you, right? You're dismissed. Go back to hunting down criminals and whatnot. Go back to your fiancée. Go jump off a cliff! I don't need the drama; I've got enough to deal with."

Lane and Reyn both groaned at our fight, but Remy took action. He stood between Bastien and me, his wary hand up to tell Bastien to back off. *"If he doesn't leave her be, I can knock him out with some hawthorn powder. But this is Bastien the Bold! Princess Rosie, he's Untouchable. I might be hanged if I do that."*

"For Heaven's sakes! Don't dowse him with whatever hawthorn powder is." Then I turned my head to scowl at Bastien. "Leave, Bastien. Just go. You're freaking Remy out. You don't want to be here, and I don't want you here. It's a pretty clear win-win."

Bastien's face soured in confusion at my words. "Huh? Rosie, how'd you know about hawthorn powder?" Bastien whipped his head to Remy. "Are you trying to dose me? That'd be just about the last thing you did, Healer."

I rubbed my hands over my face. "I can't explain this all over again. Reyn, would you deal with your village idiot?"

Reyn cast me a look that told me I wasn't helping matters, but grabbed Bastien and all but dragged him into the main room of the home, filling him in on the whole psychic talking thing.

Remy fell to his knees again, scooping up my hands and pledging his loyalty to me.

I bit down on my lower lip, confused and very turned around. It began to dawn on me how very little I knew about this world, and just how dangerous that could prove to be.

26

SNAKE SPAGHETTI

*R*emy took the bundles Bastien had left on the floor and all but ran to my side on the mattress, pulling my bare leg onto his lap and gingerly peeling off the bandage. Lane and I both made noises of surprise when we took in the horrid purple bruising that engulfed my whole calf. I could see the puncture wounds because they were black with spindly lines that crawled across my leg. The whole thing looked, well, not good. "Aw, man. That's gnarly. Can you fix it? Can you make it better?"

Remy's hands trembled slightly with trepidation and wonder. *"I'm holding the leg of the Lost Daughter of Avalon. So young. So beautiful. Her skin... so soft."*

I yanked my leg out of his grip, and cried out at the sudden movement that hurt my whole body. I hissed at the jarring discomfort, but refused to cry out again. My eyebrows furrowed as I cast him a look of supreme scolding. "Dude, be cool. I can hear your thoughts. All of them, not just the ones you mean to tell me. You've got like twenty years on me, at least."

Remy was horrified, and to be fair, he was in a rough spot. He wanted to be heard, but guarding every thought could only last as long as you never had a bad one. His thoughts were rambling now, pushing together too many apologies to make much sense.

Lane understood enough to put her foot down. "This is what I was talking about. You can't let just anyone take that vow, Rosie. The Brownie who takes the Vow of the *Guardien* would be with you every day. They eat with you, live with you, sleep under the same roof." She pointed her finger between Remy and me. "As noble as your intentions probably are, my daughter's not moving in with a stranger who's old enough to be her..." Her voice trailed off, and I knew she'd caught herself before the word "father" made its way to her lips. "It's not going to happen. And Rosie? I know it's my fault you don't know anything about how Faîte works. I know you don't like me making rules for you, and back home, you didn't need me to all that often. But here? I hate using the parental 'just trust me,' but in Faîte it'd be really great if you deferred to me until you get the hang of things. Is that cool?"

I muscled through my inner teenager's gut reaction and admitted the facts to myself: I had no idea what I was doing here. I'd almost just saddled myself with a man who... who was perfectly nice, but was perhaps not the best fit for a lifetime of palling around with. "Okay. I guess that makes sense. But you have to explain things to me, even if you're afraid I won't like them. I can't go up against all the bad things I'm supposed to be stopping if I have no idea what I'm getting myself into." My leg was burning now, any movement hurting it as the air kissed it with its jagged teeth. "I don't know enough about this big adventure to know who I should be on it with."

"That's fair." Lane cupped my cheeks, gearing up to impart wisdom to me. I felt my heart flutter, and knew she was about to hit me with something important. Lane was gentle, letting the fire in her eyes burn her truths into my soul. "Your greatest adventure will be with yourself. Everything else is a minor plot point. Avalon is not your big adventure. A man is not your big adventure. You, baby. You're your own adventure. The sooner you understand that, the simpler everything else becomes."

I blinked at her, absorbing the truth in her words and letting them relax my shoulders. Maybe she was right. As big as all of this seemed, perhaps understanding myself and how I fit into the world around me would be the thing that could light the way. Confusion always accompanied the unknown, but if I could investigate and learn about who I was, then perhaps the rest of it wouldn't seem quite so harrowing. "Thank you, Lane. I think I needed that."

Lane took in my twisted expression and dropped to her knees. "Honey, what's wrong?"

"It hurts! It's burning all over again! The air, it's... Ah!"

My leg started twitching on its own, and I watched with horror as the black puncture wounds began to seep green pus down my calf.

"Bastien! Did you get the *guérit* root?"

Reyn paused his lecture long enough for Bastien to answer from the kitchen. "Yeah. It's right here." He entered the room, grimacing at the state of my leg. "Oh! I didn't realize it spread that deep already. I worked as quick as I could, but the root's hard to come by. I went through five healers before I found one with any to spare. Paid way too much for it, too."

"Are you actually complaining about saving the princess' life?" Lane asked imperiously, her nose in the air. She was always so chill with me; it was surreal to see her shaming Bastien like a true royal.

Bastien shot Lane a hard look that told me he wanted to bite back, but knew he was in no position to. "Here you are, Duchess." He pulled a gnarled piece of what looked like ginger out of his pocket and handed it to Remy, who was afraid to look at me.

"Normally I'd have a patient just eat the root, but the poison's been in you too long. You'll have to eat part, and I'll have to cut open your wound to put the rest directly into the bite."

"What? Cut me open? Are you sure it has to go down like that? I like the eating it idea." I knew my voice was giving away my dread. Images of medieval bloodletting and other various torturous medical practices flashed in my mind. I shot Lane a look of sheer panic, but she only returned it to me amplified.

"You're cutting my baby open?" Her eyes were wide with fear, taking in Remy's grim nod with dread. When she turned back to me, her voice tried to be light and reassuring, fooling no one. "It's alright, sweetie. If that's what Remy says he needs to do, then that's what'll happen. It's nothing as scary as what you're thinking."

"It'll hurt," Remy warned me, obscuring Lane's pep talk. *"There's no getting around that. I'll need you absolutely still, too."* He mimed to Bastien to hold me down, but Bastien couldn't understand what he wanted. Poor guy. I couldn't imagine trying to practice medicine without being able to speak.

I spoke through gritted teeth as the heat spread up to my knee, making the joint immobile and adding a new layer of fear to my already panicked state. "No. I can hold still on my own."

Bastien addressed Remy, confused. "What do you need me to do?"

When Remy insisted I tell him, I groaned, wishing I could disappear. It wouldn't be fair to Remy if I only translated the things I wanted him to say. That would make me just as evil as Morgan, cutting off his words when they displeased me. "Bastien, Remy has to cut my leg open to put part of the root in. There's no time to numb the area, so he wants you to hold my leg still while he... while he ccuts me open. But you don't h-have to stay. You can go." My voice quaked on the last few notes.

Though neither of us wanted him to, Bastien softened. "Hey, yeah. Of course I'll stay." His shoulders relaxed as he let the fight he always had on standby die inside of him, so he didn't bite at me while I was already so thoroughly down. Lane whimpered as Remy got out his tools. I tried to look in the pouch to see what sort of torture devices he had to use on me, but Bastien blocked my view with his wide shoulders as he knelt next to me atop the mattress. "Look at me and nothing else. You don't need to see what he's got."

"Princess Rosalie, can you ask Reyn to start boiling the root with a sliver of ginseng? I'm giving him half, and he needs to boil it, and then mash it in with some water. Then he needs to strain it so you can drink the tea."

I explained everything to Reyn, who took a few seconds of being impressed by me before realizing I was speaking on behalf of Remy. "Ah. Yes, sir. Right away." Reyn all but ran into the kitchen with half the root and set to work.

Lane sat on my other side on the bed, holding my hand and conjuring up the worst fake smile I'd seen in a while. "It'll be fine, Ro. Just a few minutes of a little sting, and that's all."

"Thanks." I tried to offer a smile to her. "I appreciate the obvious lie and the spirit in which it's given. After this, can I get my real clothes back?"

"Of course. I'm sure Bastien doesn't mind lending you his shirt, though. It's the very least he can do after letting those snakes bite you." She shot him a glare, which he ignored.

I heard Remy sharpening something metal, and I wanted to see what it was. There was a sick fascination to identifying the weapon that would be used to cut me up, but Bastien blocked me again. He shook his head and moved off the bed, making sure to cup his hand to the side of my face so I wouldn't look at whatever Remy was doing. "Let's get you situated. Here, lie down." He motioned for Lane to move, and she scurried off the head of the bed. The two were careful as they turned my body and lowered my head to the mattress. I bit back a scream when Bastien moved my legs to rest on the straw mattress, and worried how much worse the pain would get when it wasn't gentle fingers, but a knife touching me instead. "Oh, man. It's turning blacker. And is the swelling getting worse? Remy, the black is spreading! Hurry!"

"We need Reyn in here to catch the snakes when they spill out. The root will kill most of them, but it won't do to let one of us get bit when you've got the only guérit *root for miles inside of you."*

"Wait, what? When the snakes spill out of where? Are there snakes in your house, too?"

Remy put words to what Lane and Bastien were afraid to say. *"The snakes are inside of you. The sadique snake bites its prey and leaves behind a few of its eggs to plant themselves inside the body. As the black spreads, so do the offspring. Once they reach your heart, you die. We've got time, but they have to come out now. Otherwise they'll fill your body until it bursts, and your body gives birth to hundreds of sadique babies."* Then Remy paused, and I could tell he was talking to himself. *"No, it won't do to find the Compass and then lose her to something like this. It has to be now. Just ignore her screams when they come."*

I'd been cool through an awful lot, but this set me back big time. I went from scared to full-on freak-out. I started slapping my body all over to kill the snakes hatching inside of me, crying out when the slightest movement caused agony to rip through my left leg. "Get them out of me! Get the snakes out! Hurry!"

"I'm mashing!" Reyn called into the room to inform us of his progress. I could tell he was going as quickly as he could.

Bastien cast Remy a look of deep disapproval. "Did you tell her? Why? She doesn't need to know all that."

Remy nodded with his head bowed and kept sharpening his tools of certain death. He stood and retrieved a pair of thick leather gloves from a chest near the wall, and I caught a glimpse of a scalpel that was too large to be precise. "Mom, make it be over!" I begged, not caring how pathetic I sounded. My imagination was working overtime, picturing millions of snake babies worming their way through my arteries and bursting the pipes that kept me scoring goals and, you know, living.

Lane shushed me and centered my head on the pillow, positioning herself above me so that when I looked up, all I saw was her upside-down face. Her tears dripped down on me, and I realized how much my fear was scaring her. Whenever I hurt myself, she cried worse than I ever did. When I was bummed about failing a test, she took it even harder. She was my biggest advocate, and aunt though she was, I saw in her green eyes that she was my mother, through and through. I took a deep breath and tried to let my body go limp as her tears peppered my face. "I'm sorry, honey," she hiccupped as she wiped them away.

Reyn came in with the tea that smelled like hot, fishy garbage. Bastien nearly got himself slapped when he straddled my thighs, but then he leaned down and wrapped his arms around me in a gentle hug so he could lift me slowly for the tea. Reyn pressed the cup to my lips as Bastien held me to his chest. I didn't want to feel comforted by Bastien, but that's exactly what settled in my soul as the tea filled me with its acrid taste. I downed half the cup like a champ before Reyn pulled it away and took a sip. Bastien did the same, as did Remy and Lane. "It's in case we get bit when the snakes... well, you know," Reyn explained. "I boiled the water, so whatever poison's in it hopefully won't get into us."

Remy's hand on Bastien's arm told him what I already knew. It was hammertime. Bastien called over his shoulder, "Abraham Lincoln! It's dinnertime." He whistled for my bear, and Hamish followed in behind him. "Tell

Hamish to wait in the living room. I don't know if the snakes will try to eat him, or if he can handle the poison. Not worth the risk."

"Hamish, wait in the living room. I'll be right out, okay?"

Hamish was furious, yelling at everyone in the room just where they could shove their nuts as he stormed out. Abraham Lincoln was given a sip of the tea, and got ready for the dinner of a lifetime when I explained what was about to happen. Bastien laid me down again, only this time he remained on top of me, his heavy bulk crushing me down into the mattress so I couldn't move much. Reyn donned a pair of long leather gloves that looked like the kind welders used.

Lane's upside-down face gave me a forced smile that cleared out the medical chatter I could hear Remy saying to himself as he poised his weapon. "Laney?" I whispered. "Will you sing the song for me?"

Lane started crying afresh, nodding with a relieved grin that I wouldn't stay mad at her forever, and that even though we were in a different world, we were still us. "Steady, Bastien. She's stronger than she looks. Make sure you hold her still."

"On it." His body tightened around me, arms and legs locking around me to make sure I didn't spasm and rip my leg open farther than could be sewn up. He smelled like Christmas, replacing the stench of the hot dumpster tea with presents and bows and colorful sugar cookies that tasted boring but looked gorgeous. He pressed his lips to my cheek, then shifted so our temples rested against each other in a silent apology and forgiveness. It reset our constant battle to a state of temporary surrender, which apparently we needed at least once a day. "I've got you," he promised me in a whisper that, despite everything, actually did reassure me.

"Please don't leave me," I begged him. My voice was barely audible through my shame – I would rather risk him getting bit than have to suffer alone through a surgery with no anesthesia.

"I'm not going anywhere, little Daisy," he promised.

Lane started singing my favorite song just before the knife cut into me with delicate precision. "'Wouldn't it be nice if we were older? Then we wouldn't have to wait so long. And wouldn't it be nice to live together in the kind of world where we belong.'"

I stopped breathing and held in my oxygen as long as it would stay inside of me. I knew as soon as I let the breath go, the pain would be too much to muscle my way through.

"'Wouldn't it be nice if we could wake up in the morning when the day is new? And after having spent the day together, hold each other close the whole night through...'"

That was all the air I had in me, and when I sucked in the next lungful, agony tore at my insides, announcing my white-hot torture to the room. I screamed, and Lane's hand went over my mouth to stifle the noise. I tried not to thrash around, but Bastien's grunts informed me that I was unsuccessful in getting my body to obey. The knife burned as Remy worked, tearing through my flesh as if it was butter.

When the scalpel was moved away, I felt something ripping at my skin from the inside and spilling out of the incision in barfy ribbons. I thought it was blood, but when Abraham Lincoln started slurping, his fear for me replaced by the joy of gluttony, I realized the snakes were starting to pour out of my calf. I screamed at the pain. I howled for the horror. I was past the point of being able to cry – the pain too intense for mere tears. My leg wasn't just on fire anymore, it was emptying itself of acid that felt like it burned as it left me. It wasn't just my leg, but something in my stomach started pulling downward from its hidey hole behind my belly button. I wanted to scratch it out of me, but Bastien was ready. He tightened the wrestling hold he had on me, squishing the air from my body as the snakes poured out of my opened leg like hot spaghetti.

My breath came in barely-there hiccupped bursts of life, and went out of me in exhales of endless torment. I could hear Abraham Lincoln slurping his dinner of snakes that had been hatched and grown inside of my leg. I was too grossed out to put anything in proper order of freak-out in my mind. Lane's tears rained down on my face, reminding me not to pass out.

The snakes finally seemed to be dwindling down, slithering out two by two, and then dropping out one at a time right into Abraham Lincoln's open mouth. I sobbed at getting a reprieve, and I struggled against Bastien for a full breath. He only moved enough to let my arms have a little motion. "Hold onto me. The worst part's still coming, sweetheart."

"What?" was all I eked out before Remy dug into my open wound with his hand. He spread the paste made from the root into the long slice to make sure anything still in my body that shouldn't be there would die. I felt him touch my bone and screamed myself hoarse as Bastien held me in place.

My fingers dug into Bastien's sides, taking a little of my torture out on his skin. He took it like a champ, gritting his teeth as I raked at his flesh under his shirt that had hiked up in our wrestling match. "That's right," he hissed. "Dig a little deeper, Daisy. I know it hurts. Make me feel it." He kissed my cheek again, wincing when I started clawing harder. "I'm sorry, honey. I shouldn't have dropped you in there. I was trying to keep you hidden. I wasn't thinking. I do that sometimes – get the job done without thinking it all the way through."

I thrashed beneath him, punching him in the side. I didn't have enough wind-up to really do any damage, but it was enough to deliver a decent sting. He let out a few "oof"s as he permitted me to beat on him while Remy sewed me up and wrapped the wound. The gash felt about a million miles wide, but Remy hid it beneath the wrapping. Bastien's hold on me softened slowly through the whole ordeal. He let me hit him as many times as I wanted while the pain still rippled through my whole body in haunting echoes of "this'll never be over."

When my arms exhausted themselves punching his sides, I brought my tired hands up and slapped him across the face. "You hurt me!" I shouted at him, my voice hoarse from all the screaming. "You threw me down there and didn't care what happened! All because you were embarrassed I saw your scars and heard about your army life. Well now *I* have a scar! Are you happy?"

Bastien had let me punch him without hesitation, but the slap across the face seemed to really hurt him. My intent was to smack a little sense back into him, but really it smacked a little sense into me. He watched my sadness with wide eyes and finally saw the depths of the damage he did when he went off on people and shut down like that. Though I'd just been cut open and sewn back up, Bastien was the thing that wounded me. He was the thing that made me bleed.

My mouth fell open, appalled at my own behavior. That he'd brought out the worst in me wasn't such a big surprise. That I'd let someone get to me so much that I'd lashed out certainly was. Bastien was careless with me, so I slapped him. I didn't recognize myself. "I... I... I shouldn't have done that. I'm sorry," I said quietly, as if we were the only two in the room, which we most certainly were not.

He leaned in, breaking eye contact at the last possible second, to let me get the full effect of his eyes that seemed

to see straight through my hesitation for what it was –
attraction. "Don't let me get away with it," he whispered.

"You hurt me, Bastien. You scared me and you let me
get hurt on your watch, in your house. I'll have a scar now
because of you. It shouldn't work like that. You shouldn't
be the thing that hurts me – not when you were supposed
to rescue me."

Bastien kept his mouth shut through the defiance in
his eyes, and nodded. "You're right. I'm sorry."

My fight finally went out of me, and my sweaty arms
slumped to the sides, my chest heaving like I'd just run a
marathon. I had plenty to hurl at him, but no energy with
which to make my fury better known.

His legs uncurled from my thighs as he leaned to my
right. He slid between me and the wall on the bed,
slumping in relief that the worst was over. He traced the
slope of my cheek with his rough thumb, looking at my
sweaty face as if I was something precious and delicate. I'd
never had a man look at me like that before. He kissed my
cheek again, knowing that was the most I would permit
him to do. Then he growled to the others, "Get out of here.
She needs to rest."

Reyn was still coming down from the adrenaline high
of watching snakes birth from a human, and then seeing
his BFF crumple like a piece of paper with a girly love note
written across his chest in bold letters. He helped Remy
pack up his tools so I didn't have to see the things that
would only add more colorful illustrations to my night-

mares. Then he helped Lane up off the floor, who was sobbing as she cleaned up my blood using a fallen sheet on the wood floor. When I'd been in grade school, I'd thrown up all over the kitchen, unable to make it to the bathroom in time. Flashbacks flooded me of Lane in the exact same position, mopping up my mess while worried tears cascaded down her cheeks in my honor. I'd known then and I knew now – the woman who cleans up your puke is your true mother. Though I still had questions for her, seeing her gather up the bloody sheet with nothing but love in her eyes for me, I knew I was hers, and she was mine. Mine, all mine.

Bastien stood and lifted me only the once, so a fresh sheet could be laid down for me. "Go on out and get some air. I'll watch her."

Lane hiccupped through her response, her face still wet and a sob on her lips. "Thanks. Not out of your sight." Lane exited in Reyn's arms, his handkerchief clutched to her face as he led her on wobbly legs to the kitchen.

"Call for me if you need anything. Otherwise don't move your leg. The stitches are still fresh, and you can't put any pressure on your leg." Remy paused to smile at my halfhearted wave of acknowledgement. *"It was a privilege to talk to you, Princess Rosie. Thank you for hearing me. Rest well."*

"Anytime, Remy. I'm always here to listen." My voice was shaky and my sigh uneven as the door finally closed, leaving me with an audience of just the one. Bastien settled in next to me on the bed, unwilling to leave just yet.

"Making yourself comfortable there?" I bit my lower lip through the pain that kept knocking me over the head in waves.

"You asked me not to leave you, so here I am." He reached over my body and tugged the shirt I was wearing downward to cover my naked thighs. He pulled the sheet up over me, careful not to let the material scrape over my wrapped wound. Then he held my hand, giving me something to grip through the internal fire that wasn't through screwing with me yet. Bastien kissed the tip of my nose, offering up a crooked smile that endeared me to him. "I like you in my clothes."

I don't know why that struck me as funny. Probably because the second sexiest moment I'd ever had happened when snakes were pouring out of my body like vomit. I brushed my nose to his, widening his grin to that of a churlish boy who needed a good scolding. "I like you in *my* clothes," I told him. "I think we should trade. You've got nice boobs. You could totally hold your own."

Bastien laughed, snorting into my hair. "Thanks. I don't think I need to tell you how nice yours are." He observed my expression twist from teasing to torment as the misery struck me afresh. Though there was no scalpel in my leg anymore, the nerves inside weren't aware the danger had left us alone for the moment. Bastien let me squeeze his hand through the agony, and when it left me again, he kissed my knuckles. "I'll be right back. Get you something for the pain."

"What makes you think I'm in pain?" I joked.

"I'm good like that." He was careful as he climbed over me, pausing to do a pushup over my body just to make me snicker. He returned not a minute later with a cup and a rag that was wet with warmed water. "Liquor for the worst of it," he said quietly.

He moved slowly as he helped me to sit up, tipping the cup to my trembling lips to let the green-colored licorice-smelling gasoline-like liquid trickle down my throat. The numbing effect was strong and quick, and as he laid me back down, I thought to myself how weightless I felt. My limbs were no longer a problem. After a couple minutes of quiet, nothing was a problem. I'd never had anything that strong, and wondered if it was magical liquor or something.

Bastien wound my hair up above me over the pillow and dabbed at my face and neck with the rag, sweeping the sweat from me so I was a little more comfortable. I tried to reach for him, but my hand was too tired to commit to the effort. He caught my fingers and started rubbing my arm. "What do you need, Daisy?"

"Stay with me. Just until I fall asleep. I don't like sleeping alone." I watched the contented smile spread across his handsome features, stretching his lips and dimpling his cheeks in the roguish way I couldn't help but be attracted to. "I want something happy to remember for the next time you turn into a jackweasel on me."

Bastien made a slow seduction of climbing up my body

and kissing my cheeks, brushing his lips across mine as he switched from left to right. I was so needy for him, despite everything. There was something about him that resonated with me. We both guarded our innards probably a little too zealously, clamming up or lashing out when we were poked with the wrong stick. Bastien checked the door twice to make sure it was locked, and then he settled in between the wall and me. He dragged his knuckles down the slope of my face and fingered the collar of his shirt on me. "Goodnight, Princess Rosalie of Avalon."

"Shut up."

Bastien sniggered. "'Night, Rosie." He touched the tips of my eyelashes as the lids swept shut. "Daisy. Roses have too many thorns. You're a daisy, if I ever saw one. No matter how angry you think your bite may be, I see the softness."

"Goodnight, Bastien. The snakes," I muttered sleepily.

"Remy got them all. Don't worry."

"Don't let the snakes get me."

"I've got you," he promised, kissing my cheek. "I won't let anything hurt you. From now on, if I'm around, you're safe."

It was a beautiful promise. A pretty vow that stayed with me when my breathing evened out as I lay on the straw mattress, surrounded by his arms and his piney scent. I cuddled into his side, closing my eyes as the gasoline I'd downed pulled me into a deep slumber.

27

MRS. ROBINSON'S NEW DRESS

*I*t was morning when I finally woke, though which day it was, I couldn't tell you. My leg had been redressed while I'd been out, but it was still pretty useless for actually standing on, and forget about walking. Instead of Bastien beside me in bed, Abraham Lincoln was snuggled up to me. I tried not to let him feel my slight dip of disappointment at not being able to keep any man other than Judah in my bed for a single night. "Hi, baby," I crooned to Abe, letting him lick my hand before he snuggled his face to my breasts.

Hamish made his presence known in the form of drowsy cursing if we didn't keep it down. He was on the far edge of the pillow, curled up with his tail tucked around him and under his chin, like a furry body pillow.

I couldn't quite get out of bed, so I sent Abraham Lincoln for Lane.

"Hi, baby," she said to me, making me smile. Her brown curls were in such disarray; I couldn't believe she hadn't been head-banging all night long. "You sleep well?" She was carrying a plate of eggs and fruit, which my stomach screamed for.

I didn't hold back, but shoveled bite after bite in my mouth as we spoke. "I'm not going to get used to the fact that all these years, you never slept. No wonder our house would always be clean when I got up."

"I've got my tricks," she joked, sighing contentedly as Reyn came into the room behind her and coiled his arm around her waist. "You hungry? Want to rinse off?"

"Can I seriously take a shower here?"

"More or less. They've got their ways of making running water. Especially at a healer's house. You're just not allowed to put any weight on your leg, so I'll have to help you. That cool?"

I nodded and scooted to the side of the bed on my own. Lane bent over to help me up, but Reyn stopped her. "Let me." Reyn scooped me up with his lean musculature, jostling my leg only the tiniest amount. I wasn't sure how I felt about Lane's boyfriend carrying me like a baby. I also wasn't sure how I felt about Lane having a boyfriend, but Reyn seemed like a nice enough guy. Lane had been without a man my whole life; I would never begrudge her this. It just took a little getting used to.

Reyn brought me into the bathroom and held me until Lane got the supplies situated. He lowered me slowly, letting me use him as an anchor until my good foot touched down on the floor.

The shower was difficult to get both of us inside with me in my bruised state, but the struggle was well worth the effort to get the sweat, blood and memories off me. I waited on the stool in the bathroom after we finished, toweling off as Lane dressed in what could only be described as a Renaissance fair dress. It was dark green with cupped sleeves topping the longer sashes that covered her arms. Her breasts were on display more than usual, and the gown that showed off her hourglass figure had a skirt that flowed down like an emerald waterfall of material, brushing across her sandaled toes.

"Whoa, dude. You look amazing. That looks crazy natural on you, yet still totally strange, because I've never seen anything like it on you before."

Lane smirked at me. "Thanks, babe."

The dress she slipped over my head was much the same style, but it was a dark pink – a color I rarely wore, due to it matching my name too closely. I didn't want to be the girl named Rosie who only wore rose colors. Too nursery rhyme-ish. I looked down and got a sizeable eyeful of my own cleavage, which I never displayed to the public. Even my sports bras were pretty modest, and I wore a jersey over those. "Um, yeah, I can't wear this. What happened to my jeans?"

"This is what the more affluent people look like here. We have to meet these new allies as ourselves. After that, we can wear peasant clothes. Much more low key. You'll like those better." She smoothed out her dress, and I could tell by the millions of emotions crossing her face that she didn't know how to feel about being in her hometown, wearing the clothes she'd worn before leaving with me. "I never thought I'd be back here."

I stood on one leg only and leaned on the wall. I brushed Lane's long, chocolate-colored hair with Remy's wooden comb that was missing a few teeth. "So, Reyn, eh? You two get into any trouble last night? Do we need to have *the talk*?" I teased her. She'd given me the same speech when I'd gone to prom, reasoning that even though she was my date, if any guy got the glad eye for me, I'd know how to handle myself. She struck a good balance between covering all the bases and giving me space to make a few choices on my own.

"Ha. Ha. Ha. No. Reyn's sweet, but he's a kid. He's practically your age. I'm enjoying it while it lasts, before he realizes how very different we are."

"Hello. *You're* not even your age. He's what, like thirty years old? That's hardly a kid."

"It's hardly thirty-eight."

"I can't even remember the last guy who made you look twice." I pulled her hair back and started braiding one long line in a plait down her back. "I think it's time you looked twice at this one. Reyn's a good guy. Come on. 'Here's to you, Mrs. Robinson,'" I teased, making her cringe.

"What about you and Bastien?" she asked, not so artfully changing the subject. "He's got a few smiles for you."

"Yeah. He's tricky. I'm waiting this one out to see if anything sticks. He's confusing."

"The funnest ones always are." Her smile faded. "Just be careful. He's been around several blocks, if you know what I mean."

A fist knocked slowly on the door. *"Princess Rosalie? We should probably get going if we're going to make it there before the others."*

"Huh? Get going where?"

Lane's head whipped from the door to me and back again before revelation shown on her face as she threw her head back. "Ah. Is that Remy? I don't think I'll ever get used to you being able to do that."

"To meet the Council. If you'll come on out, I'll redress your leg and we can be on our way."

"Sure, Remy. I'll be right out." Lane served as my crutch while I hobbled to a chair at the kitchen table.

Reyn was right there alongside her, lowering me down to the seat with his eyes on Lane the whole time. "You look... I thought you were beautiful as Lane Avalon, but now? Now you're a queen." He sunk down to his knees, and for a second I was scared he was going to propose or something. He clutched her hands, staring up at her as if she was the most incredible woman he'd ever laid eyes on. He was not wrong. Lane was made for the dress, not the other way around. She always knew what to do, what to say, and how to be.

Except this time. She bit her lower lip – our signature stress marker. Right then I saw the stark differences in our worlds. While Reyn needed only a few days to be completely convinced that Lane was the one for him, that kind of logic was completely lost on me. By the look of shock on Lane's face at Reyn's unabashed devotion, I could tell she was more from my world than his. He sensed her discomfort and stood, holding her hands between them as he faced her with unconcealed affection.

"Okay, okay, smooth operator," Lane smirked, trying to pass it all off as a light and breezy non-moment. "I think we should get going before you charm the pants offa me." She looked down and gasped at her dress. "Well, whataya know? It's already working. No pants."

Reyn gave her a look that was far too adult for my liking. Suddenly I went from third wheel to mother. I cleared my throat. "Alright, kids." I clapped my hands three times to reel them back before Reyn up and proposed prematurely, and consequently pushed her away. "Let's go see the Council or whatever. What am I supposed to be doing?"

Reyn turned to me, and surprisingly still had a friendly grin for me even after I'd cock-blocked him. "It's a meeting of the minds who are against Morgan le Fae. There's someone from every free province there. They need to meet you, talk with you so we can all agree what first priority is." He turned to Lane. "Do you want to lead the way, or shall I?"

"Reyn, I haven't wandered these woods in years. My last time was probably before you were born." Lane's levity died on her lips, her eyes closing at putting her foot in her mouth. She was the boot-in-the-mouth girl when she was nervous around a guy.

Reyn tilted his head to the side to size up Lane's nerves. Then a lazy look of complete and total chill swept over him when he realized she was more nervous around him than he was around the Lost Duchess of Avalon. He pulled her closer, ignoring me, Remy (who was packing a bag in the bedroom), Abraham Lincoln and Hamish as he touched his lips to hers, pulling out her lower lip so she wouldn't be able to bite it, now that it was in his mouth. He sucked on her lip as her eyes closed and her knees weakened.

I shooed the animals into the bedroom with Remy. I tried to hobble after them as best I could, but my leg wasn't seaworthy just yet. Remy ran to my side, intuiting my needs before I could admit to them. He scooped me up in his capable arms and shut me inside with himself and the animals. My hand flew over my mouth, and a giddy childish squeal birthed on my lips at Lane being so totally taken by the sweetest guy I'd met in a long time. I didn't care about the age gap. I only cared how the young'un was treating her, and so far all the flags were flying high.

"Do you think they'll stay here?" Remy asked, bringing a

halt to my party. He lowered me to sit on the bed so I didn't hurt my leg further.

"What do you mean? Like, in your house? I thought we were all going to the Council together."

"I meant in Faîte. Do you think they'll stay here in Avalon, or do you plan on going back to your world after you help us with ours?"

"Huh. I haven't really thought much about it. I didn't know it was an option to stay here. I don't think I know enough about your world to make that kind of decision."

Remy's thoughts were disjointed and scattered in fragments, so I tuned out and pulled Abraham Lincoln onto my lap, snuggling the teddy bear I would never get too old to cuddle. He stretched his back out and lifted his chin as he flopped over on my lap, offering up his full belly to me for a good scratch. I loved how much he trusted me, and vowed to protect him so he didn't have to worry about abandonment anymore.

I heard Bastien walk in on the two makeout buddies, apologizing left and right as he ducked into the bedroom with wide eyes. "Um, did you see that?" He wore a blue and green flannel with his jeans, and it looked like he'd showered and shaved since I'd last seen him. His dark brown hair was wind-tousled on top and stuck up in the back, giving the perfect model lumberjack of a man just enough of a visual flaw for him to appear like he wasn't photoshopped. He jerked his thumb over his shoulder, adjusting the full quiver that was slung on his back.

"They're making out!" His eyes fell on my dress before they widened. "Oh, I didn't realize you'd be wearing... But that makes sense. Reyn said he was taking care of your clothes, but I didn't... We're presenting you as yourself, so yeah. Wear that." He addressed my breasts, and then recalled how rude that was. "I almost didn't recognize you without that stupid t-shirt."

"Oh, you with the sexy talk. Shut up."

"That's, um, I..." He cleared his throat and tried to regain his hold on the conversation.

Remy sniggered in his mind. *"I've never seen Bastien the Bold tongue-tied before. Give him a fleet of soldiers, and he doesn't hesitate. But put him in front of a beautiful woman and he doesn't know his right foot from his left."*

"You ready?"

I swallowed a meek smile at Remy's compliment. No man had ever called me beautiful before. "As I'll ever be. But give them a couple more minutes. Lane hasn't been kissed in ages."

Bastien looked up at the ceiling, avoiding my eyes and the dress that was too tight around my bust. "Yeah, fine."

I crossed my arms over my chest to give myself a little modesty and heard Remy chuckle in his mind at our predicament. *"Ah, youth. Enjoy it while you can."*

28

CARRIED THROUGH THE WOODS

I was uncomfortable being so exposed in the dress. When Reyn offered to carry me, I politely declined, not wanting to shove my boobs in my aunt's boyfriend's face. "I'm fine. I can walk."

"No, you can't. The wound's not nearly healed, and your stitches are fresh. If you tear something? Princess Rosie, be sensible."

"Oh, hush. I'm fine."

Bastien stood at the door, his quiver slung over his shoulder and a look of determination on his face. "I can carry you there."

"I really, really, really don't think that's necessary. It's just a little sore, is all. Remy's just being overprotective." I shot Remy a look that told him to be cool, but he ignored me and shook his head at Bastien, vetoing my rule.

Reyn cast Bastien a look of concern. "I truly hope they receive her favorably."

"It'll be fine. Up you get, Daisy." Before I could consent, Bastien had me scooped up in his arms, making me feel more like a damsel than I was comfortable with. My leg jostled a little, making me hiss through my teeth at the sting. "You alright?"

I nodded through my gritted teeth. "Do it to it, Action Jackson Bastien."

"Huh?"

"Just go."

He hiked me up so my head was resting on his shoulder, with my arm wrapped around the nape of his neck to steady me. I held tight to him, feeling exposed on too many levels as he carried me over the threshold of Remy's home and out into the openness of nature. The birds overhead sang to me, letting me know Dahu sent them to watch over me and make sure I was granted safe passage. It was the sweetest thing.

Hamish ran in circles around us at warp speed, chittering his excitement at finally being able to interact with nature. Abraham Lincoln whined at Bastien's heels, wishing Bastien would put me down so he could give his daddy a bear hug and be carried.

Bastien backed up, clutching me with a snarl as he glared at the sky through the trees. "What's happening? This isn't normal. If Morgan bewitched the birds to follow you, we won't get far."

"Nah, they're alright. They're here for me. Dahu, the deer-unicorn in charge sent them." I reached out my hand, letting one of the smaller birds rest on my finger. I brought her up so she could address Bastien. She chirped and tilted her head to the side as she explained that Dahu was worried I wasn't being looked after. "See? She just said the same thing." I took my arm from around Bastien's neck and stroked her delicate brown spotted feathers, wondering if spots were to birds what freckles were to humans. "Sweetheart, could you go on ahead and scout out the path? And please have a few of you trail behind, if you don't mind. We need to make sure no one follows us. You're such a pretty little bird. Thanks for this, by the way. You guys are off the charts wonderful."

She chirped her agreement and flew off with her flock. Bastien frowned as he watched the birds split into three groups: one to go ahead of us, one to trail behind and one to fly overhead. "I don't like this," he muttered, his jaw tense.

I leaned my head on his shoulder, allowing myself to feel safe in his thick arms that I'm sure had never dropped a girl on her head. Pretty sure. I sighed heavily. "Oh, you know, I don't care." Then I took a chance and tilted my chin up so I could plant a kiss to the side of his neck. The seed of kindness and gratitude for him helping me while I had snake babies spilling out of my leg planted itself in his skin. He smelled of hard soap and Christmas trees. I wouldn't let him slip back into his surly I'm-a-tough-guy dramatics if I could help it. I nuzzled my nose to the side of his neck until I saw goosebumps break out on his skin. He tried to suppress a shiver, but I caught the cuteness.

"Knock it off," he groused quietly as he walked down the path from Remy's home toward the thick smattering of trees that lined the forest.

"Do you really want me to stop?"

"No," he admitted. "But I might drop you if you keep it up. That feels... Save it for the next time you get me in your bed."

The very adult turn the conversation took made me introvert afresh, but there was nowhere to hide. I was in the hot guy's arms, with no clue of what to do with him. "Okay," I said stupidly.

Remy was carrying a burlap sack on his back. *"How far is it to the council?"*

I asked his question for him, and Reyn responded. "It's pretty deep in the woods. It's on the border between Provinces 1 and 3. We'll be there before midday."

"No one's actually told me what we're walking into, you know. A little heads up goes a long way if you want me to perform like the princess monkey I'm supposed to be."

Reyn held his elbow out for Lane when he reached a tree with a complicated root system that jutted out into our path. She took his offer with a girlish tint to her cheeks that I rarely saw on her. Guys hit on her all the time at the gym where she was a personal trainer, but those passes barely registered with her. A simple touch from Reyn's hand, and she's as bashful as a schoolgirl. "We're going to a private tribunal of sorts," Reyn explained. "It's all unofficial and hidden from the army and Morgan le Fae's eyes and ears. It took us a long time to fish out the right spies, but there's someone from each province who'll meet with us where we're going. Think of them as the official and unofficial chiefs. Sure, the Daughters of Avalon rule the provinces, but not much of the day-to-day stuff goes down without these guys' say-so."

"Yikes. Then why'd you dress me up in this gown? Shouldn't I be in my jeans or in something that shows them we're not useless aristocracy?"

"I've got a change of clothes packed for both you and the Duchess."

"Remy's got your stuff, plus a few things for the road," Bastien confirmed.

"You're coming, too?" I asked Remy hopefully, glad our team was growing.

Abraham Lincoln was getting sidetracked watching the birds. He almost ran into a tree, but Hamish caught him in time.

Reyn replied, "We couldn't talk him out of it. Honestly, having a healer in our group wouldn't be a bad thing."

"The Duchess won't let me take the vow to be your Guardien, but that doesn't stop me from staying with you till the end. You can hear me. I haven't had a voice in years. Even if you didn't have so grand a quest placed on your shoulders, I would still follow you, no matter where you ended up."

I reached out and chucked Remy's shoulder, sharing a smile with him before holding onto Bastien's neck again. I pressed another kiss to the space between his jaw and his ear, my fingertips slowly tickling the unruly brown hairs at the base of his neck. Bastien tripped, but caught himself before we both toppled forward. The pain of my leg moving too much tore up the left side of my body. My arms wrapped tighter around his neck as I breathed through the sting. "You only have yourself to blame for that, you know," Bastien whispered to me.

"I know, I know."

"You keep that up, and you won't just get your first kiss. I'll take you behind one of those trees and let you do whatever your hands want to me. This dress should come off easily enough."

I wanted him. Maybe not the whole getting freaky behind the trees part just yet, but the kiss for sure. I watched his mouth as he carried me through the woods behind Lane and Reyn. His sculpted lips were tempting me, luring me in. I'm not sure if it was the whole surviving the snake babies thing or if it was our constant back and forth, but I began to sorely wish he wasn't engaged. I lifted my head, suddenly remembering that I was in another woman's fiancé's arms, toying with his neck and teasing him as if I could do anything about my crush.

But I couldn't, so I wouldn't.

It was as if Bastien could sense my daring warring with

my conscience. "Put your head back on my shoulder. I liked it there."

"I like it there, too," I admitted, indulging in the intimacy I'd spent my whole life without. I was finally the girl in the hot guy's arms. If only Judah could see me now.

We walked for a long time without speaking, instead listening to the birds overhead and trying not to overhear Lane and Reyn being cutesy with each other.

"I can't believe you raised her all by yourself in a foreign land. You're amazing."

Lane waved off his compliment. "Rosie was easy. It's the foreign land part that was hard at first. Adjusting to life without magic. Learning the law of the land. Trying to stay hidden long enough to get my bearings. It wasn't easy. We were homeless for a while, you know."

I swallowed hard, wishing our baggage wasn't being spilled out for Reyn, Remy and Bastien to dissect at will.

Lane continued, and as much as I wanted to, I couldn't begrudge her taking this one opportunity to vent. She'd been through a lot, more than I could've guessed with the whole having her feet in two different worlds thing. I mean, it's not like she could run off to a shrink and vent. "Rosie and I snuck into abandoned homes when we first came here. It was scary, and we had nothing. Absolutely nothing. For a while, I was terrified I'd taken the royal daughter and would have to watch her starve to death in my arms."

"Slow down," I whispered to Bastien. "Let's give them some space."

"Quiet. I'm trying to listen."

My fingers gripped the meat of his shoulders. "But I don't want you to listen! This is private. It's my childhood, and I don't want it spilled out for everyone to hear. Lane can vent to Reyn just fine, but you don't need to know this stuff."

"Daisy," Bastien said in a voice that was laced with pity. That stupid pity was the reason only Judah knew about my childhood.

I struggled against him. "Let me down. I can walk fine on my own."

"You know that's not true." He looked down at me with an unfathomable expression, as if trying to figure me out without having to dodge around all my obstacles. "Why don't you want me to know you?"

I slumped in his arms when it was clear he was stronger than me, and that I was being a donkey about the whole thing. "Because it's not pretty. It's not princess stuff. And it's private. You don't need to know my business. Would you want me poking into your childhood? You want to talk about your time in the army? You want to sit there and listen while someone tells the guy you... Just let me have a little privacy. It's my life, and you don't need to know about it."

I squirmed inside of myself with every sentence Lane divulged to Reyn, praying she wouldn't mention my low

GPA, the fact that I'd been suspended for fighting four times, expelled once, or that despite my best efforts, I still had a hard time reading above a kindergarten level. I really didn't want Bastien to know about the reading thing.

"You're a real pill," Bastien murmured under his breath. "If I'm going with you through Avalon, it doesn't hurt to know who I'm working with. Who I'm protecting."

I closed my eyes, listening to Lane confess all the things I hadn't had to think about. I hadn't had to find food for us. I'd been barely old enough to walk through the whole transition. I heard the passion in Lane's voice and knew that as mad as I wanted to be about the whole secret life thing, I couldn't hold against her all that she'd kept from me to ensure I had a childhood. We'd made it. It was because of her I was alive.

"Being homeless in Common isn't the same as it is in Avalon. You can just cut down a few trees and build yourself a hut to get you through. In Common? You have to have money first. Identities. It's a whole process that took me a while to figure out. It was worth it, though. My Rosie's in college. That's a big deal. Only really smart people get college degrees, and my girl's up there at the top with the best of them. She's going to get a degree and make something of herself. She'll have opportunities I never could've dreamed of at her age. So all in all, I call the whole thing a success."

"I think you're amazing." Reyn held back none of his

admiration, his hand atop hers that was wrapped around his elbow. "And no man ever caught your eye?"

Lane chuckled, blowing a raspberry. I could tell she was nervous. "Nah. I never had time for any of that. Being a mom was the best thing in the world, and I wasn't about to screw it up by gambling on the wrong guy. Besides, Rosie's abilities were harder to hide in the beginning. I didn't want to start something with a guy that was based on a lie. Didn't seem right."

"Strange that her magic stayed active when you went to Common. I wonder why that is."

Lane shrugged. "My theory is that it stayed in her because it wasn't just magic, it was her birth blessing. All the magic that wasn't part of her blessing faded away, but the Compass stuff and the talking to animals? That stayed. That's my guess, anyways."

I wanted to shove cotton in my ears to keep from hearing the theories and all the talk about me. I didn't need to be part of the conversation. The birds distracted me just in time. Two of them flew down and chirped that no one was around us for a long distance, and that we were safe for now. I cleared my throat. "Hey, the birds are saying there's no one around us for a good long while. We're not being followed."

Abraham Lincoln whined at the bird who'd garnered my attention, and Hamish harped on him to can the drama. Hamish was mesmerized by the forest. The trees were green from root to tip, and the bark had a sort of

310 | MARY E. TWOMEY

armor-looking scaly quality to it. The bark looked like an old person's skin, sagging off the trunk and wrinkling to show its true age. I wanted to touch the flaking off bits, but knew we couldn't stop for a nature exploration.

I felt terrible for Bastien, making him carry me for as long as we walked. It was way longer than I thought the hike would be, but Bastien didn't complain. When Remy asked (through me) if he could carry me so Bastien could have a break, my arms tightened around Bastien's neck. Bastien replied with a curt, "No. I brought her into Avalon. She's my responsibility. I'm fine."

After several hours of Lane and Reyn flirting, and me cuddling Bastien midair, the birds began to chirp to me that there were people up ahead. "Are we getting close to the Council? Because the birds are saying we're headed straight for a few people."

Bastien's arms were starting to shake, so he hiked me up. "Good. Shouldn't be too much farther."

Reyn dropped back next to us. "You know, Bastien's not really known for being under anyone's thumb."

"Your point?" Bastien groused.

Reyn cleared his throat and met Bastien's eyes. "It might help her make a good first impression if you were, you know, submissive for once," Reyn suggested to his bestie.

It was a thing of luck Bastien was carrying me. Otherwise, I think Reyn might have seen a far more violent reaction than a mere grimace. "Think again."

Reyn held up his hands. "Hey, I'm just thinking about how it'll look when you start arguing with her like you do in front of the others. They'll think they have license to talk back to her, too. We have to set a precedent."

Bastien's teeth ground together behind his lips. "It's your lucky day, Commoner. Enjoy this. It won't be happening again."

"Excellent," I said in my evil villain voice. "So if I ask you to dance for me?"

"Do you want me to drop you on your head? Because I'll do it."

Reyn groaned. "Oh, this is going to go swimmingly. I can already see the Council's respect for you going down the drain. Well, it was a nice idea while it lasted."

I leaned up and pressed a kiss to Bastien's cheek, holding the other side of his face so I could stroke his jaw and relax him. "I'll play nice," I promised. "Relax your butthole."

Reyn sniggered, but Lane did not. "You can't talk like that as a ruler, babe," she informed me. "It's my fault for not grooming you, but try to think proper British royalty, rather than palling around with Judah. The Queen of England probably doesn't say 'butthole'."

I frowned. "Now, how do you know that? I bet those royals say all sorts of saucy things behind closed doors."

Lane sighed. "They'll follow you if they think you can be the next ruler of Avalon. But if they can't respect you, they'll see you as a ruler they can manipulate and walk all over." She tapped the bottom of her chin. "So keep your posture straight, chin up, don't let them talk over you, and don't say things like 'butthole'."

"Well, there goes half my vocabulary."

Bastien looked morose, like he was carrying me to my doom. "This was a bad idea. We should've gotten Roland first."

I fiddled with his flannel shirt's collar. "I have to wait for the animals to tell me when they find the Cheval Mallet first. You guys are seriously overestimating my Compass skills."

Reyn led the way, making sure to secure Lane to his arm. I wasn't sure if it was so she looked like a proper lady with an escort, or if it was to ensure no other man tried his luck with her. Either way, she seemed happy on his arm, which was the only thing I cared about. "Tell me I still look the part," she said quietly to Reyn, her voice tinged with uncertainty. "Tell me I'm not the homeless teenager with a one-year-old."

Reyn stopped our procession and turned to face her. "You're a queen if ever I saw one. The first time I laid eyes on you, I knew I would follow wherever you led. The others will see it in you, too." His gaze was intense, as was the nature of their instant connection. He pulled her arms to loop around his neck, and his hands fell to her hips, luring her closer. He was gentle with her, his lips touching hers so delicately that I heard her whimper softly into his mouth.

I closed my eyes and buried my face in Bastien's neck to give Lane a little privacy. Bastien chuckled at my obvious squirm. "You're such a maiden," he whispered, teasing me.

"Is that like, slang for virgin? Because no kidding. I don't like the public love stuff."

"One day you will."

Though I wanted to argue, I took him at his word. "I'm nervous, Bastien," I admitted. "I'm not so great with new people."

"Stop fidgeting, and no one will know you're scared." He softened, resting the side of his chin to my forehead. "You'll be fine." He carried me forward toward the Council, who stood at attention when they saw Lane enter the clearing.

29

BAYARD THE BUTTHOLE

*B*eing an introvert is a tricky thing. You have tons of stuff you want to say, that might even be the right thing to say, but you find you can barely open your mouth to mutter a meager "hey, guys," without thinking it through ten times. It took me a while to open up, but we didn't have that kind of time. I had to fake it. I had to pull on my inner chatty Judah and summon the decorum of the Queen of England.

Or I could chicken out and play the Incredible Mute Rosie Avalon, which was nothing to sneeze at. I rock pretty hard at charades.

Bastien sensed me clamming up, so he slowly lowered my legs to the grass, leaving me his arm to lean on. He stood at attention by my side, and the stiffness of his hard body made me stand straighter. He was so casual with me, I forgot that he'd been the right hand of the captain of the

Queen's Army once upon a time. I wanted to drop his arm and run away from the new eyes that fell on me, but guessed that wouldn't be super appropriate. Plus, you know, I couldn't walk all that far on my own yet.

Reyn moved forward to address the ragtag group of prairie-run misfits, his voice more regal than I could make people believe I could be. It was clear he was the son of a public figure. "Thank you for meeting on such short notice. I trust our vow of secrecy will hold even after I introduce you to the newcomers Bastien and I have brought to you today. Allow me to introduce you to Elaine of Avalon, the Lost Duchess of the fallen Ninth Province."

There were several murmurs and gasps. It didn't take more than five seconds for everyone to get down on one knee, their heads bowed after getting a good eyeful of Lane. It was surreal to see Lane with her chin high and shoulders back, taking in the reverence with a "Yes, this is what you should do when I enter your presence" kind of noble and imperious air to her. Reyn left her side and moved back to stand between me and Remy, offering his arm to me, so I had Bastien and him to lean on.

"My Lady," began one of the four men, who was one of the hairiest dudes I'd ever seen. I mean, not quite Chewbacca level, but almost. His arms, legs, neck and chest were covered in dark brown hair that billowed out of his capri-length burlap pants and tunic shirt sleeves. "We've waited so long for you to come home. Your emerald. Is it safe? Did it survive with you, or does Morgan le Fae have it?"

"Wildman, what is your name?"

"Bayard, Duchess. Bayard of Province 3."

Lane nodded once in greeting. I'd never seen her look so regal. "And how is Province 3? Tell me what's come of your duchess since I've been gone."

Bayard was easily six feet tall, but he kept his head bowed respectfully. "Your sister, Duchess Gliten, was killed seven years ago in a battle between our land and Morgan le Fae's. Gliten's husband, Duke Ferdinand the Grave, rules what's left of our land in her place."

I knew Reyn had caught her up on which of her family members were alive still, but I could tell Bayard's phrasing hit her afresh. "Very well, Bayard. And to whom is your loyalty?"

I don't think I'd ever heard Lane say "whom" before. My palms began to sweat when I tried to picture myself being so proper. In my imagination, I said "who" when I was supposed to say "whom", and then went to go shake hands and slipped on a banana peel, throwing the hem of my dress over my head.

My imagination didn't like me so much.

Bayard looked up at Lane with steely resolve in his brown eyes. "My loyalty is to the people in Province 3. We've done whatever we can to survive, but it's not enough. If you could bring hope back to our land, I would serve you as my queen until my last breath."

Lane nodded once, looking every bit the ruler I knew she had in her when a teacher tried to fail me yet again.

"Very well. I'll see what I can do about locating my hidden gemstone. If your people will have me, I'll travel to Province 3 with it, staying there for a time until enough prosperity can be restored to your land. Then I'll move to the next province until we've all had a chance to heal a little."

"Thank you, your grace," Bayard said with a bow. "Avalon's been needing you."

Her eyes glinted dangerously as her tone sharpened. "I've heard rumors that neighboring provinces have been attacking the people in Morgan le Fae's land." I watched the mix of hairy men, and I'm guessing royals, exchange wary glances. "Her people are not to be targeted anymore. She doesn't care about them, only herself. Hurting them only brings death and destruction on innocent women and children. It doesn't do a thing to take her down. It doesn't unite Avalon against her. All it does is oppress her people, and trust me, they've suffered enough at her hands." She paused to look at each of them. "If you want my gemstone to visit your land, you'll see to it that the provinces stop attacking each other. Those who attack will see nothing but more death that they'll bring down on their own heads. They won't get a peek at my emerald." Her finality was inspiring. She was so in control, so regal. If only they could see her bumming around in her sweats with me, sticking fruit roll-ups to our noses to see whose would stay stuck the longest (mine).

Bayard took his time standing so he could tower over her, giving her the full scope of his broad, hairy shoulders and thick neck. He looked stern when you got past the initial willingness to play ball. His chest puffed, as if he'd been built to tear down aristocracies that didn't work. "You have no right to come in here after twenty-one years of knowing nothing about our struggles and tell us to lay down our swords. Province 1 is no victim. They eat well, their women get pregnant easily, and their land is booming. If they would give back the jewel they stole from us, we would have no reason to fight. Until then, we'll take from them what we can to feed our own."

Lane turned her head, as if she was finished discussing the matter. "Do what you like, but my rule won't change. The children of Province 1 didn't steal the jewel, nor can they give it back to you, but you're punishing them for Morgan's crimes. I won't bless lands who continue on like that." She stood back and addressed the group as a whole, no doubt sensing she couldn't keep reasoning with Bayard if he was stuck in his stubbornness. "Our plan is to get back my emerald to buy the provinces some time. Then I plan on finding Morgan's stolen jewels and giving them back to the kingdoms they came from."

Bayard scoffed, and I hated him a little bit. No one treated Lane like that. "You're promising something you can't deliver, Lost Duchess. Oh, how very lost you are. You don't think we've tried to find the jewels? You don't think we've searched and sacrificed with everything we have to get them? It's no use. She's hidden them so well, no one could find them if we tried for a hundred lifetimes. Your promises are pretty, but we've lost the use for pretty a long time ago."

There were three other men I didn't know. One was older, maybe mid-fifties, and graying at the temples. Another was maybe thirty years old, dressed in a mix between royal and military garb, and looked like he'd stepped off a runway with his lean and muscular body. He had perfect blond Ken-dolled hair and shiny teeth, but his blue eyes held a touch of kindness and sincerity.

The fourth dude in the circle had too much hair, like Bayard, but it was red instead of brown. The red fur guy had a pinched nose, looked about two inches shorter than me, and had a surly snarl on standby that he invoked when Bayard turned on Lane, happy to gang up on her. "I've got plenty of uses for pretty, but none of them's bossing me, I'll tell you that much." He sidled up next to Bayard and hitched up his burlap britches, spitting on the grass between himself and Lane.

I couldn't take it. Crossing the best woman in two worlds deserved a reckoning. I couldn't remember my introverted tendencies when I gripped the guys' arms to hobble forward. "Look, you arrogant jackfishes, if Lane says she can find the jewels, then you'd best believe she'll deliver. She's not a pretty little prom queen you can pat on the head and ignore. This is the best offer you've gotten in decades. I suggest you take your heads out of your hairy buttholes long enough to see the miracle standing right in front of you."

Crap, I said butthole already.

The group was quiet, but I heard Remy worrying they'd retaliate with physical violence for my mouth. Reyn closed his eyes and took a deep breath that told me I'd said the very wrong thing the first time I'd opened my mouth.

Bastien wasn't nervous. His mouth curved slowly into a knowing smile, as if he enjoyed watching me invite the throwdown. "I'd listen to her, guys."

Bayard postured, snarling at me in a way that should've made me cower. "Handmaidens don't get a vote here. Don't make me shut your mouth, little one."

Instead of backing down, I dropped the guys' arms, leaned on my good leg and motioned to Bayard to come and friggin' get it. "Bring it, you belligerent prick. Lane's too nice to take you down, but I'm not." Then I jabbed my finger to the shorter furry guy with red hair. "And you! Insult Lane again, and you don't want to know what!"

Bayard narrowed his eyes at me, deciding whether to fight me or laugh me off. Dude didn't understand that I was no joke. He threw out his hands. "Duchess, control your lady's maid. I appreciate her loyalty to you, but her mouth would be better appreciated if she were on her knees." He let out a crass laugh at the pervy joke. The redhead joined in while Bayard let loose a few pelvic thrusts to illustrate his filthy point. It was then I realized that both the Wildmen had horse tails that matched their respective fur color. Like, actual horse tails that swished out when they did pornographic pelvic thrusts.

The other two men did not laugh. I mean, Bayard had to have been like, forty-five. You'd think after a certain amount of time that people grow up out of the frat house.

"Rousseau, I think I've found someone feisty enough to warm your bed, old friend," Bayard teased, elbowing the redhead.

Rousseau hiked his burlap britches up again, and waved his arm to dismiss me. "Nah. You know I don't like the ones who talk back."

"Sex jokes? Really? Really?!" I made to take a step forward, my fists up to show him what I thought of his off-brand of humor, but Bastien whooshed past me in a breath.

"Say it again," Bastien dared, his retractable knife drawn and pressed to the coarse curly brown hairs at Bayard's neck. "Tell the Lost Daughter of Avalon just how you like it."

Beneath his inch-long beard, Bayard paled as his mouth fell open. "The what? That's not... Bastien, explain yourself!"

Reyn postured beside me. "Allow me to introduce you to Princess Rosalie – the Lost Princess of Avalon." The two men I hadn't spoken to yet gasped and went down on their knees, bowing to me like I'd done something impressive.

Bastien spoke through gritted teeth. "Only you all know that Reyn and I left Avalon to find the Compass last year. Well, we did. We found her. Now if you'll keep your manners, I'll let you keep your life." It was clear Bastien was the most feared of the group. Bayard held up his hands, but Bastien wasn't satisfied. "On your knees. Isn't that how you wanted her?" He shoved Bayard to the ground with a sneer.

Reyn helped me hobble forward next to Lane. The men were in a row before us, each one on his knee in fear at what they'd just been caught laughing at, or doing nothing to stop.

"Bastien!" Reyn barked. "Put down your knife. The rule that we don't draw swords against each other still holds true, no matter how much one might deserve a good neck shave." His eyes glinted dangerously at Bayard, whose head was bowed.

Bastien tucked his knife away into his belt, but crossed his arms over his broad chest to remain firm that I would not be the joke in this group. His anger was clear as he set down the new law. "We didn't have to show you the Compass. We didn't have to bring her here and tell you a single thing. We could've gone hunting for the Jewels of Good Fortune on our own and brought them back with none of you the wiser. We brought her to you to see if you wanted to help, to see if you wanted in on the biggest heist in our history. I bring you two women, and this is how you are?" His hand flew out in aggravation. "Rosie's a maiden! You don't joke like that in front of the Lost Princess."

I harrumphed, embarrassed. "Would you knock it off? My virginity isn't a marketing point. It's private," I scolded Bastien.

He huffed at me. "Well, do you want me to let them make jokes like that about you? You want me to just sit back and do nothing while he acts out a full-on..." He stopped short, lips sealed to keep from letting the fight escalate. His caramel eyes looked down at me with a steely desire to protect all that I was. Though he didn't get it perfect, the loyalty was there.

I placed my hand on Bastien's arm and bumped my cheekbone to his shoulder. "Thanks. I get it." I watched him nod, losing none of the fire in him that held us in the unspeakable moment where he declared that he was on my team, and I didn't kick him to the benches.

Lane cleared her throat, bringing me back to the problem at hand. "Right. So yeah, I'm Rosie Avalon, or the Lost Daughter of Avalon or the Compass or whatever. I only just learned about this world and Morgan and all of it like, a week ago. So if I get something wrong, be cool about it."

Lane stepped in, sensing I was going down too casual a road to be respected by them. She probably wasn't wrong. "On King Urien's orders before he got too sick to speak for himself, he begged me to take Rosie to Common, where Morgan wouldn't look for her. I raised her as my daughter for the last twenty-one years, and only came back because Morgan sent spies who tried to abduct Rosie. Apparently, Morgan's desperate for the last stones, and she needs the Compass to find them. Now, Rosie doesn't have a firm handle on her abilities, but she's willing to work on them to help us find Morgan le Fae's jewels and return them to their rightful owners."

"Forgive me, Duchess," Bayard begged, his head bowed to address Lane's shoes. "If you spare my head, I'll give you my sword. I'll follow wherever the Compass leads and help make her footsteps safe."

Several similar promises popped up among the ranks. Lane drew out the tension in the group until I saw sweat running down Bayard's nose. Finally she reached forward and tilted up his chin, meeting his wide eyes with a glare that made me flinch. "I raised Rosie. She's *my* daughter, and you'll treat her with respect due to the new throne. When we take Morgan down, you'll remember this day that you spoke to your duchess like I was a Commoner. You'll remember the day you were a scoundrel to your princess. You'll remember, and so will I." She released his chin, and I saw that even though he could overpower her, he submitted. He knew his life was in her hands – hands that had spent many a night sewing my game jerseys after I'd torn them. Hands that had braided my hair, washed dishes, taken out the trash, and done so much that a duchess should never have to do. "For now, you can serve your princess with your sword. We need all the help we can get."

She stepped back as Bayard let out a loud gust of relief. The men all stood, shoulders back and a readiness painting their features. Bayard was eager to redeem himself. "How can I serve you, Duchess?"

30

LEGIT LANCELOT

*T*he men stood like they were readying for battle, each one with his shoulders squared and hands ghosting over their weapons out of habit. "First things first," Lane ordered the group. "Abraham Lincoln? Come on out, love."

Hamish and Abraham Lincoln bounded out from their hiding place, Hamish yelling angrily while Abraham Lincoln begged me to pick him up with a pathetic whine. "I can't pick you up, baby. I can barely stand." I leaned heavily on Reyn and Bastien as Lane explained my whole talking to animals and the healers thing.

Remy clicked his fingers to gain the attention of Bastien, miming that I needed to sit down before my stitches tore. "Here. You did good, Daisy. Take a load off." Bastien lowered me to the grass, waving off the men's concern when my bear cub climbed into my lap.

The dashing Ken doll guy wandered off and came back a minute later with a thick stump he rolled onto its side in front of me. "Lady Rosalie, I'm Duke Lancelot of the Fifth Province. I can't let you sit in the dirt like a peasant. Please, allow me." He wasn't one of the hairy ones, but had sun-kissed skin and a charming smile. I remembered he was one of the two who didn't laugh at Bayard's crude joke.

I blinked up at him in confusion. "Your name is Lancelot? Like, legit Lancelot?" I handed Abraham Lincoln to Bastien, who gave the others a boastful grin at being able to hold a bear like it was nothing.

Lancelot had a clean-shaven face and a kind smile that matched the sincerity in his eyes. "Well, I actually go by Lot, but since we're being well-mannered with a princess and the Lost Duchess being present, I thought I'd be my most formal."

"Lancelot is an impressive name where I'm from."

"Really? It's not all that uncommon here. Easy now." Reyn and Lot each took one of my arms and lifted me, lowering me gently to the stump. When Reyn explained my injury, a few of the guys winced. "You shouldn't be out of bed," Lot said by way of a warning.

"It's fine," I lied, trying not to be the kid in a dress in the middle of seasoned warriors. "Just a little sore to stand on."

Lot softened as he watched me muscle through the jostle when Bastien placed Abraham Lincoln back in my arms. Abraham Lincoln was such a mama's boy, and I loved it. Lot frowned down at me. "You're in pain. What's your healer done to help with that?"

Remy explained the different herbs, and I relayed the message, blowing their minds when they realized I was speaking on behalf of Remy. The men drew closer, standing as near as their fear of my teddy bear would allow them.

Rousseau had his red hairy hand on the hilt of his sword. "Is it magic? Can you teach us how to control the beasts of the forest?"

"She doesn't own me!" Hamish gave Rousseau a piece of his mind, running in between us and waving his fists in the air at the notion that wild things could be controlled.

"I don't manipulate them," I explained on Hamish's behalf. "I only talk to them. Big difference. You try controlling another person, and you'll have a revolt on your hands. Same thing with animals. They sometimes do me favors because I listen when they talk. That's all anyone really wants most days – someone who hears them."

Lot was closest and knelt at my feet, only a few inches from me. His white dress shirt was fitted to showcase his lean but obvious muscles, and his beige pants didn't have a stain or a crease on them. "Your majesty, I've never seen a bear so civilized. How do you keep him from tearing at you?"

I shrugged. "His mom died when one of the provinces poisoned the Mousseuse River – I'm guessing Province 3?" I raised my eyebrow to Bayard, whose neck shrunk at the unwelcome attention. "His mom died when they tried to cross over into another province, passing by Morgan's soldiers. He was all alone when I found him. He thinks I'm his mommy." I addressed the group as a whole. "So whoever's poisoning Province 1? Knock it off. You're killing the unicorn-deer babies, and you murdered Abraham Lincoln's mother."

"Unicorn-deer?" the older man inquired. Of all the men, he looked the most distinguished. His shoulder-length black hair made room for a few streaks of gray, which only made him more striking in that well-bred nobility kind of way. I don't know how guys could get older and go gray and look just as handsome as the young guys, but he rocked the George Clooney bracket. He pressed his hand to his chest. "I'm Henri, your grace. I'm Duke of Province 2. At your service, however you'll have me." He said "Henri" like a true Frenchmen, letting me know a casual "Henry" wasn't within his vocabulary. Everything he did looked grand and purposeful. Just the sound of his regal-speak made me sit up straighter. He watched me with calculating interest, though I couldn't get a good read on him. His green eyes would catch mine, and then his gaze would flit to Lane. The way he regarded Lane was civil and proper, but there was something deeper buried there. Lane's eyes had the air of forced calm, while Henri looked like he wanted to say something to her, but he never did.

"Um, thanks. Yeah, the deer with the unicorn horn sticking out of their foreheads."

Bastien looked as if my incompetence pained him. "It's called a *cerf*."

"Oh, whatever. The *cerf* fawns are dying, so quit poisoning the river, whoever's doing it. Hurting animals for no reason? It's like, the quickest way to get on the universe's kick-me-in-the-teeth list."

Bayard dipped his head toward me, playing the role of the humble servant so Lane didn't off-with-his-head him. "That was my men. I'll have them stop immediately. Give me a day, and the water will be back to normal."

I nodded to him, taking in his stiff demeanor. Though he really did seem like he was willing to play ball, I could sense a grudge in him, some sort of deep-rooted frustration. "Thank you."

Lot was entranced, playing chicken with his daring as he watched my bear with eyes that were filled with trepidation. "I've only ever fought with bears. I've never seen them so tame with a person before. Do you think he'd let me touch him?"

"I dunno. If he bites your hand off, then probably not. Let's try and see." I grinned at Lot's horrified expression. "Just kidding. Abraham Lincoln's cool. Here." I reached out slowly with my free hand and picked up Lot's sturdy wrist. He was magazine level model of handsome, so I knew my cheeks were pink when I made contact. I kept my eyes from his features so I didn't turn into a mouse just yet. I felt his pulse quicken as I moved his hand to the scruff of Abraham Lincoln's neck. My fingers tangled through Lot's

330 | MARY E. TWOMEY

as I showed him how to pet my puppy without incurring unnecessary wrath. "Be real gentle," I warned when I felt Abraham Lincoln stiffen. My nerves didn't translate to animals. In fact, when I was most uncomfortable around people, I was most talkative with them. "It's okay, baby. Lot won't hurt you. He just thinks you're the most beautiful thing he's ever seen. Can't fault him for that." I kissed his muzzle while Lot stroked his back, marveling at the beast who was not such a beast after all. My bear rested his head over my breasts and sighed like a baby. I really was becoming his mother. I'd been missing Wilbur and Penelope, who now had no one to tell them stories about dashing pirates. Abraham Lincoln was a good suture to that painful cut.

Lot drew closer, and I could feel his breath on my cheek. I kept my eyes downward, unable to look up at him if my life depended on it. "This is incredible. Is he coming with us on the journey?"

Bastien cleared his throat, calling the meeting back into focus with Hamish on his shoulder, standing at attention. "We'll need to find Roland first. He represents Province 4, so we move forward with him."

Bayard scratched a patch of thick chestnut hair above his elbow. "Bastien, we loved Roland as much as you did, but he's gone. The Cheval Mallet took him right after it took Duchess Avril."

Lane's mouth tightened at mention of her sister being cooped up in the Forgotten Forest. My spirits lifted at the fact that I had a cousin to find, and now an aunt. My family was growing larger, and I couldn't wait to get to them.

Bastien postured as he stood next to the stump I was still seated on. "Rosie can talk to animals. Plus, she's the Compass. I think between those two things, she can find Roland for us."

Lane's voice was quiet, but still drew the attention of everyone there. "We need the Cheval Mallet because before I left, I went to Master Kerdik to give him back my emerald." She ignored the gasps and pressed on with her story. "Master Kerdik didn't receive many apart from the nine Daughters of Avalon back then, and Reyn tells me he hasn't been seen much in the last couple decades. I told Master Kerdik to take back all the stones, that they were causing more harm than the good he meant for them to do. He wouldn't do it. He said we had to surrender the stones willingly. So I did." She tucked a lock of hair behind her ear. "So did Gliten and Heloise." Then to me she explained, "My sisters who ruled Provinces Three and Four."

Everyone was in an uproar at this. The quiet calm I'd tried to instill in the group was gone. The men were on their feet, shouting above each other to make sure Lane knew just how super pissed they all were. Even Reyn and Bastien were shocked, though they didn't yell at her.

It took a while for Lane to rein them all in, but finally she was permitted the space to continue. "Master Kerdik said he'd keep our stones safe from Morgan le Fae. He'd make sure they stayed hidden until it was time. I didn't know what he meant by that, but he said I'd know when and how to find them if I ever needed them back. Then he summoned the Cheval Mallet, put them in a pouch and tied them to his flank. I never saw them again." She turned to me, and as one, the others craned their necks in my direction. "Now that Rosie and I have come back, I'm guessing this is the time he was talking about."

I raised my hand. "Can anyone give me a rundown of who still has their jewels, whose gems were stolen by Morgan, and which ones were sent off on the Cheval Mallet?"

Duke Lot inclined his head to me humbly. "Of course, your majesty. Morgan le Fae has her own jewel from Master Kerdik, plus she's stolen or cajoled the jewels from Provinces 2, 6, 7 and it's rumored she also has the jewel from Province 8, as well. So that means Morgan has five jewels in total. She's acquired most of those provinces as her own, and they live with the bounty those jewels provide. Since Duke Henri surrendered his gem willingly, he was able to keep Province 2 as his own. Since Provinces 2 and 3 border Province 1, they share in a portion of the bounty, though they are not without problems."

I frowned. "So then that leaves the jewels from Provinces 3, 4, 5 and 9 that are lost."

Lot spoke up. "Actually, I rule Province 5 in my late mother's stead, and we still stand with our jewel safely hidden." He said it without unfounded pride or aggression he wished to lord over the others. He was simply stating the facts, and even had the grace to lower his chin as he did so. Dude was classy, that's for sure.

I tried to keep track of it all. "Okay, then that leaves three lost jewels, is that right?"

Lane's chin rose. "Not quite so lost, actually. My Rosie is how we'll find the three missing stones, and help rebuild Avalon."

I wanted to hide from the unrealistic expectation that I knew anything about finding horses or jewels or any of it, so I buried my face in Abraham Lincoln's fur. At least when I was "Remedial Rosie" no one looked at me like I was the answer to worldwide devastation. They assumed I was too stupid to answer even the most basic of questions, so lofty things like world peace weren't even presented to me.

"Mama, it's okay. I love you," my bear cooed. Abraham Lincoln's belief that love would conquer all was a sweet reminder that maybe it could, if I simply learned to let it. Lane loved me, thus we survived being homeless in a new world. I don't know when I stopped putting so much faith in the simple things, but I vowed to be a little more like Abraham Lincoln, and let love drive a few more of my doubts away.

31

BARE LEGS AND BLOOD RACING

*B*ayard began running his mouth that I knew couldn't stay tamed for more than a few minutes, but I didn't pay attention. Birds started flying toward me, calling my name with a warning that chilled my bones. *"Princess! The Army! The Queen's Army is coming! They're looking for Reyn! They've been ordered to kill him if he won't come in. Run!"*

I blurted out the message the birds gave me, interrupting Bayard and ignoring his indignation at my rudeness. "Go! You all have to run. Who can hide Reyn?"

"I won't run. They can ask me whatever they like." Reyn stood tall, but he looked more stubborn than capable of putting up a good fight against an army's brutal interrogation tactics.

I shook my head. "Look, the birds aren't giving me the

impression that the soldiers will take playing dumb for an answer. Your name was on that roster," I reminded him.

Bastien hung his head. "Whose province is closest? Who can hide him?"

"I won't hide! I'm here with you all as an equal. Would any of you hide? I represent Province 2 with Duke Henri in this tribunal, and I won't cower like a dog!"

Duke Henri jerked his thumb over his shoulder. "My castle is closest. Everyone can camp with me until the army passes by. We'll leave to hunt for the Cheval Mallet as soon as we're packed for the journey."

"How far behind us are they?" Bastien asked as he took Abraham Lincoln from my arms and handed him to Lane. The men all protested at the duchess being too near the wild animal, but there just wasn't time for a lengthy conversation about it.

A bird landed on my knee and then hopped off when Lot and Bastien each grabbed one of my arms to help me up. She chirped that they were just now entering the woods, but they were instructed not to stop until they found Reyn and brought him in to pay for his crimes.

"They're just getting into the woods, but they don't want Reyn for questioning. They've already made up their minds that they're going to punish him."

"But I didn't kill Captain Burke! I'll be given a fair trial."

"By your own father?" Rousseau scoffed. "No one

would believe he could give his only son a fair trial. You'll be hanged for certain."

Bastien hung his head as I leaned on Lot's arm. "They know it was me. They know I did it, but they can't hang me because I'm Untouchable. So they're going after Reyn to get at me." This brought out several deferential gasps that Bastien had taken down the hook-nosed, pancake make-upped bad guy. "They know hanging you would absolutely destroy me, Reyn." He nodded to Henri. "Running is our best option. I won't see Reyn hanged for something I did."

"It's something I should've done," Reyn postured with defiance, his chest puffing out and a sneer coming to his lips, which were better put to use smiling. "For what Burke did to you? Brother, I should've gutted him ages ago. For what he did to my sister?" He shook his head. "I've murdered him too many times to count in my mind."

Bastien shook his head. "Enough. We run to Duke Henri's Castle, and leave from there after we've packed. They kill you, and there's nothing left for me, Reyn. I'm serious. I can't watch that go down."

Reyn cast aside his bravado and threw his arms around Bastien, gripping him tight, even though Bastien didn't hug him back. Reyn took no offense, but seemed to under-stand that there were some things his BFF was simply not capable of doing in public. "Then we'll run together, brother."

"Together," Bastien confirmed.

Lot led me toward his horse. It was white with gray

spots on the rump that were totally gorgeous. "Wise choice, old friend. Come. We have horses enough to each take one of you with us. Princess, come with me."

It wasn't often I saw panic well up in Bastien, but that's exactly what choked his words when they squeezed out of him. It wasn't belligerence, but actual fear. "No! We searched too long for them. I won't let her ride off on some guy's horse."

"'Some guy?'" Duke Henri postured, as did the others. "You brought them here to meet us. Surely you trusted us enough for that. Remember the vow we all took, Bastien. We swore to take down Morgan le Fae and restore our lands. If one of us runs off with the duchess or the princess, that can't happen." He looked sharply around at the others. "Agreed?"

Bastien still looked torn, but swallowed hard as he nodded. "I know." The others muttered their consent that we would ride together, and Bastien's shoulders began to relax a little. "Okay. Lane, you go with Henri. His horse is the fastest." I noticed he chose the oldest man who hadn't been pervy toward her.

"I can *lancer* her," Rousseau offered. While I didn't know what "lancer" meant, Bastien and Reyn were very much opposed to it.

"*Lancer* Remy instead," Bastien ordered, casting a look of gratitude to Remy, who didn't put up a fight.

Reyn turned to me and explained, "Rousseau and Bayard are Wildmen. They can be in one place and transport themselves to another in a matter of a few blinks. *Lancering* someone is taking them with you when you go."

Reyn and Duke Henri helped Lane up on the horse that looked well-groomed, like his master. She looked like she was trying on a pair of old shoes that she couldn't believe still fit her after all these years. "Just like riding a bike. I'm a little rusty, though." Henri pulled himself up behind her with the agility of a man who was used to bridling his own horse. He carefully wrapped his arms on either side of her and lifted the reins with a silent nod of solidarity to Bastien. I caught the stiffness in Lane's spine and guessed that for whatever reason, she knew Henri, and hated his guts.

Remy moved to Rousseau, gripping his hand and giving me an encouraging smile that promised all would be fine. Reyn moved to Rousseau's other side and picked up the furry red hand, catching Lane's eye with an adoring look that told her he would see her again in a matter of minutes.

Rousseau farted loudly, and then started to grumble. "Sure, sure. I can take the hit. It don't cost me a whole load of extra magic ta *lancer* two men. No, I'm fine."

"I can lancer the Lost Princess, if you don't want her on a horse," Bayard offered.

When Bayard waved me forward, both of us were hesitant, but Bastien was more direct with his feelings. "Not in this lifetime. I won't be parted from Rosie. We searched too long, and trust you all as I do, I just can't."

He slapped his flat stomach. "It's a gut thing. I'll just carry her."

I was leaning on Lot's arm, but I reached over and held Bastien's hand with my free one to calm his fears. I usually had pretty good d-bag radar, and trusted Lot to get me where we needed to go. "It's alright. It'll just be for a little bit. And we're all riding together, right? It's totally cool." The birds started screaming that dozens of the two-headed pit bull dogs were running ahead of the army. "You can't outrun the dogs that are on their way here, especially not carrying me. We have to go on horse. I can reason with some of them, but dozens? They'll bark to their masters before I even have the chance to calm them down."

Lot's fair eyebrows furrowed together. "Be reasonable, Bastien. Even if you can outrun the army, you'll be useless when you reach Duke Henri's castle. We might have to leave as soon as we get there, and we can't have you using up all your energy on this." He clapped Bastien hard on the shoulder, and then grabbed the reins of his horse. "Here, I'll saddle up with Bayard. Take her on my horse. Does that make things easier?"

Bastien gusted out so much relief, I hadn't realized he was that apprehensive about the whole thing. I felt bad for the guy, knowing how much he held inside like a temperamental volcano. "Yes. Infinitely better. Thanks, man." He dropped my arm and engulfed Lot in a two-fisted handshake that was reserved for someone who had just saved him from an ulcer. He pulled away and turned to me, his gaze determined but no longer overly worried. "Alright, Rosie. Up you get."

I'd seen people riding horses in movies, but being next to one for the first time was a little intimidating. The horses were far bigger than they looked on TV. The seat was as tall as my head. "I, um, you're going to have to help me. I've never ridden a horse before."

"*I can carry you to Duke Henri's castle without guidance,*" the horse assured me.

"Well, that's a good thing, but I'm just not sure how to get up on you. My leg is busted."

The horse whinnied, startling me. "*I can help with that. For the* Voix, *I can do anything.*"

I leaned my forehead to his neck in thanks.

Lot and Bastien each took one of my hands to hoist me up, but before they could, the horse's legs folded underneath him and he sat down in the grass. Lot was beside himself, thinking his horse was dying or something. "Marquis! What's wrong, old friend?"

I hobbled next to Marquis and rubbed his flank. "He's fine. He's sitting down so I can get on him without hurting my leg. Help a girl out?"

Bastien was more used to my animal-speak than Lot was. He was careful as he lowered me and set me atop Marquis' white back. I knew it was probably more appropriate to ride sidesaddle, but I felt like I might fall off that way. I hiked up my dress to my thighs so I could sit more comfortably. Lane caught my lack of decorum and sighed,

"Thank goodness. I hate sidesaddle. If I can ride like normal, I can hold Abraham Lincoln." She sat up in the stirrups and wrapped her other leg on the side of the horse so she could ride more securely.

Henri kept his eyes straight ahead, though I could tell he was disapproving of the scandal that were her toned, bare legs. He cleared his throat. "We meet at my son's stables, not at the main castle. No one bothers him there."

"Your son? Which one?" Lane asked, and I thought I detected a note of hope in her voice.

"I have only one son," Henri ruled, his tone firm and final, leaving no room for kindness or questions. "Damond can be trusted with a secret like this."

Seeing a bear atop a horse was, I'll admit, pretty funny. Abraham Lincoln snuggled his aunt while Hamish scurried up to ride in his bear friend's lap, knowing Abraham Lincoln would give him the best seat in the house. "I hate you so much," she growled to Henri, who looked like he couldn't have cared less, and was glad to have the true feelings out of the bag. "Let's go, guys," Lane insisted. At that, Rousseau farted loudly and vanished with Reyn and Remy both scrunching their noses.

Bastien waited for Marquis to stand before getting on behind me. His arms wrapped around my sides, caging me in so I didn't fall from my perch. One hand gripped the reins while the other clutched my stomach, causing me to sit up straighter. "Lean against me," he instructed, while Lot mounted with Bayard and we started out at a trot toward the east. I tried to recline against Bastien, but I was too nervous. The jostle of the horse didn't feel natural to me, so my body was stiff against the jerky motion.

"I feel like I'm going to either fall off or go flying forward! I've never ridden a horse before." Every jolt of the horse pained my leg, which made it doubly hard to relax.

Bastien pressed his hand more firmly to my stomach, pulling me tight to his chest. "I've got you," he whispered like a promise I needed to hear. "If you loosen up a bit, you'll move when my body does, and we'll be riding the horse like one person. It'll feel easier that way." The others started galloping, but Bastien knew I wasn't ready for that. My body was rigid and my nerves were at the crest of what they were capable of dealing with. It may not seem like riding a horse would be too much, and really it wasn't, but it was on the cusp. Marquis kept up a steady stream of encouragement, but the movement still felt unnatural to me.

Suddenly Bastien's hand on my stomach climbed up toward my ribs, tracing slowly back and forth under my breasts. His voice came out low and seductive, making my eyes flutter. "I won't let you fall, Daisy. Trust me." When the others were far enough ahead, he bent his head down and kissed my shoulder, then moved his ticklish breath further in toward my neck, dragging his lips upward towards my ear where he whispered, "Your bare legs are driving me crazy." He reached down and cupped my unin-jured calf, moving his hand slowly up to the underside of my thigh, indulging in my gasp. "No doubt that's the first female leg some of those guys have seen in a few years. What a grand unveiling it was."

"Bastien, we can't. You're engaged to Reyn's sister," I said, but my protest was weak.

"Close your eyes."

They were already on their way to shutting with every pass of Bastien's thumb under my thigh. My hand reached behind me to tangle my fingers in his hair, pulling his head forward so I could feel his breath on my skin. Without warning, he snapped the reins, leaning us forward as Marquis began to gallop through the woods. A scream stuck in my throat as the trees whipped by us, narrowly missing our legs and heads. "Bastien, this is too fast!" A thrill went up my spine at the adventure of it all. The danger pressing in around us as Marquis picked up his speed fueled something primal in me you just couldn't tap into in the steel cage of a car. The wind whipped at my face and streaked through my hair, making me feel alive in my fear. Alive was such a beautiful place to be.

Bastien held me tighter, kissing the back of my neck. "Tell me you're not excited right now. Tell me part of you isn't loving this." He snapped the reins again, and we went impossibly faster, with Bastien leaning me forward so my front was almost laying on Marquis. "Tell me my world doesn't make your blood race." I could feel Bastien's heart pounding in time with Marquis' gallop as he gripped me, keeping me safe on the edge of danger.

32

NOT KISS AND NOT NICE

I expected the stable we were to meet at might be the size of a small barn with two or three stalls in it. What greeted me was a sixteen-stall two-story building that looked immaculately kept. Though the homes we passed along the way were mostly simple one-room huts, there were welcome mats laid out on the entrance and cheery paint colors that made everything look new and spring-ish. The air smelled crisp, like it was right about time for nature to do its thing and bloom like crazy, but aside from the forest, a few sad looking orchards and the occasional bush, there wasn't much nature to speak of. The crisp smell came from the air that blew a little too hard, even after Marquis came to a stop inside the massive barn.

I was trembling on the horse, one hand locked on Bastien's wrist and the other gripping the bridle like I might fly totally off the planet if I let go of it. We were the last to arrive, and the others were each in their pockets of conversation as they decided how best to proceed from here.

Reyn reached up his arms to help me down, but I shook my head so quick, I wasn't sure he saw it. "Come on down, Rosie. I'll help you."

Bastien gently pried my nails from his wrist, hissing at the sting. "I told you we'd be okay, and would you look at that? We're here just fine. Now go on down to Reyn." He dismounted off the horse like it was nothing, his head level with my hips now.

I shook my head too quick again, and couldn't unclench my jaw to get any words out. The gentle understanding in Reyn's eyes let me know I was acting like a baby. For all the sports I'd done, I'd been in total control of my body the entire time. Being on a horse had been a surrender of power I couldn't justify, even after we were parked.

Lot broke away from his conversation with Henri and Bayard. "Here. Marquis is a bit taller than your average field horse. I'm sorry, Princess. Let me help you." Before I could decide whether or not I was ready, Lot grabbed the reins and led Marquis toward the back of the stable. It was a slow walk, but even that spooked me. "Here, you can get used to him now without all the running through the woods." He clipped a feedbag onto Marquis' muzzle after taking out the bit. Lot rubbed his flank with steady, strong hands. I could hear Marquis' gratuitous moaning over the food that he loved because it never changed, no matter the province. Those thoughts were interrupted only by the occasional affection for his owner. Lot looked up at me, his short windswept blond hair falling back from his face. "You let me know when you're ready to get down." He kept up the steady stream of physical assurances to Marquis to let him know that he loved him, and not to move too much so he didn't spook me. It was considerate of him, and I appreciated the kid gloves when I'd been thrown into a world that was so unlike my own.

Bastien strode up to us to check on me. "You're being a baby, you know. Everyone here grew up riding. You're going to look weak to the Wildmen if you don't calm down."

Lot cast Bastien a look of dismay, but I was past mere looks. Of course Bastien would be the thing to loosen my tongue and send the daggers flying. "Am I crying? Am I throwing a giant hissy fit? No. So leave me alone about it. That was my first time on a horse, you know. Most people learn at a walk, not whipping through the woods with an army behind them! I don't like being off the ground." I admitted. "I like my feet on the grass, where I have a little bit of control."

"This foot?" Bastien inquired, sliding the slipper off my good leg. He gripped my foot and ran his fingers along the arch, tickling me and pretty much asking to be punched.

"This is the one you like touching the ground? Well, then get off the horse, you little mouse."

Lot's wide mouth twisted into a goofy grin, but he remained on the other side of the horse in case I fell. "Come now, it's alright, Princess."

I jerked and twitched on the horse, trying to rid myself of Bastien and his "hilarious" ways of getting me to loosen up. "Let go! I'm gonna fall, you jag!"

"How can you fall if you won't loosen your grip on the bridle? I could do this all day long."

I laughed without meaning to when the tickle grew too much. Then I wrenched my foot away and kicked out at him, narrowly missing his nose. "Get off me! Reyn! Control your village idiot!"

Reyn cast us both a look of borderline exasperation. Hamish jumped off his shoulder to skitter over and yell at Bastien. "Alright, kids. Keep it down while the grownups are talking."

Bastien snatched up my foot again and set to work on the lucky spot. I knew I wouldn't last long against the tease. I let out an angry belly laugh, alternating between scowling and smiling, not sure which emotion I felt anymore. I let go of the bridle to smack Bastien's hand that reached like a spider for my knee. He suctioned his hand just above the kneecap, making me howl at the hard tickle I couldn't escape.

All he needed was for me to let go. He didn't even look bothered that I smacked the hands that dragged me over the side of the horse by my knee. He grinned like a fool when I slunk to my feet in his embrace, my leg tingling where he'd touched it. "That was dirty," I grumbled, catching my breath.

"They're your feet. Maybe you should wash them if they're filthy."

I looked up into his eyes, daring him to back away before the attraction that swirled up in me at the least opportune time took me over. Something in his gaze shifted, and I saw the laughter going out of him, replaced by a serious longing that simultaneously scared and excited me. The butterflies in my stomach mutated to pterodactyls that swooped through me, both urging me forward and warning me to pull back. Bastien removed one of the arms he had wrapped around my waist and thumbed my lower lip, watching the curve like it was something fascinating.

Like *I* was something fascinating.

His eyes closed as he leaned down, and before I could make an informed decision on what I wanted to do, I pulled back, bumping into Marquis and making him grunt in a "Hey, man. I'm eating here" kind of way.

Did I want to kiss Bastien? Of course. My whole body was screaming for him. But that didn't change the fact that he was engaged. We were also in a barn filled with people. I didn't want my first kiss to be ruined of intimacy because everyone was watching me be vulnerable.

As scared as I'd been on the horse, facing Bastien's look

of confusion as it melted into a cold, reserved expression was even more intimidating. "Bastien, we... I'm sorry, I..."

"Forget it. Stop overreacting to everything. It's just a horse." With that, his warmth froze over, and he turned to make his way back to the others, tossing my slipper over his shoulder as he walked away.

I balanced on my bare foot, feeling the packed dirt floor beneath me anchoring my stunned body to the earth. A hard pit weighted my stomach, even though the pterodactyls were still in full swing. *I should've kissed Bastien.* Reyn's sister didn't even know she was engaged to him. What was stopping me? The thrill of my first horse ride adventure? The sexy dress? The hot guy who in some ways totally got me, but in other ways might never?

I couldn't put a lick of weight on my busted leg, so I leaned on Marquis while I tried to figure out a way to get my shoe back on without sitting on the ground. My spirits were low as Hamish brought me my slipper, chittering to me that Bastien was a tool, and not to think twice about it.

I tried to smile at Hamish as I leaned down to take the slipper, but Lot stepped out from the other side of the horse and intercepted the footwear before I could pitch myself off-balance. He was quiet as he knelt before me on one knee. Sizing up my injury dilemma, he slowly pulled me down to sit on his thigh, my arm on his shoulder as he fitted the slipper back onto my foot.

Lot smelled of freshly cut wood, and didn't act like my butt on his thigh was any inconvenience at all. We didn't speak, but his eyes were filled with understanding he couldn't possibly have for my situation as he looked deeply into my wounded gaze. His fingers gently wove themselves through mine, playing with them carefully, as if I wasn't the dude chick born without a libido or a desire to be swept away. He touched my hand like it was something special. Like *I* was something special. I hadn't felt the right kind of special in a long time. "Thanks for letting me take a ride on Marquis. He really loves you. Trusts you."

Lot's smile was wide and touched his blue eyes at the slightest upswing of emotion. "That's good to know. I very much rely on him, too. When we get a bit of time, I'll take you out on him myself. We'll go slow, so you can get the hang of riding."

I couldn't look at him anymore; he was too handsome in that dashing Disney prince sort of way. "Thanks. It'd be nice not to look like a total idiot next time."

"You didn't look like a total idiot. You're a girl who just needed things to go a little bit slower. There's nothing wrong with that. I hear in your world they get around in tin cans on wheels."

I snorted through a laugh, thinking he was joking. Upon looking at his attractive face, I realized he was not, and that I had just snorted while sitting on his thigh. *Smooth, Rosie.* "Sorry." I turned my attention back to our fingers that looked strangely pleasant together. "No, they're called cars, and they go a lot faster than horses, but you're buckled in and encased on every side, so you can't fall out all that easily. A lot tougher than a tin can."

"Fascinating, all the things the Commoners have done without the use of magic. Maybe later on, after you've known me a little longer and can look at me for more than a fleeting second, you can tell me about your home in Common." My cheeks turned pink at his words that were spot on the mark. Yup, I had zip experience with men. When a good-looking guy acted like I might actually have a chance with him, and paid me any kind of attention, I ran away like the giant chicken I was.

I nodded, touching the back of my hand to my cheek to cool the burn of chagrin. Lot caught on and smiled. "How about we rejoin the others before they plan the whole thing without us?"

"Yeah, okay." I stood, but Lot didn't let go of my hand. Instead he looped my arm through his, letting me lean on him as I hobbled ungracefully toward the arguing.

33

POISONOUS POPPIES

"*D*on't be a tool, Rousseau. We don't have time for everyone to go home and pack. Bring back extra supplies for everyone from your place." Lane had long since dropped her queenly airs after the arguing that seemed never-ending. For a Council that was supposed to work together, they didn't actually get along all that seamlessly. Too many alphas in one barn. "Go now. Bayard's already left with a much better attitude than the one you should be ashamed of."

Rousseau farted loudly and grumbled about Bayard having more gold to work with to replenish the supplies we all would need. But eventually he complied, disappearing without too much more huffing over the matter.

Henri had closed us inside the stable, locking it so no one would see us and be able to report back that Reyn was back in his hometown of Province 2. He kept craning his ear to the door every so often to see if he heard any signs of the army, but there was nothing. "I'm going to my castle just down the way. See if I can't get us some more supplies."

Bastien raised a finger. "I'll come with you."

"You sure you can leave your princess?" Henri asked with a hint of teasing to his tone.

"I'm not needed here, and she's not my anything, old man." Bastien spoke loud enough for everyone to hear my public dismissal. My jaw set, and I kept my chin high so I didn't shrink like I wanted to.

Remy's voice was kind, bringing me back to earth. Or Avalon, I guess. *Sit down, Princess. Let me look at your wound. I can redress it before we leave. There won't be much time once everything gets going.*

"Sure." I dropped my hand from Lot's, regretting the loss of the gentle contact. Though, he made me so nervous that it was probably for the best that I got a bit of distance. My palm was sweaty due to nerves, which was, you know, totally the opposite of sexy.

"Does this hurt?" Remy asked, pressing two fingers a few inches under the line of stitches.

"No. Just a little bruised, but nothing more than a sting."

"What's that now?" Lot asked, watching the exchange with tented eyebrows in the center of his forehead. "Your leg is bruised?"

"Oh, I was just talking to Remy. He's asking if it hurts."

"Fascinating that you can hear him. We thought it was only the animals you could talk to. I wonder what other hidden languages there are for you to uncover."

"Well, I never had an ear for language back home, so here's hoping it's always this easy down here."

Lane sat next to me, and Reyn followed to take the place on her left. "How's my girl doing, Remy?"

"He says I'm totally fine, and should heal in a day or two," I lied, not liking the fawning.

Remy looked up at me, tilted his head to the side and touched a finger to my sewn cut, holding my leg still while I hissed through gritted teeth until a howl escaped me. *"You know I said no such thing. It'll be at least a week before you can try walking on it again. And there's no telling what sort of damage the snakes did to your muscle."*

"Okay! Okay! I give! He said it'll be a week at least." When Remy removed his hand with a mollified nod, his words hit me afresh. "A week?! But we're supposed to be finding the Horse to Nowhere. How can I do that if I can't even walk? Come on, Remy! Don't you have some magic Jiu-Jitsu you can whip out?"

Remy put on a comically serious face and waved his hands over my leg as if casting a spell. Then he wiggled his fingers and pretended to zap the healing into me. *"Is that about how you pictured it? You can dance now. Give it a try."*

"Ha. Ha. Whatcha got in there, Lane?" I asked as she rifled through her backpack. "Spare set of crutches?"

"Yes, that's exactly it. Pack up nice, don't they? I was

thinking maybe we could get changed into regular clothes, since the whole meet and greet is over, and we'll be traveling incognito after this. Be a little more ourselves? Whataya say, girlfriend?"

"I've never loved you more. Give me those jeans!" I snapped my jaws at the bag, pretending to eat the air separating me from clothes that felt normal and didn't leave my boobs totally exposed.

Remy finished wrapping my leg, groaning at me when I told him I had to get up to go into a horse's stall to change. *"I just rewrapped it. Please be more careful this time. You're putting too much weight on your leg."* He clicked his fingers to Lot, who helped me up gently. His long arms were careful with me as I leaned on him with my clothes tucked under my elbow.

Lot walked me to a stall that was far enough away that I wouldn't be seen by the others, turning to me before leaving. "I'm just over there if you need anything. Will you promise to call for me?"

I nodded, though I knew that would never, never, ever happen. If I needed help getting dressed, I would sooner fall on my face before letting him see me half-naked. I could barely stand in front of him fully clothed. "Thanks."

Lot brought my hand to his lips and pressed a delicate kiss to my knuckles, pausing before returning my sweaty hand to me. "Oh, no. Now I've done it. You were too shy to look at me before, and I fear I've just sealed it. I would take back the kiss, but I just can't bring myself to regret it. Funny, that."

My cheeks were red, and as my eyes climbed to his face to see the all too pleased grin he wore, I reached my peak of frustration with myself. "Alright, alright, you. Get out before you melt my brain with all your gentleman stuff. That's... Guys don't do that to me in my world, and it's tripping me out."

He lifted my hand again and brushed his lips back and forth across my fingers, warming them with his breath. "'Gentleman stuff?' You'll have to be more specific."

"The whole Disney prince on a shining steed thing you've got going on. Quit doing the... Just quit it!" I huffed through his laughter. The sound was easy and fun, like he was used to enjoying the things that encouraged happiness. I pulled my hand out of his and palmed his face with it, earning a laugh from him as I pushed him out of the stall. "Quit being a boy. I'm changing, so out you go."

"As you like it, Princess Rosalie." He bowed to me, and then laughed as I swatted at him to stand up straight. Hamish came to stand guard for me, since Abraham Lincoln had just dozed off for a nap in the hay with Marquis.

I tugged on Lane's navy-colored softball t-shirt jersey from when she joined her gym's team a few years back. It was washed to perfection, giving me that soft hug only the best old t-shirts did. Her top was a little snug on me across the bust now, but it was a far sight better than the princess porn dress, so I didn't complain. She liked her tops tight, while I liked mine easy to move in without showing the world my stomach by accident.

The jeans were mine, and fit me beautifully, covering my bandage so I didn't look like a cripple on first glimpse. My indoor soccer shoes gave me the same "I sure missed you, kid" that I winked at them with.

When I came out, I didn't expect fanfare (which Lane gave me in spades), but I also didn't expect Lot's face to fall. "You're dressed like a peasant," he remarked with obvious disapproval.

I shrugged, guessing it was best to let the cat out of the bag now and clue him in that I wasn't Cinderella. "Well, in my world, that's what I am."

"We're not peasants," Lane corrected me, frowning as she did up her hair in a messy ponytail. She wore a tight purple t-shirt with a yellow sun on the chest, and skinny jeans with her sneakers. "We're working class. That's nothing to sneeze at, Lot."

"My apologies, Duchess." Lot bowed to her and trotted over to help me back to the group.

A pop like a firecracker sounded, and when I turned toward the noise, there was Bayard, in all his horse-tailed glory. "I brought all I could take without raising suspicion. Rousseau's not back yet?"

"No, but he left after you," Reyn replied.

We turned our heads as one to the door when we heard a horse riding hard toward the stable. Reyn and

Lane ran into one of the stalls to hide, and Remy to the stall next to them. Lot scooped me up and ran me across the way to another.

The door opened and a young woman's voice called out, "Duke Lancelot? Lot! Are you in here?"

He pressed his finger to my lips and set me down, showing himself to the newcomer. "Gwen! Good to see you. How's your father, the Great Duke Henri?" A second set of boots entered, and Lot greeted the heavier tread. "Damond! I was just resting Marquis in your stable. I hope you don't mind."

"Duke Henri's at the castle answering questions about Reyn!" The girl said in a harried whisper. "Damond and I are to take you all to the bridge, where he and Bastien will meet you once they're certain they're not being followed. Hurry!"

Lot slapped his hands together, and we fell out of the stables like overstuffed decks of cards on a bad shuffle. Lane shoved our dresses in her backpack and ran behind Gwen, who looked to be a few years younger than me. She was tall and dressed in a gown like we'd been wearing, her blonde hair pinned back in the front and hanging loose halfway down her back behind her. She had a rounded nose and thin lips with eyes that darted around the barn nervously. Honestly, she looked nothing like her father.

Damond grabbed the reins of two different horses without making time for introductions. He looked more like his father, with the black hair and angular features.

"Get on!" Damond called to me after throwing a saddle on the beige horse that was just as tall as Marquis.

"I... But I..." I knew this wasn't the time for hesitating, but I seriously didn't know how to even mount the horse with two good legs, much less being down to one.

Lot pulled Marquis up from his nap, with Abraham Lincoln ambling out next to him with a yawn. "She can ride with me," he ruled, running to lift me up and place me on his horse.

"Ah! A bear!" Gwen cried out, stumbling back and pulling out a short sword. "Get back!"

Reyn scooped up Abraham Lincoln and handed him to Lane once she was settled on the beige horse. My baby clung to her, confused why he'd been woken from his nap so abruptly. Reyn grabbed Hamish and settled him in his shirt pocket before mounting a dark brown horse with spots on his hindquarters.

Another firecracker pop sounded, announcing Rousseau had rejoined our group just in the nick of time. "Whoa! Hold on a moment! What's going on?" He waved his red furry hands to calm Gwen's horse, whom he'd spooked.

"Grab a horse and ride with us to the bridge!" Gwen instructed. "Duke Henri's being questioned about Reyn, and they're sure to check Damond's stables before they go. Hurry!"

I expected some sort of oomph and "this sucks for short people" kind of thing from him, but he surprised me by blinking and transporting himself atop a horse with all the gusto of a fart and a firecracker pop. It felt so much like cheating after the unladylike grunts I'd done to get into place with my bum leg. "I'm ready," Rousseau said, his overstuffed pack on his back. "Everyone ride at a pace that doesn't rouse suspicion until we reach cover of the woods. Then ride on out as fast as you can."

Damond mounted his horse with long legs that looked well-seasoned for the job. If these were his stables, his wiry frame was perfectly at home in them, whispering to his gray horse before calling to us. "Let's go!"

Lot pulled himself up behind me, his hands far more polite than Bastien's had been. Lot kept his hands on the reins, trusting that I could balance on my own and hold on. I tried not to make a fool of myself, but a tiny squeal of fright escaped me as Lot directed Marquis forward slowly, so as not to trample anyone when we first exited the stable.

The fresh spring wind picked up and I shivered in my t-shirt, holding tight to the bridle as goosebumps broke out on my skin. Twilight had settled in, the sun setting on the prairie behind the brightly painted huts. They lined the horizon in little clusters of tightly-knit communities. The grass was sparse, but enough to make the path we traveled down appear green, though the reddish brown dirt was easy to spot through the patches of growth. It was as if nature was doing her best to thrive, but meager survival was the best it could do.

Marquis picked up his pace to match the rest of the

horses, who were cantering in front of us. "Are you holding up alright, Princess?" Lot asked, his jaw resting against my temple once the horse hit a predictable rhythm.

"Uh-huh!" I lied through my gritted teeth. Bastien had found a way to get my body to relax against his, but I couldn't do that with Lot. He was a proper prince, and I was, well, me. I felt like Lucille Ball on a walrus. "Are we almost there?"

Lot paused before answering. "No, sweet girl. It'll be many hours before we reach the bridge."

"Bastien and Henri, are they okay?"

Again, that telling pause. "I'm sure they're fine. They'll meet us at the bridge. They may even beat us there. The castle's closer to the bridge than the stable was." He boxed me in tighter with his elbows. "I'll get us there safely."

I had no choice but to trust Lot. My nerves at his handsome face dissipated a little since I couldn't actually see him. The sun set as we rode on, making my stomach tie in knots at all the things we couldn't see in the dark. Our path was lit only by their blue moon (like, an actual blue moon) and the stars. Though, the trees seemed to keep even those lights from us at times. I closed my eyes so I didn't hiss or squeal through my closed lips when the errant branch flew at us too quickly for my liking. I didn't know Lot, but I was forced into trusting him. I didn't do so well in those kinds of circumstances.

When we raced out of the woods finally, the prairie greeted us. The wide expanse of nothingness was broken up only by pink poppies that we ran past at warp speed. We charged through the green field that stretched on beyond what I could see in the dark. The few bunches of flowers gave way to a meadow that was utterly blanketed with thousands of the pink beauties, so close together you could barely see any grass. The poppies smelled like bubblegum and perfume, cloyingly sweet, but invigorating all the same. We'd gone from sparse nature to booming Mother Earth – or Mother Avalon, or whatever.

I heard Remy shout, *"Princess! Try not to breathe if you can help it!"*

"What? Why can't I breathe?"

Reyn called to us, "Lane! Rosie! Don't breathe until we pass the *étouffer* flowers!"

"Huh?" I asked stupidly.

Lot answered for Reyn. "Do you not know about the *étouffer* flowers?"

I shook my head, freezing as Lot buried his nose in my hair to muffle the fresh air that came at us. He held the reins in one hand and covered my nose and mouth with the other. I could still breathe, but it was tampered with the polished scent of his hand. He leaned me back so my shoulders were stuck to his chest, my head tilted skyward as he clamped the back of my head to his shoulder. I let out a whimper at being restrained by a man I didn't know, while riding a horse I wasn't totally comfortable on.

The bubblegum smell mutated, and something icy and sharp like menthol on steroids floated into my lungs when

I accidentally gasped at Marquis' impromptu leap. It started out just a little annoying, but after a few shallow breaths I couldn't help but taking, the ice turned into daggers that needled my throat all the way from my mouth and down into my lungs. The menthol spread like fire into my chest, filling my breasts from the inside and making them feel like they were heavy and burning with a cold sort of fire I couldn't escape. My pain came out of me in a choked gasp with very little volume to it, but my rigid spine and hands that clawed at my chest told Lot that I'd breathed the bad stuff.

Lot swore loudly. "She's been infected!" he announced to the group. We were completely alone in the prairie, and now I knew why. No one would dare come out to smell these flowers.

Gwen moved her horse to ride beside us. "Are you sure? We're out of the flower patch now. Try some fresh air, Princess!" she sounded worried, which did nothing to calm me.

I tried to answer, but breathing was so painful, I couldn't get any words out. I felt like a fire-breathing dragon, only I was afraid if I opened my mouth, I would exhale glass shards. I wanted to run smack out of Avalon, but my head was still clamped to Lot's shoulder. His hand was over my forehead now, allowing me as much air as I could suck in through my narrowing esophagus. He kept my face tilted skyward, the blue moon looking down at me with a worried "Dang, girl," feel to it. I felt claustrophobic inside my body and squirmed when the air I sucked in wasn't enough. Not only were there glass and needles inside of me, but air was growing too thick to suck down. I clawed at Lot's hand, but my aim was clumsy from the blinding pain. "We have to stop!" I worked out in a gasp of agony.

"We can't stop!" Gwen insisted, morose. "I'm sorry, Princess! I'm so sorry! If we stop now, the army might see us."

"Just breathe, sweet girl. I know it hurts." Lot spoke low in my ear. I could only just make sense of their words through the fire that raced around inside of me, rekindling the moment I thought I'd earned a reprieve. "Gwen, she can't keep on like this! She has to lie down!"

"There's nothing you can do for her now, Lot. It'll pass through her on its own. Just make sure to hold her steady when the tremors come, so she doesn't fall off Marquis."

I let out a strangled cry of agony as their words of doom and a new layer of sunburnt pain ripped through my insides. "What's happening to me?!"

Reyn called over his shoulder to us, "It's the *étouffer* poppies. You weren't supposed to breathe them in. It's my fault. I didn't warn you properly in time. Your body will survive it, but it's going to be painful, Princess."

Gwen shouted to me from my right as her horse galloped at our side. "First comes the ice and fire, then the numb, then the spiders, then the tremors, then the drowning, then the sweats. The important thing is to breathe.

The more fresh air that goes into you, the faster everything will work its way out."

Lane was towards the front of the group, but pulled her horse to Lot's other side to stay with me as best she could. "Rosie? Baby? It's okay, honey. It's going to be fine!" I heard the same lie in her voice as when she'd tell me we totally had enough money for rent the night before it was due. Then I heard her turn to Reyn and let a portion of her fear loose. "She can't stay on the horse the whole time! No one can stay still enough to ride through the tremors!"

"I've got a firm hold on her!" Lot shouted to the group, his voice determined.

The ice traced down my legs until my toes were screaming at me with phantom frostbite. My fingers were totally useless, but they were molded onto the bridle, so they stayed there, willing me to believe that they wouldn't let me fall. The menthol cold felt like it was traveling inside of my spine, freezing me and making me squirm to put out the clutch of death the foreign element had on me.

When André René Roussimoff was only forty years old, he'd had back surgery. It was so hard on him that he'd had to wear a back brace to wrestle after that. I kept that factoid in my mind to center me through the pain. If André could make it through actual back surgery, then I could handle a little freaky Avalon torture magic. I mean, it was a field of poppies. How dangerous could a flower actually be? In my imagination, it wasn't Lot's hand on my forehead, but André's massive mitt. My giant's calm, steady presence gave me strength that only he possessed. He could produce a thick-lipped smile after a rough wrestling match. If he'd breathed in the poisonous poppies, he would find a way to deal with the pain gracefully.

Lot's hand on my forehead was too clumsy with fear to be comforting. "It's alright, Princess. Just hold on. I'll get us to the bridge, and from there we'll find you a place to lie down and sweat out the poison."

"P-poison?" I eked out. André held me tighter in my angst, willing me to buck up and handle it. He'd gone through far worse in the wrestling ring, and my guardian angel wasn't about to desert me now. The flames in my veins only seemed to be growing hotter with each breath I took, so despite my need for oxygen, I took in as little as possible – until my lips and fingertips started to tingle with the ominous warnings that I was going to pass out if I didn't get more air. I took in as deep a breath as I could, letting out a closed-lipped noise of panic. Lot muffled the pathetic sound by moving his palm from my forehead to my mouth. I didn't want to be the girl who screamed. I could handle pain well enough, but this was from the inside, and totally foreign, which didn't do a whole lot to calm my peaking nerves.

Lot's voice was gentle as he tried his best to calm me. "There, there. I know it hurts. Let it out. I can muffle the screams." When I didn't take him at his word and kept my slow whimpers as the only noise I would permit, I heard the panic in his voice. "I'm sorry, sweet girl. I'm so sorry. It'll be over soon."

It was a precious lie he told me, but as the hours passed while we rode through the night, the fire did not quell. It only mutated into something darker.

34

SPIDERS IN MY BRAIN

I don't know how long it was that I couldn't feel my body. I was stiff like a board as we rode through the prairie that seemed never-ending. Bayard remained as quiet as the others out of respect for what he referred to as "living through a slow death."

He was not wrong. Lot was whispering encouraging things into my ear, but I couldn't focus once something started nipping at the inside of my big toe. I wanted to jerk it away, but I couldn't move my body at all. The only sensation I could feel was the something that was crawling on the inside of my big toe. It moved slowly, and then started prancing, daring me to swat at it. It danced in defiance with a "you can't catch me" vibe I did not appreciate. Then just when I thought my irritation couldn't take anymore, the spider duplicated himself. Now there were two tapdancing spiders inside my foot. One in my big toe, and one in the toe next door. I kept my mouth shut through the slow torture that filled my foot, one toe at a time. Then the spiders infested both legs with dozens, and then hundreds of tiny imaginary arachnids. They all fought for dominance inside my body as I screamed in my mind. Hamish shouted for me, and Abraham Lincoln moaned his worry that another mama would up and die on him.

"When the spiders start, don't bat at them," Bayard instructed. "Ignore them and breathe through it, and they'll move through your body. People bruise and scratch themselves up pretty bad, thinking they're actual spiders that can be smashed. They're not, so best hold still when they come."

I wanted to scream that they were already inside of me, but I decided to endure this one in silence. I'd carried on enough when Remy had sliced open my leg. I wouldn't be the weak one in this group. I wouldn't let them look down on me. I would learn the ropes of Avalon if it killed me. I kept my limbs absolutely still, giving the spiders inside of me the mental middle finger, daring them to do their worst. It wasn't a matter of freaking out anymore; it was a battle of wills – Avalon's torment against my Commoner's pride.

Abraham Lincoln promised to eat all the spiders out of me if only Lane would let him down. It was sweet, and totally gross.

My oversized wrestler guardian giant shushed me in my imagination, letting me know that he wasn't scared, so I didn't have to be, either. I pleaded with André to make it all be over, allowing him to see my fear, while I did my best to conceal my terror from the others. In my mind, André gave me a simple smile and hugged me, saying nothing, but giving me that serene look that chased away nuisance terrors.

I would not cry out. I would not cry at all. If this was what I had to do to get through with this whole mess, I would do it without losing myself. The spiders crawled up into my chest, filling out my ribs like a thousand little pinpricks of annoyance mingled with my own personal horror. I tried to breathe through the torture, but each breath brought only more spiders into me, multiplying them until they filled my arms.

I could move my limbs now, but I refused on principle. I wouldn't dance for the things that tortured me just because they finally granted me the freedom to move, the jags. It was a battle of wills at this point to decide who would be in control of my body – me or the hordes of spiders. I wouldn't make it harder for Lot to hold me upright. I wouldn't be the wuss in front of warriors. Lot was sweating, his arm muscles tensed around me as he held the reins in both his hands, urging Marquis onward, despite the horse's polite groans to me that this was really more than he bargained for.

When the spiders danced behind my eyeballs, I pursed my lips and gave them all the filthiest curse words I could think of. I gripped my thighs tight to keep from clawing at my eyes and letting them know that they'd won.

"Have the spiders started yet?" Bayard asked, his tone respectful over Lane's quiet weeping. We galloped together, but other than the clip-clopping of hooves, they were mostly quiet, as if scared I might scream and give away our location.

"No. I don't think so," Lot answered. "She's still stiff as a board. We're almost to the bridge, Princess," he cooed to me. "Once we're there, we can get you down and back to Duchess Elaine."

I wanted to cry out for Lane, but knew if I did, it'd break her heart not to be able to make it all better. Part of her prowess came from my blind faith that she could do anything, heal any injury, and be the person I needed in any and all situations. I wasn't about to hand her a problem she couldn't solve. That would crush her. So I kept my mouth shut and listened to her and Abraham Lincoln cry together in each other's arms.

"I see the bridge!" Gwen announced, and I heard everyone breathe in one collective sigh of relief. "Duke Henri!" she called, racing ahead, her golden locks whipping out behind her. "The princess has been infected by the poppies! Help!"

I tried to pay attention to my surroundings, but all I saw was Bastien charging out to meet us on foot. His sturdy black boots pounded through the prairie, his arms pumping with a determined look narrowing his eyes and his mouth. "Give her to me!" he called to Lot as Marquis began to slow.

Lot waited until Marquis came to a stop before lifting me with shaking muscles that had been tensed for too many hours. He lowered me into Bastien's outstretched arms, and immediately I was engulfed in a warmth that made the terror scurrying around inside of me less of a threat. Bastien was there, and somehow that was a good thing, but I was too turned around to examine just why that was. "What's going on? What stage of it are you in?"

Lot's breath was labored. "She's numb. Next come the spiders."

I gripped Bastien's back, holding him as tight as he held me, my face buried in his solid chest, as if he could chase away all the bad things. I was going mad, and tired of the chase. "She's not numb! She's standing and holding me. Rosie, what's happening now?"

I closed my eyes and whispered as Lane ran to me and held me from behind, pressing my front tighter to Bastien. "The spiders are i-in m-my head now. Almost g-gone."

"What? No. Rosie, we mean it'll feel like spiders inside your skin. In your body," Lot said, dismounting and shaking out his arms.

I nodded, jostling the spiders around and feeling them shift to new crevices, threatening to make each one their home. "In m-m-m-my head," I whispered, clutching Bastien tighter.

Bastien smoothed my windblown hair back from my

face. "Okay, then. You're doing great. Everyone I know who's ever gone through this has damn near clawed their eyes out. Just hold onto me." He kissed the top of my head, feeling my anxiety at Lane's audible sobbing. I didn't understand how he knew exactly the right way to hold me, when I didn't even know how I preferred something as intimate as that. His arms around me were strong, his grip firm and reassuring, letting me know without words that somehow he would handle the bad things that ate at my brain. In that moment, he was André Roussimoff, incarnate.

Lane fretted aloud, "Baby, it's okay to let it out. I know you're freaking out! Tell me how I can help you!"

Bastien took one arm away from me and squeezed Lane's shoulder. "I get that you want to help, but you're going to scare her if you keep this up. You want to be here for her? You can't cry like that. She's trying to hold herself together, and the waterworks aren't helping. Why don't you and Henri find us a place to keep her quiet once the tremors start?" His voice wasn't unkind, but it did carry a direct command. "It won't be easy to move her once the spiders leave her."

Lane nodded, sobbing into my hair and kissing me about twenty times before she ran off to find a place in the prairie for me to lie down unseen if someone should happen by us.

"Th-thank you," I whispered, closing my eyes and holding tight to him. Bastien didn't save me from the spiders that infested my body, but he stayed with me when the bad things refused to leave. As much as I didn't understand his mood swings, I was grateful for him all the same. When the spiders filled my ears, I could still hear, but it made my ear canals itch like none other. If I had a Q-tip, I'd jam that sucker way too deep in there. I had a feeling that was a no-no. "H-hold my arms d-down," I begged, not wanting to hurt myself.

Bastien clamped my forearms between his ribcage and his biceps, keeping me in place while he held the back of my head. He pressed my forehead to his chest to center me. "Breathe in," he instructed, and then waited for me to comply before he said in his low voice, "Breathe out. You're doing great." My exhales grew more panicked when the spiders seemed to be taking up residence and multiplying inside of my brain. I thought they'd wander around for a minute and be gone, but apparently they couldn't get enough of my skull. Bastien seemed to understand, and squeezed my jaw, massaging my cheeks with his thumbs. "I've got you. Hold onto me. You want to scratch your eyes out? Scratch me instead." I'm not sure he expected me to take him at his word, but I did, digging my nails into his back and making him tense up as he held my face steady. "That's it. Deeper, Rosie. Harder, baby," he grunted. I complied, feeling a little more in control, now that my hands had a purpose. "Make me feel it. I left you in the stable with no one to guard you. Make me pay for it."

I had a feeling Bastien would be fantastic at dirty talk.

I clawed him deeper, leaning my chin up and opening my mouth so I could bite into his shirt. Only instead of just his shirt, I latched onto his chest, chewing on the skin there as the spiders tortured me by lingering. They dared me to bat at them, to smack myself over and over across the face while they laughed and laughed at how they got me to dance for them.

Bastien swore at the sting from my bite, but it only seemed to fuel his determination to stay with me, to talk me through the insanity I was keeping neatly bottled up as best I could. I bit him over and over across his chest, breathing like a horse through my nose. The spiders lingered when they should have been running. *I* wanted to run, but Bastien held me tight, letting me hurt him just so I wouldn't have to suffer alone.

"That's right, Daisy. Tear my skin. I hurt you when I left with no warning. I wanted to kiss you so bad. It's driving me crazy, thinking about your sweet little mouth. When you turned me down, I didn't understand." He winced when I ground my teeth together, piercing his chest and sucking my spit into my mouth as I seethed through the slow torture. His voice came out pinched. "I get it now. You don't want to waste your first kiss on someone who's taken. You're a decent person, even when no one is watching to make sure you follow the rules."

The spiders were dissipating through my hair now, leaving me to catch my shallow breath and begin to process all my body had just been through. "It's over," I gasped, pulling fresh air into my lungs. "They're gone. The spiders are gone." I glanced over my shoulder to make sure they weren't actual spiders leaving my body in droves. They'd felt so real, but I saw nothing scurrying away through the night across the grass.

"Okay, then I've got to move you quick. The next wave's coming, and I don't want you out in the open when it starts." His tenor picked up with a thread of distress as he scooped me up and ran to the bridge toward Lane and the others.

"Take her under the bridge," Henri instructed Bastien. "It's the best we can do."

"What's happening? It's not over?" I hated how pathetic I sounded, but seriously, one wrong inhale and this was the crap I got? So far, Avalon pretty much sucked.

"I've got you," Bastien promised. He ran to the bridge that looked about long enough to fit five cars and one minivan underneath in the gentle river below. He ducked under the bridge and laid me in the muddy embankment. We were on the three feet of shore between where the bridge began and where the water lapped at the dirt. He rolled me onto my stomach and slowly crawled on top of me, flattening his body to mine and squishing the air out of me.

"Bastien, what are you doing? Get off me!"

"Sorry. Am I crushing you?" He tented his body by raising himself up on his elbows. "In a second, the tremors are going to start. I need you on your stomach so you don't swallow your tongue."

"Wait, what?" The familiar panic I thought I'd given the boot home reared its ugly dragon's head again, spitting in my face. "Tremors? This sucks super way bad!" I said angrily.

Bastien crushed his pelvis to my butt and wound his arms over mine to pin them above my head with his forearms. One of his legs wrapped around my good leg so it stuck up in the air like a foolproof wrestling hold. "It'll pass, like everything else. The more you breathe, the worse it'll feel, but the quicker it'll move through you. So breathe. That's the one thing I can't do for you. You're in charge of breathing, and I'm in charge of everything else about this."

"Bastien?" I whimpered, closing my eyes.

"Yeah, Daisy?"

I wanted to ask him to take me home. Home to bad TV, good junk food and a warm bed. I wanted to see Judah and let him bore me with computer talk. I wanted to take the finals I'd studied so hard for. I wanted to show Bastien all those things, but I chickened out and reached for a joke instead of the truth. "Bastien, tell me the truth. Does this turn you on?"

He wasn't expecting a joke, and I wasn't expecting his answering snorty laugh and a few comedic pelvic thrusts above my butt that made me chuckle. His laugh when he was caught off-guard was goofy and had an unpolished note to it before he smoothed it out to a refined chortle. It was imperfect, and totally endearing. "After this, we can do all sorts of things that turn us both on. How about that?"

"I'm sorry I pushed you away. The engaged thing is really throwing me. And I didn't want my first liplock to be with everyone right there, watching me screw it up. It's all just a little confusing right now." I swallowed hard. "But if I ever did want to, you know…" I couldn't even say the word "kiss", I was such a chicken. "It would be with you."

"Hey," he tsked me, brushing his stubbled cheek to my smooth one. "You don't get to apologize for that. You can say you're sorry for all sorts of things, but not that one. I was a jerk. You're right. Your first kiss should be with someone who isn't tied down."

"Speaking of being tied down, this whole poisonous poppies thing? Total drag. Let's never do this again." I fidgeted under his weight, but he had me so pinned that I barely moved. It was a testament to how much I was beginning to trust him that I didn't freak out and buck like a bull coming out of the pen in a rage. "What a waste of having a hot guy on top of me."

Bastien leaned his cheek to mine, and I could feel his smile.

"Rosie?" Lane called, inching toward my head under the bridge. I couldn't see much, but I didn't need sight to know she was still bawling. "Honey, have the tremors started?"

"Nope. It's really fine, Lane. Honestly. It's not nearly as

bad as you're all making it out to be." I tried to keep my tone light to spare her worst fear. I knew mine was anything bad happening to her, and that hers was anything bad happening to me. "Hey, do you happen to know where a girl could get some popcorn around here? I could use a treat to pass the time."

Her tone came back sharp. "Don't start making jokes. Not now. I know you're in pain! I know how scared you must be. I was with my sister, Tyronoe, when she inhaled the poppies once. She tried to claw her eyes out in my arms! I can still hear her screaming through it!"

I closed my eyes, trying to maintain my hold on the battle that was only midway through. Bastien lifted his head, surprisingly calm. "Hey, I've got this here. You want to check on Reyn for me, though? He used way too much magic yesterday using concealment charms around Remy's house. I told him I'd do it, but you know how bull-headed he can be. He needs to sit down, but he's stubborn. Can you ask him to sit with you and make it seem like it's for you, not him? He has to recharge, or he'll be useless once we reach the Inn." He flashed her a grin that looked so friendly and sincere, I nearly bought the charade.

"Sure. Of course I'll check on Reyn for you. You'll call when the tremors start and Rosie needs me?"

"Of course. Bye-bye now." He waited until she left, and then we both let out a long sigh. "Better?"

"Much. I don't like her to see me in pain. It hurts her too much. I don't want to put her through that." I was a master at faking my smiles for Lane. When the kids at school couldn't see past the fact that I was the ugly girl, I tried not to let her know how much it tore me up. My angst quickly became hers, and I loved her too much to let her suffer as much as I did.

"I know. I get it." We both felt my foot starting to twitch of its own volition. "Steady, now. Just think to yourself, 'Bastien's got me. Everything's going to be fine.'"

"Has anyone ever died from this?"

"Not while I'm around, no. That's all you need to focus on. I'm here, and I've got all the moves." He thrusted his pelvis pornographically above my butt again, making me laugh at the most inopportune time.

The twitch started in my toe, but moved quicker up my body than the other things had done. My whole leg started spasming, and then the other. "Ah!" I cried out without meaning to. "Oh, my leg! Ow! Oh, make it stop!"

"Remy!" Bastien barked over his shoulder. The healer came quick, ready to help. "Hold her injured leg down. I can't do it without hurting her more. She's flopping around so much, I'm afraid she'll tear something."

Remy grabbed my foot and slammed it to the wet grass, holding my leg steady. The seizure that moved like a wave up my body began to shake me with a force I couldn't comprehend. *You won't die if we keep you pinned like this. You won't hurt yourself this way."*

Bastien smashed the side of my face into the grass to keep my head from thrashing around. He shoved his finger sideways into my mouth just before my teeth started to chatter. I felt him wince when my seizure increased the tenacity of my bite.

After a few minutes that seemed like hours, I figured the wave would be gone. But of course, it wasn't. Why would Avalon cut me such a break? The seizure kept me locked in a high point of terror, unsure when my body might just up and peace out on me. Every muscle was tensed and vibrating like a tuning fork; I was scared it might never stop.

Bastien leaned his weight on me, crushing my shoulders to the ground so my neck didn't have as much room to jerk around and suffer real damage. I wanted to weep and moan and throw any number of fits, if only it would get me out of this mess. We hadn't even really started trying to find Roland or the missing gems yet, and I'd had snakes pouring out of my leg, a non-anesthesia surgery, and was being pinned down by the heaviest guy alive all because I breathed wrong. Something had told me from the beginning that finding Roland and the gems wouldn't be as easy as following my inner GPS.

Someone was shouting something to Bastien, but I couldn't focus enough to understand what was going on. All I heard was Bastien growl, "I'm kinda in the middle of something here! I'll sort him out once I'm finished with her!"

Bastien shifted, crushing the air out of my lungs. I tried to let him know I couldn't breathe, but I couldn't form words; my teeth were chattering so violently. I managed to suck in a breath that felt... wrong. Though I knew I wasn't underwater, the sensation of drowning overwhelmed me as my limbs began to loosen from the hold the seizure had on them. Like a deflated balloon, I collapsed in the wet dirt. Bastien carefully removed his finger from between my teeth, leaving me with the piney taste of his skin mingled with the rust of his blood in my mouth. "Bastien?" I gasped. "Bastien! I can't... breathe!"

He rolled me over so I was thoroughly coated in mud, and before I knew it, his lips were on mine. Renewed shock flooded me, electrocuting every pore in my body that this was my first kiss, and I was totally unable to participate in it. Then Bastien squeezed my cheeks, popping my mouth open so he could blow into it. He pinched the bridge of my nose and blew in a steady rhythm, forcing air in where it felt like there was only water. Remy moved around us so he was positioned at my head. He brushed my filthy hair back from my face and pressed down on my forehead to keep me still. *"It's going to feel like you're drowning, but it's not really water in your lungs. The danger is you'll think there is, and you'll stop breathing on your own. Bastien's forcing in air, so your body won't give up on trying to breathe. This phase passes quickly, so best be as calm as you can while it moves through you."*

I wanted to shout at Remy, to hold his head underwater and tell him to be calm about it. Bastien jerked my chin up so my shoulders were slightly elevated, giving him a clearer shot down into my lungs. It was more than the minute I could hold my breath underwater. It was more than ten times that, but Bastien was determined. In that moment, I was grateful for his stubborn nature that wouldn't give up on me, even when I'd pushed him away.

35

BASTIEN THE BULLY

*S*lowly the air he forced into me became easier to hold onto. I couldn't do much with my arms, so I turned my head to the side so he'd stop breathing for me. Bastien let out a strangled laugh filled with too much anxiety. "See? I told you I'd take care of it. You're alright. The worst is over. Once the sweat breaks out, we can cool off in the river. Who's amazing?"

I know I was supposed to respond with a hearty "Bastien's the king!" but I felt heavy all over, weighted with too much Avalon. I wanted to hug him or at the very least, sit up, but I couldn't move my arms. They were there, but too exhausted and rubbery from the tremors to be of any use. Bastien took a few minutes on his knees to catch his breath, rubbing his chest with one hand and leaning against the underside of the bridge with the other to steady himself.

"Remy, stay with her for a minute while I go check on Reyn. Be right back, Daisy." He hoisted himself out of the muck and stumbled toward the others.

I closed my eyes and let my body rest for the few moments it was granted respite. I tried to tune out Remy's medical fretting, letting my mind wander to the almost kiss I'd just had – because I was poisoned into thinking I was drowning. And it wasn't actually a kiss, it was CPR. I wondered if my first real kiss would nearly stop my heart as much as this had. I wondered if it would be Bastien, and how my conscience would wrestle with doing something that was so intimate with an engaged man.

Dew broke out on my forehead, and Remy quickly scooped out water from the creek to spoon over my hair, cooling me and making me feel a little less icky. "Thanks," I whispered.

"I could've helped you through the stages," he told me in a quiet voice. *"Bastien wouldn't let anyone near you, not even me. He only consented to letting me hold your ankles because he couldn't manage it."* He waited a few beats for that to sink in before he started on a different topic. *"I became a healer because it's what my father expected of his children. He was the only healer for the entire village, and there were times the work-load was too much. By the time I was ten, I'd seen many a man die on our kitchen table. I wanted to be a knight in the Queen's Army, but I knew I would serve the land better helping out father."*

I clumsily reached my arm over my head and fished

around until I found Remy's hand. I couldn't give him the reassuring squeeze I wanted to, but the sentiment was there. "That sucks, Remy. For what it's worth, I think you'd make a good knight. You rode your horse like friggin' Zorro or something. You're amazing."

"Who?"

"Never mind. I'm sorry you didn't get to be the knight you wanted."

"But you see, I did. My brothers and sisters who took up Father's profession have been able to sustain the surrounding villages for a while now. Doing this? Picking up and leaving my village on a mission from the Lost Duchess and the Lost Princess? Riding alongside Bastien the Bold, two of the most decorated Wildmen, Duke Henri and Duke Lot? It's more than I could've dreamed. I'm trying to say thank you. Thank you for choosing me as your healer. It's nice to know that at forty-five, one can still feel like a boy on an adventure."

I tried to maintain the thread of conversation, despite how exhausted the whole ordeal left my body. "I'm happy for you. You totally rode with the best of them. I wouldn't be alive if it weren't for you cutting those snakes out of my leg." The sweat was thick on me now, and crazy uncomfortable. "Dude, I gotta wash off. I'm super way disgusting."

"I can help you with that."

Before he could help slide me down the embankment into the river, Bastien stumbled back to us, kicking off his shoes and rolling up his jeans that were muddy at the knees. "She still sweating out the poison? Reyn needs you to check on him, Remy. I did what I could to steady him, but he's still a little out of it."

"What's wrong with Reyn?" I asked as Remy's thoughts turned worried. He left us to help where he was more needed.

"Nothing's wrong with Reyn. Everyone gets a little worn out. You try keeping yourself, a duchess, and a princess safe, while riding on a horse for as long as he did yesterday and see how you like it." The angry note in his tone was back, and I could tell that by asking about Reyn, I was stepping on a nerve. Something was very wrong with Reyn, something maybe not even Remy could fix, but I knew better than to ask any further.

I didn't bite back. I decided to let his anger sizzle out in the open so he could examine it untarnished by my reaction. He unbuttoned his flannel shirt, turning away from me as he took off his white t-shirt underneath. I knew better than to look at him, though the desire was there. I loved his larger than life hard body, but it was clear he did not. He glanced at me out of the corner of his eye, as if daring me to look his way with any hint of even thinking about his scars. He moved to stand in the creek, friggin' shirtless, highlighting the unavoidable fact that I was sweaty, gross, and stained with mud. He was strong, and I had a hard time pushing myself up to sit. I crawled over to the edge of the creek a healthy few yards from where he stood.

"I'm over here," he informed me, as if I'd chosen distance from him by accident.

"And I'm over here. Your mood swings seem like they need a little space." I leaned over and splashed water on my face with shaking hands that screamed at me to go to sleep. My eyelids drooped, and my lower lip fell slack as a string of drool fell into the river. Sexy, I know.

He huffed, as if he had any sort of right to be exasperated by me. "Rinse off for real. You're filthy." He sloshed over me, cupped his hands and dumped water over my head that was bent down over the creek.

The simple pressure of the water was too much. It threw me off-balance and tilted me forward. I collapsed into the creek face-first, not even caring that I could barely lift myself up. After drowning with no water anywhere near me, drowning in two feet of river seemed like a fitting way to go.

Bastien pulled me up, his eyes wide with worry, startled that his "help" had been the thing that upended me. He sat me up in the river, making sure I was steady before letting me go. The water lapped at my ribs, soaking through my clothes and cooling me with merciful ease. "Sorry about that," Bastien muttered.

I stared ahead into the dark, holding my arms around my ribs. "I'm used to you by now."

Bastien stammered a few huffs, irritated that he was required to keep his attitude in check. Eventually he acquiesced, deflating with a humble, "I really didn't mean to tip you into the river like that."

"Be nicer to me," I said without putting any icing on the correction. I was tired of his constant push and pull, and wanted it to stop.

"Don't tell me how to be."

"Be nicer to me," I repeated. "Being Untouchable has turned you into a raging dick. Avalon may act like you're God's gift, but man, what a waste."

Bastien spoke through gritted teeth. "Don't act like you understand what life's like down here. You don't."

"You survived the Queen's Army, got yourself a second lease on life, and this is what you do with it? This is who you are now? This is how you talk to women?" I shook my head. "Total waste."

I could feel Bastien's hard gaze on me, trying to figure out my moves when I'd already laid my cards out on the table. I knew who I was, and had been pretty clear on that front, but he was still guessing. Finally, his shoulders dropped. "No one talks to me how you do."

"It's no surprise to me you've surrounded yourself with people who cower to your almighty temper. It's what all bullies do."

Bastien frowned, his eyebrows knitting together. "I'm not a bully."

At this, I looked pointedly up at him, not saying anything, but letting his own conscience stir to see if there were enough pieces of it to resurrect into something real.

Oh, how I wanted something real. In a land of make-believe, it was the one thing I craved.

When he finally spoke, it was my turn to feel the blast of surprise. "I didn't used to be a bully, anyway. You can't ask about Reyn. It sets me off when people... Just leave him be. He's been through enough."

"For the record, telling me what I'm allowed to care about is super way controlling. Not the best way to shake the bully persona you seem so fond of. Reyn's a good guy; I'm allowed to ask about him if he's hurt."

Bastien exhaled, closing his eyes. "You're right. I hate that you're right. Reyn's not... And I'm..." He motioned between the two of us. "I'm not good at this."

"Understatement, buddy." I pulled my knees to my chest as I sat in the water, shivering. Each shudder was painful, and I was desperate to get to a point where my body wasn't under such duress. "I don't feel so hot," I eked out through chattering teeth.

"Yeah? Well, you look amazing," Bastien responded sarcastically. He bent over and mussed my filthy hair, kneeling next to me in the river.

"You're a jerk," I mumbled, and then moved to all fours so I could dunk my head under the water. When I came up, remaining on my knees, I could feel him watching me in the dark that was lit only by the blue moon and the stars. "Be who you wish you were, Bastien. Don't be who they tried to break you down into. Then they win. You may have lived through everything they put you through, but if you spread your venom like this, then you still work for them. Don't be bitter and old. Be amazing and young with me."

Bastien ran his fingers through his hair several times before his movements calmed. "I can't imagine a better offer. Next time you ask about Reyn, I'll try to be good." He took in a long drag of air to cleanse his soul. "Next time you step on a landmine, I'll try not to blow up."

"I forgive you," I offered, though he hadn't actually apologized. I let the gentle lapping of the water be the only conversation between us for a few beats, and it seemed to ease the volatile nature of who we were together.

I reached up a shaky hand to rest on his wrist, making sure my voice warbled with weakness that wasn't too far off to fake. "B-Bastien?" I choked out.

"Yeah, honey?" He bent further to hear my quiet request.

His little terms of endearment always caressed my heart with a coo of sweetness, knowing how prone he was to shutting down all signs of a softer side.

I gripped Bastien's wrist and yanked, pulling him forward with all my diminished strength and leaning sideways so he fell right into the water next to me. He stood up, soaking wet, deciding between fuming and laughing. I managed a wan smile that caught his lopsided one at just the right moment. "Thought you could use a bath."

I saw the glimmer of play dance in his eyes mere seconds before he pounced. "You think so? I think *you* need a bath!" He dunked me under the water, pulling me up a breath later when he saw how out of it my body actually was. "You shouldn't start a war when you can't back it up with a real fight," he scolded me. "Get over here."

My chest moved unevenly as Bastien sat down in the few feet of water, pulled me across his lap and cradled me. I was weightless for the span of time that I was in his arms. Sure, you could blame that on the water, but any scientist will tell you water's only so buoyant. It was playing with Bastien that made me feel lighter. He made a horrible day end on a smirky note.

"That poison's no joke," I admitted. "Thanks for, you know, not letting me bite off my tongue."

He held up the finger he'd shoved in my mouth during my seizure. "I'll be needing a month with your healer after the number you did on my finger. I mean, would you look at that? If you're hungry, eat some berries, not me!" He displayed the cut and marked-up index finger to me with a wounded expression as he leaned against the embankment. It felt so natural, laying around with him. "You bit up my chest, too. I didn't know you had such a strong jaw."

I pressed his sore finger to my lips and kissed it. "Bastien?" I leaned into his arm that was supporting my back.

"Yeah, baby?"

I smiled at the flirty address that felt so very natural. "I have a question, and I want a straight answer."

"Hit me."

"Do you think Reyn's sister knows she's engaged to you?"

Bastien grew serious, studying my fingers as he laced them through his. "I don't see how she would. She fell asleep before I went to her father."

"So she wouldn't care if I kissed you?" I asked quietly.

He slowly moved his head from side to side. "No. She wouldn't care. I'm just Reyn's angry friend to her, nothing more."

My face was dripping just as his was, but I couldn't wait another minute to press my lips to his and see what all the fuss was about. "Bastien?"

His words came out husky, his caramel eyes blinking unrequitedly at me through his long, wet lashes. "Kiss me, Daisy. I'm dying for it over here."

No one had ever been dying for a kiss from me before. I leaned in, doing my best to ignore the alarms screaming in my head that I didn't know what I was doing, and might mess up my very first kiss. Lane had told me that when it was with the right guy, I wouldn't question myself so much, that I'd just go for it, and it would feel right. Easy. Like I'd always known how.

My wet lips lightly brushed across the crest of his, and our eyes swept shut to remain as sealed in the moment as we possibly could. My heart was pounding as I leaned a millimeter closer, ready to take the plunge I'd been waiting for.

36

UNCLE, COUSIN AND HIDDEN SNEERS

"*H*urry! Bring him down here. They're coming!" Rousseau splashed into the creek a few feet away, breaking us apart with a blast of reality. He ducked under the bridge with us, crumbling the romance. We'd had a near-death experience, coupled with the blue moonlight encouraging us to make the most of our up and down connection, but I'd taken too long to make my move.

"Soldiers marching this way," Bayard announced. He helped a barely upright Reyn hide with us under the bridge.

"Of course," Bastien grumbled. "That just figures. Where are the others?"

Bayard set Reyn down next to us in the water, his chin drooping downward toward his chest. "Are you kidding me? What've you been doing down here while we sorted it all out? We need the Princess to calm the horses, to tell them to be quiet and lay together in the woods."

Bastien was on the job, lifting me out of the water and carrying me to the thick smattering of trees to our left. "We're picking that kiss back up just as soon as we get a minute to ourselves," he informed me. "Now do your thing, horse girl."

"I've been called worse."

Lane's face was streaked with tears and pinched with anxiety that broke when she saw me. She abandoned the horses she, Henri and his two children were trying to calm in the thick of the woods as the troops marched toward us in the distance. "Baby? Rosie? How're you feeling?"

I shrugged, trying to pass off my torment as no big thing. "I'm totally fine. It was more annoying than anything else." I rapped my knuckles on Bastien's chest. "Could you let me down? I've got to go sit with the horses."

Bastien lowered my legs but held tight to my hand, walking my exhausted body through the forest and over to the horses with Lane, who steadied my elbow. I tried to hobble with pep in my half-step so she didn't worry, but it was a bad acting job. My good leg wasn't up for the task of supporting my weight, but I cheered it on all the same, telling my body this was no time to punk out on me. Lane kept tight to my side, letting me get her all wet, and stood with me while I talked to the horses. I'm pretty sure I freaked out Damond, who let out a noise of distress when the horses he hadn't been able to calm down each laid one by one next to each other, tucking their heads down so they didn't move around and make too much noise. They lay nestled tight together like giant kittens, all but purring up at me.

"How did you do that?" Damond balked, more scared of me than the army we could hear marching in our direction.

I opened my mouth to answer, but Bastien whispered, "Gwen! Help me with Reyn. This spot isn't as hidden as the patch of rocks the others are hiding behind. Everyone should hide there who isn't needed here."

He made to pick me up again as Gwen ran past us, but I backed away, leaning on Lane. "Go on. I should stay with the animals in case one of them gets spooked."

A shadow of hesitance was swept up in a look that mutated into total fear on Bastien's usually stoic and self-assured features. He held onto my hand with a firm command to his grip. "No. I'm your guard. I won't be apart from you."

Lane's arms around me gently pried us apart. "I've got her, Bastien. She's right. We won't be able to keep the animals quiet without her once the troops come."

"But... I don't... This isn't how it should be!" He let out a frustrated growl. "Don't let go of her for any reason. Got it, Lane? I mean it. Her hand doesn't leave yours until *I* take it away from you. No one else."

Lane lowered her voice. "You're going to have to ask a whole lot nicer for her hand one day when you finally grow some manners. I've been looking after Rosie for her whole life. Now, go!" Lane harrumphed as she turned and helped me over to the animals. "That boy's getting on my last nerve. Telling me to check on Reyn when you're in pain. Telling me how to look after my own daughter."

I let Lane get her anger out, knowing she usually simmered down shortly after she vented. My teeth ground together at being treated like the broken wheel on the wagon. That was way worse than being treated like the ugly girl growing up. I'd at least been useful, which was an attribute I clung to.

Lot came out to help Lane, but I didn't even have the sanity to let the butterflies rise up in my belly at the sight of his princely features. I held my head high even though I was sopping wet, injured and ready to fall over. Lane toned down her mothering and helped me to sit down between Marquis and Damond's gray horse. They were pressed tight together, so I floated between their backs, cradled comfortably in the warm nest of bodies they provided. "Alright, kids," I said to the animals as Abraham Lincoln ambled to me and plopped his muzzle across my hip. "I need you to keep very still. Stay absolutely silent until I say so. Those are some super bad guys coming our way, and if we're careful, they'll keep right on walking."

Gwen's horse whined to me that Gwen was too far away. "I know, sweetie, but even if the soldiers come close to her, you can't make a noise, otherwise they'll find her and take her away. Everyone just close your eyes and take a little rest. You all rode so long today." I looked up at Lane, who was sweating as she held my hand. "Do animals sleep here?"

"Most of them, yes. Just like animals where we're from."

Henri had his hands on two horses, sitting next to his son, who was comforting two more. They had the same longer nose and angular features to them. Damond stroked his horse's flank, his eyes focused on the army that marched ever onward. He couldn't have been much more than eighteen, but there was a sad determination in his eyes that made him appear far older. "Aunt Lane, dip your head lower. I'm worried they'll see you."

My head whipped from Damond to Lane, my eyes wide and my body suddenly feeling a jolt of renewed vigor that I knew wouldn't last long. "*Aunt* Lane? She's your aunt? You're her nephew?"

"Yes. I haven't actually met her until this trip, but yes. My mother Tyronoe was her sister." I saw Damond clearly, his fair complexion made to look even whiter next to his jet black short hair. It was styled on top in a swoop that moved backwards over his head like a frozen wave with too much product in it. "You didn't know that?"

"But does that make us cousins? Like, real blood relation cousins?"

Damond cast me a look of disbelief mired with amusement. "Well, yeah. I thought you knew that. Duke Henri is my father, your uncle by marriage."

The best kind of shock ripped through me, making it feel like Halloween and Christmas all rolled into one. My head whipped toward Henri, my mouth falling open. "Henri? Are you really my uncle?"

Henri's voice came back to me with the hint of affection to it. "Yes, Rosalie. I didn't know if Lane had told you, so I was waiting until we had a moment to more properly introduce myself."

My smile beamed at Damond, and I leaned over Abraham Lincoln to give him a high five, which he didn't understand the mechanics of. "Dude, that's awesome! You and Gwen are my cousins? After this Jewels of Good Fortune nonsense, we're going to have so much fun together! I always wanted a cousin. Now I've got two, plus Roland, plus an uncle? Today rocks!"

Damond chuckled, his eyes crinkling at the sides. He had a pencil eraser-sized birthmark next to his right eye that moved upwards with his grin. His face didn't look practiced with genuine smiling, so I made a mental note to remedy that during our time together. "I've never known anyone who survived the *étouffer* poppies and had such enthusiasm for the day less than an hour later."

Henri cleared his throat. "Gwen is adopted, so she's not your actual cousin."

My nose scrunched, confused at the left-field information. "Oh. Well, in my world, there aren't those divisions. If you're adopted, you're legally family. So to me, Gwen would be just as much my cousin as Damond and Roland."

Henri's eyebrows rose and fell in a beat. "What a nice system. Morgan le Fae doesn't recognize adopted children as able to sit on the throne, which negated the whole reason for adoption in the first place."

His words tasted sour in my mouth. I mean, it sounded like he only adopted her so he'd have a female heir to sit on the throne someday. I remembered that the society was run on a matriarchal system, so I guessed he'd been desperate to have a daughter, but his workaround to that hadn't been honored. Still, it was Gwen's life, and to hear him speak so dismissively about his own daughter felt... wrong. I was glad Gwen was across the way, hiding with the others.

I didn't know if I was allowed to speak my feelings on the matter, since Lane remained mute, so I tried to switch the conversation to a lighter note. "Well, I always wanted a cousin, and now I have three. Tell me about growing up here, Damond. You take care of the horses? That's super cool. What about Gwen? What sort of magical awesome-ness does she get up to?"

Damond looked like he'd never been paid such focused attention before in his life, and didn't know what to do with it. "Um, well, yes. I keep the horses. Wish I could understand them like you can. That would make every-thing easier for me. Gwen gardens a lot. She's trying to cross pollinate a mandrake with a ginger root to see if it can enhance the healing properties."

"Is that even possible?" Lot asked from his spot at the

end of the row. He scooted in next to me atop the horses when Marquis' head craned around to be nearer him. They were sweet together. It was clear Marquis loved Lot.

"That's super amazing that Gwen is so creatively minded. You both sound wicked smart."

Damond chuckled at my phrasing. "Hopefully less wicked and more smart. What else do you want to know?"

"Um, you're a prince? Maybe start with that. Seriously, you don't know how to market your awesomeness. Is your castle huge?"

I could hear the amusement in Damond's voice. "Well, not compared to yours, but yes, it's sizeable. Around the footage of Lot's family's, I'd imagine."

"Mine? What are you talking about? Lane and I have a two-bedroom apartment. It's cozy." That was my delicate way of saying it was very small.

"Thanks for that, baby. She's being nice. Our place is tiny. Your bedroom is probably bigger than our whole flat, Damond." Lane spoke with her head down, crouched next to Henri at the horses' rears. There was a healthy foot of distance between them, and I could tell by the stiffness in her shoulders that even that amount of space from Henri wasn't enough for her.

"I'm sure you're joking," Damond said, though I could tell by his furtive looks that darted between Lane and me that he wasn't certain at all.

"Laney?" I asked, keeping my tone light. I'd been so caught up in how all of this was affecting me that I hadn't checked in on how all the drama was crashing down on her. I would rather have asked her in private, but we hadn't been granted much time alone. I was just meeting my cousin, but she was just finding out that she had a nephew and a niece she hadn't known about. And just like that, they were already grown. "You alright, baby girl?"

"That's exactly what I am, sweetness." The pinched flavor of her reply told me she wasn't okay, but was waiting until she had a down moment so she could break down without an audience.

"How's your magic holding up? Are you having trouble finding your way back to your mojo?"

Lane pfft'd, as if using magic was child's play to her. "Give me another week in Avalon, and you don't wanna know the damage I'll be able to do with my magic back on tap and fully restored."

"If only invisibility was one of the tricks in your arsenal. Then we could sneak into men's bedrooms." I shrugged at Lot's chagrinned noise of astonishment and uncertain chortle. "What? It's so we can steal their cell phones and tie their shoelaces in knots. What were you thinking?" I shook my head to scold him in mock astonishment. "Oh, you're sick. Just disgusting, Lot. I'm a lady."

"My apologies, *Lady* Rosalie." My bravado was always worst when I was sickest, and my jokes at their stupidest. A wave of utter fatigue swept over me, and I leaned more securely into the two horses I was sandwiched between. Lot lowered his voice. "I'm sorry I didn't get off the horse sooner or ride faster. You were so still; I had no idea the spiders were already taunting you while we were still riding. How did you do that? And I should've warned you about the *étouffer* poppies. I didn't realize you didn't know about them."

I shifted Abraham Lincoln to sit on my lap to make sure he wasn't seen. Lot shifted closer to me. "It all worked out. But yeah, assume I know nothing about your world. A heads-up the next time I'm about to be poisoned would be helpful." I yawned. "At what point are we breaking for the night? I know it's go, go, go, but I don't think I'm up for much more tonight."

"How do you mean?" Henri asked from his place further down the line near Lane.

"Sleeping. I know you all don't need it, but I do."

Lane's voice was quiet. "Yeah, I meant to mention that back at the whole meet and greet."

"Why does she sleep?" Henri asked with an accusation directed at Lane. "She's not a Brownie who's promised herself to a family; she's Fae. Plus, she's her mother's daughter, and Morgan's loaded with magic. The apple can't have fallen that far from the tree."

"She talks to animals, Henri. That actually requires a lot of magic. She's been like that since she was a baby. Always slept through the night so she could go play with her furry friends. Also, the whole Compass thing plays a part in it."

"Well, she must stop all that now! We can't be taking

three or four hours to stop so she can lie down. The longer we can move through Avalon without Morgan knowing she's here, the safer we'll all be."

I shot Henri a look of confusion. "Three or four hours? Try eight, pal."

"Eight?" Henri was scandalized. "No, no. Rosalie, you must stop at once."

"Oh, you want her to stop talking to animals now? Convenient timing. We need her to keep the animals calm when the soldiers get here." Lane wasn't usually so irritable, but I could tell she didn't like conversing with Henri at all.

"Enough. Do as I say, Rosalie. Elaine, you have no idea what you're doing with her, clearly. If she's sleeping that much, you're in over your head. The only reason she would need to sleep that much is if her magic was broken, like Reyn. If you've allowed her to carry on like this, you have no idea what you're doing. I can take over parenting the child, since you clearly don't seem up for the task."

I balked, but didn't bother with a reply. I didn't much like being bossed by people I'd known for a day. I super didn't care for people talking down to Lane.

Lane usually took it in stride when people gave her parenting advice, but she had zero tolerance for Henri. "You know, you were always like this. Even to Tyronoe, may she rest. You think you know best, so you bulldoze everyone else and tell us all how you think it should be done, forgetting the fact that your plan makes no sense!"

I could tell Henri wasn't used to being so openly defied. It was like he and Lane were just waiting for the right moment to unleash their hidden sneers they'd reserved just for each other. "I'll have you know that my children have never slept a wink beyond their first two years of life, because I know how to manage my household. The magic in Rosalie is pure. It shouldn't need recharging that often. You're running the child ragged."

"She's *my* child, and you know nothing about what she needs."

Henri bristled, his voice dropping to a low stream of perpetual judgment. "I know that as much as you wished for a baby of your own, Master Kerdik never gave you one. Your womb is closed. That's why Morgan let you be her nursemaid when you lived here. Stealing Rosalie was wise for the kingdom, but it also served your own agenda of getting a child. That doesn't mean you know what you're doing. Rosalie calls you by your first name."

"Okay, that's enough!" I turned to glare at Henri. "For starters, don't talk about Lane's womb like you know anything about owning a uterus, because you don't. And that's a real low blow, making her feel bad for not being able to have children. Secondly, she has a child, and it's me. *I'm* her daughter. She gave up having a life, having money, having anything to raise me, not to mention forfeiting a ninth of a kingdom and a castle and all that. Thirdly, I don't always talk to animals, but they're always talking to me. It's not Lane running me ragged. It's me finding friends in a different way than you do. As much as you think you know what it's like in Common, you don't, so back up off her, man. Lane's my best friend, and I won't let you run her down like that."

Henri was quiet a few seconds, and when he answered, I could tell he was well adept at ruling nations with his iron voice. "Young lady, you'll speak to me more respectfully."

"Earn my respect, then. It's lazy and entitled to just expect reverence because of your age or your title. I don't respect anyone who talks down to Lane like that. And doing that in front of your own kid? Bringing up her 'closed womb'? You're verbally punching her in the face after having not seen your sister-in-law in over two decades. I gotta say, not having an uncle isn't something I missed out on, if you're any indication of the fun."

Henri spoke through gritted teeth. "Elaine, I suggest you take a switch to your charge at the very first opportunity. She needs to be taught some respect."

I opened my mouth to tell him exactly what he could do with his switch, but Lot leaned over and pressed his finger to my lips, sealing the insults inside where they simmered along with my anger. "Quiet, now. You've said enough."

Lane let out a slow chuckle that started to sound evil after a few beats. "Oh, Henri. Parenting advice from you? Really? Why don't we have a nice, long conversation about Draper. Then you can tell me the wisdom of your ways."

Henri's hand swooshed through the air. The sight was so strange, it didn't register that he was about to slap her until I heard the smack that whipped her chin to the side. I gasped at her quiet yelp, horrified. "Apologize," Henri demanded, sounding like a superior ruler in desperate need of some overthrowing.

37

NOT YOUR PUNCHING BAG

*A*braham Lincoln howled, and let loose a terrifying growl that told everyone he was very much undomesticated, no matter how much we wanted to fool ourselves otherwise. He loved Lane, and didn't take kindly to her being slapped around.

Anger. White hot fury rode through me, yelling at my weakened body to get up and rip, tear, kill. Lot saw my red rage rising, and moved over to position himself between me and Henri, the warning in his eyes telling me to back down. When I lunged forward clumsily, he intercepted, pressing me down to lay in between the horses. I struggled against Lot for the space to get up, but he held me in place with embarrassing ease. "No, Rosie. You don't go against Duke Henri. Stay put." The betrayal I felt at Lot's restraint resonated deep inside me, severing off any attraction I might have felt towards him. "You have to stay hidden!" he protested, pinning me to the cool grass next to Marquis.

"Listen good, you waste of a crown. You'll watch your back around me," I spat to Henri the second Lot's finger moved from my mouth. "Lane? Honey, you alright?"

"I'm fine, baby." I could tell she was crying. I hated it when she cried. "Don't listen to this, okay? It's not about you. It's old drama we haven't worked through yet. You're perfect just how you are. Don't stop talking to the animals. It's good for you, and it makes you happy. We'll find time for you to sleep. We'll keep hidden, no problem." She sniffled, and I hated Henri more than I hated anyone else in that moment. I'd gotten a brand new uncle and turned him against me and Lane in the span of a conversation. Miss Personality, at it again.

I struggled against Lot to get to her, but Lot was too strong, and I was too weak. Marquis remained still, though he voiced to me his distress that his master and his friend were fighting right next to him. Lot remained over me, keeping me pinned as his eyes searched in the distance for the army. "I thought you were one of the good guys," I whispered, angry at Lot for keeping me in such a submissive position when he should have been defending Lane's honor.

"I am," Lot promised. "I didn't warn you about the *étouffer* flowers because I thought you knew. You told me to warn you about things that were different in our worlds. People don't go against the Dukes. Henri? Ferdinand the

Grave? And Duke Isengrim back when he was still alive? The dukes rule what's left after Morgan wiped out the other provinces. You can't change Duke Henri, but you can surely die trying. As angry as you are at me now, I'll risk it if it keeps you alive."

I wanted to argue with him, but he was so sincere, and his eyes were tinged with sadness. I gave him one more fruitless struggle before collapsing in a pose of surrender I would never have done on my own. "Laney? I'm here. I'm right here for you." I tried to keep the fear out of my voice and spoke only to her. "I got a scholarship because of you, because you push me the right amount. I was on track to finish the semester strong, too. I don't have any cavities, I have a good job, good insurance, can change a tire, and was happy back home because you let me be who I am. All that's because of you. Don't you let someone who hasn't seen you in twenty-one years make you question how good you are at being my mom. I know who you are. Don't let some jaggoff make you question that." The insecurity I tried never to give a voice to crept in. I'd often pictured my life if Lane hadn't stepped in and claimed me after my birth mother fake died. I would've ended up in foster care, and who knows where I'd be then. There's something about being adopted that makes you extra grateful, and therefore I didn't cause as much teen havoc as the other girls in my grade growing up. I knew how lucky I was. "You didn't make a mistake, taking me."

I could hear Lane's heart breaking. "Oh, Ro. You're the

best part of my life. You're nothing in the same universe as a mistake. You did all those things yourself. I told you, hun. Don't listen. It's not about you. Henri and I have a lot to sort through."

"Well, he can sort through it on the business end of my fist. You hear that, Henry? You come near Lane again, and I'll Texas Justice your ass so quick, you won't know what hit you. Lane is my mom, not your punching bag!"

Henri was livid. "You need a day in my stocks, child."

"And you need a—" I was in high gear, but Lot covered my mouth.

"Enough," Lot warned. "You'll get yourself killed at this rate. Breathe, Rosalie. Breathe. And Henri, you're a fool to strike a Duchess. She holds more power than you do, so you'll know your place, instead of trying unsuccessfully to force either woman to cower to you." Lot stiffened, his head looking up toward the road where the soldiers were nearing us. "Everyone, quiet! This isn't the time. The army's near, and finding Roland and the gems is more important than this fight. Not another sound!"

Lot leaned down, pressing his chest on my shoulder to stay low and make sure I didn't fly off the handle again. He released my mouth and his grip on my arm, but he remained on top of me. "Henri's out," I whispered in his ear. "I'm not going anywhere with someone who hits my mom."

Lot hung his head, pressing his forehead to mine. "I know. I thought you might say something like that." His breath tickled my lips, and partially pinned as I was, I felt totally at his command. "I'll talk to Henri. Properly, how it's meant to be done. I'll see what I can do to smooth things out. I'm a duke; trust me to know how this works."

"I don't want them smoothed. I want him gone!"

Damond leaned toward us and spoke up for the first time since it all went south. His whisper was barely audible while Henri and Lane were distracted with their quiet bickering. "What about me? I didn't hit anyone, but I'll have no choice but to leave if Duke Henri says I have to." It struck me, not for the first time, that neither Damond nor Gwen called him "Father", but instead used his proper title.

"I'll take care of it," Lot answered. His whole body was tense as he kept his eyes on the soldiers. I tried to follow his lead and focus on the greater danger, giving up my claim on the fight when he whispered a gentle, "Quiet, now."

The soldiers neared the bridge, and my heart started to pick up its pace when their black boots pounded on the wood, marching too near where Bastien, Reyn and the others hid behind a smattering of rocks. There was a hairy man like Bayard and Rousseau who stood off to the side next to a guy in a medal-bedecked uniform. I could only assume the pressed red uniform jacket meant this dude was the new captain. The Wildman had a pig-nose, and a panflute clutched in his brown fur-covered hand. There was an enormous black bird on his shoulder, and they both scanned the forest without blinking.

The Wildman let out a short whistle, and Lot covered my ears in fear. The black bird was over a foot long, with a wingspan that was four times that. I gasped when she rose up at the whistle to circle the area – a majestic bird soaring, and clearly on a mission. She looked carefully through the trees, and I knew when she landed on a branch overhead and craned her long neck down, that she'd found us. Dread churned in my gut as I tried to think up a possible solution. She was about to open her beak to alert her master when I whisper-shouted, "Hey, you don't want to do that. Come and talk to me after your people leave."

Lot covered my mouth again, but I bit him. He was an easier one to shake off than Bastien, waving his hand to rid himself of the sting from my canines. "What are you doing? That's a tracking bird! They'll find us!"

"She's already found us. I'm trying to make sure she doesn't tell her owner. Let me do what I do." I turned my attention back to the trees, speaking so quietly, I'm surprised the sound even reached her. "Go tell them that no one's here, and you can swing back and talk to me after they leave. Deal?"

The bird hopped on the branch like it had to pee, her thoughts too excited and jumbled for me to make sense of. All I caught was a grateful, *"The* Voix! *The* Voix! *Wait here!"* before she flew off to perch on her master's shoulder once more.

One of the commanders stood to the side, watching the uninhabited trees with a skeptical eye. Lot clutched me tighter, his lips moving to my cheek and exhaling into my ear. "Steady now," he whispered, making my body forget that it had just been restrained by him a minute ago.

The pig-nosed commander waited until his men were over the bridge before peering down into the space below. I let out a gust of air when he passed over the bridge and moved away from the cluster of rocks the others were hiding behind, leaving our group of royal misfits to our nefarious deeds.

38

LOT IN LIFE

*I*t was a long wait before anyone dared to move, least of all me. Lot and I were in a game of chicken, his lips hovering half an inch above mine. "Such a fair mouth for such angry fight to come tumbling out of it." He touched my upper lip with his thumb, cupping my cheek in his palm to see just how pliable I was. I was a mixture of weakened from the poppies, and weak in the knees from the touch I wasn't accustomed to. I was more used to the slaps on the back and one-armed dude hugs. Lot looked at me and handled my skin as if I was something breakable. I couldn't remember the last time I was allowed to be breakable. His breath was sweet when he exhaled in my face. "That was incredible, the way you spoke to the tracking bird. I have to kiss you, Rosalie. You saved us." His sincerity mingled with an earnest pleading, a request for him to remain a gentleman while giving in to his boyish desires.

Being desired is a heady thing, and one I wasn't used to at all.

My body was total jelly, and my brain was confused and turning rapidly to mush. "I don't know," I mumbled. "Bastien. He... I..." I didn't know why I felt a loyalty to Bastien. Dude yelled at me almost as much as he struck up normal conversation.

Lot nodded, leaving his lips right where I could close the small gap and take them. "Very well. I'll wait and see how that ends up. Know this: I'm quite taken with you. It's not many who would have the strength to stand up to Duke Henri. Fewer still who can command a tracking bird trained by the Queen's Army."

I spluttered, the butterflies and pterodactyls back and zooming around in my belly at full force. Marquis was in my ear, rattling off all the things he loved about his master, and how happy he would be if I stayed with them.

Abraham Lincoln was not so convinced. He bumped his butt against Lot, backing him away from me as the army safely passed without so much as a pause in our direction. *"No,"* he whined to me. *"Daddy. Mommy should be with Daddy."*

"It's not as simple as all that, guys. I'm not ready for that kind of thing here. Not like this. Not when I can barely stand."

"Apologies. You're right." Lot backed away, confused when I tried to sit up next to him.

"Not you. I was talking to Marquis and Abraham Lincoln. They're all about marrying me off."

Lot wrapped his arm around my shoulders to make sure I didn't collapse backwards, and turned me so I could rest my back against his horse. "Good boy, Marquis." He smiled at my chuckle. "I take it Abraham Lincoln's on Bastien's side?"

"There's no sides. I'm not the commodity you're thinking I am. Once you both realize that, it'll be business as usual. Hold on." I heard my new feathered friend from high up in the branches. "Hey! Come here, buddy." I waited for the bird to swoop down, surprising me with how big she was. She was the size of a scarlet macaw, but completely black. Her feathers were like wet leather, soft and tough. When she perched on my crisscrossed legs, Lot jerked away, leaving only his hand on my shoulder. Henri and Damond whispered noises of distress, but Lane knew I could handle a bird. Sheesh.

Her name was Seven, and she let out a constant stream of worry that her insubordination would be found out.

"Hey, I've got you. You're alright. Now tell me what the Army's doing out here."

"The judge's boy. They want the Untouchable, so they're after the judge's boy. I see him over there behind those rocks. I should tell my master!" Seven fretted.

"No, no. You don't want to do that. If you do, Reyn will

die. That would just break my heart. Do you want to break my heart?"

"You can hear me! I can hear you! I won't break your heart. You're the Voix! *You're my Voix!"*

"Aw, that's sweet. I can see why the army likes you; you're so kind. Pretty, too."

"So I can't tell my master I can see the judge's boy? That I can see the Untouchable?"

"No, you can't tell him that. It's our secret." I smoothed her feathers, smiling when she told me how she liked them preened. "Man, you're stunning."

Lot's voice was even, but taut with tension. "Rosalie, that's a *Buteur*. Do you have those in your world?"

"We have birds, but not with leathery feathers like this. So cool."

"That bird is a trained killer, used by the army to incapacitate its enemies with a single cry. It's no doubt watching for Reyn and Bastien."

"Oh, well that's alright." I kissed the side of Seven's head. "She won't tell anyone on us. You feeling alright, baby? What's this?" I pointed to a missing patch where Seven's armored feathers were missing from her breast.

She opened her beak to chirp a quiet reply. *"My trainer cut me. Let me stay with you! If you hide me until they pass, they won't be able to find me. I can't ignore his whistle! I can't disobey! You have to keep me with you."* Seven flapped her wings, letting me know she'd rather risk her luck with a bear than go back to her master.

"Oh, sweetie. It's alright. You can stay with us. We could use you, to tell you the truth. Would you mind helping us out? Flying overhead occasionally to look for trouble? We're trying to stay out of sight."

Seven took flight, soaring overhead, and crossing back and forth to get a good picture of what might still be coming for us.

She descended as quick as she could, scaring Damond. *"They've all gone ahead. They didn't see you, and there are no more coming this way. But you have to keep me from the whistle, otherwise I have to obey!"*

"Okay, Seven. Okay. Tuck on in here." My fingers were clumsy after all my body had been through. "Lot, help me. We have to cover Seven's ears so when the flute sounds again, she doesn't go running to it. She wants to stay with us, but she's afraid the flute will make her narc on us."

"Narc? What's that mean?" Lot shook his head. "This bird is dangerous, Rosalie. Not a pet."

"Hello, I've got a bear in my lap. I think we can handle a little bird."

"I have half a mind to break its neck so it doesn't render us all unconscious with a single squawk."

I clutched Seven to me protectively. "You keep that kinda talk away from me," I shout-whispered.

No sooner had the words left me did I hear a panflute let out three sharp notes that summoned Seven. For some reason, it made me want to come closer to the sound. Seven begged me to make her stay, to be more powerful than the whistle. I was doing my best, but knew I was too weak to restrain anyone. I swore, whispering to the others, "She's got to go back to her master. I don't know if he'll force the truth out of her with that flute thing. Lane, hold her for me and cover her head so she can't hear the flute!"

"I've got her, baby," Lane assured me, taking Seven from my hands and tucking her to her breast. She muffled the bird's hearing and clamped her beak shut with her fist, giving me a brave smile I hoped was even a little bit sincere.

I moved to stand, but Lot anchored me to the earth once more. "We aren't in the clear yet, Rosie. Wait here a little while longer."

"The song! I need to go to it," I protested, unsure of my own reasons.

Lot clutched me tight so I didn't go where my body wanted – toward the Wildman with the panflute. "No, no. It's magic, is all. Stay with us."

"Something's wrong. I have to go to the dude with the flute! He's calling me."

Lot held me tighter, stroking Abraham Lincoln's fur as my bear debated ambling toward the sound. "You can't go, Rosalie. You have to resist it. It's a trick of the Wildmen. It's one of the magics that belongs only to their species. They can persuade you with their music. Sing a different song in your mind. That usually helps."

"How come it's not working on you?" I asked, my teeth gritted as I fought every urge inside of me that wanted to go toward the enemy. My veins started to pull in his direction, guiding my body where the music wanted me to go.

"It is. I'm just more trained in resisting it. It's merely a suggestion, Rosie. Just say no to the temptation."

The flute felt like it was singing straight into my brain. "I have to go there!" I ordered Abraham Lincoln to go to Lane, and made to stand again. Lot's arms full-on restrained me in the next heartbeat, holding me back as I struggled with an urgency that surprised us both. "Let me go!" I begged. "He needs to know where Reyn is. I know! I know!"

"Rosalie, quiet!" Lot's hand went over my mouth, and though I felt the incredible desire to shout to the Wildman where Reyn was, part of me was grateful Lot kept me from obeying the flute. He crushed me down into the grass all over again, covering one of my ears with his free hand. His lips spoke into my other ear, trying to drown out the sound of the flute that felt never-ending. "You don't want to tell him where Reyn is. Reyn's with us. He's following you as his princess, so you must protect him. Resist, sweet girl. Resist. Focus on my voice."

I was so confused, and felt both desires with equal urgency and not enough logic to see either decision through. I began to thrash around, whimpering at the total split in my personality – wanting to run to the flute, and also stay away from it. Fear poked at me that I could be divided so easily. I pointed in Reyn's direction with a shaking hand, and though the army was long gone, part of me felt right in obeying the flute. Straight through my self-loathing, an itch was soothed at my compliance.

"No, no. Quiet now. Why is it so strong in you?" Lot weighted his body atop mine, foregoing social propriety and crushing me down into the grass. I clawed at his ribs, but found no relief in the defiance.

39

ONE FOR ME, ONE FOR LANE

*W*hen the flute finally stopped, I collapsed back into the grass, breathless but still wanting to find the Wildman and tell him exactly where Reyn was. "Help!" Lot whispered to Lane and Henri.

Lane scowled at Lot. "Get off my daughter!" she shout-whispered at him.

"She's as susceptible to the Wildman's flute as a child! She's trying to tell him where Reyn is."

"What? Rosie, calm down. Take a breath. Resist it, baby." She moved over with Seven and knelt by my head. She handed Seven to Damond, who was nervous at being so near the deadly bird. Lane bent down and covered both my ears while Lot remained atop me, covering my mouth and pinning me down so I couldn't go where my body wanted.

It didn't matter, though. It didn't matter because I

wasn't the one who told the Wildman something was up. In the exchange of the bird from Lane to Damond, Seven blurted out that there was a man nearby. She caught herself too late, and whipped away as fast as she could to divorce herself from the sound of the flute that controlled her every bit as much as it did me. She ripped through branches and slammed her head into an unyielding tree trunk on purpose to knock herself out, so she wouldn't rat out Reyn anymore than she already had. It was a sacrifice that scared me, and broke my heart.

The army had already moved on, leaving the military Wildman to move around on his own. I'm guessing he had his flute he could use to summon them back if he came across Reyn. I tried to break free from Lot's grip and point to where the dude was wandering around too near the rocks for my liking.

"Stay still! It's alright, Rosalie. Quiet now."

They didn't know what Seven had told the soldier. They didn't know the Wildman was working on a hunch that his bird might have found a man who could be Reyn. I tried to tell Lot with my eyes all of that, but if you can believe it, Lot doesn't speak eyeballs.

Henri stood up straight the second he caught on that I was trying to save the day as much as end it for us. With stealthy feet, he moved through the woods and around toward the rocks. I could hear the metal *"shink"* of his sword sliding from its sheath.

The hairy soldier with the horse's tail heard it, too. His

head whipped in Henri's direction. He put his panflute to his lips to call for backup, but Bastien and Bayard charged out from their hiding place, running at the man with their knives and swords ready.

Henri charged as well, meeting the onslaught just as it started. The Wildman cast down his flute and pulled out a sword, clashing with Bayard, whose heart, I could tell, wasn't in the throwdown. Maybe it was a brotherhood of the horsetail thing. Bayard kept him from running off toward the soldiers, but none of his slashes were aimed to kill.

Bastien didn't pull punches, especially when he was armed with a knife against a sword. I yelped into Lot's palm as Bastien stabbed with a quick hand and twisted his knife in the soldier's side. Henri made a quick slice along the throat from behind, and the two lowered the soldier to the grass as he choked on his own blood. I saw Bastien whispering something in the soldier's ear, and guessed it was the same army deathbed prayer he'd given Silvain. My heart sank for Bastien, and I worried at how many of his former friends he would have to kill before his world was put right again.

My internal scream was on repeat in short bursts of horror as I watched the gutting and then the cover-up. The blood on the ground was quickly covered with torn bits of grass and dirt. The soldier was wrapped in his own red cloak to stem the flow of blood. Bastien hoisted up the 5'11" Chewbacca and marched him into the woods, not coming out for five minutes until the body was sufficiently hidden.

Lot kept me crushed to the ground, in case I tried to run off again. I didn't, though. As soon as the soldier died, the desire to run to him and spill the big secret deserted me in the next second.

Henri came back to us, catching his breath at the very inappropriate position we were in. "Lot, get up right now. Young lady, you'll control yourself. It's just a little song. You can't go running off after every distraction that comes into your ears." He huffed at me. "Even children know that."

"Apologies, Princess," Lot offered for Henri's sake. "Are you okay now?"

I nodded, letting my body go limp with compliance. When he let his hand move from my mouth, I bit my lip against my embarrassment. "What was that? I couldn't stop myself. It's like, the whistle called and I couldn't keep myself from running to him to rat out Reyn. I'm so sorry!"

"The Wildmen are gifted with the ability to persuade behavior through their music. Most feel the pull, but the simpler the mind, the more easily it can be coaxed into following the tune." Henri looked down his long nose at me imperiously, not bothering to hold back his true feelings about my usefulness on this trip.

Lane sneered at him as she helped me to sit up, patting my back in support. "You're calling the Princess of Avalon a simple-minded fool?"

"If not for Morgan's rule that only children born into

the crown could sit on the throne, then Gwen would also be a Princess of Avalon. In fact, before Rosalie showed her face, Gwen was the closest thing our kingdom had. Gwen would never have been so easily persuaded by the Wild-man's flute. My adopted daughter is of the highest quality."

It was like being punched in the gut and then repeatedly pushed until you were a pile of nothing on the floor. I kept my head down, lest Henri know he was right on the money. I wasn't smart, and I had the mediocre grades to prove it. Judah could glance at his books and ace his exams. I had a tutor, notecards, study sessions, meetings with professors and countless lucky guesses on tests to get a mostly passing grade.

Lot stood, squaring his shoulders to Henri. "Know your place. Morgan le Fae is the queen, and we are only dukes. Your children and any that I may bear will not share equal status with Rosalie."

Henri postured, looking down his nose at Lot. "Of course yours wouldn't be on equal status. You didn't marry or come from a Daughter of Avalon. You were merely next in line to rule Province 5 when there was no more blood-line to speak of."

Lot's nostrils flared, but he kept on-topic. "Simply being born Morgan's daughter puts her above even us. You'll not run down a member of our Council."

Henri and Lot invested twenty seconds in a staring contest before Henri broke the tension with a lofty scoff. "If this is the state of the royal family, I think a revolt is in order. I shudder to think of the damage such a suggestible girl could do to Avalon."

Lane pulled me up, rolling her sleeves and gearing up for a reckoning on my behalf. "Rosie, go get the others. Tell them to get ready to move to wherever we're holing up for the night. I'm going to have a few words with your uncle."

"My adopted daughter won't be accompanying us on the trek," Henri informed us. "It's not proper for a woman to travel with a pack of Wildmen and an Untouchable. She was allowed to come this far only because you all needed an escort. I have high hopes for Gwen, who had no trouble at all resisting a simple flute, and no trouble resisting giving her affections to two different men." He narrowed his eyes at Lot in accusation. "Damond will be escorting his adopted sister home."

"Duke Henri?" Damond questioned. I could tell by his shrink back into his turtle shell that the simple address was on the furthest edge of daring he could go. I started hobbling away towards the direction I'd seen Seven kamikaze herself, but I could still hear them all well enough to crumple my shreds of self-esteem into a ball and throw them all in the trash can. So much for getting my new uncle to like me. He'd guessed right – I was stupid.

"That's up to you," Lane replied. "Gwen's your daughter."

Uncle Henri's nose rose in the air. "Yes, and there's still plenty of hope for her to marry well, though I can see you've given up hope with your daughter. I won't have Gwen's reputation tarnished."

"Screw you!" I barked, picking up the dazed bird and clutching her tight. I pressed the side of her head to my breast and stroked her feathers, cooing gently to her to make sure she knew I appreciated her sacrifice. I was no good with people; my place was with the animals, who never once implied I was stupid, or cared about the odds on my marrying marketability.

Lane put her hand on mine when I hobbled back into the fold, quieting me without shutting me up. "Henri, you hold the scepter in your province, but out here, we're equals. If anything, Rosie's in charge. She's the one we're counting on. It's her you'll need on your side if you want us to find the missing Jewels of Good Fortune and save Avalon with them. You haven't had to think about how you talk to people in a long time. Probably not since I left Avalon. But here it is now. Learn to follow, or go home."

"You dare speak to me like that?" Henri's chest puffed out, looking kingly and a little scary. Marquis was worried and stood with the other horses. Abraham Lincoln roared at Henri, scaring Seven, who flapped her free wing to fend off my bear.

Bastien ran to us, stopping short when he saw me holding what was apparently the deadliest bird in Avalon. "Whoa! Rosie, let go of that bird!"

Lane stood, her fight face firmly in place as she squared her shoulders to Henri. "You don't get it, do you.

430 | MARY E. TWOMEY

All she has to do is announce herself, and she could have you bowing to her in front of the whole kingdom. She's above you, Henri. She's above me. She's Morgan le Fae's daughter! She'll have the best of the best suitors lined up around the block, no matter what you think of how she was raised."

My head whipped to Lane in time with Henri's scandalized gasp. "Is that true?" I asked. Bastien's expression hardened, but really, what else was new? He was always pissy about something.

"Of course it. is. Morgan owns the most land after she took the flailing provinces as hers. She has the most power, and you're the only heir to her throne. You're second in power only to her."

I could tell Henri wanted to retaliate with either physical force or a royal edict, but his face grew purple with the rage he stuffed inside. "Very well," he said, his voice barely controlled. "This is where my household leaves you. Come back with the gems, and I'll forgive all your offenses."

I scoffed, my hackles raising. "We won't be even till I black your eye for smacking Lane around. Say what you want about me, but don't you touch what's mine." I pointed my finger to the dirt, my sneer firmly affixed to my lips. "Lane's mine! You got that, son? You keep that in mind when your people are starving, and you have nothing to choke down but the pride that landed you with no allies in all of this."

"Please!" Damond spoke up, coming to stand between Lane and his father. "Let me stay as your representative, Duke Henri. Then when Rosie finds the jewels that have been lost, and those that have been stolen by Morgan le Fae, all will be forgiven and our land can heal. Please, Henri! Take Gwen and preserve her reputation. Tell the kingdom I'm off breaking a new foal or something. Don't throw it all away just because you don't like the princess. Your feud with her isn't as important as the safety of the entire Second Province!"

In that moment, I saw clearly that Damond fought for his people, and Henri fought for himself. I promised myself on the spot that I would learn from Damond. I would do what I could to help Avalon, not just myself.

Henri sneered, looking like a snake. I couldn't believe I'd ever wanted an uncle. "Very well. Damond can stay as the vote for my province. See to it he's returned to me without the lack of grace your daughter has."

Bastien's eyebrows pulled together in the center of his forehead as he put together enough pieces to form an opinion. "Hey, now. The whole point of the Council is that we're allowed to speak like equals. Just because we've never had women in the tribunal before doesn't mean anything's changed."

"Bastien, get Lane over there with the others," I said, doing my best to amble up to Henri without jostling Seven too much.

"No, Rosie. It's over," Lane insisted. "You're not fighting

this one for me. I told you, it's got nothing to do with you. It's all old stuff."

I handed Seven to her, despite the bird's insistence she stay with me. "I don't give a crap what it's about. No one's allowed to hit you. Not while I'm here. Would you let someone smack me around? He hit you, so I get to black his eye. Fair's fair."

Lane didn't answer, but she pointed her finger in my face, her lips taut with a silent command that I back down. I was supposed to be able to understand hidden languages, but I didn't need that gift to hear her unspoken words loud and clear. She would handle her shiz how she handled it, and I would accept her decision.

"I was scared for you," I admitted in a whisper, lowering my shoulders to submission. "I don't like that guy."

Lane's shoulders lowered, and her expression softened. "Oh, Ro. I know, baby. Me neither." She wrapped me in a hug that sandwiched Seven between us, transferring my bird's body back to mine, where she felt safest. "I love that you would've clocked him for me. The very second I'm ready for that, I'll let you know."

"I've got you," I reassured her. It had made me rally when Bastien said that to me, and apparently the senti-ment was transferrable as I watched Lane straighten with self-respect not even Henri could strip away when our hug ended. I held her gaze with concern for her shining in my eyes. "I know who you are. Don't you listen to a word any fool says who hasn't seen you in twenty-one years. He doesn't have a clue."

"Thanks, baby." She broke out in the giggles. "'Texas Justice.' That was awesome."

Bastien made his way to my side, clicking his tongue at his horse to come over to us. "Oh, man!" I said, holding my damp shirt to my nose. "You stink like you bathed in farts, Bastien!"

He rolled his eyes and jerked his thumb over at Rousseau, who was with Remy helping Reyn out from under the bridge. "That's him. He lets it fly when he's nervous. Being so near the bridge while the army was crossing over was no joke."

"Well, then let's get going. Hopefully the ride will blow some of that stink off you. Ho! It's like rotten eggs!"

"You're saying you don't want a piece of this anymore?" He lifted the tail of his flannel shirt to present his perfect posterior to me, giving it a graceful shimmy to lure my eye and draw out my giggles.

I swatted at his butt. "You overestimate your good looks. Nothing can overpower that stench. Let's go."

His hands went around my waist to hoist me up, but my feet remained planted on the grass. He pretended to lift me as if I was a small car, making dramatic "oof" noises with his face pulled into the most comical strain. "Too heavy! Can't lift you!"

He pretty much deserved my elbow in his solar plexus, which was exactly what he got, letting out a real "oof" and doubling over. "Am I the first woman you've ever met?"

Lot, Damond and Henri all backed up, their gasps flying and their hands up to make it clear they hadn't been the ones to lay a hand on the Untouchable. Bastien waved off their concern that he would have me hanged because I gave him a taste of what he deserved. He rubbed his stomach and leaned his hand on the brown horse. "You're hardly my first," he jabbed, a suggestive smile teasing his lips. "Up you get." This time he was smarter and lifted me easily onto the horse.

"Are you two about ready?" Lot asked, trotting by us with a resigned look.

"Just about." Bastien cast up a dimpled smile, though I could tell he was just as uncomfortable as I was in our damp clothing.

Henri shook his head at me. "This is exactly the kind of behavior I was talking about. Crass and uncivilized. It's a good thing you've got your birthright, Rosalie. No one would be so foolish as to follow you otherwise."

Lane rose to my defense, but Bastien's slow motion turn held more of a threat. He moseyed up to Henri like a cowboy, staring him down with nostrils flared. "It's a good thing you married well, because no one would believe you were a man otherwise," Bastien growled. "Get on your horse and ride back to your castle, palace boy."

"Always big words from an Untouchable. You're responsible for no one. I have a whole province to think about. A fool on the throne is almost as dangerous as the wicked queen we have now."

I swallowed down the hard truth Henri doused me with. He'd nailed it right on the head. I was a fool. I couldn't read. No one would elect a president who couldn't read the Constitution.

Bastien let out a cruel snigger, his finger raising in Henri's face. "I've always known who you were behind the gallant waving to your people. I see you. Talk down to Lane or Rosie again, and we won't need words. I'll just..." Before he could finish his sentence, he popped Henri across the face with his solid fist. "That's for calling the Lost Princess of Avalon a fool." Then he turned to Lane. "Did he lay a hand on you?"

Lane's mouth was open wide in shock, but mine was still functional. "He slapped Lane across the face and insulted her."

Bastien gave me a nod of solidarity, knowing I'd needed to punish Henri for hurting what was mine, and that Lane stopped me. He didn't hesitate to finish the job, and socked Henri again in the same spot. It wasn't full-force, but it would leave a shiner for sure. "That one's for the Lost Duchess of Province 9." I postured that he'd landed the blows I hadn't been permitted to throw. Bastien wasn't finished, and tugged Henri forward, bringing his knee up into his groin. "That's for going against the Council. Rosie and Lane are in the circle, and I won't have you talking down to them. Go home and enjoy lording your power over people who still fawn over that sort of thing. We've got actual work to do." He let Henri collapse in gasps and curses into the dirt. Bastien's hand settled on Lane's back, causing her to posture. "I hear about you smacking around a woman again, and I'll take my turn using you as my punching bag. Represent your province better, Henri, or I'll have something to say about it."

40

THE WILDERNESS BEASTS WE ARE

*H*enri held Bastien's gaze a few beats before spitting a mouthful of blood into the grass. When he'd gathered his bearings after Damond righted him, he summoned his daughter with too much bravado in his voice. "Gwen! Get on your horse. Leave the beasts to the wilderness."

My hand found its way into Bastien's when he moved from Lane's side to my horse. Maybe his fingers sifted through mine to calm himself down, maybe to calm me down – I wasn't sure. Either way, Bastien met my guarded expression as I looked down at him from my place on the horse. He squeezed my fingers and spoke quietly to me. "Henri is not Avalon, Rosie." He took a chance and did something gallant, kissing my knuckles like a true Prince Charming. Something feminine and tender welled up in me at the sight I knew I'd be playing on repeat for a while. "*I* am Avalon, and I'll follow your lead any day."

I mouthed my sincerest thanks before he mounted behind me, wrapping one arm around my waist and taking the reins with the other.

The people and the horses were sorted out so we each had one (except me and Lane), and Henri and Gwen would ride back on one together. Gwen was confused when she joined our group with Reyn, Remy, Bayard and Rousseau, but her downward tilted head told me she knew better than to question her father. Damond hugged his sister, whispering something in her ear that made her stiffen as she nodded.

I could tell Gwen wanted to say something in parting to me, but she kept her mouth shut, nodding discreetly to the smile and wave I conjured up for her. They rode off, and the tension began to simmer down among the ranks.

So soon our little group lost two of its members, for better or worse. I didn't know much about Avalon, and even less about carrying out the mission we'd tasked ourselves with, but I knew we couldn't do it fighting the whole way. Duke Henri hated me, and if he was any indication of how the rest of Avalon might receive me, I didn't have high hopes for sticking around after the wrongs in the land were put right.

I kept my eyes on my shoes after Lot saddled up on Marquis with too much hesitance. Lot met Bastien's eyes, saying more than I wished he would in that span of silent warning.

"Let's go," Bastien said, his voice hard as his arm tightened around my stomach. It wasn't possessive, but there was an air of belonging that I couldn't quite put my finger on. I couldn't decide how I felt about that, since Bastien so clearly belonged to someone else. His chin looped over my shoulder, so our conversation could remain between us while the others climbed up on their horses. "You're tensing against me. I need you to relax."

"I don't know what I'm doing!" I admitted in a pained whisper, clutching Seven to my chest. "All that stuff Lane and Henri were talking about, is that true? That my status is..." I couldn't even say it. There was no way I could be above someone like Lot, who'd grown up here, and been bred for ruling his province. "I don't want to be in charge of a nation I know nothing about. And what if my Compass goes on the fritz? What if I can't find Roland? What if you guys are putting your hope in me, but I can't find the Jewels of Good Fortune?"

Bastien pressed a small kiss to my neck, his voice steady when mine wavered. "You've got this," he assured me. "You've got this, and I've got you. We'll figure it out together. You don't have to worry about any of that now. All you have to do is go on a little horse ride with me. Do you think you can swing that?"

I softened, letting my spine curve against his chest. "You'll stay with me?"

I felt Bastien's cheek lift against mine as he smiled. "Boy, are you going to be sorry you asked that. Remind yourself when you get sick of me that you wanted me to stay." His voice turned husky, pulling a blush from my face. "You want me."

I turned bashful, my neck shrinking and my chin turning to the side. "Shut up about it."

The others were ready, and turned to me for instruction. Reyn spoke for the group with a kind smile on his sweat-soaked face, as if the sight of Bastien making me squirm gave him peace. "You're calling the shots, Princess. It's to you to lead the way toward the Jewels of Good Fortune, and Roland, too." He shifted Lane in front of where he sat on the horse, his hands at home on her waist.

Reyn's unshakeable faith in my abilities made me desperate not to disappoint. I gulped, trying to tune into my churning guts, but they were too nervous to speak clearly and give me any sort of direction. "Let me think for a second."

Lane pulled their horse over to me, raising her chin with a calm smile that told me she wasn't worried at all about me delivering on all the hype. "Know who you are, Rosie. Remember: this is not your big adventure. *You* are your greatest adventure. This is just another jaunt along the way. No big deal."

I shot her a weak grin. "I love when you fancy it all up with words like 'jaunt'."

Lane sniggered, and then composed herself. "You're the Compass. Listen to your gut. What is it telling you?"

I guessed that I couldn't admit that my stomach was more at home barfing right now than doing anything useful. When Bastien's large hand palmed my stomach, I took in a deep breath, allowing him to steady me when I felt flustered. "Close your eyes," he whispered. "Don't look at the world you see. Find the jewels you can't see."

My roiling guts started to calm, refocusing on the deep voice that was saying all the right words. It was as if the ping-pong balls popping around in my stomach dropped down, and then formed into one ball that tugged me to the right. My finger followed suit, aiming us where my internal GPS insisted the jewels were hiding. "That way."

Bayard and Rousseau straightened, their skepticism starting to lift, now that I'd actually claimed my gift and started using it.

Bastien obeyed, turning the horse and starting us at a walk down a path toward the right. With us in the lead, no one saw his hand snake below the hem of my shirt. No one gasped at the scandal of Bastien's palm on my bare stomach, except for me. He thumbed my navel, letting loose a dark chuckle at my needy squirm. "Are you ready for it?" Bastien asked, implying too many things with the simple question.

Instead of overthinking, I leaned back on his chest and let my body relax, allowing his hand to make itself at home on my stomach. He didn't treat me as if I was the ugly girl (though he'd seen me with my hump, lazy eye and bad skin), but rather the woman with whom he loved to sneak little flirts. I liked being that woman, and clung to the tease he offered with a shy smile. "I don't think I'll ever be ready for you," I admitted.

He buried his face in my neck, and then cracked the reins. He startled the horse, setting us off to lead the way into the unknown. We rode deeper into Avalon, to the childhood home I couldn't remember, but now knew I could never forget.

Love the book? Leave a review.
(Unless you want me to hex you with a charmed necklace from Lane, which I can totally do)

41

LOST GIRL

Here's a free preview of *Lost Girl*,
book two in the Faîte Falling series.

"Not to be a downer, but I've been through the ringer, and I'm playing my Commoner card. I have to sleep, guys. It's a lousy habit of mine, and I can't shake it." My joke fell flat when the identical looks of doom were displayed on Bayard's and Rousseau's hairy Chewbacca-like faces. Every mile of distance we put between us and our enemy was another exhale we all desperately clung to. We'd been riding for hours into the night, moving in the opposite direction of the Queen's Army.

My mom's army. Morgan le Fae, the most hated, feared

and revered queen Avalon had ever seen was my birth mother – a woman whom I'd thought died while bringing me into the world. Apparently, she took the wicked queen thing to a whole new level, poisoning my dad so he couldn't overthrow her. King Urien remained sickly and weak, tucked away in her castle like Sleeping Beauty. I'd always pictured having a dad, but he'd been more the Superman variety than the damsel in distress kind of dude.

Whatever. I now had a dad who hadn't abandoned me. He may not be Superman, but he wasn't a deadbeat, either. Bonus, for sure. I kept having these fantasies of me walking into the castle I'd been born into and calling out his name. Somehow, just the sound of my voice would be enough to break the evil queen's spell, and he'd sit up with new life. My father would know my voice, though he hadn't heard it since I was a year old, and he'd instructed his sister-in-law, Lane, to take me away from Avalon into a world where Morgan le Fae couldn't find me. In the words of the immortal Will Smith in *Independence Day*, "'Welcome to Earth.'"

Morgan had been given an enchanted gemstone from the illusive Master Kerdik, just like her eight sisters. Unlike them, she wanted more. She stole enough of their Jewels of Good Fortune to make her province the most bountiful one in Avalon. I guess she wanted like, vats of fruit instead of mere buckets of the stuff. I dunno. All I knew was that some crazy shiz was tied to those gems. The women in the provinces without the gems had a harder time getting pregnant, and the land wasn't as plentiful. Not cool.

While I was horrified and ashamed that this was my family tree, the little girl part of me still kind of wanted to meet her, to see her face. I'd never even seen pictures. I wondered if we might have the same heart shape to our faces, the same skin that tanned easily, and if we have the same uphill battle brushing out the tangles from our brown, wavy hair. I wondered if she was dyslexic, or if that struggle was my blight to contribute to the family tree.

Remy's unspoken voice wafted into my tired mind. *"I wish I had something that could rouse you. I've been trying to keep quiet so I don't exhaust your magic further. I'm so sorry, Princess."*

"It's fine, Remy," I answered him aloud, cluing the others into our psychic conversation. "Not your fault. I like our conversations. It's normal for me to be tired."

Bastien sighed heavily – a sign of his attitude not taking a much-needed vacation. "There's nowhere to stop, Rosie. Just sleep on me."

I was already leaning my back to his chest as he steered the horse we shared. I wasn't totally stellar at riding horses, only talking with them. It was part of my birth blessing, I guess. I can speak hidden languages (though I got a D+ in Spanish by the skin of my teeth. Go figure). I can also find things easily enough to be called the Compass. The horse I was riding on was named Pierre, though he hated his name. He wanted to be called Fleur-de-lis, which was his favorite flower. Having a flower name myself, I couldn't begrudge the guy a little happiness. I let my hand rest on Bastien's thigh as we galloped through the starlit prairie, a smile teasing my lips at his barely audible intake of breath. Though we'd been connected for hours, each brush of a touch painted a crackle of something new and exciting between us. "As great a pillow as you are, I don't really think I can fall asleep upright on a horse."

"I'll catch you if you fall."

I ran my fingers along his left arm that held the reins, loving how the muscle in his scarred forearm popped out when he tensed up. "That's only like, the greatest pickup line ever."

"Is that so? Is it working on you?"

"I almost just invited you back to my bed. To keep me cozy while I sleep, of course, but still. It's a step up from the stables," I teased him. It was a flirt I couldn't help but indulge in. We hadn't even kissed, though I wanted to a thousand times over. "But seriously, folks. I do need to sleep at some point." Apparently the only reason I required sleep as a Fae was because I used a crap ton of magic when I spoke to animals, or people who had a hidden language. I contemplated cutting back on that, but it really wasn't an option. I was a foreigner here, and the animals had my back. With Remy having his tongue cut out, as Morgan had done to all the healers long ago, he was overjoyed to be able to speak with anyone. I didn't have the heart to tell him I was falling asleep.

"I can help with the sleeping problem," Damond volunteered, guiding his horse to our side with his hand raised, like the proper young lad he was. I mean, he was probably a year or two younger than me, but he seemed so much older and controlled. "You might not like the place, but it's safe. Safer than anywhere else, but that's only if we can get you in without announcing you. No one will bother us. The Queen's Army is clear across Avalon into a new province by now, so they've already swept this area looking for Reyn. We need to feed and water the horses. Refuel a little. The princess can rest then." He cleared his throat. "Duke Henri doesn't know I come here, though, so this stop needs to be kept secret." It would be strange to an outsider to hear a son call his own father by his regal title, but it made a little more sense after meeting the pompous and nasty Duke Henri. That my cousin had grown up into such a well-mannered and kind young man was a wonder.

Bayard nodded curiously that the obedient son had secrets from his old man. "Yep. Fine. Lead the way, kid."

Damond bristled at Bayard referring to him as a kid, but he was too polite to correct him. I knew the feeling. In a group of rulers and warriors, we were the young-uns. "When we get to the village, let me do the talking."

Bayard caught Damond's eye and nodded his approval, his horse's tail swishing back and forth in time with the horse he was riding. Chewbacca never looked so cool. "Look at you, taking charge now that Daddy's gone. Good for you, kid." Bayard was slightly less hairy than the shaggy horse he rode.

"Yes, well. Follow me. The princess looks like she's barely alive anymore."

Rousseau turned his hairy red head to me and winced, letting me know I looked exactly as terrible as I felt. "Oof, you're right. If sleeping cures that, then let's get the princess a bed. I'll take her there myself." He winked at me, earning my middle finger and a blown kiss. I'd quickly learned that Wildmen were kind of pervy, if Bayard and Rousseau were any indication.

When no eyes were on us anymore, Bastien placed a kiss to the space between my shoulder and my neck, making me shiver through the chill of the night that nipped at my damp jeans and t-shirt. Lane had Abraham Lincoln (my brown bear cub) tucked closely on her lap, but every now and then he whined that he needed me to hold him. Hamish (my squirrel) was happy to be in the lead with Damond, always seeking out new nuts and adventures. Seven flew overhead, but not too high, staying close to make sure her black, leathered wings weren't spotted above the trees. She was a fantastic lookout bird, turning traitor from the Queen's Army to come hang with me.

We rode for two hours more before the sparse trees lining the prairie started giving way to a hint of civilization in the form of a city's wall. It had hooks with hanging lanterns shedding light on the perimeter. When we trotted up to the wooden wall made of trees that had been cut in half and stretched several feet higher than our tallest horse, Damond dismounted, motioning for us to do the same and hand him our horses.

Lane moved to me, gripping my hand that wasn't in Bastien's. She had a sixth sense about things sometimes, and I could feel the tension in her grip. "Stay close," she insisted.

Reyn held her other hand, looking gaunt and sickly. His dark features were harder to see against the night, but the circles under his eyes were visible even under the flickering lantern's light. The shadows that danced on his face made him look like he was coming down with the flu – only he wasn't. This was one of the things I wasn't allowed to ask Bastien about, because he'd flip his shiz and turn into a sullen brat. He was protective of his bestie, not wanting anyone to know what was obvious – Reyn was a very sick man. He might even be the kind of sick that didn't get better. It had something to do with his low supply of magic, but if I sniffed any closer to the problem, Bastien's bark turned painful.

Damond looked over his shoulder, pausing as he raised his fist to knock on one of the trunks of the great wall. "Um, Lot? You might want to keep your head down. You won't want to be seen here. Aunt Lane? Rosie? Um, you might want to cover... all of that up." He motioned to our whole bodies, and like a dummy I looked down.

Right. I had boobs now. Lane had changed my appear-

450 | MARY E. TWOMEY

ance with some magical object, making me go through life on earth with a hump, a wonky eye and a fair amount of acne. When Bastien ganked my concealment necklace, my skin cleared up, my eye and my posture straightened, and my chest... grew. I looked like Lane more than I ever had before, and wasn't sure how to gracefully handle going from being the ugly girl no guy wanted to ask out, to attracting attention without meaning to. It was a steep learning curve.

Lane pulled a sweater out of her backpack and put it on to iron out her obvious curves. Bastien took his flannel off so I could thread my arms through it. It fit me like a dress, but it was the coolest I'd felt in a while. I was finally the cheerleader who got to wear the jock's letterman jacket. I was the girl the hot guy was looking at. "Thank you. Is this my invisibility cloak? Am I totally incognito now?"

The corner of Bastien's mouth tugged upward. "Keep your head down. I wish we had a hat for you or something."

"Here," Lot offered, taking his gray riding cloak from his shoulders.

Bastien frowned. "You need to keep your presence here hidden, too. Dukes don't come to places like this." He looked over me to Damond. He took out another flannel out of his pack and slid it on himself, flipping the collar up to obscure his neck tattoo. "The Lost Village? Really? I don't want Rosie here, and I can't imagine Duchess Elaine should be seen in here, either."

Seven made her home in my arms, tucking her body inside the cloak Lot fashioned around me. Lot took his time tying the lace at my neck. The hood flipped over my head, and just like that, I was the grim reaper. Or like, a super-fly Hobbit or something. Lot studied Lane, and then tugged the hood of her sweater over her hair. "It's the best we can do. I'll sacrifice my reputation for the safety of Avalon."

"Thank you for looking out for Rosie," Lane said, touching his wrist.

"Of course," Lot replied with a modest smile. His perfect blond hair wasn't even windswept from our long ride – dude was just that smooth.

Damond held his ground against the wariness in the others. "If she doesn't announce herself, I highly doubt anyone will know it's her. Keep your heads down, and don't make eye contact."

"Why are we hiding in here?" Lot asked, his brows furrowed. "Only scamps end up in the Lost Village."

"Exactly. No one's going to look for us in here." Damond moved a stray black hair back to join the others that were slicked back in a wave. He had naturally paler skin than mine, but he looked white as a sheet at what we were about to do. *Awesome.*

I whispered comfort and affectionate reassurances to Seven, who remained in my arms under my cloak.

Abraham Lincoln let go of Lane's leg and reached up for me like a toddler, but I was too weak to support myself on my bum leg for too long. Blame it on the in-home surgery I'd had that removed a million snake babies from my calf muscle.

Bastien took Abraham Lincoln from me, hitching him on his hip like a baby. "There you go, little buddy," he said quietly, revealing his soft side to me. I couldn't help but swoon at the cuteness. Bastien looped his arm around me, holding us together. "I know you want your mama, but you'll have to settle for your dad until we get settled."

My heart did a happy little skip that Bastien was playing house with me and our cuddly love child. He leaned down to kiss my cheek when the others were distracted, warming my whole body to his touch. "Stop seducing me," I admonished him with a blush. "It's working too well."

Bastien leaned his head down with an impish grin. "Never."

Damond knocked on the wooden wall, and a single stump opened halfway up the twelve-foot expanse to reveal a sort of window. A scared man's round face looked out from it. "Who goes there?" He looked out from his window that was about the same height as Damond's head. "Oh. Hey, kid. You here to see your brother?"

I heard Lane's intake of breath and saw her lift onto her toes. Her eyes were wide with excitement, and something that looked like nervous regret.

Damond stood on his toes to be better seen. "Yeah. I brought him a healer, some new girls, a couple clients and a few horses. He said he needed them. I hired these Wildmen to help me bring them in." He jerked his thumb to Rousseau, Remy and Bayard, who were right behind Damond, holding the reins of their horses after dismounting.

The man in the window was only a pudgy head who leaned back to take notes with a quill and parchment before leaning forward again. "Alright. You picked quite a night to visit. The Queen's Army was just in here yesterday, searching through the place for the Judge's son from Province 2. Boy, do they make a mess when they come through. Draper's probably still recovering. But go on in. You know I won't turn you away."

The window shut, and something that sounded like a lever turned from the inside, opening up a door that was seven trees wide. Bayard and Remy went in guiding their horses with careful steps, while Damond led the way.

Reyn and Bastien sandwiched Lane and I between them, with Lot taking up the rear. I ran my tongue along the roof of my mouth, worried that we were going somewhere I didn't understand, and might be doing something that might be more dangerous than we could handle. I wished we weren't downwind of Rousseau. His nervous stomach kept letting noxious gas out with a blast after every third step.

Damond shuffled ahead, leading the way through the

cobblestone village that was decidedly shady. There were loud fistfights coming from a street to our left, and angry bickering over who broke whose window to our right. The sound of the quarrel was broken by a woman's scream that pierced my ears with the passion of a good horror movie howl. I shrank into Bastien and brought Lane tighter to my side.

The night was lit by intermittent lanterns that highlighted trash in the street. The city reeked of piss and neglect. The shops we passed by reflected the crime city factor, missing the cheery push to bring in newcomers. Instead we were greeted with filthy storefronts and clientele that milled about with surly scowls that concealed none of their shady intent. Several toppled carts were left half on the street, and hay was strewn about in the middle of the main road we were headed down. There were no houses, only businesses with stucco roofs and barred windows. Though Damond was a couple inches taller than me, he looked small leading the way. I worried for him having made this trip before without us to back him up.

A woman in her mid-sixties with thick ankles and a torn and stained housecoat flew out from one of the buildings. She didn't give any care to who could see up her tattered brown outfit, nor did she care that I could smell her armpits even from the distance Bastien kept me as his arm tightened around me. I winced when I caught a peek of her panty-less, pudgy butt through an ill-placed slit up the back. "Damond! Good to see you, sugar pie. Tell me you've got an hour to spare for me. I see good things in your future, boy. I've got a special price on fortunes tonight. Only one silver coin for an hour. I'll never charge so little again!" She gripped onto his collar with fingers that should know better. She had green eyes, like Reyn, so I knew she was a Rétif. They were supposed to be good at trickery. While Reyn used his deceit to try and appear healthy when he was clearly not, and Lane had used hers to hide me from Avalon, this woman apparently used hers to predict the future.

Damond shook her off as politely as he could. "Not now, Gerta. I've got to see Draper. Then maybe tomorrow, if I catch you."

She cackled through the night, truly sounding like a witch. "If only your father knew you came here. He'd tear the whole place down rather than let his precious boy ruin his good name in our village." She winked at him, leering without apology. "Come ruin your name with me, boy. You've never had so much fun."

She was missing one of her front teeth and breathed heavy when she spoke in his face. I could only guess by Damond's reactive jerk backwards that her breath wasn't all that appealing. "Not this time, Gerta. Try your luck with one of the Wildmen after they help me with my delivery."

Bayard gave her a clear "I'll pass," but Rousseau looked her up and down appraisingly. As if on cue, Rousseau let out a loud, spluttery fart that exploded out his back end. Match made in Heaven.

456 | MARY E. TWOMEY

"Let's keep moving. These horses need to be watered." Damond led the way, pulling the horses forward down the darkened street. He turned right at the end, introducing us to what could commonly be known as crime central in any world. There were men out on their front porches, shaking hands with scowls as they traded coins for pouches. There were two dudes brawling in the middle of the street, getting in punches over someone named Celine.

"Damond! Not so fast. You know you don't get to pass through without a stop at my place." A man with a beer belly and no shirt on held open his front door. I didn't want to guess what kind of toll Damond paid to get through to see his brother. "In here, boy."

Damond's voice shook, but he stood his ground. "Not today, Norris. I've got to see Draper."

"You brought my payment, didn't you?" He slammed his door shut and waddled toward Damond, who stepped back on instinct.

Bastien gripped my hand, and I could tell he was debating between keeping a low profile and beating the snot out of Norris. Bayard handed his horse to Lot and stood next to Damond, his hand heavy on my cousin's shoulder. "What sort of payment?"

"A silver coin. Don't care whose pocket it comes from. Your money's just as good here, Wildman. But if you want to pass, you pay to walk down my street." He touched Damond's chin, and I flinched when Damond jerked away guiltily. "I take other payments, too. Isn't that right, boy? One way or another, I get my hand in your pocket."

Lane was shaking with grief, but I was trembling with rage. My voice came out quiet, but each word was punctuated with a rage that was bubbling up inside of me. "At what point am I allowed to kick that guy's butt? I mean, I'm supposed to be discreet, but I don't think that's as important as ending this dude." Seven burrowed against my abdomen, her wings stiffening at my tension. My sweet bird begged me to stay quiet, not wanting to risk me getting hurt in a fight. I could hear Hamish's angry chittering from Reyn's pocket. My squirrel didn't understand all the politics of the situation, but he knew when I was pissed, and took my causes on as his own, like a true friend.

Bastien held tight to my hand, anchoring me to the spot. "Your identity stays secret. Let us handle it. Keep your head down."

Bayard reached his beefy, hairy fingers out and gripped Norris' face, squeezing his cheeks until Norris squealed. "I tell you what. I'm going to go make sure Damond makes it to where we're headed, and then I'm coming back for you. See how you like getting your payment from me."

Bastien moved me closer, securing me to his side protectively. I held onto Lane's hand, ensuring she didn't leave my sight. Her head was bowed beneath her hoodie, but I could see her jaw was set in deep planning mode. I didn't want to be on the business end of whatever she had in store for Norris.

Norris let us pass by after Bayard released him with a knee to his groin and a punch across his face. "L-let's go," Damond said, and I desperately wanted to hug him, to tell him it was going to be alright.

Damond led us down several more streets, fending off aggressive street urchins and a few jags who tried to steal the horses. Bastien set Abraham Lincoln down, and the two of them defended the horses while Lot and Remy guarded Lane and I, who were unarmed. Abraham Lincoln bit one of the attackers, and raked his claw across the leg of one of the others.

"That's right, buddy!" Bastien called to his fur baby. Bastien landed a few punches on the robbers, knocking two of them clean out with a force Mike Tyson would envy. The entire fight was over in a minute, but Damond admonished all of us to try harder to keep a low profile. Bastien offered up a "What do you expect?" kind of shrug I adored him for.

The streets themselves grew filthier as we neared the three-story building with a stucco roof at the end of the street. It appeared to be the grand finale of the city, with the cobblestone ending at its imposing doublewide entrance. There had been mud on the road and some spilled food, sure, but soon we were stepping over glass and out and out garbage.

My nerves were shot when we arrived at the noisy bar

with too many drunk middle-aged and older men inside for me to be chill. We peered through the scummy window, making sure to keep a healthy distance from the drunken brawling that was happening inside.

"This is no place for us to stay!" Lot scolded Damond in a whisper that could barely be heard. There was a piano that played off-key, but no one seemed to mind. The men's attentions were all glued to the scantily clad women who danced for them all around the large common area. There were women dancing on the bar, women sashaying from table to table, women wearing sheer swaths of fabric that left nothing to the imagination, and a few women wearing absolutely nothing.

Damond was firm. "Do you really think Morgan will search for her here? This is the best we've got. Rosie has to rest, and her leg is only going to get more injured if she keeps on like she is. This is the best I can do, so keep quiet for a little longer until I can get us a room. Wait here. I'll be right out."

Damond disappeared inside, and none of us spoke of the strippers earning their keep, but remained in stunned silence until he came back. Damond's smile broke the uncertainty, spreading wide across his face. "We can take the horses to my brother's stables around back. Draper's meeting us there! Hurry!"

I hadn't known Damond had a brother, but that was on the long list of things I didn't know about my own family.

We scurried around back, looking over our shoulders

and making sure we weren't followed. Everyone exhaled in unison when Remy shut the stable doors behind us, though Bastien and Reyn kept tight to Lane and me.

"*I don't know about this,*" Remy warned me. "*The Lost Village is no place for a lady, or men who want to go about a life unscathed. You'll stay near Bastien, Princess.*"

I glanced up at Bastien, and the sight of him holding my bear again warmed me down to my toes. "If you insist."

Continue the series with *Lost Girl,*
book two in the Faîte Falling series.

ABOUT THE AUTHOR

USA Today bestselling author Mary E. Twomey lives in Michigan with her three adorable children. She enjoys reading, writing, vegetarian cooking, and telling her children fantastic stories about wombats.

While she loves writing fantasy, dystopian, and paranormal tales for her readers, Mary also writes romance under the name Tuesday Embers, and cozy mysteries under the name Molly Maple.

Visit her online at www.maryetwomey.com, and sign up for her newsletter, so you never miss a new release.

Made in United States
Troutdale, OR
12/17/2024

26791466R00289